T0366169

LIES, *Lust,* and SILENCE

CLAIRE MILES

PARTRIDGE
A Penguin Random House Company

To order additional copies of this book, contact
Toll Free 800 101 2657 (Singapore)
Toll Free 1 800 81 7340 (Malaysia)
orders.singapore@partridgepublishing.com

www.partridgepublishing.com/singapore

1

The little girl was frightened. She had been ever since she was taken. She didn't understand why she had been bundled up and removed from her home. She did not know where her mother and father were or why they wouldn't come to get her. The only face she saw was the young woman who came to see her every now and then and brought her food.

Not that the woman wasn't nice to her, she was. She was always kind and often just held her close and gave her hugs. But it was not the same as when her mummy and daddy held her.

Often the little girl would cry. She would sit on the bed or the floor and cry, not knowing where she was. She looked around at the room as she did every day. There was nothing much in it except a bed, a toilet, and a sink. It had a hard, cement floor which was partially covered with a large mat.

She often lay on the mat when she got tired of lying on the bed. To pass the time she counted the patterns on the mat. There were exactly fifty, pink, swirling roses. She liked to think that these roses were the ones her mother had planted in the gardens at home.

When her mother cut them, she would ask the little girl where she should place them. The young child had a favourite statue. It was the statue without eyes—*the blind statue*. This was where they always placed the fresh roses.

But where she was now, there was no blind statue and no roses. There was a very small kitchen which also had a sink.

She searched the cupboard in the kitchen where she found a supply of biscuits. These were stored in an old tin. The little girl checked the cupboards several times during the weeks she had been there. There was no food other than the biscuits.

The woman told her to lie on the mat every day when the sun shone through the high windows close to the ceiling in the bedroom. She told the child that it was important to get as much sun as she could otherwise she may become sick. The child washed herself every day from the sink in the bedroom and changed her clothes.

When the woman came, she took the clothes the little girl had worn the previous day. She brought them back washed and smelling fresh the next time she called. She left them in a dilapidated, cardboard box—the type that was seldom noticed.

The woman told the child that she must always keep her clothes covered with a towel. That way, no one would realise she was in the room.

The girl did not suffer nearly as much as when she had first arrived. Her memories were hazy, but she would never forget the pain as long as she lived.

She found it hard to look at the source of her pain. It was easier to pretend nothing had happened. She told herself that she was still the perfect, little girl her daddy had told her she was.

She was his princess, the most beautiful girl in the world. She liked to imagine she was back with mummy and daddy when they would go for walks; when daddy would lift her up over his shoulders when she became tired. She kept trying to remember their faces. This was something she feared she might forget.

When she finally got out of the room, she wondered if they would look the same. Would she know who they were? Would they know who she was? The girl started to cry again. She put her right thumb in her mouth.

Sucking her thumb made her think of her other hand—the hand she pretended was perfect. She desperately wanted both her hands to be perfect. She wondered what her parents would think of her now. Would she still be their beautiful princess? But they weren't with her and they never came for her.

She could never work out when the woman would come. Sometimes it was every day, sometimes every second day and never at the same time. This was when she ate the biscuits that were in the old tin.

There was only one entrance where she was kept. When anyone entered the room, the girl heard the rattle of the door being unlocked and opened.

It was late afternoon when she heard the door rattle. As quickly as she could, she scrambled under the bed and lay still, hardly daring to breathe.

"You can come out now, Sarina," the woman said as she entered the bedroom.

The girl crawled out from under the bed. The woman carried several bags of clean clothes, fresh food and other items. The child sat on the edge of the bed watching her. The woman sat beside her.

"How are you today, Sarina? Have you been able to find any sun?"

"A little, but it didn't last long. What have you brought me? Did you bring the coloured pencils?" The child looked excitedly at the bags.

"I did. I also brought you some books. If you like we can read them together. There's one about a princess and another about mermaids. Which one would you like to read first?" The woman placed the clean clothes in the cardboard box.

"Not the one about the princess. I don't want it. I don't ever want to read about princesses." The child put her thumb back into her mouth and started to suck furiously.

The woman sighed, puzzled. "Then we will read the one about the mermaids. I want you to keep up with your reading. It's very important. How is your hand today?"

As she removed her right thumb from her mouth, she put her left hand behind her back. "I don't want to talk about my hand either. I just want to go home."

"I wish you could go home too, but it's impossible. You have to stay here and be very quiet. Remember what I told you. If you hear any noises outside or close by, you must be very quiet. If anyone ever comes through the door, you must remember what to do." The little girl nodded as the woman spoke.

"You must hide under the bed and not make a noise. And keep your pencils and books hidden in the bottom of the box and cover them up with the towel. Promise you will do that."

The woman was very serious as she took a warm meal of savoury mince and mashed vegetables out of one of the bags she had brought with her. She gave the child a spoon and told her to eat.

Sarina always ate what the woman brought. She always remembered what her mother told her—*You'll never have curly hair if you don't eat your vegetables, Sarina.*

Her father always winked at her when her mother told her this. Her daddy was so funny, always making her laugh. After she ate her meal, Sarina sat beside the woman and together they read the book about mermaids.

It was almost dark when the woman told her it was time to leave. Saddened by this, the girl sucked on her thumb again.

"Come on Sarina, show me." The woman took the little girl's thumb out of her mouth and then removed the bandage from the child's left hand. She took the girl's left hand in her own and spread both their hands out together on the bed.

"It gets better in time. The pain will go away and then you tend to forget it. It just takes time," the woman explained.

Together they looked at their left hands, spread out beside each other on the bed, one big, one small, but both missing their little fingers. Their scars were almost identical. Not neat and tidy, but rough with over-granulated tissue that was red and angry.

Sarina blinked away tears as she took the woman's right hand in hers and felt along the scar where her second finger should have been.

"That's why, if you ever hear anyone, you have to be quiet, Sarina. That's what will happen if they find out you're here."

The woman dare not tell the girl that what would happen would be far worse. Both their lives would be in jeopardy. She would do all she could to protect the child for as long as she could. She hoped her courage wouldn't fail her.

"You go to bed now. I'll try to see you tomorrow." The woman held the little girl in her arms and kissed her warmly.

In between a fresh lot of tears, the little girl sobbed. "Don't leave me, Maria, please don't leave."

The woman spoke gently. "Do you still have it? Do you remember to keep it in your pocket? It helps me and I know it will help you."

The woman reached into her pocket and pulled out a small wooden object—no bigger than a fifty-cent piece. "See, I've got mine and I keep it with me all the time."

The girl also dug into the pocket of the long pants she wore. She held a similar object in her small hand. She was always careful not to use her left hand.

"I keep it with me all the time. I think about the lady on it as well. I ask her to help me get back to my mummy and daddy. Do you think she's listening?"

"I'm sure she is. I tell her things and she listens to me. She always helps me but sometimes it takes a while."

The woman grimaced as she said these words to the little girl. In her wounded heart, she was wondering if anyone ever listened to her. But she had to have hope. Isn't that what she'd been taught? She again begged the image of the lady to hurry up and get them both out of their predicament. She didn't know how long she could carry on. It was very testing keeping the child safe.

Maria put Sarina into bed then pulled the covers over her. The little girl put her right thumb back in her mouth and thought back to what it had been like before she had been taken.

She remembered all the people her mother and father used to know and wondered what they had all been doing as she was having her finger sliced off.

2

Miriam, Sarina's grandmother, was a changed woman. She no longer feared the abuse that her previous husband, Alan Farraday, had frequently dished out. He had been dead for ten years. Even her dreams about him had ceased. She was now what people described as a normal person—not completely normal, but almost. She still had visions but they were seldom alarming, not like they used to be.

Her current vision was disturbing and similar to one she had experienced years ago. She had seen a female child with bloodied hands and knees as a wild beast stood behind her. It was like something out of a horror movie. The beast was half-man and half-dog, an evil looking creature, intent on harm.

She shuddered, trying to force the image out of her mind as she went to her bedroom and grabbed her beads. She went outside and sat under the poinciana tree with her beads held firmly in her hands and rattled off some prayers.

The red blossoms of the tree surrounded her, but neither the prayers nor the blossoms made her feel any better as the image stayed with her.

Eventually when she felt calmer, she went inside to her husband, Sam Calhoun, a retired medical doctor. He was quite elderly, but while his mobility may have suffered, his mind remained sharp. Miriam enjoyed her life with him.

They seldom spoke of their past history together. It had been a long history, starting from when Miriam was a young child and he was a young medical doctor.

Miriam was undecided if she should tell her husband about her vision. She wanted to, as it had been very graphic. She decided not to, as her husband had patiently put up with her strange ways for many years. She was sure he did not want to be burdened with any more of her disquieting visions.

Rather than talk about visions, she talked about their family. Although Sam had no children of his own, he thought of Miriam's children as his. In one way or another he had been involved with them for most of their lives. Now there were grandchildren as well. Their lives were very full with the wonders of family life.

Although Miriam didn't know it, most of her children were fully occupied with more than the wonders of family life on the night Sarina Farraday disappeared.

On that particular night, Miriam's five sons were very busy. Like their father before them, they had their needs and these needs had to be satisfied. They were all big, healthy, strong men.

Mitchell Farraday, the eldest son who was in the military was unmarried. He found adequate relief for his needs on his occasional visits back to his home town.

He did not want or need a constant partner as he had his career and his extensive family. He had no difficulty finding willing partners. The ever changing tourist population satisfied his urges.

Although if he were honest with himself, he would have to admit that his lifestyle did not completely fulfil him.

Miriam's second son, Michael, was totally devoted to his wife, Denise. They never tired of each other. Their initial meeting had been tumultuous, but they had persevered with the relationship. They married and were now the proud parents of twin sons, Gabriel and Raphael and a daughter called Sarina. These children were the light of their lives.

The third son, Mark, had been very active with his wife, Tiffany. After he had spent his energy, he watched TV with their son, Arlo. His wife informed him that she was slipping out for a short time to the all-night gym for her regular exercise routine.

If Mark thought it strange that she needed even more exercise, he did not comment. He loved spending time with his son, watching documentaries.

Malcolm, the fourth son, was also busily engaged. But not with his wife, Carrie, who remained at home being depressed, suffering from chronic fatigue, anorexia and smoking pot. Malcolm found their marriage worked well with interludes spent with women he employed in his restaurants.

He was willing and they were willing. Most of these women only worked a few weeks before they moved on. This reduced any complications. On occasions, his conscience did trouble him when he thought of his young daughter, Lucia.

The fifth and last son, Matthew, was not as experienced as his brothers but was doing his best to catch up. He had an occasional girlfriend. It was no great love match, so he wasn't too upset when he found out that she also had interests. But the arrangement was satisfying to them both. Neither would be too upset if it fell apart.

Mark and Malcolm's good friend, brother-in-law and neighbour, Danny Smythe was out and about, but also not with his wife. He had told his wife, Maryanne, he had a school meeting to attend.

They had three young children, Hope, Lizzie and Harry. He did attend occasional meetings, but much preferred to meet up with Tiffany, Mark's wife.

On the night that Sarina disappeared, the Farraday brothers and Danny Smythe were all fully occupied with their activities. But when word got out that the child was missing, their pursuits were forever changed. Life would never be the same again for any of these men.

3

Danny Smythe arrived home just after midnight at the property where he lived with his wife and their three children. His conscience was unsettled. It was no good trying to tell his wife that it was an exceedingly long meeting. She wasn't a fool. No one was that keen on school meetings and none lasted until midnight.

He loved Maryanne but since the arrival of the three children and especially the last baby, Harry, she was not the same. She was moody, ill-tempered and had no interest in sex. When they had first started living together after the birth of their first child, life had been one big blur of kissing, touching and endless sex. But when the first flush of this new found love dimmed and two other children came along, the romance began to wane.

As he drove in from the main road to their home, he cut his lights. He then drove very quietly before pulling up some distance from the house. His excuse for doing this was to preserve the integrity of the new lawn they were trying to establish out the front of the house.

Closing the car door softly, he walked to the house where he removed his shoes and lay on a recliner chair on the front veranda. He did not go inside as he had no wish to wake the children and especially not his wife. He promptly went straight to sleep. Mosquitoes or crying children did not disturb him. It may not have been the sleep of the just, but it was the sleep of the sexually exhausted.

Maryanne was no fool and neither had she been fooled by the lights being cut on his vehicle nor the fact that he was sleeping on the veranda. This excuse of not wanting to wake the children was wearing thin.

Maryanne was flabbergasted that her husband could think that she would not hear him turn off the motor of his vehicle. She was awake half the night looking after his children, especially Harry, who only slept a few hours at a time before waking again and needing attention.

She thought back to another man who had caused her great distress—her father, Alan Farraday. Her memories took her back to how she wished he would remain permanently asleep. She had similar thoughts about her husband.

If not permanently asleep, then she would like to see him pay for the distress he was causing. Or if not him, then the slut he was running around with. One of them should be made to pay. Maryanne knew for certain that he was seeing someone. She could smell the perfume on his clothes.

She sat nursing her youngest child and thought of all the ways she could make her worthless husband pay. Unlike the time with her father, she had no tablets to induce an endless sleep.

When Harry finally fell asleep, she put him back into his cot then went to check on their other two children. Ten year old Hope lay on her side, sleeping soundly. Their next child, Lizzie, slept peacefully in the bed beside her.

Maryanne's thoughts were tormented. *Damn Danny, why couldn't he be satisfied with his life? If he would just give me more time to get over Harry's birth, they could get back to the way it used to be. Being endlessly tired was no fun.*

Their business might not be doing so well, but they could still be happy. Weren't their precious children enough for him? She felt like waking him up and telling him to get up every couple of hours and feed Harry. See how he'd like that.

She went back to bed and had just fallen back to sleep, when the baby cried out again. She let him cry for what seemed like hours, although she knew it was probably only minutes. She was sure there were more teeth coming through.

She held him in her arms, swaying from side to side. She heard Danny snoring outside on the veranda. This made her very angry. Not only was he cheating on her, he was also getting a full night's sleep, while she was awake most of the night looking after his children.

The sun's rays were appearing over the horizon when she came to the end of her tether. The baby kept waking; Danny kept snoring. Not even the mosquitoes buzzing around were enough to disturb him.

As she walked into the kitchen to get a drink of water, she saw her husband's fish-filleting knife on the sink. It was his favourite knife in the whole house. It was the knife that had filleted any number of fish of all shapes and sizes over the years.

"Well," she murmured. "Danny boy, let's see if your favourite knife might wake you up."

She checked the children again; they remained asleep. Then she picked up the knife and walked out onto the veranda. She sat beside him, amazed at how contented he looked. She pushed him over onto his side to give her enough room to sit beside him. Looking down at him, she held the knife to the side of his face.

"Wake up, darling husband," she whispered, keeping the knife steady in her hand. She wasn't prepared for the way he jumped when she spoke to him. His hand rose up and knocked the knife. The sharp-tipped blade nicked his face.

He opened his eyes immediately. "Geez, Maryanne, what the hell do you think you're doing?" His hand went straight to his face, where the blood was beginning to ooze. When he saw his bloody hand, he gasped. "What on earth have you done?"

"Not nearly as much as I would like to," she answered calmly, watching with fascination as the blood started to pour down the side of his face. She continued holding the knife.

"What's with the knife? Are you trying to kill me or something?" He stared wide eyed at his wife sitting close beside him. "Give me the knife, Maryanne and we'll forget what you've done."

"More like what you've done, Danny boy. Goes to show there's more you can do with this knife than fillet fish. If I ever find out just who the slag is you're chasing after, I might fillet a piece of her as well."

"I don't know what you're talking about, Maryanne. I told you I was at a school meeting. Now give me the knife."

He tried to grab the knife, but she hung onto it, grappling with him. He grabbed her wrist, but she fought against him. He started swearing at her, trying to reclaim the knife.

"It's a dangerous knife, Maryanne, give it to me." As he spoke these words, Maryanne tried once more to pull the knife from him, as she did so, it penetrated his forearm. There was a moment of silence as they both watched the knife slice deeply into his left arm.

The gash opened and blood oozed out. Initially there was only a small amount spilling onto his skin before the flow of blood began to cascade down his arm, into his hand and through his fingers. Maryanne dropped the knife. She stood staring at Danny as the blood oozed down onto the floor.

"Get some towels or I'll bleed to death." He held his bleeding arm in his other hand, pulling the separated skin edges together. "Move, Maryanne, get a towel and then call Mal".

Maryanne looked at the wound and then back at Danny. Her mind was boggled. Here was her husband sitting beside her, with his arm opened up and blood seeping down the chair onto the floor. She heard his words but could not fathom what was happening.

Her husband pushed her towards the front door. She hurriedly moved in the direction of the bathroom, intent on finding the towels that he had told her to get. She grabbed a few towels and ran back to her husband.

When she saw his arm and the blood streaming over the chair and the floor, she screamed, "Danny, what's happened to you? What's wrong?" Her husband looked at her in astonishment.

"I've been cut, Maryanne, my arm has been cut open."

He watched in continued disbelief as his wife wrapped the towel tightly around his arm. She sobbed and screamed.

"Why are you bleeding like this?" Maryanne continued to sob as she kept her hands around her husband's bleeding arm.

Danny began to realise that his wife's mind was beginning to unravel.

"Phone Malcolm and tell him to get here fast. Go to the phone in the kitchen and dial Mal's name. Tell him to get here right now; tell him it's an emergency. Go Maryanne, hurry."

He pointed back to the door that led into the kitchen. Maryanne followed his orders as if on automatic. She picked up the phone, scrolled through until she found her brother's name. As if in a dream, she pressed the button.

The voice that answered was slow and groggy. "Hello".

"Danny says you have to come right now. It's an emergency." Maryanne's voice was at high pitch.

Her brother was instantly awake. "What's wrong, Maryanne? What sort of an emergency?"

"It's his arm; it's been cut open. There's blood all over the place. You've got to come, Mal. Please come quickly." Maryanne slammed the phone down and raced back to her husband.

Danny was sitting back on the recliner, taking deep breaths; the towel was soaked. Maryanne took one look at it and ran to get more. "Should I phone the ambulance, Danny? Maybe that would be a better idea."

Her husband looked at her again in puzzlement. "I don't think so, Maryanne. Once Danny gets here he can take me to that doctor's place in Cooroy. They open early. Someone there should be able to stitch me up."

He worriedly regarded his wife. Her agitation was genuine. He saw the wringing of her hands and the worried look on her face.

"What happened to you Danny? Did you do this while you were fishing?"

Danny looked again at the knife which had slid down the edge of the seat of the recliner. The entire incident was overwhelming. Maryanne kept changing the towels. Her hands were shaking as she dabbed at the cut on his face.

"Yes, Maryanne, that's how it happened. I was fishing in the creek."

Maryanne sounded exasperated as she spoke. "I keep telling you to be careful. You shouldn't be out there at night alone. I knew this would happen. I wish Mal would hurry up. You stay here. I'll get you a drink of water. That helps when you're losing a lot of blood." She got up to leave.

"Maryanne," he spoke softly to her. "Take the knife with you, clean it up and put it back in the drawer. Would you do that for me?"

He watched as she picked up the knife and went back into the kitchen. He heard the tap running, so guessed she was washing the knife. She returned quickly with a jug of water. They heard the sound of a vehicle at the same time. They looked up to see Maryanne's brother, Malcolm, driving towards them.

Maryanne ran down the stairs to meet her brother. "Thank goodness you're here, Mal. It's Danny. He gashed his arm while he was fishing. It's very deep and will need stitches. Please hurry and get him to a doctor."

Malcolm followed his sister up the stairs, took one look at Danny with the blood soaked towels strewn around him.

"We better get you to a doctor fast, Dan. You don't look so good. You can tell me all about it once we're on the road."

Malcolm helped Danny down the steps and into his car.

"What the hell happened? You've been fishing for years. You've never done any damage like this before."

As they left, Maryanne called out, "I love you Danny."

Danny Smythe looked back at his wife, now with tears streaming down her face. He mouthed the words, "I love you too."

What was going on with his wife? His thoughts were bewildered as he tried to make sense of the switch in her personality. One minute she had sliced his arm open and the next it was as if she knew nothing about it. Granted, he was not the best of husbands, but did that warrant her taking a knife to him? Had she actually been planning to kill him?

There was one aspect in this bizarre episode that pleased him. If Maryanne wanted to believe that the reason for the deep laceration on his arm was due to a fishing accident, then he would readily go along with it.

Danny was determined that none of the Farraday brothers would find out that the knife wound was inadvertently caused from his interlude with Mark's wife.

It was Michael Farraday he feared most. If Mick ever knew about the affair, Danny knew he would be dealt with.

The second Farraday brother might not be as robust as before he was shot, but one thing was certain, he never wanted to be on the wrong side of him.

He had to be convincing if his story was to hold up. A fishing accident would save both his and his wife's involvement in any further unwanted questions.

"It was just one of those things," he explained. "I guess I wasn't paying enough attention in the half dark. It serves me right. I'll have to be more careful in the future."

Mal gave no indication that he did not believe him. "Catch anything?"

His old friend shook his head. "We can go to Sam's old medical practice in Cooroy? I've heard they open pretty early."

Mal kept glancing at Danny who was very pale; there was more sweat on his brow. The sight of more blood made him drive faster.

"If I can get in and out quickly, you can drop me back home and then get home yourself. By the way, how's the family?" Danny did his best to keep the conversation away from his injury.

"Lucia is good. Carrie's just the same—nothing much changes."

Danny made no response. In his opinion, Malcolm's wife was a lost cause. He couldn't understand why he had stayed so long. If he had a wife like Carrie, daughter or no daughter, he would have bailed years ago. Malcolm was a very good looking man, with his slim build, dark hair and eyes.

All Miriam and Alan Farraday's children were similar in looks. Malcolm never had any difficulty in attracting women. Danny's thoughts returned to his own wife. He wished she could return to the laughing woman she once was. He was fearful that she might also be a 'lost cause'.

The medical practice was a ten minute drive. Within minutes they pulled up outside the refurbished building they had visited when they were very young.

Fortunately the door was open. "This place must open up with the birds," Danny commented, as it was still very early.

There was a receptionist at the counter. As they walked in together, she looked at the clock hoping they would realise the practice was not yet open for business. She then realised she had left the front entrance open by mistake.

It was unusual to have a couple of men walk in this early, especially as it was not the weekend when sporting and alcohol-driven accidents were most common. They both looked tired. She was very wary; not only was she alone with two strangers but there were drugs on the premises.

She saw one of the men stumble. The darker of the two helped him sit then walked over to speak to her. "My mate's not too good. Do you think you could get someone to patch him up?"

She looked over at his mate and saw the blood-stained towel wrapped around his arm. "Oh, I see. What's happened?" She immediately felt relieved as they appeared genuine.

"Knife wound, fishing accident," the dark haired man replied.

The receptionist, who looked like a teenager, sprang into action. "Better come straight through and we'll take a look."

She gestured for them to follow. By this time, the wounded man was perspiring even more. The dark haired man walked beside him keeping him steady.

She took them into a consulting room. Malcolm helped Danny onto the bed and carefully lifted his arm out. As this occurred, there was a fresh ooze of blood come through the towel.

The receptionist went to the sink and began washing her hands. "I'll have a look first to see what we're dealing with."

Danny had his eyes closed, happy to have someone repair the deep laceration on his arm. Malcolm was confused as he watched the young woman unwrap the towel, wondering what she thought she was going to do. Eventually, it got too much for him.

"Where's the doctor? Shouldn't there be a doctor here to fix this?"

She turned around and looked straight at him. There was disdain in her expression. "I am the doctor."

He was taken aback by this. "Geez, I'm sorry. I didn't mean to imply anything. It's just that you look too young to be a doctor."

He didn't know what to say. He felt a fool. He thought she looked as though she should still be at high school. Her dark hair was tied up in a ponytail and her skirt was so short it barely covered her long legs.

"You think you can fix this up, Doc?" he asked, trying to sound apologetic. It was obviously not the right thing to say as she regarded him with an exasperated sigh.

"Of course," came her curt reply.

Malcolm looked down at Danny's arm, avoiding her scornful eyes. The blood flow was beginning to lessen.

"How did you manage to slice yourself up? It must have been an awfully big fish." The doctor examined the wound.

She kept working as she said. "Just because I might be young, it doesn't mean I'm not competent."

Then her disparaging tone changed as she considered the problems she faced. "I might need some help though; there's no one else here as yet. Would you mind locking the front entrance? The office staff will be here shortly. You can't be too careful."

She gave him another disdainful look as he left to lock the door.

When he returned, she was again scrubbed up and looking very professional. "You might want to hold his arm while I anaesthetise around the edges."

Malcolm did as he was asked. He washed his hands and then donned the gloves she gave him and followed her instructions. He watched as she talked to Danny.

"You say you did this while fishing?" she asked again.

Danny took his time answering. "After fishing, I was home cleaning up when the knife slipped. Stupid, really, I should have been more careful. Guess it was half dark at the time. That couldn't have helped."

"What about your face? How did that happen?" she asked, keeping her hand steady as she sutured the arm.

She had already placed a small dressing on his cheek. Danny still looked uncomfortable, like he wished it was all over and he could get out of the place.

"I'm not too sure. I must have nicked it when I gashed the arm. I can't really remember."

She kept working, aware the dark haired man watched her every move. He saw her slim wrists cutting and stitching. His close scrutiny annoyed her. Every now and then she would lift her eyes and look straight into his.

It wasn't the time or the place, but he couldn't stop his eyes from lingering on the tight shirt that showed just a little of her cleavage. When she turned around to get the dressings to cover the wound, his eyes automatically looked at her legs. About the only thing he knew about doctors was old Dr Sam Calhoun who had married his mother—and he looked nothing like this doctor.

His wife visited doctors all the time but he didn't know any of them personally. All he knew was that he paid for the visits and the numerous pills that she took. There was visit after visit, to this and that kind of doctor but nothing seemed to renew the spark she once had. Nothing made any difference to her wellbeing.

He thought of the woman he had been with the previous night and compared her to the doctor. There was really no comparison. This woman was not only good looking but extremely intelligent as well.

By the time she finished suturing Danny's arm, she had advised him how to look after his wound and the need to be more careful. He watched as she gave Danny an injection. Malcolm wasn't listening to a word she said. He was too mesmerised by her.

She looked at him sternly and repeated "What about you— have you had one lately?"

He didn't have a clue what she was talking about, but replied with the only response that made any sense.

"As a matter of fact I have, but I wouldn't mind another one."

Hell, he thought, *doctor's had certainly changed since old Dr Calhoun's days. They didn't waste any time getting personal, and he wasn't even the patient.*

"That's encouraging. How long ago? Was it in the last five years?" she asked in total surprise.

"Well, yes, I'm pretty sure it was more recently than that."

"Not many men of your age ever remember to have one. I guess I should congratulate you." She looked him square in the eye again, so he gave her his megawatt smile.

It didn't seem to work as she ignored him and spoke to Danny.

"That's got you all fixed up now. Just remember what I told you and come back in a week, or before, if you have any trouble. So take it easy and lay off the fishing. See the ladies at reception before you leave so they can get your details."

She followed the two of them to the reception area. As they reached reception, she touched Malcolm Farraday's arm. He turned around, wondering what she wanted this time.

"By the way, it was a tetanus shot I was referring to."

She gave him a wink, and he returned it with another of his brilliant smiles. He heard her laughing as they left. As soon as the two men were gone, Dr Zaylee Lang waited until the office staff processed the visit; she then checked Danny's medical record. There was no other history available so she quickly wrote up his notes.

She wondered about the large laceration on his arm. It was deep and long. It had also required many sutures and considerable expertise on her part.

It was unusual for a fisherman to be smartly dressed in jeans and a fitted shirt. He did not have the look about him of a man who had been fishing all night. There was no fishy odour. She was almost certain she could smell either after shave or perfume on him. Maybe he had showered before the accident.

She wondered about the other man with the drop-dead good looks. She would always remember the smile. She knew he had eyed her off throughout the procedure. She had felt his eyes roam over her.

Serve her right, she thought, *she should get out of her school girl habits and wear more suitable clothes.* She wondered what his name was. She ambled out to the office staff and casually asked if they knew who the other gentleman was as he was asking about tetanus injections.

The receptionist looked at the doctor as if she were mentally deficient. "Don't you know? He's one of the famous, or should I say infamous, Farradays. I'm not too sure which one. There's a heap of brothers and they're all very good-looking. But the word is, they're trouble and you're better off keeping away from them."

The doctor was taken aback by the woman's explanation. "I thought you would have known—this practice used to belong to old Dr Sam Calhoun who married their mother after his first wife had died. The story goes that their mother was a bit odd. She had a monster of a husband. There was a shooting a long time back but I don't remember all the details."

The receptionist had exhausted her tale and turned to get back to her work. Dr Zaylee Lang decided she would look up the files of these infamous Farradays as soon as she had a spare minute.

On that same morning, Michael and Denise Farraday were in bed asleep when they heard a vehicle pull up out the front of their home. They had lived in the same home for ten years.

Over the years, they had three children. They had married, as did two of Michael's brothers, Malcolm and Mark, and their sister, Maryanne.

"I can't believe she's here this early. When I said early, I didn't mean before the sun came up." Denise struggled out of bed, telling her husband to hurry and get dressed.

They had a long day planned. They had many business interests and had arranged to fly to Sydney with their accountant, Dax Webster. They intended to return by nightfall so as to be back with their children.

They heard their visitor shutting the door of her small car. It wouldn't be long before she would be bounding up the stairs ready to start the day. Denise made it to the front door as their child-carer for the day, Mia Lamont, came up the front stairs. She was one of those endlessly, cheerful people.

The two women hugged. Then Mia started chatting, telling Denise what she had organised for the children. She liked to have activities planned for when they returned home from school. She was keen to get started.

"First off, we'll have a cup of tea; then we'll get the children ready for school. By that time, they should be awake." The two women went to the kitchen. Mia was always welcome in their home and often cared for the children when their parents went away.

Mia loved children. She owned a child-minding business. Not that she had any head for business or for managing staff, but Michael and Denise, along with their accountant, Dax Webster, looked after the business side of things. If there were staffing or parent issues, Denise would sort them out.

Mia was fortunate in being able to take time off when she chose. She had capable staff. Besides, she loved all the Farraday children, not only Michael and Denise's. She always made a point of being available when asked.

"Can I wake them now?" Mia waited for Denise's approval before disappearing down the hallway to the twin's room.

"Come on boys, time for breakfast." There were groans from Gabe and Rafe. Two dark-haired, identical faces looked up at her. She pulled the sheets off them. She knew them well and saw herself as an aunty, although she was no relation. She even had the same dark hair and eyes, much like all the Farradays.

Having no family of her own, she considered herself part of the Farraday family. Other than her good friend, Francine and the Farradays, she was alone in the world. She had been raised by her grandmother who had since died. The memories of her mother were very painful so she avoided any thought of her.

Once she saw the boys were moving from their beds, Mia went in search of Sarina. She was an endearing child and very pretty. Except for the frequent nightmares that plagued her, she was a carefree child.

Mia entered Sarina's bed room. She saw the bundle of sheets and blankets strewn across the bed. At first, she thought the girl was curled up underneath, so she tip-toed over and whispered, "Sarina, wake up, it's time for school."

There was no response. Mia pulled the bed linen back and saw the bed was empty.

She called out again, "Sarina, where are you?" It was unlikely the child would be playing a joke on her by hiding at this early hour.

Again, there was no answering giggle. Mia looked under the bed and in the wardrobe, but still could not find her. She went back to the kitchen where both parents were packing lunch boxes.

"I thought she must be out here having breakfast," Mia spoke to both of them. "She's not in her bed."

"I haven't seen her. She hasn't come out yet," her father replied. "I'll go and find her."

Michael went in search of his daughter. Meantime, Mia kept chatting to Denise but when he returned, both women instantly noticed the concern etched on his face.

"She's not in her room. The boys haven't seen her. You search the house, Denise, and I'll look outside. You come with me, Mia."

They began searching the immediate area outside the house. Not finding her, they then searched further out onto the open areas around the house and along the track to the entrance of their property.

The property where Miriam and Alan Farraday's children had been raised had never been named, but when Michael and Denise married, he called the place 'Sunshine' because he said that as long as he lived, Denise would always be his sunshine. She was the person who would always light up his life.

He jogged to the entrance, looked around, but there was no sign of his daughter. Mia checked the sheds. She looked under the benches and shelving that held a variety of plants and seedlings. She kept calling out the child's name. There was no answer.

When they returned to the house a distraught Denise was beginning to panic. "Where could she be? I checked her early in the night and she was asleep in bed. Michael, where is she?"

He went to his wife and held her. "We'll find her, Denise. I'll call the boys and get them out here. If she doesn't turn up, then we'll call the police."

He began phoning his brothers and Danny Smythe. Fortunately, his oldest brother, Mitch, was still in town. Michael explained that Sarina was nowhere to be found. There was no need to further express the urgency of the situation.

Michael's four brothers and a tired Danny soon arrived. They immediately organised themselves to check different sections of the property. The tracks and paths around the house were searched a second time. Danny said he would notify their sister about what was happening.

When he told Maryanne, she began crying. She said she would keep their children home for the day until Sarina was found. She did not ask how he was. If he thought his wife's behaviour was strange, he did not mention it to her brothers.

Matt, the youngest brother, had joined the police force after leaving high school. His reason for this was his admiration for his sister-in-law, Denise, who had been a detective before marrying Michael.

Matt was intelligent and dedicated. As it was his day off, he was not in uniform. Like his brothers, he was aghast at the thought that his niece was missing. After having searched the areas close to the house several times, he called his brothers together and said it was time to officially notify the police.

Other than a few looks of dismay between the missing girl's parents, there were no objections. Michael and Denise had a tumultuous history with the local police.

The family kept searching. None of them wanted to think the worst which was that Sarina could have fallen into the creek which flowed close to the house. It was not always such a gently, flowing stream.

It had been known to rise rapidly and had the power to cause havoc and damage to anything along its banks or in its path. There was a water hole as well, not far from the house where children and adults had swum and played over the years.

The police were quick to respond. A missing child was a worst-case scenario, deserving immediate attention. Matt, being one of their own, was the spokesperson. He advised his colleagues of Sarina's disappearance. The parents of the missing girl were in a daze of panic and disbelief.

There was talk of a child-abduction alert. But before that occurred, the decision was made for a further search of the property. Everyone involved was hoping the little girl would be found before this drastic step was taken. The state emergency service was called in. Before long, an army of men and women in orange uniform arrived. They soon began another search of the property, including the creek and the waterhole.

A few of these people involved in the search could remember back ten years ago to the days when there had been a similar search on the property. This had occurred on the day when two men had died and Michael Farraday had been shot.

It was also the day when the skeletal remains of Mia Lamont's mother, Mandy Lamont, had been found buried in the earth inside a shed. This shed had been partially swept away by the raging waters of the now peaceful creek.

The parents and twin brothers of the little girl were questioned again and again. They could add nothing further other than she had been put to bed and was asleep when checked later in the night about 10pm.

None of them knew she was missing until Mia had arrived very early and discovered the girl was not in her bed. The police could gain no further insight from the distraught Mia. Between her tears, she could only reiterate what they already knew. So the child abduction alert was activated.

Michael's brothers began to feel useless. How do you comfort a father and mother when their daughter has disappeared? The couple had withstood many bad incidents in their life, now they were facing another.

Malcolm phoned his wife. He hoped she was sufficiently alert to understand what he had to tell her. When she answered, she sounded reasonably coherent. When he told her what had happened, Carrie Farraday screamed out in dismay. Their housekeeper, Mrs Potter, immediately went to comfort her.

As she collapsed back onto her bed, Carrie handed the phone to Mrs Potter. Malcolm explained that he would tell his daughter that her cousin was missing. Lucia and Sarina were of similar age and good friends. Lizzie Smythe, Maryanne's second child, was also of a similar age.

Mrs Potter stayed with the child while her mother buried herself in her bed. When Carrie wasn't asleep, she was crying. Mrs Potter feared for Lucia's well-being. Her mother was always sick and her father was always at those restaurants of his—who knows what he got up to?

From Mrs Potter's point of view, Malcolm didn't get up to much with his wife. She had her suspicions, but that was all they were. He was too good-looking and charming. He was also surrounded by countless women.

She worried about Lucia. As she had free rein with handling the house-hold expenses, Mrs Potter purchased a disposable mobile phone for Lucia. She told the little girl it was only to be used in an emergency. It was to be their secret. If Lucia ever needed to contact Mrs Potter, she could use her very own phone and her parents would know nothing about it.

Also in secret, she taught Lucia how to use the phone. She again stressed that it was only to be used in an emergency or if she was frightened. They had a weekly practice so that Lucia knew how to use it. Lucia thought this was a wonderful treat and enjoyed their weekly secret conversation.

Mark also phoned his wife. She was naturally shocked. She told her husband she would tell their son what had happened. Arlo was the oldest of the male Farraday cousins. He was also good mates with the twins.

Arlo remained at home with his mother on the day of his cousin's disappearance. Tiffany was tempted to phone Danny but caution won out. She realised it was better not to tempt fate, especially on a day like today.

Instead she told her husband to bring the twins to their home as they could stay with Arlo. It would be better for them emotionally to get them away from the property. They could play video games or watch TV. Mark was grateful for his wife's thoughtfulness.

Mitch, in spite of his many relatives, often felt very alone. There was no one person he could confide in about his fears, dreams and hopes. He had his army buddies and his brothers but they had their own lives and interests.

He thought about his niece, Sarina. He remembered his brother hoisting her up on his shoulders and teasing her about her loose tooth. Mitch felt a huge emptiness inside him. He could not define what it was or how he could fill it. He imagined it was too late now.

Danny soon became exhausted; this was plain for all to see. He went home to rest. The large bandage around his arm gave testimony to the reason for his exhaustion. The story of the knife wound paled into insignificance in comparison to the missing child. He returned home to Maryanne and their three children.

Maryanne took one look at her husband. When she saw the sadness in his face, she told him to lie down and rest. The children were put into their rooms. She asked Hope to watch the other two. Taking him in her arms, Maryanne lay down beside him.

Matthew was bewildered. He had no idea what could have happened to his niece. The worst-case scenario was that she had fallen into the water hole or somewhere else along the creek. It was impossible that she could have been taken.

He wouldn't allow his thoughts to travel in that direction. Not that he considered being drowned in the creek a better alternative. He sat on the back stairs of the house and stared out at the hollow log not far from his eyes. He wondered if Michael or Denise ever went near it anymore. They never spoke of it, so he guessed they had probably forgotten about it.

Sunshine had always been Matt's home, right up until he joined the police force. He hoped one day to become a detective, the same as Denise had been. His dog lay by his side, panting after another scout around the property.

"Where can she be, Billy Bob? What's happened to her?" He spoke to the dog. It looked at him as if it understood that something dreadful had happened. Matt stroked the dog's head.

After a time, Matt was joined by Mia. Together they sat on the back steps in silence. They had known each other for years, ever since the discovery of her mother's remains on the Farraday property.

She often called Matt her little brother. He had been twelve when she had first met him on a terrifying night ten years ago. Mia and her friend, Francine, had ended up spending the night in this very house. Mia and Francine had been teenagers at the time.

"What do you think's happened to her?" Mia asked, again feeling tears spring into her eyes. She was a very emotional person. At times, she wondered if there was something wrong with her.

"I don't know," Matt replied, "but it doesn't look good. She's been missing for hours. They say the first twenty-four hours are critical. The police divers are doing a second search of the water hole and the creek so we should know something soon."

"No, please don't think like that," Mia grabbed his hand and held it. "She's probably just hiding or gone for a walk."

"Thanks for trying, Mia, but I don't think so." He let her hold his hand. It was comforting sitting on the back steps with her, away from everyone else.

They remained holding hands, her eyes staring at the steps in front of them. Spots on the cement stairs began to blur in front of her. She shook her head, trying to clear her vision, uncertain about what she was seeing.

"What's that?" she asked Matt, pointing to the bottom of the stairs.

He looked to where she was pointing. "Oh no—it looks like blood."

He was down the steps examining the brown spots within moments. He rubbed at one of the spots then tasted it.

"It tastes like blood. We better get the sergeant." He glanced back at Mia who looked like she was about to burst into tears. "Don't touch anything, Mia, and look after Billy Bob for me."

Mia stepped back up onto the veranda away from the brown spots. Her crazy mind tried to think of all the reasons why there would be blood on the back steps of the Farraday home. She was imagining simple things—like one of the twins stubbing their toe or a bird flying into a window. She blocked all thoughts of Sarina from her mind.

Mia was trying to keep Billy Bob quiet when a contingent of uniformed police arrived. Instructions were given for everyone not connected with the search to keep away. They were now looking at a possible crime scene. Matt hurried along the path beside the veranda. When he reached the end, he vaulted over the edge. He took Mia back inside the house.

Michael and Denise were sitting inside the room that the family called the prayer room. Miriam and Sam had joined them the moment they were informed that their granddaughter was missing. Mia, again crying, sat beside Miriam as Matt explained that blood had been found at the bottom of the back steps.

Shock seeped into all of them. Their worst fears were being realised. Denise and Michael held onto each other. Denise was sobbing quietly. Michael looked vacantly out through the window. His usual calm and confidence was deserting him.

There was nothing that could compare with the pain he now felt. He could feel a rage boiling inside him, but there was no one or thing to direct his rage at. There was no longer a violent, abusive father or his evil half-brother, Jack Smith. They were both long gone.

Miriam started muttering away, pulling out her beads and saying her prayers. The old doctor looked at his wife, hoping desperately that she wasn't returning to the bad old days of her mental health problems. She had been well for so long. If anything was going to tip her over again, it would be something like this.

Matt stayed with Mia until she had calmed down then went in search of his other brothers. Billy Bob followed him. His words were greeted with silence and shock. Whether it was Sarina's blood, no one could be sure as yet. It wouldn't be long before forensic teams arrived and the results known.

Exhaustion was evident on all their faces. Not the exhaustion of the search but of the immensity of horror at their niece's disappearance.

Matt wanted to be by himself, so he took off with his dog, again walking around to the back of the house which was now crawling with police and other investigators. Billy Bob was sniffing along the veranda where he had vaulted over the railing.

This was outside the range of the crime scene tape. The dog began whining, dragging at something he found near the edge of the cement base of the house. Matt glanced down at his dog. That was the moment he saw it.

If screaming was acceptable, then that is what he would have done. He would have screamed like a girl, like Mia would have. Instead he jumped back, took some breaths and bent down to pick up what had caused his dog's agitation.

It was as he had thought. He had known what it was from the first glimpse, but had told himself it was impossible. He picked a small finger up off the ground. Immediately he had done so, he realised he should not have touched it. He sat back down on the ground, again in shock, before calling out to the police.

Two constables arrived within seconds. Matt was well known to them as they had worked together. They looked at their colleague, sitting on the ground, pale as a ghost and barely able to talk.

"Look," was all he said, showing them the finger. The two constables were quick to act. They called their sergeant over. There was no doubting what had been found. Matthew stayed sitting on the ground while the finger was taken from him in gloved hands and placed in an evidence bag.

How long he sat there he wasn't sure, probably not long? He rubbed Billy Boy and told him he was a good dog. He stood up and with the dog behind him, returned to tell his family what he had found.

This latest piece of information was met with even deeper shock and despair. Matt found he could not stay with Michael and Denise. They were too distressed. He left them in the prayer room together.

Mia followed Matt to where his brothers were grouped together. When he announced this latest find, they were again shattered. If dogs could cry, he was sure Billy Bob would follow Mia's example.

Words could not express their shocked feelings. Their worst fears had come true. Mark and Malcolm thought of their own children and how they would feel if one of them was missing and their finger had been found.

Mitch thought of his own daughter—the daughter he had never seen. He didn't even know her name. What sort of a father was he—nothing but the worst kind? But he knew that if anything happened to her, he would move heaven and earth to help her.

5

Francine Hamilton stood by the side of her husband, Brad. For months now, she had watched him wither away. He was half the man she had married seven years ago. She had loved him so much back then and still loved him to this day. The intensity of desire had diminished as he lost his strength and his body weight, but the love remained.

It broke her heart every day to see him barely able to walk. It was an insidious disease that crept along, gradually sapping his energy and vitality. She held his hand, the weight of his pending death heavy upon her heart.

They had tried for a child, not at first, but after a few years of marriage. But nothing had happened. Now Francine was beginning to think that she would never have his child. He would be gone from her before she could give him the greatest gift that a couple could hope for.

Maybe the disease that racked his body had been the reason. Who knew? Maybe it was she who was unable to conceive. One thing was certain—they were not going to go through any IVF at this stage of the game.

She had heard of couples who had kept sperm for later fertilisation with an egg—to be used after aggressive treatment or sometimes even after death. But this was not for Francine.

As she sat beside her husband, she thought of her empty future without him. The seeds of an idea had been developing in her mind. If it hadn't been for the wretched disease that was taking her husband, she would not be thinking about such drastic means.

She had her business, which was becoming fabulously successful. Her boutiques were called Lady Francesca and carried the finest clothes. Francine had always been addicted to clothes. She prided herself on style.

As she sat beside her husband holding his hand, she spoke quietly to him. "I have to go away for a few days on business. There are fashion shows I need to attend."

Brad glanced at his wife, admiring her blond hair and fine features. When he had first seen her, he had thought her the most beautiful woman he had ever laid eyes on. He still thought it today. If it were possible she was even more beautiful today as she was now in her late twenties and reaching the full maturity of her beauty.

Francine was already packed for her few days away. She had arranged for the woman who did her domestic chores to stay with her husband. She left instructions to make sure he was taken care of—that his every need was met. The woman had proven herself to be very reliable. Francine paid her well for her services.

There was still one important thing she had to do before she left. She had not yet completed her dressing, but she had showered and rubbed fragrant lotion into her perfect skin. She went to her husband and hopped into bed beside him. She knew he always liked her in red, so she had pulled on her most alluring lingerie.

She propped herself up on her knees beside him. He had his eyes closed, whether asleep or not she wasn't too sure, but she was determined that he would wake up and make the most of her before she left—illness or no illness.

Her hands touched him, rubbing his chest and his now concave stomach. Where had all his musculature gone? She looked at his thinning hair, once dark and glossy. His legs stretched out long, thin, and pale before her. She started kissing him.

She heard him groan. "I don't think I can, Francine. I don't have the energy."

"You don't have to do anything except lie here, I'll do the rest."

She glanced down at him. She could see that there was little response. She could feel his ribs under her tongue. If she opened her eyes, she could count them; they were so pronounced. She felt him start to respond, nothing much but it was probably as much as she was going to get.

They were both naked. She slid on top of him. She couldn't tell if it was pleasurable for him. It certainly wasn't for her. But one had to persevere if goals were to be achieved. She lay there for several minutes, pretending satiation. The thought went through her mind that maybe they were both pretending.

"I'll miss you," she said, kissing him gently again on the lips. "Was that good for you?" she asked.

"You know you're always good for me, Francine. I didn't know I still had it in me. You'd better get going. What time is your flight?"

Brad looked at his lovely wife, still as mesmerised by her as the first time he had seen her. He cursed the wretched disease that was slowly eating his manhood away. She deserved so much more. He had asked her to leave him, to find someone else who could be the man for her that he could never be. But she steadfastly refused. Whenever he brought up the subject, she no longer argued with him. She just left the room and told him to forget it.

"I've got to go now. I'll phone you tonight when I arrive. I should be back in a day or two. If you need anything, call Val."

Val Richards was the woman she employed to take care of her husband and home when she was away. She kissed him goodbye and left. She could not believe the treachery she had planned. The first step had been taken, now she just had to pull off the rest of it.

She had no intention of going to any airport or catch any flight. There was no fashion show that she just had to get to. Francine could care less about fashion shows or clothes, except maybe which clothes she should wear for the next part of her plan. She had already booked herself into a small motel. She had never stayed there before and her business was not in the same area, so the chances of her being recognized were next to nil. She had booked the room in her maiden name.

After she unpacked her few belongings, she lay on the bed and rested until it was dark. She hid her identification under the mattress before checking she had enough cash on her to get through the evening. Then she came to her next big test. How to dress? She did not want to be too noticeable.

She thought back to the first time that she had met her husband. The memory of this meeting was etched in her mind. She knew exactly what she had worn. If it had helped catch Brad's attention, then she would wear something similar.

She recalled the night she had met Brad. Of course she had been with Mia. As usual they had worn seductive clothes—short skirts and tops that showed just enough cleavage to be noticed.

What she knew about men was that they liked legs, backsides and breasts; so she would wear something that emphasised these features. Her years in her dress shop had taught her that there were many subtle ways to be alluring. She chose a black, short skirt which she wore with a blue blouse that reached her waist. It was short enough to show off her trim, tanned stomach and had enough strategically placed buttons so that she could undo as many as she wanted if the need arose.

One thing she would not do was wear red underwear. That was exclusively for her husband. So she chose blue to match her blouse. The shoes came next.

High heels were her passion. But casual sandals would be more appropriate for the part she wished to play. It would be hardly likely she would feel up to wearing high heels after working all day.

Francine was as ready as she was ever going to be. After pulling on her sequinned sandals with natty straps surrounding her trim ankles, she set off to enjoy a few drinks after a long flight and a hard day's work. She had scoped out the restaurants and knew which ones appealed to the age group she was interested in.

She pretended not to notice the men who were sitting alone. But walking up and down became tedious, so she stopped and slipped inside a restaurant that was doing a roaring trade. She found a seat at the bar. She ordered a drink, not alcoholic, because she needed to stay alert.

She kept discreetly looking around. There were many couples, a few becoming boisterous as the drinks flowed. There were several men who vaguely resembled Brad but they all had partners. She was considering shifting on when she noticed a man sitting by himself at the far end of the bar.

Did he look like her husband? He was big—much bigger than Brad had ever been. He had broad shoulders and a strong build. He also had dark hair.

Well, she though, *he's the only one who seems to be available and shows a resemblance to Brad, so maybe I should start with him.* She only had two days to complete her mission.

She kept glancing at him, hoping he would notice her. All she managed to do was gain the attention of a woman sitting alone and some man who was already with a woman. If she didn't move things along, she might have to settle for another man she had noticed who wore a wedding ring. So she made her move. She would just have to brazen it out.

She picked up her purse and moved to the end of the bar. There were no available seats, so she pushed in beside him. Now she had to face the awkward part. She was out of practice. But wasn't she a successful business woman used to dealing with hard-headed clients? Surely she could manage this.

"Hi, are you alone?" she asked as the man looked at her. She saw his dark eyes light up as she shoved in beside him, her arm accidently brushing up against his. His eyes immediately observed the way she was dressed. He looked pleased.

"I am, would you like to join me?" he replied, as he moved over to let her in. "What are you drinking?"

She hadn't thought about drinks. She was determined to remain sober. But maybe he would think her a prude if she wasn't a drinker.

She said the first thing that came into her head. "White wine."

She stood quietly beside him. Her nerves were getting the better of her but she couldn't back out now. Standing closer to him, she saw that he was older than she had first thought, maybe too old for what she had in mind.

But age in men didn't seem to be as big a problem for fertilisation as it was for women. The rest of him fitted the image of what she wanted.

"Have you eaten?" he asked as she sipped her drink. She let her leg rub up against his. If he noticed, he gave no indication.

"I'm not hungry," she replied, "I thought I would drop in for a drink. What about you?"

Had she tried she couldn't have planned it any better. The two people beside her happened to bump into her, causing her to fall against the man. She made the most of it, making sure her breasts brushed against his chest. She muttered an apology, taking her time to pull away from him.

She looked at him again, and could see she had more than ignited his interest. His eyes were glued to the front of her blouse. So, like the elegant tart she was, but pretending she wasn't, she managed to flick open a couple more buttons that held her little blouse together.

"Oh, I'm hungry all right. How about we quit fooling ourselves here and just get on with it?" His big hand reached out and slid up the inside of her leg.

She wasn't expecting this. It was happening too quickly. She couldn't speak for a few moments as the hand with its thick fingers travelling up further. She thought she might choke. She stared at him, holding her breath as the fingers probed further.

This man with the black eyes and hair may prove to be far more than she had bargained for. They were in a bar full of noisy people, she was squashed up beside him and he was doing things to her that she had almost forgotten about.

"I think maybe you're right," she stuttered, still not attempting to move away from him. She closed her eyes while she waited for him to stop which he eventually did.

Then he took her by the hand, made his way through the crowd and took her outside. It was dark around the back of the restaurant. This was not what she had planned. She thought of the motel room with its soft bed.

"Do you want to go somewhere more comfortable?" she managed to say as he pushed her up against a hard, wooden fence and started kissing her. His lips tasted sweet from the drink he had just finished. His tongue slid into her mouth. At first she was reluctant, but soon found herself kissing him back. She knew he was hard. She could feel him pressed up against her.

She didn't know how he had done it, because his arms had kept her trapped against the fence, but he was suddenly pushing himself into her. She was shocked that it had happened so quickly. But wasn't this just what she had wanted?

A crazy thought crossed her mind. She was pleased she hadn't worn the shoes with the high heels or she might have fallen over. She stood on steady feet feeling him thrush harshly into her.

This was no gentle taking. Her brain was on fire, as he continued. It had been so long, she was climaxing time and again. Time was on hold until she felt him stiffen, and moan. He held onto her until both their breathing steadied.

"Now we can find somewhere more comfortable. Got any ideas?" he asked between breaths.

She straightened her clothes then took him by the hand and together they walked the short distance to the motel. She quickly opened the door and they stumbled in, not turning on any lights. The bed was in front of them. She wondered what she should do now, strip off or help him strip off.

It didn't matter as he ripped open the rest of the delicate buttons that were holding the blue blouse together. The black skirt had already been dispatched. That left her in her blue briefs and bra and the diamond studded sandals with the multiple straps that came up her slim ankles.

"I think I'm going to need the light on for this," he whispered into her hair, smelling it as he pulled out the pins that had held it up.

Before she knew it, she was flat out on the bed with the lights full on. She watched in amazement as he disposed of his own clothes. He was an incredible specimen. She swallowed hard as she viewed his rock-hard body. Her eyes followed down his body. She couldn't believe her eyes as she saw how big he was. No wonder her brains had nearly left her head as he taken her against the fence.

"You sure you know what you're doing, that you want this? If you want me to stop, you better say so right now." He was on the bed with her.

"I'm sure," she whispered, pulling his face down to hers. She surprised herself as she wanted to taste him again, to have her tongue in his mouth. She wrapped her legs around him, pulling him into her. Again she could feel his hardness rubbing against her.

"Not yet," he said as he moved away from her.

She tried to grab him, wanting to feel him on top of her again. His black eyes bore into hers as he picked up his jeans and pulled a packet from his pocket. She saw him rip it open and quickly pull the condom over his hardened penis. Damn, she hadn't thought of that.

What was the good of him if he was going to use a condom? She wanted his sperm inside her not in some stupid piece of latex. What little bit of rationality she had left, told her that she would have to outwit him.

He was back within seconds. His mouth was all over her. She felt bereft as his lips left hers and travelled over and down her body. She wanted to keep kissing him, to taste his mouth on hers. Her senses were on fire.

"Please," she whispered. He lifted his face and their eyes held.

"Please" she asked one more time so he moved up over her and entered her for the second time.

She went with him, not caring if they never stopped. It went on and on. She reached down to touch him and felt the cursed condom.

So she pushed him off her, rolled on top of him, pulled the condom off and said, "My turn now."

Her mouth was all over him. She wanted his precious sperm inside her not in some condom. She thought it was the nearest thing to paradise she had known.

Their coupling became faster and faster until she again saw him stiffen and groan. He pulled her back down on top of him and together they lay with bodies satisfied under the glare of the light above.

How long they lay like that she wasn't too sure, but he eventually pushed her off. She heard the light flick off. He was back in the bed beside her and moving over her again. She put her hand down and touched him—no condom. His response was immediate.

This made her feel proud, to think she had this effect on him. He was obviously a very virile and experienced man, different from Brad—but she would not allow herself to think of her husband. This was not the time for comparisons.

The passion continued interspersed between some sleep. Not that it mattered if she didn't get any sleep at all. After all, she had all day to catch up or for all she knew, the rest of her life. She had two days to achieve her goal, two days while she was at her peak time, when eggs were supposed to be ready and waiting to be fertilised.

She must have fallen into a deep sleep because the next thing she knew, she heard him in the shower. He wasn't going to get away that easily. A few more times might just do it. She slipped out of bed and followed him into the shower.

He was lathering himself up when she stepped up beside him. She looked up and smiled at him, unsure how to interpret his returning expression. She took the shower rose and rinsed him down while he soaped her up.

They were both ready. "Not in the shower, we might fall over if it gets too vigorous," he whispered.

He lifted her up in his wet arms and carried her back to the bed. Eventually, he rolled out of the bed again, and again headed for the shower. This time she didn't follow. She had no energy left.

When he returned, she lay on the bed watching him dress. She noticed the scars. She had felt roughened skin during the night, but she was too sensitised to take notice.

"How did you get those?" she asked, timidly touching a large, ragged scar that ran along the side of his chest

"Battle scars," he grinned, "Fighting off hungry women."

He leaned over and kissed her, not the kiss of passion they had shared during the night but a feathery brush against the lips.

"Now I've got to be going. There's somewhere I have to be. Thanks for the night." He stood up and was ready to leave.

"Wait," she called out. "How about tonight, do you want a repeat, same time, same place?"

"Lady," he answered, "you don't have to ask twice. But this time, we might try some talking as well." Then he was gone.

She stayed in bed dozing on and off until midday. She felt pleased with herself. Everything was going to plan. She had been uncertain how she would be able to manage the sex as she had never been with any man other than Brad.

Thinking about the night, it had been better than she could have imagined. It had blown her away. She didn't know sex could be like that. She remembered the feeling of her brains trying to explode out the top of her head. Surely, there must be a baby come out of it.

When she finally got out of bed, she saw the money he had left. It made the whole thing seem so much sleazier than it already was. But what did she expect?

The afternoon dragged on. Realising she was hungry she went in search of a café. She had to keep her stamina up for another night.

She showered and dressed again, this time in similar garb as the previous night. She wore the same shoes. He had loved her shoes and told her to leave them on so he could just look at her. He nibbled at the straps that covered her ankles then proceeded to nibble right up her legs.

Francine phoned her husband frequently during the time she spent away from him. She told him about the flight, about the fashion show she had not been to the previous night. There was excitement in her voice, but it wasn't due to the clothes or the fashion houses. Brad told his wife he was pleased she was enjoying herself, but that he missed her.

She tried not to be early, but couldn't help herself. She sat at the back of the restaurant at a table for two. She had just sat down when he came in. Their eyes connected. He walked straight to her. She took more notice of him this time. He was dressed in smart jeans and a trim-fit shirt. His hair was cut short. He was an incredible specimen.

"Are you eating tonight?" he asked. She said she'd have what he was having and a glass of wine. He ordered immediately. When their meal arrived, she was unprepared for the huge rump steak with the eight tiger prawns. He wolfed his down with several glasses of beer.

When she ate only a small portion of her meal, she watched as he took her plate and ate what was left over. When he was finished, he asked. "Well, come on. Tell me what you're up to?"

She hadn't expected this. "What do you mean, what am I up to? Same as you I expect. I wanted some casual sex."

"Is that what it's called? It didn't feel too casual to me." He shrugged his shoulders. "Guess it doesn't really matter what you call it. Are you ready for some more?" He hesitated before adding, "There's something about you that doesn't add up."

"What do you mean by something that doesn't add up?" She felt a little anxious at this statement.

"It's almost like you're naïve. You don't do this very often, do you?" He watched her closely.

This observation alarmed her. "Look, I'm here on a business trip. I deal in women's clothing. I felt lonely, that's all. Besides, you could have said 'no'. It wasn't just all me. I want to go now. Are you ready?"

She didn't want any more questions. She had told him enough about herself. They both stood up at the same time. He paid for their meal and drinks and walked out behind her.

"Are we going straight for the back fence or to the motel?" she asked.

He took her by the arm and laughed. "No, we'll give the back fence a miss tonight. I've had a hell of a day. Just good old fashioned sex will suit me fine. Help me forget my troubles."

"What sort of troubles have you got?" She didn't know what to call him, thinking it was ignorant not to call him by some name. "I don't want to know your name, but I should call you something."

"How about if I call you lady and you can call me whatever you like."

"Sounds good to me; you still haven't told me about your troubles. Not that I really want to know, but I guess we should talk about something. Once we reach the motel, there won't be any need for talk." She almost added, *I hope.*

He was quiet for a moment before he responded, "Sad troubles and bad troubles of the worst kind."

"Oh," she hadn't been expecting anything like this. "Doesn't sound too good; do you want to talk about it?"

"Lady, I've done enough talking for one day. All I need right now is you. We both want the same thing. So how about we get on with it?"

He watched as she opened the door. He placed his big hand against the small of her back as he followed her into the room.

They stood beside the bed facing each other. "Please don't leave me any money. It's insulting. I don't need paying. This is something I need and if I'm not mistaken, you need it too."

She saw him catch his breath, as he took her in his arms.

"Before we start, I just want to look at you."

He slowly stripped her of her clothes, leaving her totally naked except for the strappy sandals. He stepped back from her and under the brightness of the light, stared at her. His eyes devoured her svelte body, the long, blond hair strewn around her shoulders and her black eyes. The swell of her breasts and the little jerky movements she made as she swayed from side to side waiting for him, took his breath away.

"You are the most beautiful woman I have ever seen, ever been with," his voice was gruff as he held her eyes for a few more moments before taking her with him onto the bed.

The night was a repetition of the previous, even more intense if that was possible. She was more relaxed although still very heightened in her awakening sexual awareness. Sex, lust or whatever it was, overtook them both completely.

When she awoke, she heard him in the shower. It was still very early. Again she joined him. She felt his scars and kissed their tract, her tongue flicking around the jagged edges. They returned to the bed. But their time together came to an end. He told her that he really had to go. Then he kissed her a final goodbye.

"I'll be here again in exactly four weeks," she told him as he was walking out the motel room.

"I'll see you then," he replied as he shut the door.

6

The day following Sarina's disappearance was even more frantic than the previous. Denise was inconsolable. Her husband tried his best to comfort her, but his attempts were futile. He also had his own sorrow to deal with. It was as if he were in a trance. Of all that had befallen him in his life, nothing compared to this.

The police now declared the property 'Sunshine' a crime scene. It was almost a repetition of what had occurred ten years previously.

The scenario was much the same. There were numerous accusatory questions couched in an understanding and empathetic manner. There was nothing alleged as yet. There was no point in antagonising a grieving family.

There were further, more thorough, searches undertaken. They were no longer looking for a missing child, but most probably a deceased child. It was impossible now to think she had run away or fallen into the creek and drowned.

The prime focus was to find a body or a murder weapon. There was little reason to suspect that this was a kidnapping, as there was no demand for a ransom. Police searches were well on the way delving into the personal and financial details of Michael and Denise Farraday.

For a couple who lived simply, they were very rich people. They owned property, houses and businesses. Their accountant, Dax Webster, was initially reluctant to disclose any information. He said a subpoena would be required. This was easily obtained.

Dax was flummoxed by the whole incident and just a little nervous. When the Farraday's had not turned up for their flight the previous day, he had phoned Michael only to be told to cancel everything as their daughter was missing.

While this was dreadful news of the worst kind, his mind went back ten years when he and the Farradays had hatched up their deal. He wondered if this had anything to do with the missing child.

Dax Webster and Michael Farraday had forged a successful partnership and had a grudging respect for each other. Although not good buddies, they got along well. They both had their talents but at the back of Dax's mind was the danger that was kept suppressed in Michael Farraday. Dax would never step out of line with their business dealings.

Dax had married a former successful, netball player, Laura. They had two children, a boy and a girl, much the same age as the Farraday children. When he heard the news about the missing child, he told the Farraday's he would manage the business side of things which would free them up to concentrate on their missing daughter.

SES volunteers and police had commenced a more thorough search of the property, walking side by side with eyes glued to the ground for any sign of a weapon or a body. The other Farraday brothers had returned to be with their brother and sister-in-law. They in turn were questioned by police—routine questioning such as where they were on the night of the disappearance. All had acceptable alibis for this time period.

When Malcolm saw the state his brother and sister-in-law were in, he knew he had to do something. He was very familiar with depression and haunted expressions. He lived with it every day. Over the years, he had seen Carrie change from a fun-loving woman to the wreck of a person she was today.

He didn't know if he loved her or if he ever had. All he knew was that she had helped him once, and he had made a vow to himself that he would always take care of her. Besides this, there was their daughter, Lucia, who was the joy of his life.

There were no restrictions on any of the Farraday's movements, so Malcolm took the opportunity to return to the medical practice he had visited the previous day.

He had not heard from Danny or Maryanne, so he assumed they were coping as well as the rest of them—which wasn't that good.

It was Denise who concerned him the most. She had been the strength that had seen them through their time of trouble all those years ago. Now it was time for the rest of them to come through for her.

He had no appointment but hoped the connection to the name of the missing child would be enough to get him in to see a doctor. He had seen the names of several doctors on the front door. The practice had grown substantially since Dr Sam Calhoun had owned it.

His wife had seen numerous doctors over the years, probably every doctor in the town, but as far as he knew, none from this practice. As for himself, the less he had to do with doctors, the better. He hadn't been to one for almost twelve years and had no intention of changing his habits. That one time was enough to last him a lifetime.

The same woman he had seen the previous day was at reception. When she saw him, she looked at him suspiciously before asking.

"How can I help you?" The woman well remembered the scandal surrounding the family.

"I was wondering if I could see a doctor?" he asked.

"Do you have an appointment?" When he told her he didn't, she asked if it was urgent.

"I suppose it is, not urgent like yesterday, but pretty urgent." He knew the woman had recognised him.

"I'll check and see what's available. Have you been here as a patient before?" she asked.

"Not for a while," he replied, knowing full well that the woman knew he had never been near the place, at least not in years.

She looked at the appointment book and said he could see a doctor if he could wait for fifteen minutes. He told her he could. The woman took his details. The fifteen minutes seemed to take forever. At last his name was called.

He was shown to a different consulting room. He sat on the chair as he had been requested and waited. Again time passed slowly.

He looked at pamphlets advertising various medications. He had no interest in these as both his wife and his mother had spent a large part of their lives consuming any number of them. He heard the door open.

"Sorry to keep you waiting. I've been busy," He turned around to see the same woman who had stitched up Danny.

"Oh, it's you." She looked startled, again conscious that she was wearing another short skirt. She seldom had good-looking men come through her door. "Back so soon." She tried to keep her voice even. There was no escaping the little thrill she felt inside her.

"Seems like it, Doc, but not for the tetanus injection." He tried to keep his eyes on her face, but they had disobeyed his conscious thought and travelled down the length of her. She found herself doing the same.

"Please sit down and tell me how I can help?"

He felt unsure of himself. "I don't know how to say this, but my sister-in-law isn't doing too well. I was wondering if there was something you could give her to help her cope."

This was a first. She'd never heard of anyone wanting something to help their sister-in-law cope. It was a novel way of asking for prescription drugs. He didn't look the type who was used to doctors. He looked more the type to be having a few puffs of marijuana.

"It's not usual practice to prescribe something without seeing the patient. That's not the way it works. If you need something for yourself, please say so. If it's really to get treatment for your sister-in-law, then please ask her to come and see me." She was being as frank as possible with him while maintaining her professionalism.

"Well, that's the trouble, Doc. She isn't exactly able to get to see you. She's kind of holed up at home. I was hoping maybe you could do a house visit. I could take you there, if you like." It was obvious that she did not believe him.

"If you could give me a few more details, maybe I'll see what I can organise."

She had no intention of going to see anybody with this man even if he was good looking. She realised then that he hadn't smiled at her even once.

He took his time replying, "It's not an easy thing to talk about. You see my niece disappeared yesterday and a finger has been found. It looks like it belongs to her. I guess you can understand why her mother isn't coping too well."

It all became instantly clear. She was ashamed of her dismissive attitude. Of course she had heard about the missing child. She had not thought to associate the names. She searched her mind for a suitable response.

"Oh, I didn't realise. I'm sorry. I didn't make the connection. How terrible for your sister-in-law. Of course I'll do anything I can to help."

He looked upset. He has his hand on her desk, so she put her hand over his, in a gesture of sympathy.

"I've got a little girl of my own. I don't know what I'd ever do if anything happened to her. I think I'd need something more than a pill to help me cope." He paused, turning his hand over to hold hers.

She did not remove her hand from his. She could feel the tension in him. "Is there anything you could give her to help calm her down? Denise can't stop crying and Mick's not much better. I've never seen either of them like this, not even during the bad times."

She wasn't sure what the bad times were.

"I'll come straight away. I'll let the office know it's an emergency. I'll get my bag and be right with you." She quickly organised her doctor's case. She threw in a few extra items.

When she was done, she asked. "You will take me there, won't you? I'm not that familiar with the area."

"Sure, if you're ready, I'll take you there now."

She followed him out to a red Alfa Romeo. The doctor watched the man sitting next to drive at speed back to the place where his family was living in their own private hell.

Upset as he was, he noticed the smooth, tanned legs that were on display beside him. She had tried her best to pull the skirt down, but it wasn't long enough to be pulled anywhere.

He tried to recall her name but couldn't. "What did you say your name was again?"

"Zaylee, Doctor Zaylee Lang." She was waiting for his comment on her name.

Sure enough, he soon asked. "What sort of a name is that? I've never met a Zaylee before."

"Not many people have. Probably something my parents made up. They liked to think they were trend setters. I guess I'm used to people asking me about it."

"Sorry, I didn't mean anything by it. It's a pretty name, kind of suits you." He looked over at her again, his eyes on the ponytail, "I mean you look so young, like you should still be at school."

"Thanks, I think, but I'm not that young. What about you? You said you have a daughter." This left an opening for him a mile wide. She noticed the wedding ring on his finger.

"Yes, I do—Lucia. This whole business has upset her. I told her last night that Sarina is missing. They're about the same age and very close. Are you any good with kids, Doc?" Their eyes again connected but not before he had glanced at the tanned, slim thigh that was just inches from his own.

"I like to think so," she answered. "If there's anything I can do to help, please give me a call. I'll leave you my business card. It's got all my details."

"Thanks, Doc, I might just have to do that, what with her mother being how she is."

She tried to follow where he was driving. This proved difficult as it was a winding road surrounded by large gums. Before she could get her bearings, they were turning into an obscured entrance to a property.

7

"This is my home, or used to be when I was younger."

As they drove in, she was overwhelmed at the activity that was occurring. There were numerous men and women searching the areas around the house. She could also see search parties tracking along a creek. She caught glimpses of more men and women combing the various tracks and paths among the thick forest that covered the hills.

He pulled up behind a number of other vehicles. She followed him to the house where he guided her up the steps and inside. There were several, large men sitting around in a kitchen, all looking much like Malcolm Farraday.

"These are my brothers," he said. "This is the doctor." They nodded to her and she nodded back.

The scene in front of her was overwhelming. They all looked so much alike. There was also a young woman who sat at the table with them. Again, there was a strong resemblance. She thought she must be their sister.

The woman was wearing brief shorts and had tattoos visible on her legs and back. Her dress sense didn't reflect that of the men at the table. She looked very much like the Farraday men but her demeanour was totally different.

"Where are Mick and Denise?" Malcolm asked his brothers. They pointed down the hallway. Zaylee followed him down a hallway to the last bedroom. He knocked briefly on the door then walked straight in. The doctor followed him.

She was taken aback by the grief on the faces of the two people who looked up at her as she entered the room. The woman, who was very attractive, was curled up on a double-seater chair, quietly sobbing.

A man sat beside her with a vacant expression on his face. He was another replica of the men who sat in the kitchen. This man and woman seemed to have lost all their vitality.

"Mick, Denise, this is the doctor. I thought maybe she could help." The two people concerned both looked at her. The doctor again cursed the short skirt she was wearing. She vowed she would go clothes shopping and buy something more suitable. She felt very unprofessional, especially when confronted by such a sad scene.

The two people did not notice her dress sense; they didn't seem to notice anything.

The man, Mick, as his brother had called him, nudged his wife then stood up out of good manners to greet her. His wife looked at her and managed to say, "Hello".

Zaylee looked at Malcolm and whispered, "Please don't leave." He nodded to her and then sat on a stool that was shoved into a corner of the room.

She was overwhelmed. What did one say to a couple who had lost a child—a child who may well already be dead, but if not, had obviously been mutilated? She tried to recall what she had read about counselling bereaved parents but everything seemed to have slipped out of her mind.

Then she remembered something that an old professor had said in one of his lectures on loss and grief. She recalled his words, '*Sometimes it's not the words you say. It's your presence and the fact that you are there.*'

She took a deep breath, walked over to the man, shook his hand and put her arms around him in comfort.

He nodded to her before saying, "Can you help my wife?"

These would have to be about the most difficult words she had ever had to deal with. Handing out a few pills was much easier. She didn't trust her voice, so she just nodded.

The doctor looked at Malcolm who gave her a small smile of encouragement. She sat beside the distraught woman, covering her hands with her own. When she felt sufficiently confident, the doctor took Denise in her arms.

The woman clung to her, sobbing out her fears and distress. "My little girl, our beautiful princess, she can't be gone, she just can't." The woman wept quietly. "She's going to walk through that door any minute, I just know it."

She looked at her husband, "Michael, you have to find her. You have to." He regarded his wife with desperation in his heart.

"We will, Denise, we'll find her, I promise." He cursed himself for his foolish words.

He had no idea how to find his daughter. Malcolm walked over to his brother and put his arms around him. The two men stood around awkwardly observing the women, before Malcolm said, "Come outside for a while, Mick. Get some fresh air."

He glanced again at the doctor. She nodded to him. "Go," she mouthed.

As the men left the room, her eyes again met Malcolm's. For the first time that day, he thanked her with his brilliant smile—the smile that went right up into his eyes. She thought she could look at that smile all day. It lifted her spirits and strengthened her confidence.

Zaylee spoke quietly to Denise. She didn't want to give her false hope, to pretend that there was nothing wrong but she had to give her some hope. Before she could think of some soothing words to say, the bereaved woman began talking about her children, her greatest accomplishments.

She talked for a long time, about her twin boys, Raphael and Gabriel, about when they were born; about what a shock it had been when they were only expecting one.

She spoke of her beautiful daughter, explaining how she had been a difficult baby; how she hardly ever slept through the night; how she had terrible colic; how she had fevers every time she was cutting teeth. But the child had grown out of these problems and was now a perfect child—except for the nightmares.

Denise spoke of the dolls the little girl loved. She explained about the collection of Barbie dolls and the doll house where they all lived. Then she said how Sarina and Lucia loved to play together. She asked the doctor did she know Lucia. The doctor pretended she did—it was only a small lie.

She knew of this second girl from the child's father. Denise spoke on and on about her children. The doctor sat beside her. She held her hand and listened. After a time, the mother of the missing child looked around her and said.

"Oh my goodness, how I've been prattling on; I'm not usually one for chatting, that's more Mia's style. Have you met Mia? Poor girl, it's not easy for her, but we do our best for her. There's really only Michael and myself who know what happened—except for Michael's mother." Denise wiped her eyes.

Dr Zaylee Lang wondered what it was that had happened to the woman called Mia. But it was not the time to be probing into this issue.

"But I'm forgetting my manners. I haven't offered you any refreshments. My mind is all over the place. I really can't get my thoughts on track. This must be how Mia feels. Do you think you can lose your mind?"

The young doctor tried to follow the words that were being spoken at great speed by Denise. "But first for some refreshments, come out to the kitchen and we'll have some tea, or coffee, or water, or juice or whatever you want."

She kept babbling on as Zaylee followed her to the kitchen where she shooed the men outside and asked Mia would she get the cups as she had to offer this kind woman some refreshment.

The sound of silence was deafening as the Farraday brothers looked at this changed woman, who was again taking charge—but who was also smiling at them all, with a look on her face that was akin to craziness.

The men did as they had been asked and went outside onto the veranda. Fortunately, Michael was not there to see the break in his wife's mind. He had gone outside by himself. Malcolm stayed close to the doctor. He could see she was out of her depth with this strange turn of events. She looked to him for guidance, but he shrugged his shoulders and shook his head.

Malcolm was familiar with his wife's depression and fatigue. He was used to her illness although he did not understand it. But this was the strong minded ex-detective that they all knew and had relied on especially during the worst days of their lives. Only now she wasn't the same person. Denise was now an unknown.

Zaylee Lang took it all in. She noticed that the woman called Mia was obviously puzzled at the change in Denise. Whether it was the right thing to say or not, Mia told Denise to sit down and she would make the tea.

Then, as she made tea and poured it into coffee mugs, Mia started chatting to the two women who were now sitting at the table.

"Did you know that Denise is my hero? She is the bravest woman I know. When we were young, that is Francine and myself, we wanted to be just like her but neither of us had the brains or the sense. Do you remember that, Denise?"

She waited until Denise indicated that she remembered. "You know, Doctor, we were such morons. In fact, we were terrible, but I was a whole lot worse than Francine." Mia stopped to suppress a laugh.

"We used to call Michael—the divine Michael Farraday—which he was. But now I think they're all divine, the whole lot of them. We're honorary family members—both of us. Maybe you could become an honorary member as well because you've got nice, black hair and dark eyes. You look a bit like the rest of us." Mia hardly stopped to take breath.

Zaylee Lang had no idea what this strange, young woman was babbling about, but at least Denise was sitting quietly sipping her tea and seemed to be enjoying the conversation. She even laughed a few times.

If this nonsensical chatter was therapy for the woman who seemed to be losing her mind, then she was all for it. The tea drinking and chatting kept on. Malcolm stood near the door taking in the strange scene before him. Anything was better than seeing his sister-in-law curled up in a ball sobbing incoherently. He looked admiringly at the doctor who had somehow managed to quieten the household.

Dr Lang wondered who she should talk to about her concerns regarding Denise. The woman was putting up barriers in her mind to help her cope with the dreadful events that were occurring. She looked at Malcolm and decided he would have to be the one, as it was he who had first approached her. She excused herself from the two chatting women and beckoned to him.

As he approached her, she took his hand and stepped back into the hallway.

"Denise is at the end of her tether. What she needs is sleep. They also need something to reduce their anxiety. If I give you some medications, do you think you can make sure they take them?"

"Of course, whatever you say, and thanks, Doc, for what you did in there. That was really something. I really appreciate it—we all do." Malcolm rewarded her with a half-smile, but it was enough to boost her faith in herself again.

"I really didn't do anything. It was that other woman, Mia; she really helped. Who is she?" The doctor was intrigued as to how this woman fitted into the picture of the Farraday family.

"Mia, well, she's just Mia. I guess she's always been around. It's been hard for Mia but she seems to get by." The doctor continued holding his hand as more activity and noise came from outside the house.

"Sounds like something's going on," he commented as they walked outside to the veranda.

The sergeant, holding an evidence bag, was walking towards Michael. "I need to talk to you and your wife, Mr Farraday."

If Michael was conscious of anything amiss, it did not show. His family watched on in interest.

"She's not holding up too well, Sergeant, but I'll go and find her. Maybe it would be better if you came inside."

The sergeant and two constables followed him into the kitchen. The Farraday brothers watched on. They positioned themselves outside the kitchen window so as to hear what was being said.

The sergeant entered the kitchen area where Denise and Mia sat. The young doctor also walked as far as the door to be close to Denise. The expression on the policeman's face was very serious. Zaylee kept looking at the evidence bag and did not like what she thought she saw.

"It might be better if you sit down next to your wife, Mr Farraday. It will make it easier all round." The sergeant looked uncomfortable.

Mia stopped chatting. Instead, she burst into tears as the sergeant strode determinedly into the kitchen. He motioned for her to leave. She joined the other brothers outside the kitchen window. As she continued to cry, Matt stood beside her and put his arm around her shoulders.

"I have a few questions for you both, but mostly you, Mrs Farraday." Denise seemed to have shaken off some of her grief as she looked expectantly at the sergeant.

"Have you found her, Sergeant? Please tell me you have?" Her face held both anticipation and dread.

"No, we haven't found her. But we did find what looks to be strong evidence of what may have happened to her."

He held up the evidence bag. "Is this one of your knives?" He waited while both Michael and Denise looked at the bag in dismay and puzzlement.

"It looks like one the knives I keep in the kitchen," Denise finally said after staring at the bag for some moments. "But how did you find it? Where was it?"

"It was found in the boot of your car, wrapped in what looks like a pillow case. Can you explain why it was there? It was hidden under your spare tyre; any ideas how it got there?"

Denise continued to look puzzled, but Michael quickly came out of his previously dazed condition. "Just what are you saying, Sergeant? Are you thinking that my wife put it there? Do you think it has something to do with what's happened to Sarina?"

"Yes—to both your questions, Mr Farraday. That's exactly what I think. But time and forensics will tell."

Michael was disconcerted by the sergeant's accusation. Surely he didn't think his wife had anything to do with their daughter's disappearance. He could feel himself becoming enraged. He tried desperately to hang on to his usual cool composure.

The sergeant continued on with his theories while the two constables stood at the door, keeping the doctor at bay. She heard what was being said as could Michael's brothers who remained outside the kitchen window.

"What can you tell me about the pillow slip? Is it one of yours?"

Denise slowly answered. She was struggling to follow the conversation.

"Yes, it's Sarina's. It's her security blanket. It's what she sleeps with. She wraps her dolls in it. She uses it for everything. What are those marks on it? It shouldn't be dirty. I wash it every day." She went to touch the pillow slip but the sergeant pushed her hand away.

"Those marks are blood, Mrs Farraday—the same blood that was found on the knife hidden away in the boot of your car. Have you any comment about that?"

Denise looked at her husband, "What's he saying, Michael?"

Michael swallowed hard, again seeing the crazed look returning to her eyes. "He's implying that you did something to Sarina, Denise. That you hurt her."

The woman looked confused. "I did smack her one time but only on the bottom. There wasn't any blood. She was being naughty, Michael. She and Lucia wouldn't behave. They wouldn't put their toys away. Do you think that's what he's talking about?"

"No, I don't think that's what he's talking about, Denise. I think he means that you did something worse." Michael didn't know how to tell his wife that the sergeant was as good as accusing his wife of murdering their daughter.

It was the accusatory expression on the sergeant's face that tipped Michael over the edge. Not only did he have a daughter who was missing and a wife who was in the process of losing her mind, but now he was being told his wife had as good as murdered their daughter.

No one was prepared for his reaction. Michael Farraday roared, then moved across to the sergeant and grabbed him by the shirt collar.

Before the two constables could intervene, he snarled, "Listen, you smart arse prick, you leave my wife alone."

His fist bunched up and connected with the sergeant's chin. This was followed by another blow to his nose. The sergeant would have fallen but he was grabbed again by his shirt collar and slammed up against the kitchen sink. Before any more blows could be delivered, the two constables were pulling him off the sergeant.

Michael Farraday had a reputation of being handy with his fists. He had once spent time in jail for belting up a man who had hurt his brother; he was in no mood to be man-handled by two young constables.

The first constable wasn't quick enough; before he knew it, he was at the receiving end of a punch to his abdomen which landed him on the floor. The other young constable, together with the now recovered sergeant finally restrained him. He was quickly cuffed.

When Denise saw her husband in handcuffs, she started screaming. "Leave him alone, just leave him alone."

The grieving woman now became as enraged as her husband. She kicked out at the sergeant who had her husband backed up against the wall with his firearm trained on him.

"Cuff her too," he snapped to the constable. Being a big, strong man, he had no difficulty overcoming the screaming and enraged woman.

"Get more help," the sergeant quickly instructed the young constable who immediately called his fellow officers.

The Farraday brothers were bewildered by this sudden turn of events. They had never been overly friendly with the local police. Their most intimate connection to the police was through Matt otherwise they kept their distance from those involved in any form of law and order.

This attack on their brother and his wife, as well as the unbelievable accusations being made against them, was too much. A melee erupted as brothers joined in. All the brothers, except for Mitch who tried to reason with his siblings, became caught up in the defence of their brother and sister-in-law.

They were all big, strong men but so were the people involved in the investigation. Fists were flying and punches thrown. Bodies landed on the veranda floor. Eventually, as law enforcement officers battled on, and it seemed as though there would be no back down from the Farradays, the decision was made to use Tasers. Batons had not gained any control.

Mitch's efforts to restrain his brothers had proven useless. None were prepared to listen to his voice of reason. He had been gone for years and had little knowledge of what his brothers had lived through. The fight soon ended. The brothers were trussed up, arrests made, the paddy wagon was called and they were escorted to the police station. Mitch watched on in bewilderment.

Denise lay curled up in a ball again on the floor of the kitchen, hands cuffed behind her. She was again sobbing uncontrollably as her battered mind finally put the pieces together as she realised what the police sergeant was implying.

They thought she had murdered her beloved daughter. This was beyond her scope of thinking. Surely no one could ever think her capable of that. The doctor ran over to her, ignoring protests from the sergeant.

As bravely as she could, she confronted him and said, "I'm this woman's doctor and she needs to be in hospital, not handcuffed and put into a paddy wagon."

She stood up to the sergeant, who was a giant in comparison to her own slender build. She forgot about her short skirt and the hair that had come loose. This was her job, what she had been trained to do, just as it was the sergeant's to arrest the Farraday's. He began to dismiss her but she stood her ground.

"I'm calling an ambulance and she's going to hospital." She reached for her mobile and began punching buttons.

The doctor emphasised who she was as she requested emergency help. She then helped Denise stand, before ushering her to a more comfortable chair. She quickly got her bag and gave her several tablets.

The ambulance soon arrived and after receiving instruction from the doctor, Denise was bundled onto a stretcher and carried away. Both the police sergeant and the doctor were again on their phones. The sergeant wanted the woman under police guard and the doctor wanted her to get the best mental health available.

The sergeant wanted to leave. He had endured enough. Before he did he spoke to Mitch who remained sitting on the front steps in a state of disbelief as he listened to Mia sobbing. Nothing he said made any difference to her.

"Always heard you were a wild bunch; how come you missed out?" The sergeant was quick to note that this man with his short crew-cut was probably bigger and stronger than the rest of them.

Mitch Farraday gave a dismissive shrug of his shoulders. "When are you going to let them out?"

"When they are processed and make bail; if they make bail, particularly your brother Michael." The sergeant announced.

"It was just a scuffle. They didn't mean anything by it," Mitch said as he tried not to look at the blood that was drying around the sergeant's nose.

"Not by the feel of my face," he replied. "They can all rot there together for all I care."

With these words, the sergeant decided enough was enough. He called to the few remaining police and the SES workers and announced that they were calling it a day. The doctor, Mitch and Mia were advised to leave as the entire property was a crime scene.

Mitch looked to the doctor and said, "I can't do anything with her. She just won't stop crying."

8

Zaylee was exasperated and exhausted. When Malcolm Farraday had arrived at the medical practice she never expected to be confronted with the unbelievable grief of a heart-broken mother, the endless crying of another woman and a brawl between police officers and a bunch of hot-headed brothers.

She looked at this big man who had told her that Mia would not stop crying and thought to herself that he looked big and tough enough to sort out any kind of problem.

Instead she said "I'll take her with me and drive her home." The doctor guided Mia to the Alpha Romeo.

She had no other way of getting herself home other than in the car she had arrived in. The keys were still inside. Mia seemed to understand when the young doctor explained she would take her home.

"Where do you live, Mia?" Zaylee asked as she drove towards Tewantin. "I take it you do live in Tewantin," she said, hoping she was heading in the right direction.

"I don't really want to be alone," Mia replied. "You can drop me off anywhere and I'll walk home."

Her next words were very plaintive. The doctor thought she would never forget what Mia said. "Other than Francine,

Michael Farraday was the only person who ever cared about me when I was young."

Her memory took her back to the words spoken by Denise earlier in the day. "I know Denise and Michael care about you, but who is Francine?"

"She's my best friend, only I don't see her that often any longer, not since her husband became sick."

"What about your boyfriend, then? Can I drop you at his place?"

"I don't have one of those either—never have had. I don't have anyone, really," Mia replied in a tired, listless voice.

The doctor was listening to a frightened, lonely person. She had difficulty digesting how this person beside her had confessed to never having had a boyfriend. She was very lovely with long, black hair and incredible eyes much like Malcolm Farraday. The tattoos added to her allure

Not knowing what else to do, the doctor made a suggestion. "How about we get something to eat then see what's happened to your friends? It's been a while so maybe they'll be released soon."

Mia made no reply, so the doctor took this for a yes. She bought two salad rolls and milk shakes then drove to the river.

Zaylee had a double purpose. She didn't know what to make of Mia nor did she know what to do with her. She could hardly leave the distressed woman alone. As well as this, she had no idea what to do with the car. The doctor and Mia sat on a bench beside the river, each with their own thoughts while they ate.

The evening shadows had lengthened when Zaylee said, "How about we go to the police station and see what's going on? Maybe we can help."

Her mind kept seeing punches being thrown. Mia followed her back to the car, not seeming to care where they were going. She was happy just not to be alone.

Zaylee pulled up at the police station. She had no idea what she was going to do as she had no knowledge of police procedures. They walked up the stairs together to be greeted by three of the Farraday brothers being released. There was no sign of the fourth brother, Michael.

As they were signing papers, the sergeant was forcefully lecturing the brothers. They all looked subdued and were agreeing to whatever he said. The doctor stood to the side and waited until the lecture was finished.

Malcolm had not noticed her and was about to walk past, when she touched his arm. He looked like he was ready to haul off again when he saw her.

For the second time that day she was rewarded with his smile, "What are you doing here, Doc? Not that I mind." He made no effort to remove her hand from his arm and neither did she attempt to shift it.

"I had to take your car because I had no other way of getting home, and I've got Mia with me. I don't know what to do with her. She seems so lost."

"I'd forgotten about how you would get home," he said. "Not that I'd forgotten about you, though. It was a good thing you did there today, Doc, before the shit storm happened anyway." He gazed down at the young woman beside him, "Sorry about that, Doc. I don't usually swear in front of ladies."

She didn't tell him that she had heard more swearing during the 'shit storm' than she had in her whole life. "About the car and Mia, what's going to happen?"

They were outside the police station. Mark was being picked up by a blond woman in an SUV with several children in the back. They all looked very grim.

Before he could respond, Matt asked, "How about a lift home, Mal? I've been suspended from my job and don't have any transport."

Matt did not think to ask why the Alfa Romero was at the police station. The two brothers, the doctor and Mia got into the car.

Malcolm manipulated the seating so that the doctor was sitting beside him leaving Matt and Mia in the back seat. In spite of the trauma of the day, he couldn't help but glimpse her legs.

"Can you take me home first Mal. Billy Bob is still in the yard. He needs to be walked." Mal was only too happy to oblige.

Mia sat beside Matt staring blankly out the car window. He noticed her despondency and said, "You feel like walking Billy Bob, Mia?"

Mia shook herself out of her reverie, "Sure Matt, I'd love to. It might make me feel better."

This arrangement suited Malcolm. Now he would have the doctor to himself not that he intended doing anything more than enjoy the pleasure of her company.

Matt's home was an average sized house with a large yard that was totally fenced in. This helped keep Billy Bob quiet during the time when he wasn't home.

"You feel like having a drink first, Doc, before I take you home. It's been a hell of a day," he asked after dropping off his brother and Mia.

"As a matter of fact, I'd like nothing more. As you say, it's been a hell of a day." The doctor answered immediately. She surprised herself as she was not given to making rash decisions. She should go home and call her boyfriend; that is if she could locate him or if he would even answer his phone.

He drove until he pulled up behind a large building. He opened the door for her. She followed him up some back stairs where he produced a key which led into a large office. He invited her to sit down then returned with a drink full of ice and lemon twirls. She noticed he only drank water himself.

"What is this place?" she asked, looking around. There was noise from the front and cooking smells.

"It's a restaurant," he replied. "Would you like something to eat? You can have whatever you like. We can eat right here."

"No thank you." She was perplexed by the surroundings but he wasn't making any explanations. It felt good to have her with him. He watched as she stood up and commenced looking around the room.

"This is quite a big office. You could almost live here." She went to sit down on a grey sofa.

"You better not sit there," he said quickly. It was the pull-out sofa bed he used for his trysts. He didn't want her sitting there. She was special, made for better things. Before he could stop her, she was sitting down. He couldn't help but peek again at the legs which the short skirt did little to cover.

The image of her sitting on the grey lounge did not sit well with him. "Maybe I'd better take you home."

This surprised her. "Oh, all right then. I'll just finish my drink." It was the quickest drink she had ever shared with anyone.

Before she knew what was happening, she was being escorted back down the stairs and into the Alfa Romeo. Once there, he was in no hurry to get moving.

"How about you tell me all about yourself, Doc?" He said as he pulled out into the traffic.

"Not much to tell really. I went to school, then university to study medicine, graduated and here I am. I have a mum and a dad, but no brothers or sisters. Not like you," she added.

They chatted on while he drove. Before she knew it, she was parked in front of her home. "How do you know where I live? I never told you." She sounded alarmed.

"Relax Doc, I haven't been checking up on you. One of the women where I work said her husband was friends with Dr Zaylee's boyfriend. She seemed to know all about you and your boyfriend. I didn't think there could be two Zaylees."

"Oh, that's weird all the same. I'm not in the habit of telling people where I live. It didn't take you long to find out. I only met you yesterday."

"It kind of feels like I've known you forever, Doc," he looked up at the darkened windows of her home. "I better walk you in; looks like the boyfriend isn't home yet."

She made no comment about this. Instead she got out of the car in a hurry and was through the gate and started up the flight of stairs knowing he was close behind.

She could sense him behind her. If she slowed down, he would bump right into her. She was tempted to slow down, because damn it, the boyfriend was out again, not home waiting for her.

After the day she had just lived through, she knew just what Mia was talking about when she said she didn't want to be alone tonight. She was feeling sorry for herself, when he spoke.

"Did you know, Doc that you've got the nicest arse I've ever seen?" She stopped abruptly and swung around to face him. She was on the higher step so they were face to face.

"I apologise, Doc. I didn't mean anything by it. That sort of just slipped out. What I mean to say is—you not only have the nicest arse but the nicest legs as well. I haven't seen the rest of you, but I'm betting it's all pretty nice."

Their faces were very close. She could still see the smile in his eyes in spite of the dark of night. "Is this a new type of pick up? You could have told me I was petty or good looking, not tell me I have a nice arse. Not very romantic, Mr Farraday, I thought you could do better than that."

"It really hasn't been the day for thinking up smart pick-up lines, Doctor Zaylee. In case you haven't noticed, I'm not exactly dressed for a pick-up. I've been in a brawl along with my brothers and in the lock-up. Which reminds me, I'd better be getting home to the wife."

This put a dampener on the stirrings in both of them. It was like a cold bucket of water being thrown over them. But having come through the trials of the day, a little spark still remained.

He took her in his arms. Their lips met, tentatively at first and then as they discovered each other, the kiss exploded. There was no guessing where his hands finished up. They were right around her buttocks pulling her in close. No little, short skirt stopped the fingers that were pressing and massaging into her firm flesh. The feeling and touching went on until finally he pulled away from her.

"I gotta get home, Doc, still got things to do." With that he left her trembling on the top step as he drove away.

When he arrived home, he checked on his young daughter. As she was sound asleep, he covered her up then kissed her good night. He went to the bedroom he shared with his wife, showered and changed then crawled into bed beside Carrie. She was still awake with eyes half-closed

"Do you still love me, Mal?" she asked, in a weak, tremulous voice. "Don't ever leave me, Mal. Promise me."

"You know I'll never leave you, Carrie, never." With that he kissed his wife gently on the forehead, and pulled her thin, childlike, bony body against his. He lay there thinking of the day's events as he heard his wife's breathing slow down and knew she had slipped off to sleep.

9

Sarina was fast asleep in her bed at home on the night the monsters came and took her. She would always be confused by what happened. Her mother and father had put her to bed. They had laughed with her as they pulled the Dora sheets over her. She wore her Dora Explorer pyjamas and it was exciting to have matching sheets.

Lucia, her cousin, had told her she was getting too old for Dora pyjamas, but she had always loved Dora, how she went on adventures and how she could solve so many riddles. Yes, she loved Barbie, the little mermaids, and once she had loved princesses, but underneath it all she thought Dora was spunkier than the others.

She had heard her father say that her mother was spunky. That was what she wanted to be, spunky like her mother and Dora.

She knew nothing of being carried out of her bed. Her first realisation of something being wrong was when she awoke to see a monster dressed in black.

She was terrified and started screaming, but the monster clamped his hand over her mouth and said terrible words to her. She could not fully follow what the monster was saying but she did know that he said he would kill her, her mummy and daddy as well as her brothers if she didn't keep quiet.

The child was petrified not only by the monster that held her but by the other monsters that she could see in the front of the vehicle where they had taken her.

Then there were two monsters holding her down. One of them dangled a knife in front of her eyes. The monster holding her down, kept a hand over her mouth, while the other took the knife and cut off the little finger on her left hand. Just like that, with no warning.

The finger was swiftly sliced off from the rest of her hand by a thin bladed knife. The child could not scream out because of the hand held over her mouth, but in her heart and mind she was screaming in pain and anguish—wanting her mother and father.

Terror overtook her as she fainted. Her only means of defence had been the screams that were in her head.

10

Mia took Billy Bob for his walk. She put the leash on him, and let him lead her where he wanted to go. She followed behind, trying to keep up with him and to control his strong movements. She started to feel better as she followed behind the dog until she recognised where he was taking her.

She was at the back of Sundial Park. When she realised this, she had a moment of panic. This was the place where she had spent time as a teenager and the place where she had almost been taken. She glanced around and saw that nothing much had changed. It still looked run down although the lawns had been recently mowed.

There was rubbish piled around trees as well as palm fronds and branches that had fallen to the ground. They remained scattered across the few tracks that remained in the park.

As she let Billy Bob off his leash, he quickly scurried off into the bushes. She thought she would give him a few minutes running around before calling him back. She looked around for a bench to sit on but there was none, so she was forced to sit on a swing.

Not that she minded. It was a carefree feeling swinging up and down while Billy Bob rummaged through the grass and trees.

It was becoming dark, so she headed back to where Matt lived. After the events that had happened to her in this park years ago, she had seldom been back. She had been so frightened back then, not sure what was happening. It was thanks to Michael Farraday that she had escaped the man who was after her.

That was one good thing about her crazy brain. She had the ability to put things out of her mind altogether. Well, almost altogether. But the darkening sky prompted her to hurry with Billy Bob again leading the way.

When she returned, Matt met her at the gate. He had showered and changed. He took the dog from her, rubbed him down and fed him. When he was finished she followed him inside. She had not been to his home before. There was little furniture; just some kitchen stools around a serving bench and a few lounge chairs that sat before a large television set.

"What a bloody awful day it's been. I feel like having a beer. Would you like to join me?" Matt asked.

She had always thought of him as a younger brother. Not that she had ever had much to do with him over the years.

"I've never felt so lost or lonely in all my life. I can't believe what's happened. I think I'll need more than one beer to make me feel any better."

Matt showed her where the refrigerator was. He added that there was another fridge in the garage.

She went to the kitchen refrigerator and got them a bottle each. They sat beside each other on the lounge. "I haven't been drunk in years. Not since before that day. Do you ever think about it, Matt?"

"I'm not likely to forget," he replied. He noticed that her bottle was empty; he went to get them both another.

"What do you think has happened to her?" she asked.

"I've no idea. It's different from last time—with my dad and Jack Smith. They're both gone, as well as your mother, Mia. I'm sorry about that."

"Doesn't matter, Matt, it was so long ago. Anyway, let's not talk about it or I'll start crying again; how about another one?" She got up to get a refill. There were a few stumbles as she carried them back.

As she sat down, she spilled half the bottle down the front of the top she was wearing as well as onto the lounge chair. "Oops, sorry about that; I'll clean it up then I'd better have a shower. You don't mind if I use your shower?"

"No, help yourself." He pointed to the bathroom. Before he knew what she was doing, she had whipped off her blouse and began wiping up the spill that had already soaked into the lounge chair.

Matt was stunned to see Mia in her skimpy bra and brief shorts rubbing away at his lounge chair. He saw the big tattoo of a butterfly on her back. He was mesmerised by it.

"That will have to do. I'm off for a shower; you keep the beer cold. I won't be long." Then she was gone, trying her best to walk straight.

He grinned to himself as he watched her disappear. As he heard the water splash down, his thoughts turned to his occasional girlfriend. Just as well he hadn't made any plans. It would be difficult to explain the woman in his shower.

He sat back, slowly sipping his beer while he thought of his future. He'd probably lose his job, but he felt a sense of relief in being able to get some of the frustration out of his system. Not that he wanted to be fighting with his workmates, but the thought of Mick and Denise losing their daughter was unthinkable. His troubles paled in comparison.

He had finished his beer and had another in his hand when Mia returned from the shower. He did a double take when he saw she was wearing one of his police shirts. It was much too big for her, covering her down to mid-thigh.

"Hope you don't mind," she said. "It was the first clean thing I could find."

"No, I probably won't need it again anyway. Besides it looks better on you than me." He couldn't help but notice she had left half the buttons undone.

"You think so. I could almost wear it as a dress. What do you think?" She spun around, trying to flare out the ends of the shirt. As she did so, the shirt pulled up and he had a fine view of her backside. He tried not to look.

"When did you get to be so big, Matthew Farraday?" she asked. "You were just a skinny kid back when when it happened," she commented, looking down at his oversized police shirt.

All he could do was look at her as she pranced around in his shirt. "Did you get me another beer? I'm still sober and still standing, but I'm getting mighty hungry. What have you got in your kitchen?"

"Not much," he confessed.

"Well, that's one of my few talents—making a meal out of nothing. I learned how to live on next to nothing when I was a kid living with my grandmother. Come on, Matt, let's explore your kitchen."

With that she pulled him up, spilled some more beer on his lounge chair and again told him she was sorry. She promised she would clean it up later. He told her not to bother about it, that they'd probably spill a lot more before the night was done and it could all wait till tomorrow.

He followed her into the kitchen. She skipped, laughed and twirled around in his shirt, as she started checking the cupboards, pulling out whatever she could find. They drank more beer while she considered what they could eat.

"I'll tell you what the menu is for tonight. We can have either dog food or weetbix with vegemite, jam or honey. Which do you prefer?" She didn't wait for him to reply. "I know what we'll do, how about a bit of everything."

"I'm not too sure about the dog food. Billy Bob still has to have breakfast. I guess the rest of it is all right." He watched as she started spreading vegemite over the weetbix.

"Here, have a taste of this. It goes well with beer." She held the weetbix up to his mouth and he took a bite. She wiped a speck of vegemite off his lips before handing him his bottle of beer. She told him to wash it down quick or it would get stuck in his mouth.

"Just pretend its milk. It goes down better. If you shut your eyes, you can put anything with dry weetbix. You can use water, cordial or whatever you can find in the cupboard. It can keep you going for weeks."

He couldn't imagine anything worse than weetbix with cordial. He looked at Mia and wondered about her childhood, about her family. As far as he knew, she didn't have any. It was the reason why Mick and Denise kept an eye on her.

"Ready for the second course," she giggled as she sipped on another beer. "We'll have desert before I'm totally wasted." She delved into the box, pulled out several more weetbix which she liberally covered with honey. "The honey might spoil the taste of the beer but we can always finish off with more vegemite."

This time it was his turn, he held the weetbix dripping with honey up to her mouth. She giggled, took a swig on her bottle then took another bite. This time the honey spilled over the side of the weetbix and down the front of the partially buttoned police shirt.

"Oops, better clean that up." She opened the shirt up further. "You did it, Matt, so you clean it up."

He was more than a little drunk himself, so he unbuttoned the shirt altogether. As he looked at her breasts covered with drizzled honey, he took a breath, then bent down and started licking off the honey. Her breasts became taut and the nipples hardened. He couldn't help himself as his mouth covered her breast.

He heard her choked voice, "What are you doing?" Her voice was no more than a whisper. She made no move to stop him. For once in her life, she couldn't think of a thing to say. She thought she might swoon at the sensations that were coursing through her.

She might not be talking but she was making moaning noises. It was these noises that brought him to his senses. At first he thought it was Billy Bob; that somehow the dog had managed to get inside.

The half-drunken Matthew stopped what he was doing, straightened up, and then pulled her shirt together.

"Geez, Mia, I'm sorry. I didn't mean to do that. I don't know how it happened. Guess it was the beer." He grabbed a paper towel, wet it and gave it to her. "Here, you better do it yourself."

She didn't trust her voice but managed to stammer out a few words. "That's okay, my fault. Honey can do that—dribble off the weetbix, I mean."

She hardly knew what she was saying. She took the paper towel and rubbed the rest of the honey off her chest. "Maybe we better clean up. At least we had something to eat."

They cleaned up together, not that there was much to do, only put the weetbix, vegemite and honey back in the cupboard. Mia did what she did best, and that was to start chatting away about nothing.

When the one knife they had used, was washed and put back in the drawer, she said, "How about another beer?"

Before he had a chance to reply, she was off to the garage to find some more. The refrigerator in the kitchen was empty. When she came back, she had two more bottles.

"I think I'm a little drunk," she said as she sat down beside him again on the lounge chair. "Maybe I should go home."

"You don't have to Mia. I think maybe we're both pretty drunk, although the weetbix might have sobered us up a bit." They sat together, for once Mia was quiet. She had run out of things to say.

"Do you mind if I kiss you, Mia?" he asked, moving closer to her. He took the near empty bottle from her hand, put it on the floor, then leaned over and pressed his lips to hers.

After the first tentative kiss, she replied, "I suppose I don't. That was nice; want to try again."

After that, the kissing became more intense. He explored her lips, his tongue probing its way inside her mouth. His hands had somehow found their way back inside his police shirt. She loved the feel of his hands around her breasts

"How about we go to the bedroom? It's got to be more comfortable than here. Besides, we'll fall over the empties if we're not careful." He pulled her up and dragged her after him.

They were both more than a little drunk. They fell onto the bed together. Matt removed his clothes and had already pulled the shirt off her. Just as he suspected, she had nothing else on other than her tattoos and her metal piercings.

"Oh, wow, Mia, you are incredible. Can I look at you first before we get started?" He lay her down on the bed then he stood back and stared.

Her long, black, silky hair was spread out around her. He looked at her eyes shining black and glistening in front of him. His eyes feasted on her slim, lithe body, her rounded full breasts. He lay beside her, kissing and touching. Then he raised himself over her, their bodies touching.

"Are you ready for this, Mia," he asked, staring at her. He didn't think he could hold back much longer.

"I've never done this before, Matt. I hope I get it right. You'll have to tell me what to do."

It took him a moment to realise what she had said. He drew back off her. "What do you mean? You've never done it before?" There were tears beginning to form in her eyes. "You mean you've never had sex before."

She looked away as though she were ashamed. "Look at me, Mia. Don't look away."

He put his hands around her face and forced her to look at him. He thought his heart was going to stop at the hurt in her face. "Hey, don't cry. It's okay. If you want to stop, just say so."

He kissed her again, this time, it was sweet and gentle. "If you want me to keep going, you don't have to say anything, just nod your head, but you better hurry up because I don't think I can hold off much longer." He held her while he waited for her signal.

Mia Lamont, the girl reputed to be the biggest flirt in town, whose mother disappeared, who never had a father, who had no relatives, who had never had a man take her in his arms and just love her for herself, considered her options.

On this day, which was one of the worst in her life, she had to decide if this was what she wanted.

She looked at Matt, the man she had always thought of as a younger brother, who wanted to make love to her. All she had to do was to nod her head. Or shake it. She felt frightened. Then she wondered if this was where her life was leading her—to Matthew Farraday.

She swallowed then smiled at him, and nodded her head.

He kissed her lips again very tenderly. Then his mouth moved down to her throat. She started to moan, so he kept kissing her neck while his hands played with her breasts. Their bodies were pressed close together. She was quivering and groaning. Their love making commenced.

Eventually they were spent. They lay unmoving for some time before he rolled off her and pulled her close to him.

"You don't have to cry, Mia. It's supposed to make you feel better," he said, listening to her quiet tears.

"I can't help it. It was just so incredible, Matt. Thank you for showing me what to do. I could have gone my whole life and never knew what it was like." She rolled over to face him. "Do you think we could do it again? That is if you want to."

"Sure I want to, Mia. We can do it all night if you like. Are you sure you don't want to get some sleep, we're both still half drunk?"

"I've got the rest of my life to sleep, Matt. Of course I want to—right now if you think that's okay."

Matt may not have been as old as Mia Lamont but it was his pleasure to lead and hers to follow. Mia was more fulfilled and content than she had ever been in her lonely life.

The night was well and truly over. The sun was pouring in through the slatted blind. They were both amazed at the night they had spent together. They were initially shy with each other, but relaxed when they saw all the empty beer bottles and beer spills.

By the time they had finished cleaning up, they were both hungry. There was still nothing more than weetbix but this time it was relieved with long-life milk which Mia found in the cupboard. The honey was also a welcome addition. She deliberately spilt a few drops down the front of her chest and, of course, he just had to lick them off.

Billy Bob was scratching and whining at the back door. It was time for the dog to be fed and walked. They stayed together the entire day as neither had a car. The weather was fine so they walked with Billy Bob down to the shopping centre where Mia had once worked.

They bought as much as they could carry. Like a pair of kids they walked back to Matt's house.

Before they left the shopping centre, Matthew slipped into the pharmacy and purchased some protection. He had not anticipated the events of the previous night and knew Mia hadn't either. He could not believe she had never been with any one before. He had heard all the rumours about her as a youngster. He was perplexed by the whole persona of Mia Lamont.

She may be an oddity but the fact remained she was a quick learner when it came to the bedroom. All thoughts of his sometimes girlfriend disappeared. He wondered how long this liaison with Mia would continue. After another sexual encounter, he knew he had to broach the subject as Mia had little in her mind other than her new past time.

He was certain she gave no thought to protection. At least, she hadn't cried for hours and only mentioned Sarina a few times. It didn't take much to divert her from her miserable thoughts.

"Mia, are you on the pill?" he asked.

"I take vitamin pills—vitamin D. They say we don't get enough sun because we're inside most of the day, but that's all." She replied, cuddling up to him.

"No, Mia, I mean the contraceptive pill, birth control, not vitamins." He rolled her over to face him. There could be no more frolicking around in the bed until he could set her on the right track.

"You mean, to stop babies happening, that sort of pill?" She was paying more attention to him now.

"That's exactly what I mean. If you're not Mia, you better go see a doctor, that is, if we're going to keep on doing this. You do want to keep doing this, don't you?" He trailed his hand around the big butterfly tattoo on her back.

"Of course I want to keep doing it, but only with you Matt. I've never been to a doctor before except when I was a little kid and the child welfare told my grandmother I should be immunised. Maybe I could see that nice doctor who looked after Denise. Do you think that would be all right?"

"That sounds like a good idea. I'll get you there to see her as soon as I've got transport. Or maybe we could go on my bike." He didn't wait for her reply; he was on his mobile making an appointment, "How about this afternoon?"

That same afternoon, Dr Zaylee Lang was puzzled to see Mia in her consultation room. She immediately remembered how desolate she had been the previous day.

Instead she found a totally different person. At first Mia was tongue tied, could hardly get her message across, but at the same time she was cheerful and was what some women referred to as *glowing*. She was smiling and had a gleam in her eye that the doctor hadn't noticed previously

Eventually, Dr Zaylee determined that Mia was asking for contraception. When she asked about her medical history, Mia told her she didn't have any as she had never been to see a doctor before, at least not that she could ever remember.

The young doctor was perplexed. She did an examination and some blood tests, before writing a prescription. Mia was giddily happy as she left. Zaylee could not help herself as she followed her new patient out the front door.

Her eyes followed Mia as she walked towards a young man. She watched Matthew Farraday ride off on his motor bike with Mia seated behind him. The young doctor was more perplexed than ever.

11

Sarina awoke with excruciating pain in her left hand. She was terrified. There was no mother or father to take her pain away. She looked down at the hand that was causing her unbearable pain. It remained covered with thick bandages.

She again closed her eyes and told herself that it was another bad dream, like the ones she had when she woke screaming.

Her dreams were often worse when it was raining or when the thunder crackled and the lightning flashed across the sky. It was then that she would run to her parent's bed for safety.

After a time, because there had been no noise in the place where she lay, she was brave enough to open her eyes again. Shyly, she looked around and realised she was in bed in a room with high, dark walls and high windows.

She thought she would sit up but when she tried to, the pain in her left hand became worse so she cradled it in her right hand. After a time she did manage to sit up. As soon as she was upright, she again felt giddy so she lay back down in the bed, being careful not to bump her left hand.

She kept her eyes closed, not really sure if she was asleep or awake. Her most prominent sensation was the endless pain in her hand. She tried to remember what had happened to her. Then the image of the black monster returned to her. So she remained on the bed. When her hand did not hurt as much, she put her right thumb into her mouth.

She heard a noise, like a rattling sound coming from outside the room. The noise stopped; then she heard footsteps. She hoped it was her mummy or daddy or even her brothers. Even though they teased her and often told her she was a scaredy cat, she prayed they would walk through the door and save her.

But instinct told her that the footsteps belonged to none of her family. If they belonged to her brothers or her parents, there would be voices, laughing and talking. She shut her eyes even tighter and sucked harder on her thumb. Then she heard a voice speaking to her.

"Hello, Sarina. Are you awake?" The voice was soft and gentle. It gave the little girl the confidence to open her eyes. When she looked towards the voice, a woman with dark hair and eyes was staring at her. She thought the woman looked like her Aunty Maryanne or Mia—only younger.

"My name is Maria and I want to make sure you're all right. Does your hand still hurt?" The woman knew that of course the hand still hurt; that it would always hurt one way or another, if not physically then mentally. A scar on her hand might form and heal but never the scars in her mind.

Sarina looked at the woman, not speaking. "If you like," the woman continued. "I can give you something to help take the pain away. Would you like that?"

The girl nodded. The woman pulled a bottle from her pocket and poured some of the liquid onto a spoon. Sarina opened her mouth and swallowed. "I'll return as soon as I can to give you some more medicine. Do you feel hungry or thirsty?"

Sarina managed to say *thirsty* in a weak, tearful voice. The woman disappeared. When she returned she held a cup of water in her hand. As Sarina began to drink, she noticed the woman's hands.

Had she not been so thirsty she would have refused to drink because the sight of these hands frightened her. Her eyes glistened with tears. Fear was rippling across her small face as she looked at the woman who had not one, but two fingers missing.

"I have to go now, but I'll be back as soon as I can." The woman started to walk away from her.

"Where are my mummy and daddy?" The young girl asked in a tremulous voice.

This was the question the woman was dreading. How should she answer? The child needed to have some hope or else she might just pine away in front of her eyes.

"Your mummy and daddy and all your family are out looking for you, Sarina." The woman replied.

The little girl said no more as the woman left her. She was more confused than ever. If her parents were out looking for her than why didn't the woman just tell them where she was? Sarina pondered this question before she again fell asleep, cradling her left hand in her right.

12

In spite of having Dax Webster and a host of solicitors, Michael Farraday was not granted bail. All the money in the world could not help his cause. He had nothing to do all day but to wonder why this tribulation, by far the worst in his life, had befallen his family.

He received regular updates on his wife's condition. He knew she still remained under police guard in hospital, knew that she had shown little reaction when questioned or spoken to. This was not the same woman whom he loved with all his being.

He wondered if his wife, who had fought for him, protected him and had contrived to keep him out jail, would ever recover from the disappearance of their daughter. He doubted he would if she was never found.

The reasons why he had not been granted bail were extensive. It was alleged that he already had a history of violence, of brawling and fighting. He had previously been convicted of grievous bodily harm and had spent six months in jail.

He had also been convicted of drug possession and had been indirectly involved in the shooting of a man. The remains of a missing woman, Mandy Lamont, had been found on the property where he and his wife now lived.

As there was no firm evidence as to how Mandy Lamont had died or was buried, it was eventually concluded that she may have been killed and buried by either Jack Smith or Alan Farraday or person or persons unknown.

But the stigma remained about Michael Farraday and his involvement in this woman's death. Rumours died down but they did not go away altogether.

Michael and Denise were charged with the mutilation, murder and disposal of the body of their daughter, Sarina.

There was sufficient evidence to prove this allegation. Forensic testing proved that the blood found on the back steps of their home, along with the dismembered finger were those of their daughter.

As well as this, the blood found on the knife and pillow slip which were shoved under the spare tyre in Denise Farraday's car, was also proved to belong to the missing child. Added to this, the fingerprints on the knife were those of Denise Farraday's.

There was also ample motive and opportunity for this horrendous crime. The opportunity was always there—just waiting for either Michael or Denise to snap and kill their daughter.

It was alleged that they had cracked under the strain of their daughter's constant waking in the night with her nightmares and terror screams. Subpoenas into the release of her medical history revealed that Sarina Farraday had been a poor sleeper all her young life.

Her nightmares and screaming were well documented. It seemed all treatments to alleviate this disturbing condition had failed. Everyone knew how tiring it was to have a child who barely slept. Michael and Denise had endured more than their fair share of sleepless nights.

It was easy to see how it had happened—how either one parent or the other had finally come to the end of their tether, and whether intended or not, the little girl had been threatened with dire punishment which ended in this actually occurring.

The finger had been severed. Forensic evidence indicated this had occurred while the child was still alive. As there was no sign of her body, it was alleged that between them they had killed the little girl and disposed of her body—whereabouts unknown.

Even though Michael and Denise were well off, there had been no ransom demand for the return of their daughter, so that ruled out kidnapping. All other family members had alibis for the time frame involved.

All agreed that the missing girl's parents often complained of sleepless nights because of their daughter, but none had ever had reason to suspect abuse. In fact, they all told the opposite story of the parent's absolute devotion to their children and especially their daughter.

Family members also had their properties searched to no avail. Computers, mobile and landline phones were checked. Family members were told not to leave town in case they were required for more questioning.

Michael and Denise Farraday's finances were of particular interest. Dax Webster explained how Denise had come into money from her deceased parent's estate. Together, the three of them had formed a partnership that proved to be very lucrative.

Fortunately for the accountant and the Farraday's, Dax Webster's abilities for hiding and cleaning the money that Michael and Denise had produced week after week in small amounts all those years ago, was too difficult to track after such a long time.

There was no reasonable explanation for the missing child other than that she had been murdered and her body disposed of by her parents.

Denise was fighting to climb out of the haze that engulfed her. She still lay curled up in a ball, still had bouts of crying, but at the back of her mind she knew she had to fight to pull herself up and out of the black hole that consumed her. She had a husband who was again languishing in jail and twin sons who still needed both their parents.

Michael was in disbelief about all these recent happenings. His life had been shattered once when he was fifteen, now at thirty seven it was happening all over again. He lay in his cold cell with only a thin blanket and his misery for company.

13

The days following the disappearance of Sarina were difficult for Michael's brothers and his sister, as well as their respective families. The twin boys, Gabriel and Raphael remained with their Uncle Mark and Aunt Tiffany.

Arlo was their cousin and good friend, but having three boys of similar age and two being twins, there was a clash of personalities. Arlo became the odd man out in his own home. Not that the twin boys meant for this to happen, but they were both feeling the effects of their parent's being labelled as murderers.

The good natured Mark did his best to keep peace and harmony between the boys. He eventually bought them a pack of cards each and when the squabbles became too much, he sent them off to their respective room and told them to play solitaire.

Mark coped well with the boys, but Tiffany did not have the patience of her husband. She told Mark that she had to escape; to get out of the house or else she would go mad with the strain of it all.

After all, she explained, she was a Farraday as well, and wasn't he aware that they were all being tarnished with the same brush? It was not easy living in a town where their name was mud.

Danny Smythe was of similar mind. He had always loved his wife, Maryanne, right back to when she was a teenager when she had become pregnant by him at the age of fifteen. At first, when they started living together he thought he had struck paradise as sex was available to him day and night, but then more children came along, and the gloss began to wear.

But strangely enough, since she had stabbed him, either intentionally or not, their marriage had improved considerably. Even the baby was sleeping through the night, so sex with his wife was as good as ever.

He wondered about Maryanne as she seemed to have wiped the episode of the knife totally from her mind. Except for the wound on his arm and the nick on his face, it was as if nothing had happened.

The major concern was what had happened to Sarina as well as the charges made against Michael and Denise. How they had both ended up either in jail or hospital was a mystery to them all?

The Smythe children were less affected than those of Mark and Malcolm. Because of their different surnames, fewer people knew of the connection. But it remained a harrowing and puzzling time for all of them.

Danny was wary of Michael. But not for a moment did he think Michael or Denise had anything to do with their daughter's disappearance.

He thought back to the day ten years ago when Denise had shot Jack Smith straight through his forehead—stone cold dead. It was the same day that Alan Farraday hung himself. It was also the same time that his eldest daughter had been born—much to Danny's surprise. Danny had to get away from home—to escape the memories.

He told his wife he was going for a beer. He asked if she intended going to her regular yoga class. When she replied that she felt too tired, he took the vehicle she usually drove. Danny drove straight to the Royal Mail Hotel. He had two beers to help drown his sorrows when he saw Tiffany.

He made a bee-line for her, not that he had any intention of furthering their liaison. It was good to have someone to talk to about their situation; someone who had the same problems and understood all the ramifications involved.

They drank and idly talked before Tiffany suggested they go for a drive. It would give them more privacy to discuss the family problems.

Danny agreed as long as that was as far as it went. They left one at a time. Neither wanted more scandal in the family. Danny had good intentions, but if it was on offer, he knew of lots of quiet places to pull over.

Tiffany had come prepared. She knew from past experience that he often stopped for a beer. This wasn't one of his regular nights, but sometimes routines changed and luck came along.

Before she joined him, she pulled a long, black wig over her short, blond hair. She was fond of her husband, but from her point of view, it was no great love match even though her husband was besotted with her. Not that Danny was all that hot either, but life could get very boring.

Under the current circumstances, it would be unwise to be caught with her husband's brother-in-law. The black wig was camouflage. She felt confident that from a distance, she could pass for Danny's wife. Everyone knew the Farradays had black hair, and Maryanne was no different.

"What's with the wig," Danny asked, staring at the woman who had hopped in beside him.

"You can't be too careful, Danny. If anyone sees us, who do you think they'll suspect I am." Tiffany flicked her black hair around before moving closer to him, her hand on his leg.

"Let's just wait and see, Tiff. We'll get out of here first then see how it goes. It wouldn't do to get caught."

He drove until he came to a rest area off the main road.

"What's happened to your arm?" she asked, noticing the bandage.

"Just an accident, cut it with a fishing knife," he replied. Tiffany was already almost on top of him.

"Shouldn't affect your performance," her voice was husky as she started kissing him.

It was then that Danny remembered his wife's threatening words and thought of the knife that she had wielded. What had she said—something about filleting his slag girlfriend if she ever caught up with her? These words stayed with him as he made the decision to rebuff Tiffany's advances.

"I think I'd better be getting home. I'll drop you back at the hotel." She was less than pleased. He heard her groan of frustration as he headed back towards Tewantin.

"A lot of fun you turned out to be," Tiffany chided him as they began the descent down the steep section of the road. "I should have stayed home with Mark. At least he never knocks me back."

"Why didn't you then? Mark's a good man. He'd never do you wrong?" Danny had a twinge of conscience as he thought of his old friend.

He also thought of Malcolm, how the three of them had been such good friends most of their lives, at least up until the fateful day ten years ago when all their lives had changed. He wondered if this was another era when their lives were again changing.

His SUV was gaining speed rapidly. Danny applied his brakes, but nothing happened. He tried again, still nothing. The vehicle gained more speed. He dodged all the uphill vehicles in the passing lane. There were headlights coming at him at incredible speed.

It took him only a moment to realise that it was his vehicle that was traveling at incredible speed. He again tried his brakes, still nothing happened. His vehicle kept gaining speed. He tried his hand-brake to see if this would slow his vehicle. He dropped his gear to low but nothing happened. It kept gaining speed. There was no way he could stop it.

Danny screamed out to Tiffany to hold on as he tried to take the slight bend at the bottom of the hill. He was no longer in control of his vehicle. It flew into the air then spun around to slam head first into a sturdy gum. The SUV came to a sudden halt. The motor kept running, but there was no activity from the two occupants.

The first of the people who stopped at the accident scene were confronted with one dead female and a dying male. Tiffany had not applied her seat belt after her attempted encounter with Danny. Subsequently she caught the full force of the twisting SUV as it belted up against the gum tree.

Danny was thrown back onto his seat. His eyes were shut. There was bleeding from his nose and mouth. His breathing was erratic. There was no verbal response to any commands. His eyes flicked open several times as passing motorists tried to extract him from his battered vehicle.

The air bag had not been sufficient to prevent the devastating injuries to his head and chest. He was taken out of the vehicle and placed on his side. Ambulance, police and fire trucks were already pulling up beside the twisted vehicle.

For those people who had stopped to help, the sound of sirens was very welcoming. The smell of petrol was strong. Although the female passenger was dead, the police managed to extract the victim before the vehicle caught fire. A small fire had started before the fire service managed to extinguish it.

There had not been any major eruption or explosion, but the fire still managed to cause significant damage.

Danny survived until he was placed in the ambulance, when he was pronounced deceased on the way to hospital. He shook and fitted as the damage to his brain was too catastrophic to allow him to continue living. Eventually, the seizure stopped and as it did, Danny Smythe took his last breath.

Tiffany's body was covered with a white sheet after paramedics ascertained that life was extinct. As she was being placed on the stretcher that would carry her to be autopsied, one paramedic jumped back in fear of his life as the black wig slipped off her head. The wig was gathered up and sent with the body for autopsy.

The police soon determined that the vehicle involved in the crash belonged to Maryanne Smythe. The woman was identified as Tiffany Farraday. It was now the unenviable job for the police to notify the next of kin.

Questions were asked as to why these two individuals were out together at night. The family connection between the two was soon determined although why they should be together was unknown.

People speculated and it was not too hard to figure out the reason. The black wig was cause for more speculation. The consensus was that women being woman, they liked a change of appearance.

Once the preliminary identification was determined, an official identification was required. Being very familiar with the

Farraday family, the police decided that Mitchell Farraday would be the most appropriate person to ask. The scuffle with the other brothers remained fresh in the minds of police.

Mitch could not believe that both his brother-in-law and sister-in-law had been killed in the same car crash. Being a man who was used to his own secret liaisons, he quickly came to his own conclusion. His biggest concern was that it again involved a brother and sister. The family troubles just kept on coming.

The police had an unenviable job. Who to notify first? How do you tell a husband and a wife their spouses were deceased? The name Farraday was already on the lips of most people in the area—now there would be more speculation.

Mark was at home with the three boys. Thankfully they were all in bed asleep as he sat watching his favourite television programs. When he heard a car pull up, he assumed it was Tiffany. The sharp rap on the door was disconcerting. The documentary was forgotten as he opened his front door to see two police men standing there.

The two men asked if they could come inside. Mark obliged, opened the door further. They followed him inside.

He was naturally alarmed as he asked. "Is this about Sarina? Have they found her?"

The police officer in charge sat down in front of Mark. "No, Mr Farraday, I'm afraid it isn't. It's about Tiffany. Can you confirm that Tiffany is your wife?"

"Yes, of course, Tiff's my wife but she's not home yet. She left a few hours ago to get out of the house. She said she was off to the gym. It gets her down what with everything that's been going on. You know, with Mick and Denise and little Sarina. She said she was going to see a friend for a few hours after she finished her workout. Why, what's happened?" Mark was becoming alarmed as he saw the two police officers glance at each other.

"I hate to inform you, Mark, that your wife was killed in an automobile accident earlier tonight." The words were out. Now the police waited for the dreaded reaction.

He could not speak, at least not straight away. He looked at the two policemen sitting in front of him. He sat and stared and shook his head. It was if he had lost his voice.

"You mean Tiff's gone, dead. She can't be. She was here sitting on this lounge with the boys just a few hours ago. You must have it wrong. It can't be Tiff. It's got to be someone else." He was now standing and walking around and around the lounge chair, repeating the same words over and over, "It can't be Tiff."

"I'm afraid it's true, Mark. There was a terrible accident and she was mercifully killed outright. Have you got anyone who could stay with you?" The more senior policeman was very sympathetic. The younger policeman looked on. He was a friend and colleague of Matthew Farraday who would also be in for another bout of bad news.

"Maybe you could call Malcolm, my brother. I'm OK though, but I'll have to tell Arlo, that's our boy." He looked expectantly at the policeman as the younger policeman contacted Malcolm and asked him to come to his brother's house.

"How do you tell your son that his mother is dead?" he asked in a daze.

"It might be better if you had someone with you. We've contacted your brother and he's on his way. Why don't you wait till the morning? Tell him then." The senior constable didn't think he could stand much more of seeing the shock and grief on this man's face.

He was immensely relieved when Malcolm walked through the door. One look on the faces of the three men told him that something dreadful had happened.

As quickly as possible, Malcolm was informed of the tragic death of his brother's wife. They waited until the shock had passed, before making their escape. No mention was made to Mark about the passing of Danny Smythe in the same accident.

That was considered to be too much to absorb. Before they left, they discreetly pulled Malcolm to one side and informed him that Danny had also perished in the same vehicle. There was more disbelief.

"What about Maryanne?" he asked, while the shock of this double fatality sunk in.

"She's being informed as we speak. I believe you have other brothers. Do you think your brother Matt could stay with your sister?" Although Matt was suspended from his job, he remained a popular and likable colleague. "We'll contact him for you, if you like."

Malcolm mumbled his thanks as he watched the police officers drive away. He went to join his brother. What to say? Mark was again seated on the lounge chair vacantly watching the television set in front of him.

"I don't believe them, Mal. I think it's just the police being police, maybe just having a go at us for the fight after Sarina disappeared. What do you reckon?"

"I don't think so, Mark. I'm pretty sure it's true. She's gone, Mark. Danny's gone too. He died in the same accident." Mal gave his brother time to absorb this latest piece of devastating news. Danny was their best friend.

The brothers sat in silence together, not talking, just looking at a television screen where the sound had been muted. There were figures of people playing out roles on the screen. It was surreal to watch people pretending to live out other people's lives when two people close to them no longer had a life to live.

After a time, Mark spoke, "You say Danny's dead as well—in the same accident. How can this be?" He looked at his brother in bewilderment.

What to say now? Malcolm thought of Dr Zaylee and wished she could be here with him. He might just have to contact her. "It looks like they were out together, Mark. Danny and Tiffany, do you understand what I'm saying?"

"I guess they went for a drive to get away from it all," he commenced and then regarded his brother as he processed his thoughts. "You don't mean that you think they were on together, do you?"

"I'm not sure, Mark, but there's going to be talk, so you better be prepared."

Malcolm had no doubt that they had been 'on together'. He had heard the talk. He knew Danny from old. Not that he was one to talk. He'd been playing up on his own wife for years. Sex with his wife had ceased a long time ago.

It was hard to see his brother break down. Mark was a big, slow-talking man without an ounce of malice in his body. As he watched the tears pour down his brother's face, Malcolm picked up the phone and punched the button that connected him to Dr Zaylee Lang.

She answered on the first ring. "You've gotta come, Doc, something terrible has happened to Mark and Maryanne. Better come to Mark's place first." She didn't ask who it was. He gave her directions and she told him she was on her way.

He didn't have long to wait. When she saw the red car, she pulled up behind it. He met her at the gate and briefly told her what had happened. She tried to maintain her professionalism as she listened to what he said.

One look at Mark convinced her that her services were very definitely needed. She took some tablets from her bag. He swallowed them down with a slug of whisky. With his brother's help, she assisted the grieving man to bed. They sat with him for some minutes before he drifted off to sleep.

"He should sleep for several hours now. What about your sister? Will she be all right?"

"I hardly think so, Doc. Maybe it would be a good idea if you could see her as well. I could take you out to where she lives. I'll phone Mitch and let him know what's going on. He can stay with Mark."

When contacted, Mitch was unnaturally quiet. He saw no point in telling his brother that he already knew about the tragedy or that he had identified the two bodies. He had not returned to his military post due to the turmoil of his niece's disappearance and her alleged murder by his brother and sister-in-law. Now there was another tragedy. It was at these times he wondered if he was maybe better off being in Afghanistan instead of living in a place that was considered to be near perfect, at least climate wise.

14

It was getting late, damn late, and where was her no good husband. Maryanne Smythe was furious.

Her life had improved lately. She was feeling so much better since Harry started sleeping through. The two older girls never gave her an ounce of trouble.

If only Harry would keep sleeping through. Their sex life had resumed and just when she thought he had stopped sneaking around, she feared he was at it again.

Her thoughts became tortured. *Well, she had news for him. She would sort out his philandering habits once and for all.* She brooded as she awaited his return. The night wore on and still he did not return. She stomped around the house, thinking out different ways to make him pay.

Danny always kept a rifle—for snakes and other vermin. Yes, that's what she'd do. She would welcome him with the rifle. Not that she knew how to use it and not that it had any bullets in it. But it would frighten him. If he did not curtail his womanising ways, then he might as well just go. She would learn to live without him.

She saw lights coming through the front gate and heard the vehicle pull up. A car door slammed shut. She wanted to get the timing just right. Footsteps approached the front steps. That's when she flung the front door open, pointed the rifle towards the footsteps and screamed out.

'Danny Smythe, you sneaky bastard, this will be the last time you'll ever play up on me. Do you think I'm that big a fool that I don't know what you're up to? You've been out tom-catting around."

She continued her screaming and raving as two police officers dived for cover back behind their patrol car.

Maryanne was no longer capable of recognising that the car in front of her was a police vehicle. She kept screaming while brandishing the rifle, swinging it from side to side. Then there were more lights coming towards the house. She slowed her ranting while she watched the second car pull up.

She looked back at the first car and began to realise that it was not her husbands. She was confused as she studied the first car and from the markings on it, slowly realised that it was a police vehicle.

The second car came to a stop as Matthew and Mia got out. The two police officers made another approach towards her. Before she could collect her thoughts, there were now four people confronting her. She lowered the rifle as Matt was the first to reach the steps. There had been several looks pass between Matt and the two police officers. They were all known to each other and were equally perplexed.

"Maryanne, are you all right?" Matt asked gently.

"No, I'm not, Matt, I'm not bloody all right. Its Danny, he's out tom-catting around again. I told him he had to give it up or else. I'll make him pay once he gets home." She looked at the police officers standing behind her brother.

"What are they doing here?" she demanded.

"They've got something to tell you, Maryanne. How about we all go inside and sit down? You don't want to wake the children." Matt directed his sister towards the kitchen. He also removed the rifle from her hands.

Maryanne was still angry, but being confronted by two police officers, caused her to lose some of her anger.

"What do you have to tell me?" she asked in a more civil voice. Mia was hovering nearby, again almost in tears.

The senior police officer cleared his throat before commencing, "There's been an accident, Mrs Smythe. I hate to inform you, but your husband has been killed."

"Yeah, right, of course. I might just kill him myself if he ever gets himself home. He's been gone for hours, Matt. He must be like the children, having a sleep over with some tart. Well, for all I care, he can sleep over forever." Maryanne again displayed her anger.

Mia quietly asked if she would like a cup of tea. Maryanne told Mia to help herself.

She then looked at the two police officers and asked would they like a cup before repeating. "You still haven't said why you're here at this time of night, nor you either, Matt. What's going on?"

Matt remembered back to the time when his sister had tried to kill their father, or as she put it, put him in a permanent state of sleep. Her plan was that their father could never hurt his children again. She didn't really want him dead, just not be alive.

His sister had poisoned the hens in the chook house as a trial run before her attempt to put their father into a permanent sleep. She saw nothing wrong with any of her actions. The police officers gave Matt the go ahead to speak to his sister. She was gradually calming down as Mia served up cups of tea.

"Maryanne," he commenced. "Listen to me carefully. There's been a dreadful accident. Danny has been killed. He's dead, Maryanne. He's not coming back, not ever. Do you understand what I'm saying?"

Her attention was focused on her brother. "Are you saying that Danny's dead? That he's not alive, like our father and Jack Smith. But he can't be. He was here just a few hours ago. I know he's late, but if he were dead I'd know it. I know all about Danny. I know what he gets up to."

Maryanne could not grasp that her husband was gone. Matt continued, only knowing one way to convince his sister.

"That's just it, Maryanne. We don't know exactly what he was getting up to. Tiffany was killed in the same accident as Danny."

He waited to see if she made the connection and of course she did. "Not Tiffany, surely not, I knew he was on with someone. The rotten bastard, at least he could have gotten someone outside the family. Serves him right, serves them both right. You know what, I'm pleased he's dead, pleased they both are. Both Mark and I will be better off without them."

She stood up and started roaming around the house, muttering to herself. Then she would stop and talk to Danny as if he was still with her.

"I told you what would happen to you if you didn't cut it out. If you didn't learn anything from my father about running around with every tart that comes your way, then you're nothing but a fool, Danny, a stupid, randy fool. I'll never understand you, Danny, never."

It was extremely awkward for all concerned. Mia thought she heard the baby cry out so she went to comfort him. The two police officers looked to Matt for confirmation about what to do with the obviously psychotic Maryanne.

It was mesmerising for them to watch her as she talked to her dead husband as if he were still in the room with her. She continued to berate him. They could hear her tell him that he needn't think that she would continue to love him if he kept carrying on with all those women and especially with Tiffany, of all people. He could just go now and never come back—see if she'd care.

To the immense relief of everyone, Malcolm and Dr Zaylee Lang walked through the door. Matt shook his head in dismay at the two of them. He had no answers for his sister's behaviour. The doctor took only a few moments to decide that Maryanne needed hospitalisation.

She was immediately on her phone giving instructions. The police officers were arranging for an ambulance. It was a repetition of what had occurred with Denise. The ambulance arrived. The scene was worse than with Denise. Maryanne became aggressive, screaming out violent curses and displaying murderous actions toward her dead husband who she perceived to be alongside her.

She was strapped onto the stretcher with her wrists tied down. Her brothers watched in dismay as she was driven away.

Mia had settled the baby, but he was again crying as she made more tea and coffee for the gathered group. "What about the children?" she asked. "What's going to happen to them?"

The senior police officer said he would contact family services. Mia stopped him and said as she was family she would take care of them. No one made any comment about this. The police officers were none the wiser as it was assumed she was a sister or relative.

It was agreed Mia would care for Maryanne's children. Matt commented that he would help Mia. No one thought to ask how it was that Mia had arrived with Matt.

The police officers happily departed from the troubling scene. Malcolm and Matthew were left to sit in stunned disbelief with the doctor and Mia. The deaths were bad enough, but the complication of the two deceased being in the same vehicle added another dimension to the tragedy. There were implications for them all, especially the children.

Malcolm noticed Zaylee yawning. He told her he would take her home.

Matt and Mia sat together considering all that had happened. "Come on, Mia, we better get some rest. Tomorrow won't be any easier."

They lay down on Danny and Maryanne's bed, held each other before dropping off into a disturbed sleep.

Malcolm drove the doctor back to Mark's house where she had left her car. They briefly went inside to find Mitch sitting on the same lounge chair where Mark had sat when he received the news about his wife. He was vacantly watching some show on the screen in front of him. After a brief explanation of what had occurred with Maryanne, the brothers said goodnight.

Malcolm walked Zaylee back to her car. "Thanks again for everything you did tonight, Doc. It seems I'm always asking for your help. There must be some way to pay you back for all you do."

She looked up at him. There was no flashing smile this time, only sadness. "I'll think of something," she said.

Then she reached out to him, and pulled his face down to hers. It was supposed to be a kiss of comfort instead as their lips came together, the kiss became deeper and longer. His hands were around her, pulling her closer to him.

"I don't think the timing is too good, Doc," he whispered in between breaths. "I think you'd better get in that car and go before this gets out of hand."

He pushed her away, then opened her car door and helped her in. She said goodbye to him. She too was crying. She was becoming just like Mia. This Farraday family was becoming not only more and more tragic but more complicated as well.

15

Maria waited until the men left for the night. She was worried about the little girl, knowing she had to be in pain. Fear of infection was another concern. She knew more than most what that felt like. Maria made the decision that she would give the child some of the antibiotics she kept in the cupboard.

These small capsules had reduced the infection when she had sustained her last mutilation. She reasoned they would also help the girl. They might have passed their expiration date, but surely they would have some effect.

She had no idea how to get more antibiotics without causing suspicion, not only from a doctor, but also from the men who had left the house. Her fear of these men was much stronger than being questioned by some doctor for wanting medications for no apparent reason.

Keeping herself calm was difficult. She watched and listened as two of the men tuned into the radio while the other two watched television news broadcast. It was unclear what had occurred, but she knew without question it was a horrendous act. She should know. She had been at the receiving end of many of their horrendous acts.

When she was a little girl much the same age as Sarina was now, she had her mother to protect her and sometimes even her father would look out for her. But they were both gone. Her father had never returned after the visit from the nice man, Michael, and the lady detective. Her mother had passed away not so long ago. That left her at the mercy of what Sarina had termed 'the monsters'. Yes, she decided, that was as good a term as any.

She waited a little longer to be sure the monsters were gone. Once she was satisfied, she took her chance. It was far into the night as she left the main house and went to the granny flat.

If the monsters knew she had kept the child alive, she had little hope that she would remain alive as well. They had thrown the little girl away like so much garbage, not caring if her body was ever found.

In fact, that was exactly what they had done, trussed the child up in a large, black garbage bag before throwing her small body in the dumpster close to where she lived.

When she found out what had happened by listening in to the triumphant conversation of the monsters, Maria was mortified. She wasn't very brave. Her courage often failed her. Whenever she did have the strength to voice disapproval or an opinion, if she wasn't shouted down, she was belted down.

The monsters had no patience with an insignificant woman who had different ideas to theirs. So Maria learned stealth and to keep her mouth shut. She also learned how to unobtrusively listen in.

It was hard to tell if the child had an awareness of day and night, given the gross circumstances of her capture. To turn on the small light in the granny flat would court disaster especially if the monsters returned unexpectedly.

Maria let the front door rattle for longer than usual. She hoped the child would wake naturally with the sound of the rattling door. She was very young, extremely traumatised and in pain. But Maria knew she had to take her chances while she could. It was life or death for both of them.

Sarina did hear the rattling door. At the first sound, she woke instantly to find darkness surrounding her. She did not always mind the dark for this was when she often found out things from her terrifying dreams.

It was at these times when terrible images come into her mind that she used to run screaming into her parent's bed. She always wished she could sleep through the night like her brothers.

She had often talked to her mother about how she found things out in the darkness; how she knew what might happen in the future. Her mother told her that this was probably a gift from her grandmother. She explained how her grandmother had a gift and that she could sometimes tell what was going to happen.

Denise never told her daughter that whatever it was that she had inherited from Miriam seemed to be more of a curse than a gift. The endless nightmares were testimony to this.

She lay on the bed cradling her left hand. She knew it was Maria, coming to her in the darkness. Sarina waited for the woman to speak.

"Are you awake, Sarina?" the woman kept her voice very low, knowing that sounds carried easily in the night.

"Yes," the child murmured softly. "My hand hurts, Maria. It's paining really badly."

"I know, Sarina. You're being very brave. I've brought you something for the pain and something to help your hand heal. If you sit up, I'll give you the medicine. Here, let me help you." Maria helped the child bring her legs over the side of the bed and sit up. She saw her wince as she shifted her hand onto her lap.

Maria poured some medicine onto a spoon and brought it to the child's mouth. After this, she took out a capsule, opened it up and mixed it with some jam.

"Please take this, Sarina. It will help kill any germs that might be in your hand. Do you know what germs are?" Maria breathed a sigh of relief as the child swallowed the mixture.

"Yes, my mummy told me all about germs. She said that's why you have to wash your hands all the time when you go to the toilet or before you eat anything." Sarina was proud to be able to tell Maria about germs.

"Your mummy is a very clever lady, Sarina, and a very good lady. One day when it's safe, I hope I can return you to your mother."

"Thank you." The child looked so sad Maria thought her heart would burst. "But I want to see both my mummy and my daddy. Do you think you can make that happen?"

Maria brushed the hair back from the child's face. "I promise I'll do everything I can to make that happen, but I'm not sure when it will be safe enough."

Maria told the child it was time for her to leave, but before returning to the big house, she left her some more medicine in a small glass and told the girl to drink it down with plenty of water when the sun came up. Sarina told her she would. Maria lay the child back down on the bed and kissed her gently on the forehead.

As Maria was about to leave, Sarina spoke, "The monsters will be back tomorrow, Maria. They are very angry. I think they are going to hurt you. Please be careful."

Maria looked down in the half-dark at the small child. A shiver went down her spine. She wondered about the words the girl had spoken. She dreaded the coming day.

As the sun rose, so did Matt and Mia. They had briefly discussed how they would tell the Smythe children that their father was dead and their mother had been carted off to hospital. They had little time for discussion before they were confronted by Hope.

"What are you doing here?" Hope asked, looking at them both as they stood in her parent's kitchen drinking coffee. "Where are mum and dad?"

"Hope," Matt commenced. "There's something we have to tell you. Is your sister awake?" Just then Lizzie came into the kitchen dragging a stuffed toy behind her. Mia did not know Maryanne's children as well as she did Michael and Denise's.

Lizzie held Hope's hand as she saw her Uncle Matthew and Mia in their kitchen. "I have to tell you girls something." Matt commenced, hating every word that was coming out of his mouth. "There's been an accident, a very serious accident. Your daddy's been killed. He's not coming back. Do you understand what I'm saying?"

The two young girls stared at their uncle. He repeated again. "I'm really sorry to have to tell you but your daddy's dead." He waited for some reaction from the two young girls.

He saw Hope's face begin to crumble, "Where's mummy?" she asked in a barely audible voice.

Matt swallowed hard then looked at Mia for support before continuing, "Your mummy's been taken to hospital. When she found out what had happened to your father, she collapsed. The ambulance came and took her to hospital where she can be looked after."

He kept seeing the devastating image of his sister. Collapse wasn't the right word. She was raging, raving and screaming at full force on the stretcher in the back of the ambulance. It was a sight he would never forget as long as he lived. He wondered if his sister would ever be normal again.

Hope then spoke. "What's going to happen to us? What about Harry?"

Mia was on her knees in front of the two girls. She pulled them into her arms then spoke tenderly to them. "I'll look after you and Harry, until your mummy gets better. Your Uncle Matt will be here as well to take care of all of us."

She looked beseechingly at Matt. He smiled at her and nodded his head. Mia could no longer hold back her tears as she held the two young sisters. Hope was crying as well. She was old enough to understand what had happened. Her young sister, Lizzie, had also burst into tears.

Had it not been for the loud wailing of Harry, Matt thought the crying might go on for hours. He went and picked up the baby, and not knowing what to do handed the squealing infant to Mia. The cycle of tears was broken as Hope and Lizzie told Mia what had to be done for Harry.

As Danny's father had passed away a few years previously, Matt took it upon himself to notify his mother of her son's demise. She was naturally devastated by this news. Matt did not elaborate on the circumstances of her son's death, only to say it was a traffic accident. It was enough for the poor woman to learn about the death of her son without knowing he had been killed in the same vehicle as his wife's sister-in-law.

Matt felt sorry for Danny's mother. She was a nice woman who had always been kind to the Farraday brothers when they were much younger. Danny's mother had also lived through the awful experiences associated with her own philandering husband.

The next person he had to tell was his mother and Sam. He didn't know how much more he could take. Telling family of the two deaths was an unenviable task.

When the old doctor answered the phone, Matt related what had occurred. He also added that Maryanne had collapsed and had been hospitalised. He didn't add that he thought his sister had gone mad.

Sam listened quietly to Matt before he added, "I think Miriam knew something bad was coming, not just with Sarina, Michael and Denise. She still gets the visions, Matt. She said they keep on coming. It's not over yet. Take care, Matt, won't you."

Matt was puzzled. Sam had been a medical doctor, a man of science and learning and yet here he was warning him about his mother's crazy visions. He thought maybe the old doctor was becoming slightly touched as well as his mother. Or else, he was suffering from the first stages of dementia.

There were family decisions to be made, children to be cared for, and scandal to be dealt with. Mitch was left with the unenviable task of telling Arlo his mother had been killed. Mark was in no fit state to explain anything to anyone.

It was a task he had no skill at. He was ill equipped at handling anything to do with children, let alone tell a child his mother was dead. He had seen his fellow soldiers injured and sometimes die on the battle field, but telling a child, particularly his brother's child, was a far cry from his military experiences.

This time he was on his own. Mitch could see his brother was still in shock. Arlo was inconsolable and the twins weren't much better. Mitch could handle Mark but had no idea how to deal with three young boys who were also grief stricken. He phoned Matt.

After a quick few words to Mia, Matt suggested that he bring the three boys to the Smythe property. Mitch was only too happy to oblige. He soon arrived with Mark and the three boys. Mark was not angry only dazed. He got out of the vehicle, wandered around and then sat on the front steps of the Smythe home.

The day passed in a blur of caring for the children. When dusk began to fall, Mitch returned with Mark and the boys. Much as he desperately wanted to escape back to his own unit, he remained with his brother.

Mia contacted her child care business and explained she would not be in attendance in the foreseeable future. She handed over the running of the business to her next-in-charge who was only too happy to accept when she saw the pay increase that came with the job.

Francine, Mia's childhood friend, upon hearing about the recent tragedy, offered her sympathy. Surprisingly, Francine sounded happy before revealing she might at long last have some good news of her own. Mia could only think that her husband must be improving.

The following day, Mitch was back again with Mark and the boys. Thankfully, he had thought to bring food with him. Supplies of pies, pizza, sausages and bread rolls as well as treats arrived.

Five young children hoed in, all coming back for seconds. It was better than crying and being inconsolable. Even Harry put as much into his small mouth as he could. They all laughed when they saw chocolate dribbling down his face. If Harry didn't like the treats that kept coming, he just dropped them on the floor where Billy Bob made short work of them.

When the children weren't eating, they were sent off to play video games or solitaire. There were far fewer squabbles than usual. In spite of the sadness, the children were getting along. Billy Bob also enjoyed being with the children.

The day was drawing to a close. It was time Mitch took his brother and nephews home. He had grown to admire the strange woman called Mia whom he had met so many years ago, when she had blond hair and had flirted with him.

She was still an odd ball, but her ability to bring peace and harmony to the bereaved children was admirable. He still didn't know how she came to fit in with the family, but she was very at ease with them all.

She often chatted about her friend, Francine, and how her friend said she might have good news. They all agreed it was about time someone had some good news. There wasn't a lot of joy going around at the moment.

Mitch did not miss the looks that passed between his youngest brother and Mia who was filling the gap of the missing mothers. He only wished she could be caring for his niece, Sarina, as well. But that was not to be.

The food was consumed and the house cleaned up. Everyone helped out. Even Mark was showing an interest. Mitch was herding the boys into his vehicle, when two police cars approached. His first thought was that it was a follow-up visit resulting from the recent tragedy. In a way it was, but not what any of them expected.

The grim-faced sergeant marched determinedly towards the gathered family. Billy Bob was barking and sniffing around at these new visitors.

The four police officers nodded to Matt. Matt took one look at his colleagues and decided they hadn't come for any kind of social or bereavement visit. There was a definite air of seriousness about the lot of them. He didn't know how much more serious the family situation could be.

"We need to have a chat. I think I know most of you," the sergeant said.

He then extended his condolences to Mark on his loss. He nodded to the rest of the family.

"Maybe you could take the children inside," The sergeant spoke directly to Mia, who carried Harry on her hip.

Mia called the children together and took them inside. She told them to eat what they liked and watch whatever program they wished as long as they remained quiet while the police were present. Mia breathed a sigh of relief as she put the baby down. She then joined the Farraday brothers. The sergeant began speaking.

"You'll be interested to know that preliminary investigations have been carried out on the vehicle belonging to Maryanne Smythe. These investigations have revealed some anomalies. We can't be sure yet, but the crash investigation unit is fairly certain that there was damage to the brake line."

He waited while the family digested this piece of information.

"Furthermore," he continued, "it's quite possible the brakes were tampered with. It's early days yet. The fire in the vehicle is not making the investigation any easier. There are a few more points of interest, one being why Mrs Farraday was wearing a black wig. Any ideas, Mark?" he asked.

Mark did not have to pretend that he had no idea what the sergeant was talking about. All he could manage was, "Tiff had blond hair. She didn't have a wig, not that I know of."

"My officers tell me your sister was making threats against her husband. Is this true?" He directed his question to Matt who was stunned at the way the conversation was going.

"She was upset, naturally, wouldn't you be? She just found out her husband was dead." Matt replied.

"From what my officers tell me, she threatened to kill him. Is this correct, Matt?"

"I don't remember that being said," Matt replied quickly. "We were all in shock."

He had never been much good at lying. He was fearful they would start to question Mia. He knew she would not stand a chance if she was hauled into a police station and thoroughly questioned. Just then Harry began squealing at high pitch. Mia made a hasty exit much to Matt's relief.

"In the interest of finding out what caused the accident, do you mind if we do a quick search of the house? We don't have a warrant but I'm sure none of you will have any objection." This caused more disbelief for the family.

The sergeant did not wait for a reply. The police officers marched up the stairs and started to take the Smythe home apart. The children were asked to go outside. Mia, again carrying a crying Harry, ushered the children out the front door.

"They can't stay here with all this going on," Mia spoke to Matt. "How about we take them to Michael and Denise's place?

It's no longer considered a crime scene." There was unanimous agreement.

Mitch was especially pleased as he didn't think he had the patience or the talent to deal with the three boys much longer. Mark was coming out of his shocked state but still wasn't up to taking care of the boys. The biggest problem was the twins who had no parents at all to care for them. At least Arlo had a father even if he wasn't fully functioning.

The children were transported to Sunshine. This was next door to the Smythe property. Mia was smart enough to make a game out of it, telling the two girls and three boys what fun it would be to be staying at Rafe and Gabe's house.

She did not mention Sarina. The twins were excited to be going home at last. When they asked if Arlo could stay with them, Mitch readily agreed.

Mitch stayed behind while the police continued their search. He sat on the front steps, bewildered at what kept happening to his family. He heard footsteps behind him. He stood up to find the sergeant standing there with a grave expression on his face.

"Any idea what this knife is doing with blood caked around the handle?" he asked. Mitch was shaking his head when the sergeant added, "or what this is over here near this chair?" He pointed to an area of brown stain that had been partially cleaned up.

"I have no idea. I've only ever been here once or twice. I don't know much about Danny. As for Maryanne, I hardly know her either. I had left the area before she was even born."

Mitch realised how little he knew about his siblings as they grew up. He was well aware that bad things had occurred; that they were all left stigmatised by their parents—their father especially.

"I'll tell you what I think, Mr Farraday. I think a crime had been committed here. I think perhaps your sister has been involved in the death of her husband." Mitch stared in disbelief at the sergeant. "So it follows, that she has probably been involved in the death of her sister-in-law, Tiffany. Don't you or your brothers leave town. There's appears to be a lot more going on with your family than meets the eye."

The sergeant then added, "Just so you know, this property is now a crime scene. You lot sure keep us busy."

Mitch had no option but to travel back to the home where he had grown up but had left as soon as he was old enough. His mind was full of questions. He had escaped once, but it looked like the fates were against him; he was trapped once more. He made a decision right there and then, that this time he would remain to see it through—whatever fate had in store for him.

17

Eventually the children slept. Sleeping arrangements were sorted with some of the children sleeping on mattresses on the floor. For Arlo, being an only child, this was a great adventure.

The girls slept in Sarina's room where there were already two beds. Lucia often used the second bed when she slept over. It seemed irreverent to be using Sarina's bed, but the further tragedies made this a necessity. Harry presented a problem. He required a cot to sleep in. Matt remembered that there was a collapsible cot somewhere. So after further searching, the cot was found.

Mitch waited until the children were settled before informing them of the sergeant's accusation. Their sister was facing further trouble. The Smythe property was now a crime scene. None of them wanted to think that Maryanne had anything to do with the deaths of Danny and Tiffany.

As far as they knew, Maryanne had no ability to tamper with brakes. Trouble seemed to be endless for them. It was no wonder the cupboards were searched for something to help drown their sorrows.

When the supplies were depleted, more mattresses were dragged out of sheds and cleaned down. Neither Denise and

Michael's bedroom or their parent's bedroom was used. Their parent's room had been left closed up for ten years.

When the children awoke, it was to the sight of adult bodies dead to the world and strewn across the floor. So sleeping on the floor became part of their ritual. Breakfast then became a game as well with who could eat the most weetbix.

Malcolm and Miriam were notified of what had transpired with Maryanne. Miriam was devastated to hear about her only daughter. Sam Calhoun would have his work cut out comforting his wife.

Mia asked Malcolm if he would like Lucia to stay with her cousins for a few days at Sunshine. She assured him that the children were coping better than expected as they were all together. This arrangement was better for all concerned than having to deal with crying children. Malcolm quickly agreed.

Denise and Michael had yet to be notified of these latest tragic events. Matt volunteered to do this. Michael had always been his father figure, the man who had raised him and cared for him during his childhood.

They were devastated upon hearing of the deaths of Danny and Tiffany. The possible charge that Maryanne faced was another blow. Matt did not have the heart to tell either of them that he thought Maryanne had gone off her head. They all had vivid memories of what she had done to their father.

Life slowly settled into a pattern. Mia and Matt cared for the children. Mitch and Mark agreed to help. Never in his wildest dreams, did Mitch ever envisage going to grocery stores to buy baby formula and foodstuffs suitable for school lunches.

Mark trailed along, giving some measure of expertise to these shopping expeditions. There were also afternoon activities—

sports, dancing, music and all manner of interests. It was an exhausted household that finally made it to bed.

Malcolm became a constant visitor to his old home. His daughter, Lucia, had frequent sleep-overs. Being an only child, the close association with her cousins was broadening her experiences and social interaction.

She was learning to fit in, to bicker, to share, to stand up for herself. All those things she missed while living with her sick mother and often absent father. Other than the times she had spent with Sarina, this was the first real experience she had living in close proximity with other children. She even loved to sleep on the floor when it was her turn.

When the children became too noisy, Mia packed them off to their rooms. The main source of entertainment was either playing video games or solitaire. They all had their own separate pack of cards which helped reduce the bickering.

No one had any idea how long this state of affairs would continue. Maryanne remained in hospital as did Denise. Both women were making progress. Maryanne continued to claim that she knew nothing about her husband's death or that of her brother's wife.

As far as she knew, the blood on the knife and veranda floor had occurred when Danny had stabbed himself with a fishing knife. She knew nothing about cars, and certainly nothing about brakes. She had ceased her ranting about her husband's infidelity. Denise still mourned her daughter, but was now far more in tune with daily events.

Matt had three homes he was responsible for. He kept an eye on Mia's riverside unit, his own house and now the family home at Sunshine. His parent's bedroom being unused was a waste and it was time it was put to better use.

His night time trysts with Mia were becoming more difficult to manage with so many people in the house. He contacted his mother and informed her it was time to put the room to better use now that her grandchildren were all living there. Miriam was only too happy to agree.

Their parent's bedroom had been out of bounds when they were children. It was their parent's refuge. Although from the bruises their mother often sustained, it was anything but a refuge—depending on their father's mood.

The furniture in the room was old, dark and heavy. No one had any idea where their father had acquired it. Cupboards and wardrobes were emptied out and the contents discarded. There was nothing of significant value.

The queen size bed was a monstrosity. No one had ever seen anything like it. It was ugly, heavy and black in colour. It had been bought by their father many years ago.

Knowing their father, it had most probably been stolen. No one was sure how it had ended up on the Farraday property. The mattress was also old but not nearly as old as the heavy bed. It was time to get rid of both bed and mattress.

The problem was how to shift it. It had iron sides down to the floor. It was impossible to see underneath it. The bed had been sitting on the same spot for decades. A museum or antique store would be a more suitable home for it.

The strength of the four brothers would be needed to shift it. The children were at school. Mia put Harry into her child care centre while she went to visit her friend, Francine.

They were eager to complete the task. There were grunts and groans while unsuccessful attempts were made to shift the bed. Mark, being the most mechanical minded of the four, got down to examine the bed properly. He pushed and pulled, before getting his tools. He began scraping bits of metal from around the bed where the iron reached the floor.

In his own quiet way, he stood up and announced to his brothers. "Buggered if I know, but it looks like it's bolted to the floor. No wonder we can't shift it."

This caused debate on why it would be attached to the floor. No one could think of any valid reason as Mark handed out spanners, oil cans, scrapers and other tools.

They spent considerable time loosening the bolts. It was no easy job but eventually the bolts loosened and slowly turned. It was uncomfortable and tiring work causing the brothers to fortify their efforts with frequent refreshments.

Eventually the bolts were removed and the test was now to see if the bed would move. At first, there was only slight movement but then with more muscle power, they were able to shift the bed several centimetres.

"Bloody thing is as heavy as lead," Mal explained. "We'll bust a gut if we're not careful. Wish old Danny was here; he'd enjoy this."

Matt looked at his brother, sending him a message to be a bit more sensitive about Mark's feelings. But Mark only grinned and said that the only thing Danny would enjoy more, was the beer they were consuming.

"It seems like something is blocking it. Maybe we have to lift it up instead of dragging it," Mark explained.

Mitch responded, "If we can't lift it over what's blocking it, we might either have to cut it into pieces or leave it where it is."

"No," Matt replied. "The old man built this place, and if I know anything, he's put something under the bed. He never did anything without a good reason. Why do you think we were never allowed in here? Does anyone ever remember spending time in here? Not that we ever would have wanted to."

"Yeah, you're most probably right," Mark agreed. "We'll need something more to lift this bed, maybe some crowbars. I'll have a look outside to see what I can find."

The other brothers drank more beer and considered the ramifications of what Matt had said. Malcolm just wanted to forget about his father and his good buddy, Jack Smith. He drank two beers to his brother's one.

He thought then of his wife who was most probably lying listlessly at their home. He felt a pang of guilt. She had helped him way back when he was in need. He vowed he would try to be a better husband even as the image of the young doctor came into his mind.

Mark returned with tools that he reasoned would assist in shifting the bed. He handed them out and then gave instructions they were all to lift the bed over whatever was hindering its movement.

The brothers did as instructed; they lifted and pushed. Eventually, after more grunting, swearing and groaning, the bed was lifted.

"Let's take a break," Matt suggested. There was no objection. They walked outside to cool down. Matt regarded his eldest brother whom he had little contact with during his youth. Mal and Mark were together as usual, talking about whatever it was that had kept them close in their youth.

"Are you going to be hanging around for long, Mitch?" Matt asked.

"As long as it takes," his brother replied.

"Can I trust you?" Matt asked in all seriousness.

"What do you mean, can you trust me?" Mitch asked in astonishment. "Of course, you can trust me. What are you getting at, Matt?"

"Well, Mick's not here, so there's really no one else. Mark and Mal have their own problems, so I can't talk to them. So that really only leaves you, but if you're going to shoot through, then there's not much point. I'll have to figure it out by myself."

Mitch had no idea what his youngest brother was talking about, but he could see that he had a major problem on his mind.

"Anytime, Matt, I don't intend going anywhere until things settle down."

"Good, but it can wait till later. Let's get this bed sorted first." Matt signalled to his brothers that it was time to resume their task.

Mark took charge, and with two brothers lifting and two brothers pushing and pulling, the old bed moved enough so that the mystery was revealed.

"Holy crap," Mal exclaimed. "Would you look at that? It's a cover or a lid to something." The four men studied the heavy cement block that had lain centred under the bed.

"It's just like the old man to do something like this. I wonder what he was up to." Matt had numerous reasons to be suspicious about his father's intentions.

"Well, we better get moving. The kids will be home from school before we know it. They don't need to know all about their grandfather and what he got up to." Mark Farraday was already making attempts to lift the heavy cover.

They took turns trying to loosen the cover that had been hidden for so long. Eventually there was movement. Together with the help of the crow bar, they lifted the heavy piece of cement and levered it to the side.

"What the hell is this?" Malcolm asked as they gaped down at the dark hole that lay in front of them.

"Looks like a tunnel to me. Why on earth would there be a tunnel under the house?" Mitch had experience with tunnels and wasn't too keen on having any more.

"Only one way to find out," Matt replied. Already his brain was working out reasons why there may be a tunnel under the house. "If no one wants to have a crack at it, I'll go down and take a look."

The other brothers were not remotely interested in going into the dark space below them. The three brothers lowered him down. There was a drop of approximately two metres to a crawl space which was deep enough for him to comfortably move through.

"If I don't come back, you better come and get me," he shouted out as his brothers shone their torches at the disappearing legs of their young brother. Matt burrowed along a few feet keeping his torch light beaming all around him. The walls were firm with little sign of rodents or animal droppings.

They heard Matt shout out, "Oh, shit, not again," as he disappeared through the tunnel.

"Are you all right, Matt?" They were calling out in fear as Matt had not spoken for some time.

Eventually they heard him say, "Yeah, I'm OK. I just hit my head. I'm coming back out now; there's nothing down here. The tunnel only goes for a few more metres then it peters out."

Matt backed out as quickly as he could. He couldn't stop the shivers running down his spine. It was like déjà vu. He wished

Denise was with him to tell him what to do, but this time he was on his own.

The skeleton that he had crawled onto had moved and crackled underneath him. When he felt the bones dig into him, he thought he might be sick. He didn't know how he had not seen it until he was on top of it.

Matt guessed it was because it had partially seeped into the soil below, whether through ground moisture or the fluids that had escaped from the form of the body, he would never know.

It was about the worst experience of his life, worse than when he had found the finger bone up in the cave. That had frightened him, but this had scared the living daylights out of him.

He thought again of Denise and how clever she was. Trying to think as she would, he took a small piece of bone from the skeleton and shoved it deep into his pocket. Who knew what it might one day reveal?

Matt quickly moved away from the skeleton. When he reached the crawl space entrance, he tried to think what he should tell his brothers. He gathered his strength before calling out.

"There's nothing much down here except a bloody great hole and a few metres of tunnel. I don't know what the old man thought he was up to. There's nothing in here and it leads nowhere." Matt brushed the soil off his clothes as soon as he was pulled up.

"What a waste of space and effort," Matt said, pleased to back in the room. None of his brothers noticed the slight shaking of his hands.

"I say we forget the bed and put it back where it was. Maybe give it a coat of paint and get a new mattress and leave the damn thing where it was." He had seen enough of his father's old bed.

No one had any arguments. They were all tired of hauling the bed around. Soon there would be seven children to contend with.

Lifting the cement cover over the hole and dragging the bed back to its former position was not as difficult as the original move. The oil and grease used to loosen the bolts worked in their favour. The bed was back in its central place in the room. The only thing they didn't do was bolt the bed back onto the floor.

Matt said he would tighten the bolts when he painted the bed. Changing the colour would soften the bed's appearance. Most of all he wanted to forget the memory of the skeleton.

When he was alone, Matt removed the small bone out of his pocket. He looked around the room trying to decide where to leave it. He saw his mother's jewelry box which looked almost as old as the bed. He opened the lid and dropped the bone inside. One of the brothers had mentioned they should keep it for their mother as a memento.

As soon as he had realised the direction of the tunnel, Matt knew what his father's intention had been. Alan Farraday had been tunnelling towards the box-shed where he kept his stash of weapons, ammunition and drugs as well as records of his business undertakings and criminal activities.

As far as Matt knew, no one had been to this buried shed for ten years. Michael and Denise had wanted nothing more to do with it. They wanted to forget the horrors of that time. Why his father did not continue with his tunnelling, Matt had no idea? There could be many reasons. He tried not to think what his father might have done this time.

Maybe it was the skeleton that had stopped the tunnelling. How the skeleton had come to be there, probably only his father knew? Had his mother known anything about it, she surely would have objected to the bed being shifted for fear of discovery.

Worst of all was the question of the skeleton. Who had this person been? How had they died? Matt prayed that whoever it was, they had not been left to die in the dark confines of the tunnel.

He could see no point in telling his brothers. What was there to gain? There was enough sorrow and grief as it was. None of them needed any more strife in their lives, least of all himself.

Had he known the skeleton was there, he would never have made the suggestion to shift the bed. This was now another memory he did not want. He already had images in my mind of one skeleton, now he had a second.

18

Darkness was again her friend. Sarina had not suffered any terrifying dreams since she had dropped off to sleep. She knew her mother and father were very sad. She had seen them in her vision.

She didn't know how she could manage it, but she reasoned that if she could see them both looking so sad, then maybe she could use her mind to send them a message to say that she was okay; not really okay but she was alive.

She thought back to the night when the monster had cut off her finger. She knew they thought she was dead. She remembered hearing them say it was bad luck that she hadn't made it. It was then that they had shoved her into the bag and thrown her away.

This was the most terrifying memory of all when she had been in the bag. She was sure she would never breathe again. It was just as well that the bag had busted. She shut the memories out. Sarina was learning how to protect her mind, to keep out the bad images.

She decided she would listen to the night sounds and enjoy the few stars that shone through the high window. She made up little rhymes in her head repeating them over and over.

> *"Bright stars at night, please show me your light,*
> *Soft night with sweet sounds please let me be found."*

Sarina spent a lot of time on her bed listening to night sounds and had come to distinguish many of them. She knew when small lizards or geckos slithered around outside. She was used to the wind, knew when it was being gentle or when it became angry. When the wind was really angry, she could hear the crashing of palm fronds hitting the ground.

The rain was also soothing. Mostly it was soft and gentle. She had not heard cracking thunder or seen any vicious lightning strikes. The early morning bird sounds were the best of all. The kookaburras became a welcoming morning sound. She knew what crows, magpies and butcher birds sounded like. She tried to work out what they said to each other.

The crows were the best talkers. She just knew they were telling each other what to expect for breakfast. This made her wonder if Rafe and Gabe were still fighting about who could eat the most weetbix. She could still see the toast with vegemite that they gobbled down. Her brothers never seemed to get tired of arguing or eating.

The door began to rattle. It was too early in the morning for Maria to come. The kookaburras had not stated their song yet. Sarina cradled her painful hand and as quickly as she could, she crawled as far as possible under her bed.

She always did as Maria taught her. She kept her dirty clothes, pencils and books under the towel in the old box and pulled the sheet up on the bed as if no one had slept there. Soft footsteps walked towards the bed. As she glimpsed out from her hideaway she saw the feet stumble.

"Are you under the bed, Sarina?" It was Maria sounding very sad as if she had been crying.

The little girl scrambled out from under the bed, careful not to knock her hand. She looked at Maria and saw her puffy face and red eyes.

"Are you all right, Maria?" Sarina asked. It pained her to see Maria upset.

"I'm not very well at the moment, Sarina." Maria replied.

"Would you like to lie on the bed with me? This is what mummy often does when I've been crying. It helps me a lot." The little girl hopped back onto the bed and gestured for Maria to lie beside her.

"Thank you. I would like to lie beside you very much." Maria lay down on the bed beside Sarina.

Sarina took Maria's hand and held it tight. "Did the monsters come for you, Maria?" she asked solemnly.

"Yes, Sarina, they did."

"Did they hurt you?"

"Yes, they did, but not like they hurt you. It was a different kind of hurt."

"Why did they hurt you, Maria?" the child asked.

"Because something went wrong with their plan; it made them very angry. They said they had the wrong people. A mistake was made but they wouldn't get it wrong next time." Maria knew she should not burden this child with her anguish, but she was sick with grief and shame.

"Don't cry," the little girl said. "It helps if you suck your thumb. That's what I do."

Maria heard the child put her thumb in her mouth. She looked at her own ruined hands with only eight fingers remaining. To please the child, she too put her thumb in her mouth. It did not prevent her mind returning to the monsters who had again taken their frustration out on her.

The shame she felt threated to overwhelm her. She wished they had cut off another finger instead of having to endure the repeated indignities they dished out to her. There were worse things than losing a finger. She was their slave in every way that counted.

19

Relentless questioning and investigations by a team of detectives provided no further clues as to the whereabouts of the body of Sarina Farraday who was presumed murdered by her parents.

There was insufficient evidence to prove that Maryanne Smythe had tampered with the brake line that resulted in the deaths of Danny and Tiffany. But it was almost certain that somebody definitely had.

The coroner was satisfied that their deaths were caused by devastating trauma suffered when the vehicle crashed due to the brakes possibly being tampered with. Who had tampered with the brakes was unknown? But all efforts were being made to discover the perpetrator.

There was too much coincidence for these three deaths not to be connected. Files from long ago were sought. All the investigating officers involved in this recent Farraday fiasco had a good knowledge of what had occurred on the Farraday property ten years previously.

They were familiar with the details. Jack Smith was shot by Detective Denise Davidson in defence of her then boyfriend, Michael Farraday. Alan Farraday had died by his own hand by hanging himself from a beam in the largest shed on the property.

The skeletal remains of Mandy Lamont had been found buried under a shed that had been partially washed away by raging creek waters.

Back then, there had been three women who had disappeared approximately twelve years earlier. The remains of two of these women were found, one being Mandy Lamont, another being Jane Broadbent. The third missing woman Geraldine Wright, a young teenager, had never been located.

The Farraday family were kept under close scrutiny. From police investigations, there was no reason to suspect the family had any connection with the deaths of Danny or Tiffany. The only detail of note was that most of the family was again spending time at the Farraday property, Sunshine.

The children were living there and going to school from there as well. Mark and Mitch returned most nights to Mark's home. It was known that Malcolm was also spending time with his brothers although he also went back to his home each night.

Mark and Malcolm had handed over most of the running of their respective businesses to their managers, which freed them up to take care of their families.

There was little known about Mitchell other than he had been in the military for many, many years and only returned to his home town spasmodically. He had no criminal history.

The coroner had released the bodies of Danny and Tiffany so they were free to be buried. Mark could not formulate any plans for his wife's burial. Maryanne was not sufficiently mentally stable enough to organise any sort of burial for her husband.

It was left to the three remaining Farraday brothers to undertake this onerous task. Did they bury them together or separately? There were small children to be considered as well as the remaining spouses. To bury them together was as good as saying they had been on together.

After much discussion, it was decided to bury Danny at the cemetery at Cooroy where his father had been buried. Danny's mother had no objection to this. Maryanne had little to add to these arrangements.

Danny was buried with great regalia at Cooroy. He had been a popular man with plenty of good mates. His three children were a poignant site with the two girls dressed in identical outfits and Harry looking smart in baby jeans and matching denim shirt.

Maryanne was discharged from hospital. She attended with her three children accompanied by her youngest brother, Matthew. Mia remained in the background with Raphael and Gabriel. Mark was there with Arlo.

Malcolm was accompanied by his young daughter, Lucia. His wife did not attend. Carrie was not well enough.

Michael and Denise were unable to attend due to their incarceration. Denise's health had sufficiently improved to the extent that she was now resident in a women's prison. Their plight was desperate as they missed each other as well as their surviving children. They could see no clear solution to the miserable state they found themselves in and had no idea what had happened to their daughter.

Dax Webster with his team of top class solicitors was hard at work applying for bail but to no avail. Both their histories suggested bail was too risky to be granted—Michael because of his history of violence and Denise because she may be a risk to her other children.

Danny's mother wept silently in the front pew of the small church. Her sadness was magnified as she had seen her estranged husband buried from the same church. The thought of the cumulative tragedy that had occurred as a result of his philandering ways was always on her mind.

She looked at her daughter-in-law and knew just how easy it was to almost lose your mind when your husband was with other women. She had no illusions about what her son had been up to. Her heart was mostly with her three grandchildren.

The older Mrs Smythe was pleased that the health authorities had made arrangements for Maryanne to leave hospital and continue psychiatric care whilst living with her mother.

The woman, Mia, who was a close friend of the Farraday's had proven to be a god-send when it came to the children. As far as Mrs Smythe knew, this young woman had agreed to look after all the children at the Farraday property until the respective families were able to cope. Danny mother was grateful for this as her grandchildren would not have to be separated. She doubted that she would have the strength to care for the three children, particularly as there was a baby involved.

Maryanne sat in the front pew with Harry, her daughters and her brother. They listened attentively to the service. Harry grew restless. Maryanne did her best to sooth the baby. It wasn't long before both mother and baby became agitated.

Matt took the baby who continued to wriggle and squirm in his arms. It wasn't long before he looked around for Mia who came up quietly from a side aisle and took Harry. She rocked him until he fell asleep.

When the internment was over, Maryanne was taken back to her mother's home. She had been asked if she was up to caring for her children but she said she was too tired. She returned with her mother and Sam.

Maryanne said that all she needed was peace and quiet. She had her memories to live with. She was unable to care for the children without Danny. Miriam now employed a woman who came in daily to help with the home and cooking.

Maryanne's daughters, Hope and Lizzie, were left to wonder why their mother did not want them with her. Harry was already used to other faces and places.

Tiffany Farraday was similarly buried in Tewantin. There were fewer people attending than at Danny's funeral. As she was laid to rest, and the last of the soil was thrown over her coffin, Mark broke down. It was left to his brothers to take Mark and Arlo back to Sunshine. It was a solemn day when Tiffany was finally buried.

Dr Zaylee Lang had strong memories of when Maryanne had broken down following notification of her husband's death. She had seen the poor woman carted off in an ambulance, tied down to a stretcher.

She knew a little about the Farraday family as her involvement with them seemed to keep increasing and never for the better, except for one aspect—that being Malcolm Farraday.

She attended Danny Smythe's funeral as she considered him her patient. After all, she had sutured up the large gash on his arm that he said had come from a fishing accident. She continued to have doubts about the cause.

Following requests from the coroner as to the cause of the injury on Danny's arm, the police ascertained that she was indeed the doctor who had attended to the injury. She told them she was satisfied the cause was a fishing accident. She also added that she did not think there was anything sinister about how the injury had occurred.

At least this is what she had assured the police detective who had spoken to her. Doubts remained, especially after the encounter with Maryanne on the night her husband had died.

The murderous look in Maryanne's eyes caused her to question how the knife wound had really occurred.

But the smiling face of Malcolm Farraday made her keep her suspicions to herself and was the real reason she attended the funeral. She slipped into the back of the small church and listened to the funeral service. She soon spotted him as he sat alongside his brother Mark. Her eyes were drawn to the pretty, golden-haired girl who clung to his hand.

He was not accompanied by any woman who might be the wife or mother. She found this strange. The lad who sat beside Mark could only be his son—the boy who had lost his mother.

After the service, condolences were extended to the bereaved. Maryanne looked to be in a daze and was wringing her hands in agitation. Dr Zaylee thought it was time someone got her away from the place.

She noticed that an older woman, who looked very dismayed, come to Maryanne's assistance. She assumed this was Maryanne's mother. She was accompanied by an elderly gentleman who was reliant on a walking frame.

Maryanne was soon whisked away. Her children appeared to be in the care of the strange woman, Mia, who had also sought out her care. Matthew was close by, holding the hands of two, young girls.

Zaylee did not take long to catch the eye of Malcolm Farraday. He took one look at her and his smile broadened. Their eyes held as he made his way towards her. He brought the little girl with him.

"Hi, Doc," he said. She thought he was going to grab her there and then, but he held himself back, conscious of the child beside him and the rest of the gathering. "It's good to see you."

He had never been tongue-tied in his life but that was exactly what he was feeling as he stared at her. Their eyes did a dance together, sliding from each other's lips to a full exploration of their faces. The fact that they did not speak could have been embarrassing if anyone had been paying attention.

The girl tugged on her father's hand and said, "When are we leaving, Daddy?"

The spell that held them together was broken. Malcolm looked down at his daughter and said to her, "This is Dr Zaylee, Lucia, say hello."

Lucia looked up at the woman who had been staring at her father. "Hello" she said.

"Hello, Lucia. It's lovely to meet you." Zaylee was unsure if she should shake the child's hand. In the end, she gave her a brief kiss on the cheek. It was probably out of line, being a complete stranger.

"No short skirt today, Doctor," his voice was no more than a whisper, as he gazed down at her legs now partially covered by a conservative skirt. "It might not be short but it's still tight enough to show off your lovely arse."

Zaylee was mortified that someone would hear him, particularly his daughter. But the little girl's attention was taken by Maryanne's two daughters. She let go of her father's hand and went to join her cousins.

All she could do was to splutter, "You shouldn't be saying such things at a funeral. It's not respectful."

"I don't think Danny would mind. If I know Danny, I bet he's looking down having a good old perv at all the women here today, especially you." He couldn't help himself. He lifted his hand to brush a lock of hair back from her face. "I've missed you,

Doc. But things have been pretty chaotic as you could imagine. Maybe I'll catch up with you soon."

"I'd like that," she replied, before she realised what she had said. "I mean at the medical practice, that is if you are sick or something."

"I was thinking more of a home visit one night. Think you could manage that." His smile was back, teeth white and black eyes boring into hers.

"I think I'd better go," was all she managed to say as she turned away from him knowing his eyes were glued to her. Unwittingly she swayed from side to side in her haste. She blamed her shoes with the high heels which were totally inappropriate for a funeral.

In his eyes, it only made her more desirable. He thought he had better escape with his daughter as fast as he could. Dr Zaylee Lang did things to him that he had never experienced before. Not even when he had first hooked up with his wife.

20

She sat beside her husband, sadness clutching at her heart. Francine did not think it was possible for him to lose any more weight. He was skin and bone. His frail body now lacked the strength to walk by himself.

He now used a wheelchair, the best that money could buy. It was motorised so that he could take himself outside where he could sit in the sun, enjoying the simple pleasures of this life such as the sun on his face and the breeze on his skin. If the clouds became grey and thickened, then he would let the gentle sprinkling of rain fall upon his head.

He didn't know what the afterlife would bring, but it could not be much better than these few simple pleasures. Brad Hamilton knew he did not have long to live as his body slowly succumbed to the disease that ravaged his body.

His greatest pleasure was looking at his lovely wife. He loved the way she tilted her head when she spoke to him. He thought she was the classiest woman he had ever seen with her long, blond hair, her graceful neck and lithe figure.

Francine dearly wanted to tell her husband that she was going to give him the greatest gift she could. She was fairly certain that her plan had worked. She had done two tests and they were both positive, but she had to be certain, just in case the pregnancy test kits gave false positive results.

She had to be absolutely certain before she took the drastic step of informing her husband. Even though he might not be alive to hold his child, at least he would have the knowledge that part of him would live on; that she would be able to a have part of him once he was gone.

She still harboured doubts. She had to be absolutely certain she had got the timing right. She had told the man that she would see him again in exactly four weeks and now that time was almost up. She often thought about what she had done; she convinced herself it had been the right thing.

Her desire to see him again was very strong. Maybe it was just lust, because her sex life was non-existent. Didn't women have needs the same as men?

Francine now spent little time in her boutiques, preferring to spend more time with her husband. But if she was going to pull off another tryst with the man who had hopefully sired her unborn child, then she would have to pretend renewed interest in her Lady Francesca boutiques.

She was busy going through her new stock, when she noticed an attractive woman enter her store. Her sales manager was busy with another customer so she approached the woman to enquire if she could be of assistance.

The two women regarded one another with respect for each other's looks. It was only a momentary appraisal, but long enough to recognise class.

"I'm after a more conservative look, something that's classy but not provocative in any way. Maybe some suits with mid length skirts, not too tight." The days of short skirts were coming to an end for Zaylee Lang.

If there were any more like Malcolm Farraday among her patient list, not that he was her patient, she would spend all her time feeling embarrassed and fending off suggestive remarks.

"Why would you want to wear clothes that don't do you justice? You have a lovely figure. It would be a shame to hide it under clothes that don't suit you." Francine was puzzled why this attractive woman would want to minimise her good looks.

"Well, that's the thing. The work I do demands a more conservative look." Zaylee followed Francine to a rack of expensive but dull looking skirts and jackets.

"What work are you involved in?" Francine showed her what she thought were the most attractive of the particular range of conservative clothes.

"I'm a doctor. I work in general practice." The two women were examining the clothes.

"Really, where do you practice?" Francine asked, her mind already leaping ahead. If she were pregnant then she would prefer some doctor who knew nothing about her or her family. One who would not ask too many questions that would compromise her in any way.

"At Cooroy," Zaylee answered, taking several garments to try on.

"Sorry to talk shop, but are you taking on any more patients? I've heard that some doctors are overloaded and can't take on any more clients. Do you have any vacancies?"

Zaylee thought it strange that this beautiful, young woman would be asking to be taken on as a patient. With her stunning good looks, she must surely have her pick of doctors, certainly the male ones. "Certainly, just phone and make an appointment. My name is Dr Zaylee Lang. I'll leave you my card."

The two women discussed clothes and eventually Zaylee left with a collection of stylish skirts, jackets and dresses, all demurely suitable for a young medico. At the same time, she could not pass up some of the trendy, tight-fitting skirts, jeans, shorts and skimpy tops she knew would catch the eye of certain men like Malcolm Farraday.

She never gave her boyfriend a second thought. She had purchased any number of conservative outfits that was sure to dampen the ardour of any hot-blooded man. If she was confronted by that megawatt smile, she could be at risk of losing her job. She didn't think she could trust herself that much.

Francine watched the lovely doctor leave her premises. Yes, she had already decided that this woman would be very suitable in helping fulfil her plans. Another few weeks and she would be making an appointment to clarify what she hoped had already happened.

The four weeks were up. She had booked herself into the same motel. Again she had told her husband that she had to go away for a couple of days to check up on the latest fashions. He told her he was pleased that she was able to take a break.

She assured him that it wouldn't be much of a break as it was just more work. She emphasised that it was a different type of work, but work all the same. If only he knew. She kissed him goodbye, told him she would phone him often then set out on her lying, cheating escapade.

She didn't know why she got herself into such a tizz with her clothes. After all, men didn't usually have any interest in clothes per se. It was what was underneath them that mattered most. She had changed her mind any number of times about what to wear.

Finally she chose skin-tight jeans and a sequinned top. This time she wore the shoes with the killer heels. She hoped she didn't look too tall and thin.

With the heels on, she wondered if she would be as tall as he was. On this second occasion, she didn't care if she was suitably dressed or not for a quiet few drinks in a bar. She just wanted to look alluring. She realised that she was hungry for him.

She tried not to be early, but she was. In spite of changing her clothes and hair style many times, she was already at the bar waiting when he walked in. He took her breath away.

Then he was walking towards her. He was big and strong. His almost black eyes were already devouring her. Francine felt no shame as he sat beside her and placed his hand immediately on the top of her thigh. There was no welcoming kiss, just the hand rubbing seductively against her upper, inner leg.

She already had a drink, so he ordered a beer, drank it down rapidly and then told her it was time to go. There was little conversation. She got up quickly, trying to keep herself steady on the high heels. Just as she had imagined, she was almost as tall as he was. When they looked at each other, their eyes were almost on a level.

They were barely outside, before his arm went around her. He pulled her close. His big hand soon found its way to the bare flesh that was there for the taking between her skin-tight jeans and the bit of fabric that was her top.

This time Francine had been doubly careful because she knew this man was no fool. She carried no identification at all. There was no need to hide anything under the mattress. Instead she left the lot in a drawer back home where hopefully the ever diligent Val Richards would not find them.

When they reached the motel room she was again anxious. She gave him the key and he unlocked the door. Then they were inside with the bed waiting for them. She had expected him to have her half undressed already and flat out on the bed. Instead he just stood in front of her, watching her.

"The rest is up to you," he said.

She hadn't expected this. "What do you mean?" she asked nervously.

"Just what I said, if you want me, you figure it out, strip me off." He was taunting her.

She didn't like his tone nor the demeaning way he was looking at her.

"Why are you being like this? If you didn't want me you wouldn't have turned up."

She was becoming nervous. It wasn't supposed to be like this. In her dreams, he would have already undressed her, his seed being planted again and again inside.

"I don't know what it is with you, Lady. You turn up looking like a bitch in heat. I suppose next you're going to tell me that you're here trying to sell more clothes or some such crap. You're as hot as a fire cracker. I can smell it on you. You want sex, that's fine, I'm all for it. But you're also playing some sort of game."

He reached for her then and pulled her into his arms. This was what she had been waiting for. She wanted to feel his kisses, to feel his tongue in her mouth. She was leaning into him, rubbing herself against him.

"You forgot one thing," he whispered, his hands were tugging at the zipper to her skin-tight jeans. She looked at him expectantly, wondering why his hands had stopped their exploration.

"What?" She asked, "What are you talking about?"

"You forgot to remove the wedding ring. What will your husband think?" His voice was mocking and condemning.

Francine pulled away from him. She could not believe she had been so stupid. She had planned everything so carefully. The clothes, the hair, the shoes, the underwear but she had forgotten the most important aspect of all—the wedding ring.

At first she could think of nothing to say, until he continued. "If he doesn't mind, then I sure don't. There's nothing like getting a bit on the side."

"It's not what you think," she stammered, trying to come up with some logical excuse. "We've got one of those types of marriages where we don't interfere with what the other wants."

"I think it's referred to as an open marriage. Somehow, in spite of all your sexy clothes and frantic come on, I can't see you as being that sort of person." He was sitting down on the bed, observing her closely.

Francine's nervousness was being replaced with anger.

"Who the hell do you think you are, being so bloody noble all of a sudden? You didn't mind fucking me all night four weeks ago. Seems to me you're the one who has developed a conscious. What about you, have you got the little wife and two kids at home? It didn't worry you a month ago, so what's the big deal now. If you're not up to it, you can get the hell out of here and I'll find someone else."

"Fiery little thing, aren't you, and desperate? What? Isn't your old man up to it? Can't satisfy you enough that you have to go out trolling for it?"

"You leave my husband out of this. He's more of a man than you'll ever be, Mr High and Mighty with the wife and two kids at home." If she could, she would kick this arrogant man in the shins, only he would probably kick her straight back.

"Well, if he's that much of a man, what are you doing here with me? Is he blind, can't get it up, gay, sick or something?"

He heard the catch in her breathing when he said this. "That's it, isn't it? You've got a sick husband at home. What sort of woman does that make you? There are a lot of words that come to mind—slut, tart, cheater, faithless."

These were the words she knew to be true, but hearing them said out loud was more than she could bear.

"Shut up, shut up. Just shut up." She screamed at him. "You don't know what you're talking about. You don't know what it's like, day after day. No one can know what it's like."

All the shame and degradation that she had indulged in was coming back to haunt her. She started beating him with her fists, while she continued to scream at him.

"Do you think it's easy for him, for me? Do you think either of us asked for this? Well Mr High and Mighty, I hope when your turn comes, life doesn't treat you as cruelly as it's treating us."

She stopped to draw breath, looking at him with fire in her eyes. He had moved a few steps away from her, not that her fists were having any impact. "Well, no, you supercilious bastard, I hope it treats you twice as bad." She continued to lash out at him, slapping his face and pummelling into his chest.

"I hate you, do you know that, I hate you. I hate your muscles, I hate your strength, I hate your black hair and eyes and I especially hate the way you make me feel. I hate everything there is about you, Mr High and Mighty. In fact, I hope you rot in hell."

Francine was a quivering, sobbing mess. She looked at the man who had reduced her to the worthless piece of woman that she was. Everything that he had said about her was true.

She was nothing more than a slut, a faithless, cheating wife with a dying husband at home. All her intentions of having a child were just a dream—a stupid, hopeless dream. This man had taken away every vestige of pride that she had.

She sat back on the edge of the bed and put her face in her hands and sobbed her heart out. The man continued to stare at her. He was unused to crying women. His primeval urge was to throw her back onto the bed and do what she had wanted. Even in her dishevelled state, she was enough to turn any man on.

Instead he sat beside her and pulled her into his arms. She didn't resist, crying out her pain in his arms. Soothing and comforting a distressed woman was not within his experience. So he just held her, kissing her hair and murmuring soft words that she did not hear.

Eventually, the sobbing stopped. She remained in his arms until she felt her head clear of the tears that had coursed down her face.

She desperately tried to regain some composure. She was embarrassed, ashamed and guilty as charged. Francine pulled herself out of his arms. She could not look at him. She kept her head down and directed her voice to the floor.

"I'm sorry. I don't usually do or say things like what just happened. I feel ashamed of myself. I used you for my own needs. I don't know what's happening to me." She let out a desperate sigh. "I never thought I was the sort of person that you accused me of being, but that's exactly what I am—a worthless, cheating, slut of a woman."

"Don't be so hard on yourself. You don't have to be ashamed." He felt awful seeing how she had broken down.

Nearly everything she had said about him was true as well. He was no saint, didn't even come close. He had greedily taken everything she had offered him four weeks ago and would have done the same again tonight except for the vulnerability and naivety he sensed in her. All the sexy clothes and alluring demeanour she had thrown his way would never diminish the underlying goodness of her.

"Look at me, Lady," he demanded.

He brought her face around so that she was forced to meet his dark eyes. When he looked into her face, he couldn't help but see the pain that was there. "You have the most beautiful face and incredible eyes. You shouldn't be selling yourself this way. You're too good for men like me. You shouldn't be picking up guys in bars. That's not you, is it?"

His being kind to her was beginning to feel even worse than his derision. "You don't know how hard it's been. He's dying, you know. I won't have him much longer. There are times when I just can't stand it. Have you ever known how that feels?"

He still held her face in his hand, "More than you could know, Lady, more than you could ever know."

She took his hand away from her face and held it in hers.

"I get so lonely at times. When I was young, I always felt alone. I had one good friend but now I hardly ever see her. Then I had my husband, but then he started to get sick and soon there will be no one. I don't know what I'll do when he's gone. I sometimes think I'll have nothing to live for. Have you ever felt like that?"

He did not have sufficient words to reply to this. The hole in her heart seemed to be enormous, so big that there was nothing that would fill it. All the sexual encounters in the world would not mend this woman.

"Something always turns up when you least expect it." He smiled at her and her spirits seemed to lift. "How about we just hang out and keep each other company? We could always go back to that bar and drown our sorrows. What do you say?"

"Might as well. I've got the night off from my husband." She regarded him again with a shameful expression. "But I've got to get out of these clothes. As you so rightly guessed, they're really not me."

She stood up to go through her bag so as to find something more casual. She pulled out a loose skirt and top. "Better turn your head while I get changed," she said to him. "I know you've seen it all before, but this time I'm trying to be the real me."

"I think I like the real you," he replied.

He did as she had asked and looked away, amused by this turn of events. When she had changed, he took her by the hand and they walked together back to the restaurant.

He ordered drinks and a meal. She was again amazed at how much he could eat as he finished up devouring what she had left behind. They drank some more until she thought she was partially drunk.

"I think I've had enough to drink. I'd better return to the motel before I collapse. Just as well I took the heels off," she giggled.

He loved the sound of her laughter. "I'll walk you back then. I can't have my woman falling over."

She liked the sound of being called his woman. When they returned to the room, she timidly said he could stay the night if he wanted to—on the floor, she hastily added.

He should have declined her offer. Floor or bed, it didn't make much difference. So he followed her inside. She threw him a pillow and a thick duvet so that he could bed down on the floor. Then she slipped off her clothes, hopped into bed and pulled the sheet up over her.

She could hear him breathing beside her on the floor. She was unsure whether he was asleep or awake. It was more than she could stand, knowing he was so close, hearing him breathe, smelling his cologne. She slipped out of the bed and lay beside him on the floor.

He was very obviously not asleep. He wrapped her in his arms. His kisses and love-making were gentle and fulfilling for both of them and lasted the night.

21

Maria visited the young child whenever she thought it safe. Her biggest problem was that she never knew when the monsters would return. They would silently drive up, making as least noise as possible.

There was no revving of engines or horns blowing or burn outs, just the quiet noise of a vehicle pulling up and the motor being switched off. Sometimes they were together, sometimes one at a time.

She listened into their conversations as much as she could without being too obvious. It wouldn't do to be caught trying to discover their plans. So she put on her impassive face and did their bidding. As long as she did as she was told, her slavery situation was mostly kept to fetching and carrying.

What worried her more than anything was what would happen to Sarina if they ever did decide her use was no longer of any benefit. So far, she had been lucky.

They did not suspect that she had managed to rescue the child and had hidden her away in the granny flat at the back of the main house. Not that any of them ever went there, or if they did, it was very seldom.

She often thought it would be better to let the child go, to be found by passing neighbours, but this would create a massive media storm and the monsters would realise who had pulled her out of the dumpster and kept her alive.

If that were to happen, her fate would be sealed in a most terrifying way. One part of her wondered if it would have been better if she had let the little girl die—trussed up in a garbage bag and thrown away into the dumpster.

However she looked at the situation, it was better that Sarina lived—if only for her own sanity. She had come to love the little girl; had even come to depend on her.

But should Maria come to the ultimate harm of her own death, she had to devise a way for the girl to escape. She could not bear the thought of the child starving to death locked up in the granny flat. Or worse, suffer at the hands of the monsters for a second time.

It was hard to imagine the child would not eventually call out for help if she did disappear and Sarina was left totally alone.

Maria knew the monsters had gone away for a time. She had heard them talking. Whatever their previous plan was that had caused them such great anger when it had failed, was now seen as being reasonably successful. She had heard them say that the side benefits were nearly as good as the original plan.

Maria thought she would take her chances. The little girl had been locked up in the granny flat with little light or fresh air. She opened the door with as much rattling as she could manage. It would give the child ample time to hide under the bed even though she would only have to get back out again as soon as she realised who it was.

"It's all right, Sarina, it's only me, Maria. You can come on out now." The little girl crawled out from under the bed, taking care not to bump her hand.

"Would you like to go outside for a while, Sarina? The monsters have gone away, so we should both be safe." Maria observed the excitement on the child's face.

"Yes, please, Maria. Will my mummy and daddy be out there?" the little girl asked

"I don't think so. But there will be lovely sunshine and fresh air. Maybe you might be able to play on the swing for a while."

Maria pulled out a pair of thongs for the child to wear. She knew nothing about children's foot wear. She had purchased some thongs she thought would fit a girl of Sarina's age at the second-hand shop.

Maria was always extra careful when she left the house. She wanted to remain invisible, never to be noticed. It wasn't too hard because she was very insignificant. She always walked along different streets when she did her shopping so that people would not remember her.

She was a most ordinary looking person, not that she ever looked in the mirror. Her insignificance would ensure that the people who served her in the shops would have no memory of her. She seldom spoke and always smiled a quiet 'thank you' at the end of her purchases.

She chose her time well. She often watched the park over the back-yard fence and knew it was rare for anyone to be there in the middle of the day. Children were normally at school. It was usually too hot for older people to be seeking their daily exercise.

She pulled a cap over Sarina's head. To maintain her insignificance, she wore a wide brimmed hat. Taking Sarina by the hand, Maria unhooked the gate at the back fence and ushered the young girl through.

Sarina looked out at the expanse of green grass and the tall trees that were a few metres away from her. They reminded her of what it had been like at home.

Sarina looked around just in case her parents may be waiting for her but there was no one there. She followed Maria through various bush tracks until they finally came to the play area. The big swing was right in front of her. She was much too big for the smaller swing which was more suited for the likes of Harry.

Her sore hand prevented her from attaining any momentum on the big swing. So Maria pushed her, up into the air with the sun on her face and then back down again as the breeze swirled around her legs. Sarina thought this was the happiest she had been in a long time.

There was a road close by, not far from the swings. There were cars driving back and forth. She saw a lady walk along with a dog. The dog was hurrying along, pulling on its leash, while the lady hurried behind.

Maria saw her watching the woman and immediately said it was time to go. Sarina kept looking at the woman and the dog because they seemed familiar. She tried to wave to the woman but Maria pulled her away by the hand and said they had to hurry.

She took Sarina into the thick bushland that was at the other side of the park. They seemed to walk for ages along paths that were littered with all kinds of branches and leaves. Suddenly they were at the back of the house they had left. Maria quickly opened the gate and immediately took Sarina back to her gloomy prison.

Sarina thought Maria was angry with her when she had tried to wave to the woman with the dog, but she didn't scold her. Maria left her alone and went back out through the rattling door.

Sarina took out her pencils and tried to draw the woman with the dog.

When she was back in the main house, Maria breathed a sigh of relief, thankful she had taken the child out but also doubly pleased to have her back again. The child had enjoyed the outing but Maria was alarmed when she noticed Sarina was about to wave to the woman with the dog.

She supposed it was the child being friendly as this was the only person they had seen. To be safe, Maria had taken her through the various tracks in the park so as to make it seem that their house was further away from the swings than it was.

If the child ever did escape into the park, hopefully she would be unable to identify the place that was a prison to them both. Maria had much to fear, both from the monsters and from the authorities. Keeping a child hidden away even if it was with the best of intentions, would surely bring the wrath of law and order down upon her.

22

The Farraday and Smythe cousins went to the same school. The twins were full of energy and vitality as were most young boys.

Before their sister disappeared and their parents had been jailed for her alleged murder, they were considered to be some of the smartest and liveliest in their school. But over recent times this had changed.

Now they were becoming ostracised. Not that the other children openly said as much to their face, but the innuendo was there. They were the sons of killers, the sons of murderers.

There was even the odd rumour flying around that it was the twins themselves who had done away with their sister because they were jealous of the attention paid to her by their parents.

It was a harsh reality in which these two lads found themselves. Their former life had been full of fun and even some glory. They were usually top of their class, could play football and cricket. They were now experiencing a taste of what the nasty side of life could be like.

Parents warned their children to keep away from the Farraday twins. There were still people around who remembered back to the time when their father had been shot and their mother had killed a man. No amount of time or keeping a low profile could suppress the unfortunate events associated with their parents.

It started by children talking about them behind their back, waiting until they had walked past before making remarks about murders and jail birds.

Not that one could altogether blame other children. It wasn't every day that any adult, let alone children, had the experience of having the sons of murderers in the class room. They began to became notorious but not for their scholastic or sporting abilities.

Gabe was the older of the two boys, but only by minutes. In the battle for who was the leader, they were evenly matched. They would fight and squabble about everything under the sun, much to the dismay of anyone who thought to take them seriously.

Their parents learnt to ignore their many battles. Even Sarina had learnt that they were harmless when they squabbled away together.

This latest turn of events in their young lives brought them even closer. Their sense of fair play was challenged every day. It became time to learn defence mechanisms. It started with words. They learned to give back as good as they got. They were called names like 'killer' and 'jail bird'.

Other boys would make signs directed at them like a knife being swiped against a throat. One time an older boy presented them with a chicken bone and told them to have a look at their sister's finger

It became harder to defend themselves and their parents with words alone. Inevitably, fights broke out. The twins had little experience of fighting, but their education was improving dramatically.

Initially, they were bumped into, with insincere apologies like 'sorry mate'. Then the pushing and shoving started. Temper got the better of them, and they lashed back.

Their teachers were unaware of what was going on. They were very sensitive concerning the boy's welfare. But parents started to complain about the unruly Farraday twins. It was inevitable that something had to be done about them.

They were called to the principal's office and asked to explain themselves. Being the children of a family who had been stigmatised in their own youth, the twins kept their mouths shut.

Their parents had taught them to be open and outspoken, but as instinct kicked in, they went by the principle of never dobbing.

They had nothing to say for themselves about why some other lad had been punched. Fighting of any kind was not allowed. Bullying was unacceptable. The only problem was they weren't the ones doing the bullying but were the recipients.

Their cousin Arlo was seen as a victim, as too were the Smythe girls. They had all lost one parent. For the children at the school, this was a great tragedy—to lose a parent—especially for the little girls.

Then, like Gabe and Rafe, the rumour mill swung into action and it wasn't long before they too became the butt of jokes. Lizzie was too young to understand the full implication of what was being said, but Hope and Arlo had no such illusions.

Great shame was felt by the two of them, so naturally they were drawn together. Like Gabe and Rafe, they tried to defend each other as best they could. Unlike the twins, they did not experience the physical violence.

They did not have the dubious history of the twins or their more forceful natures. They kept to each other when appropriate. They did not want to be seen as boyfriend and girlfriend even though they were much too young and had no such desire or thought.

But some children grew up fast and would soon resort to teasing if it was known that Hope and Arlo hung around together. It was merely a survival mechanism.

The other two cousins, Lizzie and Lucia were much the same age. They stayed together when out in the playground. They held hands and played games together. Again like their cousins, they were surviving the ravages of school years as best they could.

They were both shy, quiet little girls who had mothers who were different—mothers who were seldom seen.

The only children, who maintained a distant friendship towards the cousins, were Dax Webster's son and daughter. The older boy was of similar age to Gabe and Rafe. The daughter was closer to Lucia and Lizzie's age.

The relationship their parents formed brought the children together. But it was not easy being friends with the most infamous children in the school. The friendship remained covert at best.

Their home life was held together by Matt and Mia. Maryanne remained with her mother. It was the task of the uncles to take the three children to visit her.

Maryanne fussed over her children but showed no interest in returning to take care of them. The Smythe children stayed with their mother for short periods over the weekends but then returned to Matt and Mia's care.

The problem of the twins was becoming a concern for the family. Matt was summoned to the school to discuss their behaviour. He had been unaware of what had been occurring. When he saw the twins after school and on weekends they were happy children. But the principal was giving him a different picture from the one he saw at home. After the meeting, Matt was forced to consider how all the children were coping.

He was out of his depth. He asked his brothers and Mia for help. There were suggestions such as counselling, another school, boarding school or if needs be, home schooling.

Mia looked shocked when home schooling was mentioned. There were enough tribulations to deal with at home. She didn't want another person in the house. Then the question arose if they should tell Michael and Denise about their twin sons.

This was put on hold. It was up to the rest of them to find a solution, to ensure the children were not ostracised and forced into a daily battle of defence.

Mitch was of the opinion that it wouldn't hurt if all the children had some experience of self-defence or martial arts. Life could take many twists and turns and who knew what the future held for any of them. This was one suggestion they all felt worthwhile.

Karate was top of the list as it taught control as well as defence and attack skills. All the children except Harry were joined up at the local club. Mitch could appreciate the turmoil the twins faced.

He decided to give them extra lessons. Their path was not going to be an easy one. They were boys without parents. They had plenty of people to love and care for them, but nothing made up for the total absence of parents.

Mia was happy to see the children's uncles take on additional responsibilities. This gave her a little extra time to herself and Matt. She loved all the children dearly but with Harry needing constant attention, she grabbed what free time she could.

This was when she told Matt that she thought she had seen a child who looked just like Sarina while walking Billy Bob near

Sundial Park. She had put Harry into the child care centre so she could check on Matt's house and also walk the dog.

While walking past the park, she saw a woman wearing a floppy hat pushing a little girl on the swing. The girl was about to wave to her when the woman lifted her off the swing and disappeared into the bushes.

"So I took Billy Bob into the park to have another look, but they were well and truly gone by the time I got there," Mia explained to Matt. He was used to Mia prattling on. She could tell a story about anything, even taking the dog for a walk.

"Sarina's gone, Mia. There's got to be heaps of little girls who look like her." Matt responded.

"Well, if she's really gone, then where is her body? It just can't disappear." Mia was becoming upset at the thought of the lost child.

"Come on, Mia, don't start crying. It doesn't do you any good." He took Mia in his arms and kissed away her tears.

"I'm worried about Lucia," Mia said. "She's seems so lost when she goes back to her home with Mal. Poor Carrie, it's a shame what's happened to her. I guess that's life. There's always some ordeal going on, look at Francine and Brad. I don't know how much longer he can last. Last time I saw him, he was just skin and bone."

"Enough with the sad stuff, we've still got time before the bus pulls up." Matt Farraday was more of an action man, not that he wanted to be insensitive. But since discovering Mia, every available stolen moment needed to be explored. The emotional stuff he would leave to her.

There were better ways to spend their free times than worrying about what may or may not be. As they again tested out the iron bed, Matt tried hard to put the memory of the skeletal bones that lay beneath them out of his mind.

At last she was home from school. Lucia had her afternoon tea with Mrs Potter who made sure she ate her fruit and drank her milk. It was part of Lucia's routine to spend time with her mother after school except for when she had sleep-overs at Sunshine. Mrs Potter was in two minds about Lucia spending so much time with her cousins.

It was clear the child benefited from the interaction with the other children, but Mrs Potter was concerned that she was seeing less of her languid mother. This routine also impacted on her importance in the household.

Mrs Potter could not fathom exactly what Carrie's health problem was. She was anorexic, hardy ate a thing, was always tired and depressed. The only time she ever showed a spark of life was when she managed to get herself outside and smoke those awful cigarettes.

She had a beautiful daughter, a good-looking husband who seemed to work day and night and a home any one would be proud of. Carrie had everything to live for.

She had every doctor and psychologist in the area to help her get better. Mrs Potter often had little patience with Carrie as she seemed to be throwing her life away, especially when she smoked those awful cigarettes. She knew a little about certain addictions. Her thoughts then turned to her brother.

Lucia ate her afternoon tea as Mrs Potter had requested. She ate as much as she could before going to visit her mother who lay in her huge bed. Lucia loved her mother very much but more than anything she wanted a mother who could take her to dance lessons or brush her hair like Sarina's mother used to.

She missed Sarina. They were best friends. She still played with Lizzie at school and slept beside her when she had sleep-overs. The three girls had all been good friends but since Sarina's disappearance, nothing was the same.

Lucia sat on the bed with her mother holding hands. When her mother finally dropped off to sleep, she escaped to her bedroom. Her bedroom was quite big with wide windows so that she could see out as far as the driveway into their home. She often saw her daddy come home in his red car.

Lucia had found another game to play. Due to her solitary existence she had turned her imagination to making up games. When she was with her cousins, there was plenty to do. There was always something going on.

At home, she played video games and solitaire but there was another game she had made up herself that took up much of her time. She only played this game when she was alone by herself in her own room.

When she stayed at Sunshine, Mia and Matt made sure that all the children took turns in feeding the hens and collecting eggs. There was Billy Bob to feed, exercise and groom as well as plants to water. There was often so much to do, there was little time to play.

They even had to wipe the table down after dinner at night and leave their plates clean before they went into the dish washer. Lucia had never had to do that at home. Mrs Potter always took care of everything in the kitchen.

Now the cousins had so much to do, they seldom had time to 'hang out'. She had heard her older cousins complain about this. She was unsure what hanging out meant, but it seemed like fun. They all had Karate lessons as well as any number of other activities after school. Life was so full and busy at Sunshine. Sometimes Lucia just wanted to spend time in her room alone.

She had thought up another game that included all her cousins. She called some of her Barbie dolls, Hope and Lizzie. Of course, the prettiest Barbie was called Lucia. She even named one doll Sarina, even though everyone said Sarina was now in heaven.

She had a very large Barbie doll house which she dragged over in front of her built-in wardrobe. She pulled out her stuffed toys and named the two that looked most alike, Gabe and Rafe. She named another one Arlo and the smallest and cutest she called Harry.

Lucia kept some of her favourite toys in the Barbie doll house but the ones she had named after her cousins she hid behind the doll house, just in case Mrs Potter thought she was silly when she cleaned her room.

At night, she sometimes crept into the wardrobe and played with the toys. Once she had even fallen asleep in the wardrobe but had woken through the night and crawled back into her bed.

Her father always came to check up on her during the night when he got home from his work. He would have been very worried if he could not find her.

23

Francine was excited about her changed status. She could not wait to make an appointment to see the doctor she had met in her boutique. At last she might have good news for her husband—something to brighten his life, to brighten both their lives.

Her husband looked frailer than ever. He was hardly eating and fell asleep in his wheel chair whenever he was left alone. Francine was afraid she would not have her husband much longer. The prospect of a baby should make these last few weeks so much more meaningful.

She had no difficulty in seeing Dr Lang. The doctor was as bright and vivacious as she remembered. Francine did feel embarrassed at the untruths she was about to tell, but the overall result would far outweigh a few, simple lies. Although they would not be simple; they would be massive.

After a cursory greeting and general chit chat, the young doctor enquired how she could assist.

Francine could not quell her excitement. "I think I'm pregnant. I did a home test and it was positive."

The doctor did not doubt her new patient's positivity. "Well, congratulations. I can see you are overjoyed. First we'll do an examination and then some blood tests. I'd like to see the baby's father as well, to check everything out."

"Oh, is that necessary?" Francine asked. She hadn't thought of that.

Dr Zaylee was surprised at the woman's response. "Just a safe guard; there are various anomalies that can occur, so it's as well to know the father's blood grouping, etc."

Francine began to panic. This was going to be her husband's baby. That was her plan. That was what had kept her going, sneaking off at night to spend time with some man whose name she did not know and did not want to know.

He was only known to her as Mr High and Mighty. What had he called her—Lady? That was all they knew about each other, except for their experiences in bed. That was all she wanted to know. It was time for some subterfuge—or the hurtful truth.

"I'm a little embarrassed. I don't think it's my husband's baby. I was away from home; you know how it is, one thing leads to another. I had a one night stand with some man I met at a conference. I'm pretty sure it's his child."

"What are you saying, Francine? Do you want a termination?" Dr Zaylee never ceased to be amazed at the myriad of concerns that came through her door. She would never have suspected this beautiful woman of cheating on her husband.

But when she thought about the smiling face of Malcolm Farraday, she knew just how easy it would be to cheat.

"Oh, no, not at all, I want to keep the baby."

"I'm a little confused," Dr Zaylee continued. "You definitely want to go through with the pregnancy. What about the man you met at the conference? Does he know? Does he want this child?"

"Well, that's a problem? I don't know who he was. I'd had too much to drink at the time. It's all a bit hazy." Francine was searching her mind for suitable answers.

"So how do you know that it isn't your husband's child?" Dr Zaylee asked. "Have you been having problems?"

"You could say that," Francine answered, thinking of her husband lying at home with hardly enough energy to scratch himself. "Yes, we've been having problems, big problems. We don't get along as well as we used to."

At least not in the bedroom, she neglected to say. "He's away a lot." Soon he'd be away for ever, she rationalised.

"You seem to be sure about what you want," Dr Zaylee replied.

"Yes, I am. I'd like to have a baby. It's about time. The body clock is ticking." Francine noticed the look of astonishment on the doctor's face. "There's no worry about my being able to keep this baby. I'm quite well off. I can afford it."

Francine had no intention of telling the doctor she was the owner of the best boutiques in town. All the doctor had to know was that she was a sales assistant working in a dress shop.

But Dr Zaylee was not interested in whether this woman could afford a child. She was very attractive and looked to be in good health. She was more amazed at her statement about her body clock. She looked as though she could have another twenty years or so left on her body clock.

The doctor completed her consultation and told Francine she would contact her very soon about her condition. Francine thanked her warmly then left. She imagined she would only have a few days to wait before she could tell her husband the good news.

The day dragged on for Zaylee. She saw various patients with no end of different ailments, but her thoughts went back to Francine and her desire to have a baby. The situation of the beautiful Francine was a mystery. The oddities of people's desires never ceased to amaze her.

But the doctor knew a lot about desires. Much as she tried to pretend otherwise, her desire for a certain man with his flashing smile and black eyes never left her for long.

She thought of his lovely daughter and wondered again about her mother. They were obviously still together for hadn't he told her on one occasion that he had to get home to the wife.

Unfortunately for Zaylee, her own boyfriend was not given to patience. She frequently started work very early. When she returned home she was often too tired to go out with him or indulge in sex. Her boyfriend was a hot-blooded man and being like most hot-blooded men, sex was never far from his mind.

If she were entirely truthful, it was not her boyfriend she wanted to have sex with but Malcolm Farraday. But he had a wife, so that was that. No amount of day dreaming could change this fact. The doctor was too wise to get caught up in a triangle—even if she was tempted.

It was too dangerous a path. Of all people, she should know. She had seen the results of people with busted relationships walk through her door on any number of occasions. Not only did they present with bruises and contusions but with broken hearts that sometimes never mended.

Thinking of her boyfriend, she considered how to ease herself out of the relationship. If she was sufficiently boring, not only in their social life but also in bed, he might get sick of her and opt out.

There would be no one happier if he walked out the door for good. But she wasn't sure if this would happen. He was very possessive and didn't like her having any other sort of life except her working life and being with him.

She was a little frightened of him. He was quick tempered especially when he was drinking which seemed to be happening more often.

As usual, she was home late and as usual he was annoyed with her. He told her he was going for a few drinks. She told him she thought this was a good idea as it might improve his mood. Of course this response annoyed him further. She set about cooking their evening meal wondering how everything had gone so wrong.

She waited for him, but as he did not return as promised, she left his dinner in the refrigerator. She was staring vacantly at the television set when she heard him pull up. One look on his face told her that Dave Norton's mood had not improved.

"You can warm your dinner up. It's in the fridge," she said as he made his way towards her.

"I thought you might get it for me," he replied, sitting down beside her. "What's this crap you're watching?"

"Just some show," she replied. "I'm really tired so I think I'll go straight to bed."

"What about my dinner?" He demanded. His mood was sour; he was busting for an argument.

"I'm sure you can warm it up yourself. If you'd been home when you said, it would have been hot." She stood up to go to the bedroom.

"You're always too bloody tired, too busy or too important. You think you're too good for the likes of me what with your fancy degrees and your upstart colleagues."

"I've never considered myself anything but what I am. I have never considered myself too good for you." She replied evenly, trying to quell his bad temper.

"You know, you're nothing but a bitch. You think you're too good for us locals. Because I work with my hands, you think you're superior to me. Well, sweet Zaylee let me tell you something. I've watched the way you swing that hot, little arse of yours around in front of any man who'll look at you. You're not much better than a slut, no better than the tarts who troll the bars."

She had listened to enough. "Get out, you hear me, just get the hell out of here. I've had enough of your abuse." She fired back at him, sick of his jealousy.

'You don't know what abuse is yet? You've had such a fancy, easy life with everything handed to you on a plate. You've never felt the hand of abuse in your life. Well you're going to feel it now." Dave Norton lifted his considerably large and angry fist and struck her several times across the face.

It was quite true what he had said; she had never been at the receiving end of any type of abuse in all her life. Her parents loved her, nurtured her and cared for her. She could not believe she was now at the receiving end of what she had seen done to many women.

She stared at him in shock, overwhelmed by what he had done to her. It took her a few moments to collect her thoughts. But when the full realisation of what had just occurred hit her, she picked up her bag and her mobile phone and walked straight out the door.

The doctor kept walking. She walked until she thought she could go no further. Her strength began to wane. Her mind was a jumble. Her brain unable to comprehend that she had been struck by her boyfriend. This was something that only happened to other women.

She wasn't sure where she was. She was aware that it was dark and she was out alone. She should have had more sense. Wasn't this how women got into trouble? How they got mugged or worse still, raped?

Zaylee was slowly coming to her senses. She finally recognized where she had finished up. In the dim lamp light she read the sign—Sundial Park. She thought of all the people she could phone for help—her colleagues, friends, or the police. At the back of her mind there was only one person she wanted to come to her rescue.

Of course she knew his number, both his mobile and the restaurant number. She had spent years training to be observant. She had coded both into her phone.

She phoned the restaurant, rationalising that he would more than likely be there. It took some time before he answered. "Hello, who's speaking?" he asked not recognizing the number.

"It's me, I'm in trouble. Can you come and get me?" When she heard his voice, the tears began to streak down her face which was now beginning to throb. It was the first time she had cried since it had happened.

He didn't have to ask who was calling. "Tell me where you are and I'll be right there." She gave him directions.

He had been longing to hear her voice, but not like this. He noticed he was low on petrol but as she sounded so upset, he didn't stop to fill up.

Zaylee sat on the swing in the dim light, wanting desperately to see the red car. As she waited, she saw several black SUV's driving quietly around the surrounding streets. The sight of these was very unnerving.

As the red car approached, she ran towards it as fast as she could. She was in beside him almost as soon as he had pulled up.

"Oh, thank you," she cried as she flung her arms around him, tears streaming down her face. He was not sure what to expect but it wasn't the usually controlled doctor virtually jumping into his arms. He could feel her distress as she cried in his arms.

"Its okay, Doc, nothing's going to hurt you now." He cradled her close while he waited for her to calm down. "What's happened to you? What's gone wrong?" He couldn't help but to bury his face in her long hair and pull her even closer.

"I don't know where to start. I had to get away. I can't stay there any longer. I didn't know where to go or what to do. I don't understand how this could have happened."

She knew she wasn't making much sense, but she felt so safe in his arms. She couldn't stop herself from bursting into more tears.

Malcolm was equally perplexed. Here was the woman he had dreamed of; the woman whom he thought was outside his reach. It seemed impossible that this lovely woman was in his arms, seeking his comfort.

He had fantasies just thinking about her. He had kissed her, held her, touched her, but that was as far as he dared let his imagination take him. As far as he was concerned she was up there in the stratosphere.

What was he, nothing more than a reformed druggie, a weak man who had to have his brother defend him? Michael had gone to jail to save his self-esteem, to give him respectability and a better chance at life?

He thought again of his brother languishing away in jail for a crime he knew he had no part in. Of all the people he knew, his brother had more principles and guts than anyone else on the planet.

Putting thoughts of his brother aside, he waited until she had stopped crying. "Tell me what's happened, Doc?"

She remained in his arms as she wiped away her tears. "I would never have believed it possible, but he hit me. Can you believe it? All I did was tell him to heat up his own dinner. Then he started calling me all sorts of names. He'd been drinking, but that's no excuse. I've never been hit by anyone in my whole life." She was again becoming unravelled.

"I take it you mean your boyfriend?" he asked, holding her close.

He thought again of his brother. There was no doubt what Mick would do to a woman basher. But he was not his brother. He didn't have his skills or strength.

"I'll take you home to my place. You can stay there for as long as you like."

She looked up at him in surprize. "I don't think that's a good idea. What about your family?"

"I don't mean the house. I'll take you to my place at the back of the restaurant. It's quiet and private. No one will know you're there. It's off limits to anyone but me."

When they arrived, he helped her out and took her up the back stairs to his office. He sat her down and looked at her face.

"He gave you a hell of a wallop, Doc. You'll probably have a shiner of a black eye tomorrow but you still look beautiful to me." He tenderly touched her face before getting an ice pack to help reduce the swelling.

"Thank you again. I really didn't know where to go. I couldn't stay there with him. But I don't have any clothes. All I have is my bag and phone." She held the ice pack to her face as she looked around his office. "I see you've bought a new sofa-lounge."

He thanked his lucky stars that he had got rid of his old one.

"I thought it was about time," was all he said.

It reminded him of her. It was made of a soft fabric in gentle colours; not at all what he would have normally purchased for a male-dominated room. "Maybe you'd like a drink, cup of tea, whatever you like?"

"Tea would be lovely," she replied, watching him get a cup and boil up the jug. He sat with her as they drank tea together. She was more settled. There were no more tears or recriminations although he could tell she was far from over her ordeal.

"How about I make up this sofa for you and you get some sleep, Doc? I should have something here that you can wear to bed." She watched as he got sheets, pulled out the sofa so that it folded down to a comfortable bed.

He soon had the bed made up. "I had lots of practice making beds when I was a kid. Now you get some sleep and I'll be back later."

"Where are you going?" she sounded alarmed.

"I have to go home and check up on things and then I'll be back. I won't leave you alone tonight." He helped her into the bed, pulled the sheet up over her, kissed her gently on the lips and then left.

He was furious at the man who had done this to her. He could understand it if she was a bitch, always criticising and nagging a person to death. But she was nothing like that. She was respectable, clever, admirable and beautiful.

She was a prize, someone to be cherished, not belted around.

He drove at speed back to his home. He had to check on Carrie and Lucia. Mrs Potter sometimes stayed the night, but this was not one of them. He was usually home late, but home nevertheless.

He pulled up in front on his home. Carrie was in bed, sleeping soundly. He watched her steady breathing, sadness overcoming him. Her thin, skeletal body lay in front on him, curled up on the bed barely looking any bigger than Lucia. He kissed her fondly on the cheek then went to check on his daughter.

His daughter's bedroom always gave him pleasure. Her bed lamp was still on. It was everything a little girl's room should be. There were pink sheets, pink pillows, pink and blue wall hangings, and even a large, pink, doll house. There was a scattering of toys all around—everything to make up for the loneliness he suspected she felt.

Since Sarina's disappearance, she seemed to have lost some of her zip. She had Lizzie and her other cousins to play with, but Sarina's loss had dampened her spirits.

He picked up a few toys as he walked over to her bed before pulling the sheets over her and kissing her goodnight. He turned off the bed lamp then left her room. Before he returned to his car, he checked the security of the house making sure his family was safe.

It was only when he was in his car and turned on the motor that the car spluttered and died. It was out of petrol. This could not have happened at a worse time. He was desperate to get back to Zaylee. She should not be alone tonight of all nights.

There was no option but to take the Yamaha. Very quietly, he left his home to return to his office. He was unaware that his daughter had been woken by the noise.

Upon his return, he did his best to be as quiet as possible. It seemed like he had been away for an eternity, even though it was his quickest trip ever. She was asleep on the sofa bed. He sat on the edge of the bed watching her, wondering what he should do. He knew what he wanted to do.

But it wasn't the right time or place. He had to be sensitive; not take advantage of her situation. All the same, it was a special night for him. He switched off his mobile phone. The rest of the world could go hang for once. The lovely Zaylee was more important.

Eventually, he slipped out of his jeans and shirt and lay on the bed beside her. He dozed off, not certain how long. The next thing he knew she was cuddling into him.

"Are you awake?" she whispered.

"I am now," he replied, pulling her in closer to him. "How do you feel?"

"Better, more settled, I'm glad you're back. I didn't want to be alone tonight." Her hand strayed to his chest, pulling at the dark hairs. "What about your family? Are they okay?"

"Both asleep," he replied. He was running his fingers through her long hair. "Maybe you better go back to sleep too, Doc. It's probably the best thing for both of us."

"I don't think I can. Do you want to just talk?" she asked, still rubbing away at his chest. He was sure she was unaware of what she was doing to him.

Talking was the last thing on his mind, but if talking was what she wanted, then talking it would be.

"Sure, what do you want to talk about?" He lifted her hand from his chest but it was only gone a few seconds before it was back again.

"You," she said. "I don't understand you or your family."

"We're a pretty boring lot, not much to talk about." His family was the last thing in the world he wanted to talk about. If she knew much more about them, then she'd probably be gone from his bed right there and then.

"What happened to you? I get the feeling something bad happened." She asked, her hands still stroking him.

"Doc, the only thing that's happening to me is you. You must have realised that by now. I want you, Doc, more than I've ever wanted any woman. If you don't believe me, I'll show you." With that he took her hand away from his chest.

"I'm not that patient or controlled that I can just lie here with you rubbing away at me. I'm trying to be sensitive here, Doc, on account of what's happened to you. I'll have to do something about it soon or else go sleep somewhere else."

"I don't want you to sleep anywhere else and I want you too. It's just that you're married with a child. It wouldn't be right, at least not to me." She pulled away from him.

"Think about it, Doc. We're both fully grown people lying half-naked beside each other in the middle of the night. It's not really the right time to be developing a conscience. You make up your mind soon, Doc, or I'll have to leave."

He gave her about two seconds to make up her mind. When she didn't move away from him he knew he could stand it no longer. He rolled her underneath him and then the kissing, touching and meeting of bodies started. Conscience played no part in their actions for the rest of the night.

24

When the first rays of the sun brightened the room, Malcolm knew it was time to leave the arms of Zaylee. He was utterly spent and could have stayed in bed all day, if she would remain there with him.

The night had been better than his fantasies. He knew right there and then he wanted her in his life if only she would have him. Somehow he would work something out that would keep her by his side or at least in his bed.

It was too soon to be considering how her conscience or his marriage to a wife whom he had promised never to leave could be overcome. His conscience was never a problem, but it was clear that hers was.

She wasn't the 'mistress' or 'the other woman' type. But he wouldn't leave Carrie. He owed her too much. He quietly showered and changed his clothes. Before he left, he went back to her and gently kissed her.

"Where are you going?" she asked, reaching for him. He noticed that the flesh around her eye was bruising.

"Go back to sleep, Zaylee. I'll be back soon. I have to check on Carrie and get Lucia ready for school. I shouldn't be long."

He kissed her again, but this time not so gently. Seeing her lying naked in front of him almost caused him to forget about his wife and daughter.

He finally dragged himself away from her. He had forgotten about his car being out of fuel and that he had the Yamaha. Once he was on the road, he felt that life couldn't get much better—except for all the endless issues of his family.

But the night with Zaylee pushed all family troubles from his mind. *He thought to himself that in life you had to enjoy the good times because you never knew when the bad times were sure to come along.*

He savoured his ride home on his bike, with the wind whipping into his face and the roar and speed of his bike keeping the image and feel of the lovely doctor alive in his body.

His red car was where he had left it. He found the front door unlocked which surprised him as he was fairly certain he remembered arming the security system the previous evening.

The house was very quiet which was not unusual. Neither his wife nor his daughter tended to wake early. His wife often slept till midday or later. Mrs Potter was not expected until later on in the day.

He quickly ran up the stairs where he first looked into Lucia's room and noticed she wasn't in her bed. It was unusual for her not to be in her own bed as she seldom ran into her mother's bed at night if she awoke.

Carrie loved her daughter but was not so keen on having the child squirm and roll around in the bed. She often complained that when Lucia was in a sound sleep, she would fling her legs and arms around and knock into her own fragile, bony limbs.

The pain was almost more than she could bear. So Lucia knew better than to run to her mother in the middle of the night if she was frightened.

He next went towards the main bedroom. He was about to open the door when he noticed brown specks on the ivory coloured carpet. Unsure how these spots occurred, he would have to ask Mrs Potter to have the carpet cleaned.

He tried to open the door but it refused to budge more than a few inches. It was not locked because they never locked the door—ever. It wasn't as though Lucia would walk in on them having sex because sex had not happened for them in years.

He pushed harder until he could see that the door was being obstructed by the bed spread that Carrie had purchased years ago when she was healthier. He eventually pushed the bed spread back with the toe of his shoe and finally opened the door to the room where he had spent many years with his wife

The sight that greeted him left him utterly stunned. He gasped then stepped back outside the bedroom again, unable to believe what he thought he had seen.

Bracing himself, he again stepped into the room. It was true. Everything that he thought he had seen at that first glimpse lay like a nightmare before him. It was not a fairy tale or a horror movie.

What lay before his eyes was the most horrific scene he had ever laid eyes on. There was his wife lying half out of the bed they shared, with her head reaching the floor and her skeletal body lying haphazardly upside down over the edge of the bed.

But worst of all, was the blood that had seeped from her pale, fragile, scrawny body onto the bed linens and carpet.

He could not believe what he was seeing. His wife, the person who had brought him back from the brink of desperation, lay ignominiously before him. He clutched his chest, fearful that his heart may stop.

He felt a pang of pain course through him. This could not be happening. He forced himself to stop his panicking emotions, to steady himself, to take some control of the situation.

Gingerly, he stepped further into the room. He could tell by the lifeless expression in her still open eyes that she was dead. He went to her and lifted her gently back onto the bed so that her head was again on the pillow instead of lying skewed over the bed side.

He did not think about the blood. All he wanted was his wife back in the bed where she had spent so much time. He could not bear to look at the gaping, bloody hole where her neck should have joined her head to the rest of her body.

Still reeling from the shock of it all, he quickly got a towel and covered her neck. He then got a clean sheet and placed this over her so that only her face was showing. The staring, vacant eyes unnerved him as much as any of the horror he had seen.

He sat down on the opposite side of the bed to try to get hold of his thoughts and emotions. He knew he had to phone the police, but for the life of him he could not remember the number. He held his mobile in his hand and pressed some buttons, but there was no reply.

Part of his brain told him there were only three digits. Eventually he got the digits right and was asked who he wanted to speak with. Did he want the police, fire or ambulance?

He stammered out police and ambulance. Then he was hit by numerous questions. Eventually he told whoever he was talking to that his wife was dead and that there was blood everywhere. He couldn't remember giving his name or address but he supposed he must have.

It was then that he remembered his little girl and he told whoever he was speaking to that he had to go and find his daughter. He slammed the phone down,

Where was Lucia? He remembered she wasn't in her bed, thinking the only place she may have gone to was into bed with her mother. He raced back to her bedroom, his eyes glued to her bed but again she was nowhere to be seen.

He looked under the bed, then around the room but could not see her. His heart was thumping in his chest. Where was his beloved daughter?

It was a large house with many rooms. He raced from room to room looking for her. When he was in the down stairs area he started shouting out.

"Lucia, where are you?" There was no answer so he ran outside to the front of his home. "Lucia, answer me, where are you?" There was no reply, but he did hear the sounds of sirens as more vehicles drove at speed down the driveway to his home.

By the time the police cars drew up, he was a bundle of nerves. He could barely speak. His words were a jumble of unconnected sentences. He kept looking around, hardly able to keep still long enough to explain his concerns to the police.

It was not until the officer-in-charge pulled him to one side, held onto his arms, slowed him down and asked him to repeat what had occurred.

"It's my wife, she's lying dead upstairs and my little girl is missing. I can't find her. I don't know where she is." He did not stop to take breath.

"Why don't you do something? Look for her; help me find her." He shook off the officer's hand that held onto him. He resumed his tortured cries for his daughter.

"Mr Farraday, I want you to slow down and tell me what's happened? You say your wife is dead and your daughter is missing. When did this happen?" Malcolm repeated what had happened.

Police and ambulance personnel entered the house, while others began searching the premises. By this time, Malcolm was an emotional mess. A paramedic remained with him.

The sight of Carrie Farraday was a scene none of them would forget in a hurry. It was obvious to all that the woman was dead and from first observations, it was clear that she had been murdered. A crime scene was declared. Crime and forensic investigation teams were called in. There was still no sign of the missing child.

Another search of the house was underway. It was unclear what other evidence may yet be discovered pertaining to the suspected murder of Carrie Farraday. Therefore it was only a cursory search of the house for the young child. Already, there was another check of the grounds underway.

Malcolm was a quivering wreck. More police vehicles arrived and with them came police with more seniority. Sergeant Andy Brown was in charge and was quickly apprised of the situation.

No one mentioned the occurrences that had recently befallen the Farraday family. No mention was made of the alleged murder of Sarina. But it was uppermost in the minds of all those police officers present that they were looking at a similar situation.

As he pulled himself together, Malcolm contacted his brothers. Very soon, there were more vehicles arriving. Four brothers stood together, all in shock and bewildered at this latest unbelievable tragedy. There was no imaginable reason for the terrible events that kept occurring in their family.

Again there were insufficient words to comfort their brother. So they remained together in silence, leaning up against the front of Mitch's SUV.

Zaylee remained at the back of Malcolm's mind while this latest trauma was unfolding. He wanted nothing more than to be back in bed with her.

But he had strong memories of what it was like for anyone involved with his family. He recalled how difficult it had been for Denise when she had been a detective and got mixed up with Michael. He considered what Denise was going through now, sitting in a jail because she was accused of murdering her daughter.

He would keep Zaylee right out of this current disaster. He cared for her too much to have her involved. He would lose her for sure, but it was better that happened than have her contaminated by his family's reputation and have her interrogated by the police.

He asked his brother Mitch for a loan of his phone. He walked away to make the most difficult phone call of his life— the one that was breaking his heart.

When she answered, he spoke in a cold voice. "Hello," he said as soon as she answered. "I've been thinking about us and it's not going to work out. So whatever we had, it's over and done with." He tried to keep his voice firm.

"So I think you better get out of there right now, and take the sheets with you. I don't want to see you again. I don't want any sign of you left behind. Any woman who sleeps with a married man is nothing but a tease and a tramp and needs a good thumping. It was no more than you deserved what your boyfriend did to you. So just get out, do you hear me, get out?"

He finished his tirade with the words. "I don't want to have anything to do with you ever again." He didn't wait for a reply as he handed the phone back to his brother.

Eventually, Andy Brown returned, ready to ask more questions. Before he could commence, Malcolm asked, "Have you found Lucia?"

"No," the man replied. "I think it might be more convenient if you came to the station for a chat about what's happened here."

The sergeant was not leaving any room for refusal. Malcolm was courteously manoeuvred into a police vehicle.

"We'd better get Dax out of bed and get the lawyers in," Matt announced to his brothers. "I don't know what's going on, but something's up. Someone is systematically killing off our family. We better make sure Mick and Denise know about this and we'd better keep a closer eye on the children."

The brothers had no option but to leave. They went to their respective homes and checked on the children. Other family members were informed and advised to be extra careful. There were decisions to be made about the children.

Two Farraday children had now disappeared. How do you tell children that two of their cousins were missing? Another aunty is dead and their uncle has been hauled off by the police for questioning.

As they left their brother's home, there were state emergency service volunteers arriving to do further searches. A child abduction alert had been instigated for the missing girl.

The room Malcolm was placed in was grey and stark. He thought again of Michael, and the number of times he had been in a similar situation, sometimes because of him. He wondered what Michael would do if he was in his place.

Malcolm kept an eye on the time and realised he had been there for several hours before the door opened.

The sergeant sat opposite him and the questions began. "Did you kill your wife, Mr Farraday?"

"No, of course I didn't. I would never hurt her. I cared for her. She wasn't well, you know. Whoever did this," he stopped to consider what he was saying, "she wouldn't have stood a chance. She had no fight in her. She was too weak, too frail—poor Carrie."

"Where were you last night? Can you account for your whereabouts?"

He hoped that enough time had lapsed for Zaylee to have left his office. "I was at work where I usually am. You can check if you like."

"We already have. Your staff report that you came and went earlier in the night. Where did you go?"

He had a distinctive car. There were not too many red Alfa Romeo's in the area. He cursed his streak of flamboyance. Even though it was unlikely, it was possible that his car had been seen near Sundial Park.

All he could hope was that no one had seen the doctor hop in beside him. "You know how it is. I had to get out of the place for a while so I went for a drive."

"Can you tell me where?"

"Not really, I just drove around then came back to the restaurant."

"The people you employ also state that they didn't see you again for the rest of the evening. Why was this?"

He was in dangerous waters whichever way he answered. The way he saw it, he admit he had spent the night with the doctor and had left his sick wife and child alone in the house or else say nothing and wait for his solicitor. This was by far the safest option.

"I'll wait for my solicitor before I say anything more."

"That's your privilege. You haven't been charged with anything; this is just routine questioning. If you know anything about the murder of your wife, it would be best to tell us everything. As for your missing daughter, heaven help us all if it's a repeat of what happened to your brother's child."

The sergeant let this statement sink in before continuing.

"What is it with you Farradays? First your niece, then your sister's husband, your brother's wife, and now your wife and child; if I didn't know better I'd say someone has got it in for you all or else you're all psychopaths. You're free to go for the time being, Mr Farraday, but don't you or your brothers leave town. I'll let you know when I want you back here again."

He could not wait to leave the confines of the room where he had been questioned. When he walked outside, his brothers were waiting for him. They took him back to Sunshine where they waited to hear if Lucia had been found. Their world was again collapsing around them.

25

The phone was ringing in her ear. Mrs Potter could not believe it. She had never had a phone call in the middle of the night, never, except the time the hospital phoned and said her husband had died from a heart attack.

When she looked at her bedside clock she could she it was in the early hours of the morning. She had no idea who could be phoning her at this hour. She had been a widow for many years. She had no children of her own but she did have a brother.

She answered her phone as quickly as possible.

"Hello" she asked, trying to keep the alarm from her voice.

"Can you come and get me, please, Mrs Potter. I'm very frightened." Lucia Farraday's voice was no more than a whimper. She knew immediately who it was.

"What's the matter Lucia? Where are your mother and father?" Mrs Potter was already out of bed, a sinking feeling coming over her.

"I don't know. Daddy won't answer his phone and mummy won't open the door. I'm really scared. Please come and get me." It was very clear to Mrs Potter that the young girl was terrified.

"You wait at the front door and I'll be there as soon as I can. You'll be safe with me."

Mrs Potter was utterly disgusted with both Carrie and Malcolm. How dare they neglect their daughter? She was such a lovely child. She supposed both parents were stoned out of their brains or drunk or both.

She knew what Carrie got up to when she ever had the energy to wake up. Instead of eating, she went outside and smoked that brain-numbing stuff. Carrie often told her that she felt better after she had been outside, but Mrs Potter knew better. It was the illegal drugs that made her feel better—not the fresh air.

It was no place to be rearing a child. As for the father, he wasn't much better. He didn't get into smoking, not that she knew, but he did drink and then there were the women.

She knew about them as well. She had seen the evidence, even though he had tried to hide it. Didn't he think she knew what condoms were? That she had been born in the dark ages. If only he knew? But she had taken herself out of that lifestyle. She was now a respectable widow.

As Mrs Potter sped towards the place of her employ, she decided she would pick up Lucia and take her to her own home. After all, she had just cause. It would serve both her parents right if they couldn't find her in the morning.

Besides, she would have Lucia back home again probably before either one of them was awake. That is, if her father came home at all. She cursed Malcolm and his women.

As she pulled up, she saw the red car. Well, at least he had made it home. She went to the front door which was open and there was Lucia, looking frightened and holding onto her two teddy bears, her small bag and her phone. She looked very lonely.

"Come here, Lucia. You come home with me and I'll tuck you into bed. I'll keep you safe."

Mrs Potter bundled the child into her car and drove to her home. She rented a small, brick house.

Mrs Potter struggled financially to get by. Women in her situation did not fare that well. She made enough to get by, but there was little likelihood her circumstances would ever amount to much more than what she now had.

Not unless some miracle occurred. She thought of her brother and wondered how he was faring.

She took Lucia into a spare bedroom, helped the child into bed, and left a small light on in case she became frightened again. She told Lucia that they would have a sleep in, then a nice breakfast before taking her back home in time for school.

Let her parents suffer for an hour or so. It would do them the world of good. It would serve them right. After all, they let their daughter suffer enough. They couldn't even come to her during the night when she was frightened. Such were Mrs Potter's thoughts.

True to her word, Mrs Potter let the child sleep in. They had a leisurely breakfast of toast and vegemite and a large glass of milk. Lucia refused anything further. The little girl solemnly ate her toast. She was very nervous.

"All right, Lucia. I'll take you home. If we hurry up, you shouldn't be late for school." Mrs Potter helped the child into her car.

As they approached the drive way into the property, the older lady noticed the vehicles that were present. The police vehicles bothered her as did the number of people milling around.

All she could imagine was that they were looking for Lucia. What had she done? In her heart she knew she had done the wrong thing. She should never have taken Lucia without her parent's permission. She had virtually kidnapped the child even if it was with the best of intentions.

Mrs Potter became so alarmed she turned her car around and headed straight back to her home. Lucia sat quietly beside her, unaware of what was happening.

As the search for the missing child and the investigations into the murder of Carrie Farraday continued, Lucia remained inside Mrs Potter's small house thinking back to the previous night when she had become so frightened. It was very bewildering.

She had woken when she heard the sound of a motor bike. As she looked out the large window of her bedroom, she saw lights leaving their property. She could see by the light of the moon that her father's red car was out the front of the house so she knew he must be home.

She hopped out of bed and quietly knocked on her parent's bedroom door. As there was no reply, she timidly opened the door and peeked inside. She could see her mother asleep but no sign of her father.

Where was her daddy? He knew that her mummy didn't like her in bed with them, but whenever she woke, he would stay in her room with her until she went back to sleep.

She called out softly for her father, but he did not answer; nor could she find him anywhere when she ventured down stairs in search of him. So she went back upstairs to her bedroom, and hopped back into bed. Still she couldn't sleep.

She closed her eyes and said the little prayer that her father had taught her: *Now I lay me down to sleep, I pray the Lord my soul to keep, and if I die before I wake, I pray the Lord my soul to take.* She said this many times, but still remained awake.

She said a little prayer for Sarina just in case she wasn't in heaven but somewhere else. Although she couldn't imagine where she might be because all the people she knew said she was definitely in heaven, because she was such a good girl.

Her world revolved around her parents, Mrs Potter and her cousins. Since Sarina went to heaven, she saw her cousins often. As she could not talk to any of the people who were important in her life, she decided she would visit her Barbie doll house where she could pretend to talk to her cousins.

She picked up a few of her dolls but then she thought of her boy cousins, especially Gabe and Rafe who ate so much weetbix. She laughed at this so she moved around to the back of the doll house to play with the Barbie dolls and the stuffed toys that she had named after all her cousins.

She opened the wardrobe door so as to give herself more room to play. She left the light off as there was enough moonlight coming through the large window of her bedroom. She talked to Gabe and Rafe, the large teddy bears that she had named after her twin cousins.

She told them how greedy they were eating so many weetbix and spilling honey all over the place. Lizzie and Hope Barbies were much better behaved. Even Harry did not spill his honey. Arlo, of course, had vegemite all around his face. Boy stuffed-toys were far less well-mannered than pretend Barbie girls.

Lucia played happily until she heard more noises which sounded like vehicles pulling up. She wondered who it could be. It couldn't be her father as he was already home even though she could not find him. His red car was out the front so he had to be somewhere. It was at this moment she heard Sarina talking to her, telling her to be careful, to hide.

Then she heard more noises like car doors closing quietly, and then footsteps coming upstairs. She knew when someone was on the fifth step because it always squeaked. It made a noise like the trees outside, groaning when the wind was strong. It sounded like there were a lot of footsteps. It couldn't be her daddy because there was only one of him.

She became frightened. She had no idea who could be coming up the stairs. She thought it might be Uncle Matt or Mark or even her new uncle, Mitch, who she had seldom seen before.

As she listening to the night sounds, she thought she heard Sarina calling to her, telling her to take care, that there was danger present.

But then she wondered why anyone would be sneaking up the stairs in the middle of the night to see her daddy. They could see him any time if they wanted to. So she hopped back into the wardrobe and pushed the door closed leaving a small gap so that she could see who might come into her room.

Lucia sat perfectly still as she clutched Gabe and Rafe, the two stuffed toys that looked most alike. Barbie was too thin and small to be much comfort when you were scared. She heard voices but could not determine whose they were.

Then she heard a gurgling noise and a thump. There were more voices, no louder than a whisper. The footsteps began to move. She heard the sound of more doors opening and then it was her door that was being opened.

Lucia held her breath and clutched Gabe and Rafe even tighter as she peeked through the gap of her wardrobe door. She saw a large figure enter her room and stealthily go over to her bed.

The figure bent down to look under the bed then began to search her room. The figure moved closer to her, shifting the doll house out of the way.

She clutched Gabe and Rafe even tighter. They were both large, almost as big as she was. She had received two which were almost identical at Easter last year. The only difference was their colours. One was brown and the other was black.

The moment the dark, frightening figure pushed open the wardrobe door, she was very pleased that the two teddy bears were so big. She kept her eyes squeezed shut hiding behind Gabe and Rafe as the door slowly opened and then was pushed shut again.

Lucia was uncertain how long she stayed hidden. She heard the footsteps move back down the stairs and then the sound of the vehicles driving away. She didn't know how long she should stay hidden, but she had to find her mummy and daddy as she had been so frightened.

She ran to her mother's room but the door would not open. Her daddy was nowhere to be found. She then remembered Mrs Potter telling her to use the little phone she had given her. She tried to call her father thinking he might be outside or still at the restaurant but he did not answer. Then she called Mrs Potter.

26

She could not believe it. As long as she lived, she would never believe the words she had heard.

Zaylee was devastated. She was in disbelief at the words that Malcolm had said. She was given no opportunity to speak before he had hung up. How could he be so cruel? She had just spent the most incredible night of her life with him.

Yet here he was telling her it was over, to get out and that she was no better than a tramp. Of all the things he had said to her that was the worst. She felt crushed, humiliated and so very hurt.

Fool that she was, she had let herself fall in love with him. Whatever love was, she was no longer sure. But her feelings for him had been so intense; so intense she could no longer bear to have her boyfriend touch her.

All her thoughts had been full of him, the way he looked at her, the way he smiled at her and then finally the way he had loved her.

She gave way to her devastated feelings. The thumping she had received was temporarily forgotten. It was the least of her problems. Her boyfriend was out of her life which was what she had wanted. But foolishly she thought she would replace him with Malcolm Farraday.

But he was far worse. He had not resorted to physical violence but he had emotionally destroyed her. She had fallen for him hard, not just for his good looks and charm but for the way he had treated her and the tenderness he had shown her when she most needed it.

She sat on the sofa bed and cried her heart out. It was early in the day. What was it that he had demanded? That she get out of there as soon as possible, and to add insult to injury to take the sheets with her. What sort of a creep asked a girl to do that?

Her moments of self-pity changed, as she indulged in the start of a black rage. A rage directed at all men. First there had been Dave Norton, now the ex-boyfriend and then there was Malcolm Farraday, the married man and father who had just spent the night whispering sweet words of love into her foolish ears and making love to her hungry body.

What they had shared was far more than just sex. She had thought it had been the gentle coupling of real love. How could she have been so wrong?

She recalled again what he had said, "Anyone who sleeps with a married man was no better than a tramp" or words to that effect. Had he not also said that she had deserved the good thumping that her ex-boyfriend had handed to her?

Her thoughts were chaotic. *It was partly his fault that the ex-boyfriend had belted her around. It was his fault she couldn't think of anything else other than what it felt like to be kissed by him and wondering what it would be like if they made love. Then when she'd succumbed, the callous bastard had thrown her out. What a fool she'd been.*

The doctor did not take long making up her mind. She stripped the sheets off the bed, and then pushed the sofa bed back into position.

She remained firm in her decision. She would just pack up and leave. There was nothing left for her. Her heart had been more than broken. It was in a thousand pieces. Her life was shattered.

She put the sheets in a plastic bag and dumped them in the first bin she could find. She did not want any part of her left behind in his office.

Just as he had asked, he wanted her gone and gone she would be, forever. She was determined that not one speck of her would remain. She gave his office a quick clean, then found a cafe where she drank nothing but coffee. She knew she looked a fright as the flesh around her eye was beginning to bruise.

His betrayal was far worse than the beating she had taken from Dave Norton. She had to get away. She emailed her place of work and explained that she had experienced a break down due to personal reasons. She informed her employer that she needed an indefinite leave of absence but would return when she felt well enough. She promised she would keep them informed of her well-being and proposed return to work.

When things had to be done, there was none more proficient than Zaylee. As she sat hugging her coffee cup she realised it was just as well she carried such a lot of trivia in her bag. She was able to cover her bruised and swelling eye with a large pair of sunglasses as she pondered her immediate future.

Her mind made up, she hailed a taxi which took her to the home she had shared with Dave Norton up till the previous evening. But that was the end of her sharing with any man. Never again would she allow herself to be at the mercy of anyone.

The rational part of her brain told her that one day she would heal, but the emotional part of her brain was disillusioned at men in general.

Arriving at her home, she was in two minds about her next move. She realised that both her car and her ex-boyfriend's vehicle were still there. She braced herself for another battle. Fortifying her courage with deep breaths, she marched bravely up the stairs, opened the door and walked inside.

Dave Norton looked sheepishly at her as she walked past him. When she looked at him, sitting there with his hangdog expression, she could not believe what she had ever seen in him. He wasn't even that good looking—nothing like Malcolm Farraday. Then she castigated herself for making such comparisons. Suddenly all her anger at him evaporated.

"Good morning," she announced pleasantly. "I'm here to collect my things and then I'm off."

She proceeded into the bedroom they had shared, collected her belongings and was ready to depart. He watched her as she dragged her belongings down the steps to her car. She made a point of removing her sun glasses so he could get a good look at the damage he had done.

"Well, that's it then, I'm off. Have a good life." She gave him her most pleasant smile as she approached the door to leave.

"Where are you going? You can't just up and leave. What about me?" he asked.

"You're a big boy, Dave, big enough to belt a woman around. As you said, I'm too good for you even if I am a bitch and a slut."

With that, she trudged down the stairs towards her car. She knew he followed her but she didn't turn around once to look at him again.

She drove away slowly in her car. As she left Tewantin, she gave a small wave goodbye. This was her final farewell to thump-artist Dave and the smiling-assassin Malcolm.

Her face would heal but she wasn't too sure about her heart. It had been broken into a thousand pieces. It had been assassinated by the treacherous Malcolm.

Zaylee knew her parents, who loved her dearly, would be totally devastated if they knew she had been at the receiving end of someone's fists. They were both gentle, kind people who had no concept of how such things occurred.

She made up her mind that she would not tell them. She would save them from this anguish by saying she was taking some time off to travel. Yes, she would travel, as far as she could from brilliant smiles and flashing black eyes. She pulled into the nearest petrol station, filled up, and then drove away.

Newspapers, radio and television were of no interest to her. She stopped whenever she felt tired, booked into motels and walked the beaches until all her energies were spent.

Sleep was not easy. Try as she might she could get neither the image of him nor their lovemaking from her mind. The memory of him stayed. All the driving and walking in the world could not erase it.

27

On the night that Carrie was murdered and Lucia disappeared, Maria was struggling to cope. The night may have been full of brilliant moonlight, the breezes soft and the temperature mild, but Maria knew that this was nature providing a cover for what she knew was coming. The monsters silently returned in their black, malicious-looking vehicles.

She was banished from the dining area where they ate pizza and pies and drank their evil-smelling spirits while they talked strategy. She often heard the word 'strategy'. They had a 'strategy' for dealing with this problem and a 'strategy' for other problems.

Maria did not really want to know what strategy they were planning, but she knew it was nothing good. From her experience, there was no good in any of them. They were evil men. None of them had done a good deed in their lives.

But if she wanted to survive, which she did now that she had a small child she was responsible for, she had to be aware of the strategies they were planning.

It wasn't so long ago that she would have welcomed death, especially when her fingers were removed because of her disobedience. On a very few occasions when she had been brave enough, she had voiced her objections to their plans. Yes, she would gladly have died only she didn't know how to do it.

She could no more slit her wrists than put a gun to her head. The memory of all the blood when her fingers were sliced off cured her of these possibilities. She didn't have a gun and wouldn't know how to use one if she did. As for slitting her wrists, this was totally out of the question. She hated knives, could not bear to touch them. She could still see the knife piercing the flesh of her little finger, could hear the bone being cut. It was an indelible imprint in her brain. Then there was the pain. Then it happened all over again with her index finger. Knives were out of the question.

Another consideration regarding the best way to die would be to use pills. But she had no access to these. Never in her wildest dreams would she ever go near a doctor to ask for something that would help her sleep—especially a permanent sleep.

The only other thing that came to mind was drowning and that would require a massive effort as she would have a long walk to get to the river or the ocean. It would be her luck that someone would come along and save her.

She had Sarina, now, so it was no good thinking about taking the easy way out. She would just have to listen in and be as smart and cunning as she could.

The monsters stole away again later in the night. When she was sure they were gone, she rushed to the granny flat to check on Sarina before they returned. She rattled the door to give the child time to scramble under the bed.

This was a worry for her especially at night. What would happen if Sarina fell into a deep sleep and one of the monsters decided to visit? It was hardly likely, but you never could tell.

As she walked through the small kitchen and into the main room, she was pleased to see Sarina was not on the bed. "It's only me, Maria. You can come out now."

The little girl wriggled out from under the bed, carefully holding her damaged hand. "It's very late, Maria. Is there something wrong?"

Maria did not want to worry the child unnecessarily but she had the ugliest feeling. "I'm worried the monsters will do something bad again. I want you to be safe, Sarina. I worry you might fall asleep and won't have time to get under the bed."

The girl looked at Maria with concern. "Something bad is going to happen, Maria. I saw it in my vision. Did you know I sometimes see things? My mummy said I'm like my grandmother. She told me that my grandmother can see when things are going to happen in the future."

"What did you see, Sarina? What did your vision tell you?" Maria asked, not knowing what to think of the child's strange statement.

Sarina sighed, "Someone's going to die. It's someone connected to Lucia. Do you know Lucia, Maria?"

Maria shook her head, aghast at what the child was telling her. "Lucia is my best friend and she's not safe. Maybe if I try really hard, I might be able to send Lucia a message and tell her to hide. It would be terrible if the monsters caught her and cut her finger off. So I think that's what I'll do. I'll put a picture of her in my head and tell her to hide."

Maria was terrified at what the child was telling her. "Oh, Sarina, let's hope that nothing terrible should happen. Please be careful, especially tonight. Nothing feels right about this night."

"I'll sleep under the bed tonight, Maria. But you must be careful as well. Do you still have your wooden circle with the picture of the lady on it? I'm going to hold mine in my hand all night and I'll say lots of prayers. I can only remember little prayers, but I'll keep saying them all night. I want us all to be safe. I think the monsters are going to get angry again."

Maria was overwhelmed at what the child was saying. She felt more miserable and worthless than ever. She sat beside the child for as long as she dared, then watched as Sarina grabbed the wooden circle from under her pillow, kissed Maria goodnight and then wriggled back under the bed.

Maria straightened the sheet making sure there was enough hanging over the side so that Sarina was hidden from sight. She returned to the main house and went to bed.

As the soft chirping of the morning birds could be heard, the black vehicles pulled up outside the house. Maria listened carefully as they were not nearly as quiet as when they had left.

There was a loud roar to their motors and no attempt was made to subdue the heavy slamming of doors as they returned to the house. This was not a good sign. The monsters were always quiet, staying out of sight, not wanting to be noticed.

There were raised, angry voices reverberating throughout the house. Maria snuggled down further into her bed and pulled the sheet up over her head. She knew it would not be long before they came for her.

For the monsters, rage and Maria often went together. Just as she guessed, there was banging on her bedroom door demanding her presence. She did not hesitate. She was up as soon as the demand came.

She kept her head down, hardly daring to look up and make connection with any of them. She didn't have to be told what they wanted. She would feed them while they kept drinking and then she would go back and lie on her bed.

She prayed Sarina remained hidden under the bed. As quickly as she could, she cooked up ham, sausages and eggs. Her hands had difficulty holding the hot pan as she was shaking so much. Her missing fingers did not make the job any easier.

She had seldom seen them in such a rage. The language was vile and the deed that they had been involved in was terrifying. Then there was the laughter as they described the despicable act they had performed. She did not fully understand when they talked about a red car and where the hell was the bastard.

She tried to shut her ears to what they were saying. It was so very true what Sarina had seen in her vision. Someone had died tonight. It sounded as though it was a woman.

Maria was devastated. "Let her rest in peace," she prayed.

There was no talk of a child for which Maria was relieved. If the monsters had gone to where Sarina's friend lived, then perhaps the child had been spared. Maria knew it was almost her time. She had finished feeding them while they kept drinking.

Their speech became louder but the main monster told them to quieten down, to remember the strategy. Then he clicked his fingers to gain her attention and pointed towards the bedroom. She knew it was time.

She was tempted to leave the pan burning on the stove so the house would burn down, but then thought of Sarina. She turned off the switch and went to her room.

They came to her one by one and it seemed to go on for hours. She did as Sarina had suggested and kept the wooden circle with the image of the lady on it, firmly clutched in her hand and prayed it would soon be over.

Sarina too had heard the vehicles arrive. Usually she heard very little as she lay under her bed, locked in her prison. But then the door rattled. It wasn't the quiet rattle of Maria arriving but the heavy sound of someone impatient and full of anger.

The footsteps stopped in the kitchen then proceeded into the room. Sarina was terrified. She knew it was one of the monsters who had cut off her finger. She just knew it.

She saw the black boots walk closer and stand beside the bed, not moving. Big, ugly boots were within her sight, just inches away. They moved around as though the owner was restless. Sarina heard vile language being spoken. She could almost feel the heat of anger coming from above the bed.

Sarina hardly dare breathe. She sucked her thumb and held onto the wooden circle. The big, ugly boots eventually turned around and then she felt the monster fall onto the bed.

She heard the heavy breathing which made it a little easier for her. She tried to match her breathing to his so that he would not hear her. But this was impossible as her little body could not get sufficient air when she did this.

She lay there silently listening to the noises that came from the monster inches above her. She let her mind say the little rhymes that she made up when things were really bad.

Monster, monster, go away; don't ever come back, not any day.
Monster, monster, I hope you die, and never again see the sky.

The child was unaware of falling asleep. The sound of big, ugly boots just inches away from her had woken her

Sarina pushed herself back against the wall because the sheet that usually hung down the side of the bed was no longer there. It was in a tangle on the floor beside her.

She held her breath. Slowly the big, ugly boots made their way back towards the rattling door. But now there was not just boots but ugly black-covered legs. They stopped on their way to the door and turned around.

Sarina almost screamed as this happened but the thumb in her mouth prevented her from doing so. Then the legs turned around and walked slowly back through the door.

The girl did not know if she fainted from fright. She thought she must have because it was hardly likely she would fall back to sleep after seeing those fearful legs and those ugly boots.

28

There was little fun to be had languishing in a prison. Denise tried not to think of her days as being worthless. But that was how it felt. Her life felt worthless for she had lost everyone who was dear to her.

Her beloved daughter was gone. Everyone said she was dead, so it must be true. Her husband was in the same situation as herself, languishing in a prison cell. Both of them were rotting away in what was not much better than an endless, boring hell.

There were her twin sons, the light of her life. From what Matt told her their lives were being turned upside down as well. What was to become of them?

When she saw the news broadcasts about Carrie and Lucia, Denise forced her thoughts to consider what was really happening to her family.

She had to accept that her daughter was gone, but enough of her spirit remained that convinced her not to accept it was coincidence that such horrific events kept occurring. There were more forces at play and none of them were good.

The detective in her was reawakening. She had spent time grieving while she waited and battled for her mind to overcome her grief. She had to pull herself together instead of being the broken woman who had somehow survived all this time.

There were other people who needed her, who needed her strength and her canny ability to sort through the myriad tangles of people's lives.

She was allowed to speak to Michael on occasions. She could hear the defeat in his voice. She knew he was strong enough to last until they were released, but it was the dreadful sense of loss that she heard in his voice that was the hardest to take. Even though he tried to sound upbeat, there was no hiding the pain that remained.

There was ample time to wonder how all their lives had come to this. That was the one thing she had plenty of—time. There was time to spend doing trivial chores, time to spend eating with the other inmates, time to listen to no end of concerns and squabbles, time to find her way in the pecking order of such institutions.

When she was first imprisoned, all she wanted was to be ignored, to be left alone. But as she came to realise that many of the women were in similar circumstances, her conscience troubled her.

So when she could, she tried her best to help those unfortunate women who seemed to be more bereft than she was. There were women who had no one to share the burden of their sad and lonely lives.

Because she had been in such a state of grief and disconnection from the world at large, some of the other inmates had thought she was unhinged. But, as time went by, it became clear to them that she was a woman of intelligence and substance.

In a way she had been unhinged. Her cherished daughter was gone, her family all but demolished. Denise had been only too happy to be considered unhinged as long as she was left alone. But the plight of others forced her to re-evaluate her situation.

Even though she empathised with many, she had no close companion, no one she could call a friend. There was one woman who always made a point of conversing with her. This woman had been charged and convicted of the murder of her husband.

Denise listened with little interest to what the woman spoke about, but over time the woman's honesty about her circumstances brought about a mutual respect.

This woman told her that of course she had killed her husband. There was no question about that. It was either kill him or be killed herself and she had chosen the former. Her only regret was her children. She had two of them and she feared for them as they had been placed in foster care. Denise could well understand her concerns.

The woman's name was Abigail Jordan.

She never spoke of her own heart ache. It was enough to listen to the gruesome tales of other women. It was not the place where spirits were uplifted yet Denise fought her way out of her depression.

There were psychopaths among the population but there was also a plethora of other women who had come to their unfortunate incarceration by the cruel demons of fate.

Abigail had opinions on everything. Denise made no mention of her relationship to Carrie and Lucia Farraday as she watched the unbelievable, breaking news reports. It was doubtful that any of the inmates made the connection of the names being the same, although the prison officials would certainly have known.

She needed to be extra careful. Her old nemesis, Sergeant Bill Boyd who had pursued her and almost strangled her to death ten years ago, would not have forgotten about how she had bested him.

Bill Boyd had not retired but had climbed up the ladder and was now a superintendent of police. He was revered for his analytical skills.

Denise smirked at this as she knew that his best analytical skill had been abusing innocent, young girls along with his good buddy, Arthur Webster, Dax's father.

Abigail sat beside Denise at the meal table when Denise suddenly asked. "What do you suppose are the main reasons for murder?"

This was totally unexpected as Denise always avoided anything other than superficial conversations. She needed to qualify her thoughts and Abigail was as good a sounding board as any.

"The usual, I suppose," Abigail replied, looking sceptically at her new friend. "Revenge, jealousy, money, power, sex or just good, old-fashioned madness. In my case it was because he kept knocking me around and I finally had enough so I stabbed him. It was worth it though. I'd do it again, only next time I wouldn't be fool enough to get mixed up with him in the first place. But you know how it is, you get sucked in by these men and before you know it, you've got a couple of kids and you're stuck."

Both women were pensive. "What about you? Why are you here?" Abigail asked.

"They said I killed my daughter," Denise answered sadly.

"Did you?" the other woman asked.

"Of course not," Denise replied, aghast at the suggestion. "This isn't a very nice subject though, is it? How about we talk about something else?"

Abigail was smart enough to detect that her new friend was through discussing anything personal.

Denise considered everything Abigail had said. Who did she know who had reason to be attacking her family? She started making a list in her head. Not Jack Smith or Alan Farraday because they were both dead and buried.

She briefly thought of old Dr Sam Calhoun but she dismissed this thought as quickly as it came to mind. He loved Michael's mother, there was no denying that. He would certainly never do anything to harm Michael or his children. He thought of Michael as the son he never had.

The memory of the disappearance of three women now over twenty years ago came back to her. In fact, the memory of those terrible days of when Michael had been shot and her subsequent shooting of Jack Smith seldom left her. Then there was the suicide of Michael's father, Alan Farraday.

She thought of Superintendent Bill Boyd and his good buddy, Arthur Webster who was now retired from his years spent as a police prosecutor. She put them on her list, but then thought this was unlikely.

Bill Boyd was at the top of his game. He would have little to gain by decimating her family even though she wouldn't put it past him to have both Michael and herself in jail for the rest of their lives if he could get away with it. Maybe he had achieved his wish for that was where they now were.

She had no doubt he would be keeping a good eye on both of them, especially on Michael. What was it he called her husband back then—her killer boyfriend? He was never convinced that Michael was not involved in Mandy Lamont's death. Michael might have buried her body but he certainly didn't kill her.

She still shuddered to this day as she remembered the superintendent's big hands around her throat as she put it to him about a hypothetical scenario of a paedophile ring involving high-ranking and supposedly respectable people. But what did he have to gain by going after her daughter or Lucia?

What about Danny, Tiffany and Carrie? He could have no possible reason for wanting them dead. Still, he was an evil man. He must be laughing his head off knowing all the tragedies that had befallen her family.

Her list was not growing very fast. There was Danny's father who had been indirectly responsible for Jane Broadbent's suicide but he too was dead. Jane Broadbent had been the second woman to disappear.

The third woman who went missing all those years ago was Geraldine Wright, who, when she was eventually found, was calling herself Geraldine Farraday. She had a daughter fathered by Alan Farraday.

Michael had made arrangements for Geraldine and her daughter to be cared for. They had little contact with them over recent years. Money was still being paid into accounts set up for mother and daughter.

These accounts remained in use so she could only assume that Geraldine and her daughter were both doing well. The daughter would now be fully grown and probably working.

She didn't want to think it could be Dax whom she had been living with before she met Michael. He might be dodgy and cunning, but he didn't have the guile to be committing murder.

There was no reason for him to be decimating her family. After all, it was due to Michael's and her efforts that he was as successful as he was. He would have everything to lose if they weren't around.

Denise could think of no one else who had reason to attack her family. Then she started thinking about motive. Of course there was the biggest motive of all, the money that had been left in the prayer room; the money that had come from Alan Farraday's long, criminal history.

This was the money that Dax had laundered for them which had set them all up financially. There could not be a stronger motive than this.

As well as the cash there was also the question of the box-shed that Matt had shown her when he was no more than a young lad. As far as she knew the drugs, weapons and Alan Farraday's journals were still there.

No one had touched them or even looked at them for ten years. No one knew anything about this hidden cache other than Matt, Michael and herself. As for the money, the only people who knew where it had come from was herself and Michael and maybe Miriam, Michael's mother.

She could never quite tell with Miriam what she was aware of. She had always been considered to be strange—an oddity. Denise thought of her own daughter and the odd visions she used to describe, much like her grandmother.

Both the cash and the contents of the box-shed were the results of Alan Farraday's criminal activities. Was it possible that there was someone else totally unknown to them who was after the money?

She gave it more thought and decided that the amount of money they had laundered was sufficient motive for murder. But *who* was the question?

It could be any one of the many coded names that Alan had left in his journals. But why take this long to come after them? Surely the people who were involved with Alan Farraday and Jack Smith would now be dead or very elderly.

Denise had chores to attend to but her concentration was not on these tasks. Her thoughts and memories were elsewhere as she performed the repetitious, prison tasks. Her mind kept taking her back to the trip she and Michael had taken the day he had been discharged from hospital after being shot.

She clearly remembered the initials—SC—and the excitement she had felt when she had figured out it was a truck stop called Sandringham Creek. It was the place where Geraldine Wright, who was calling herself Geraldine Farraday, had escaped to with Michael's father.

It was the place where Geraldine had lived in contentment and comfort. The only requirement for her free board and lodging was to provide sex for both Alan and Jack Smith. It was clear that this arrangement had continued on satisfactorily for many years until the death of both these men.

It was also the place where Geraldine had given birth to a daughter fathered by Alan. There was a little girl of about seven or eight called Maria and she certainly looked a lot like the children of Miriam and Alan Farraday.

She remembered the child was shy and nervous. She also remembered her asking what would happen to Maxie.

Denise could not recall their exact discussion but she certainly remembered Geraldine squeezing the young girl's arm when she mentioned Maxie and that she was quick to state that Maxie was their dog. Denise had been very curious about that entire part of their conversation.

It was like a revelation—like she had been thunder struck. Denise realised that Maxie was no more a dog than the prison bars that held her captive. Maxie was a real, live, living person.

Just what his relationship to Geraldine and Maria was, she had no idea, but she would bet her bottom dollar that there was some relationship to either Alan Farraday or Jack Smith. For the first time since Sarina had disappeared, she began to feel excited. Yes, she was on the hunt. The detective in her was well and truly back.

What to do? Being locked up curtailed any active investigation on her part. She did not want to talk to Michael in case she had it wrong. It was impossible to tell who might be watching her even if she was in jail. She had to be very careful.

Who could she trust enough to help her? She didn't take too long thinking about it. There was really only one person, and that was Matthew.

She was desperate to put her theories to the test and desperate to ensure that the rest of her family was safe. She was allowed phone calls so the first chance she got, she phoned Matt, hoping she had the timing right and that he would be home.

"Hello," Denise recognised the voice straight away. It was Mia.

"Hi, Mia, it's Denise. I was wondering how you were all coping." Denise knew Mia would either start crying or start chatting on about the terrible time they were experiencing which was just what she wanted.

It would make what she wanted to say all the more convincing if the call was being monitored. She let Mia talk on until she asked for Matt. Mia knew by the authoritative tone in Denise's voice that it was time for her to hand the phone over.

She spoke to a very subdued but astonished Matt. Why would the detective want to talk to him? For that was how he still thought of her. They had already spoken about Carrie's death and Lucia's disappearance.

"I can't imagine how upsetting this must be for you, Matt. You need a break, you need to get away." Matt considered how odd it was that they were having this conversation.

"It's not really a good time for a break, Denise." He replied.

"It's probably the best time to get away. It might clear your mind, help you cope. Why don't you take a trip up north? You remember that time when Michael and I went up to Mackay, when he had been sick. It's a lovely place. There are lots to see and learn." Matthew was bewildered by the conversation.

"There are all sorts of forests with trees and logs, huge logs that you would fall over if you weren't careful. It's a wonderful place, Matt, just the place for a short break. You never can tell what you might come across. Did you know you've got relatives who live up that way?"

She chatted on about trivial things. Matt answered in similar fashion but she knew he had caught on, that his mind was mulling over everything she had said. After a few more minutes she said goodbye.

Matthew had much to ponder, to get clear in his mind what the detective was trying to tell him. Denise only hoped that no one else had caught onto what she was trying to tell him.

29

Matt believed he had worked out some of what the detective had been trying to tell him. The part about the log was easy but as for the rest of it, he was not too sure. He remembered that Michael and Denise had gone to north for a short holiday. Or so they had claimed.

Even back then, Matt considered it odd that they would go off on a holiday the minute Mick had been discharged from hospital, when he could barely walk, and was still in pain after being shot.

There was only one thing for it. He needed assistance and not from Mia. Mia was not made for drama and intrigue. She was great with the children, but this was way out of her league.

He phoned Mitch, the brother whom he had very little contact with until recently. He had few memories of his eldest brother as a child. Mitch had left by the time he was born. His only memory was of the few times he returned home on leave from his military service.

Mitch sometimes stayed the night at Sunshine but otherwise went back to Tewantin. Mark and Malcolm were in no fit state to be of help. Mark was slowly pulling himself together but Mal remained a wreck. There was nothing that helped. It was as if his heart kept breaking over and over every day.

Matt realised the detective was thinking along the same lines as himself which was that someone was out to destroy the Farradays completely.

Maryanne remained with their mother and Sam living day to day, trying to be interested in her children, trying her best to lift herself out of the melancholy that engulfed her.

The Smythe property was no longer a crime scene but still she refused to return. Sam arranged for a man to manage the property. He lived in the granny flat where Danny and Maryanne had first lived with Hope when she was a new born baby. The main house was kept locked. The Farraday fortune paid his wages. This arrangement allowed the rest of the family to care for the children and for each other.

Mitch could not believe the twists and turns his life had taken. The only life he had known was the military with its discipline and strict codes of brotherhood. Now he found himself in another sort of brotherhood, that of his family or more especially the brotherhood of his own blood brothers.

He was learning about what made them who they were, about their lives and especially these most recent happenings. When he heard his phone, he would not be surprised if it was more bad news.

"Mitch," it was the voice of his youngest brother. "Can you get out here right now? I need you."

There was something in Matt's voice that had changed. It took him some time to work out what it was. Matt sounded excited. That had not happened with any of his family for a long time. He told his brother he was on his way.

He still did the shopping run and was becoming something of an expert on what to feed children. He only bought the healthy stuff or else Mia would start with her lectures. Often he could not help himself. He purchased what was sure to bring a smile to the children's sad faces—things like chocolate treats and ice creams.

Now there were two less children; this brought immeasurable sadness to him. How could two little girls be gone?

Matt was waiting for him out the front of the house. Mia was about to leave with Harry as she was going to visit her friend who was not coping well. Mitch was puzzled when Matt indicated they should wait until Mia was gone. The other children were at school.

When Mia was finally gone, Mitch asked. "What's going on, Matt?"

"It's a long story. Maybe we better go inside." Matt led the way inside as they sat at the kitchen table.

"There's a lot that's gone on that you probably don't know about." Matt explained. He told his eldest brother everything he knew especially about Denise and Michael and all that had happened to them ten years ago. He finally got to the part about the log and the box-shed.

"You're joking. You're telling me that there's a hoard of weapons and drugs here at Sunshine and that it's sitting right here in front of our eyes."

"That's what I'm telling you. Denise thinks it's all mixed up with what keeps happening to us, or at least that's what I think she's trying to tell me." Matt gave his brother time to digest what he had told him.

"I intended telling you about it a while ago but things just kept happening. I need you to help me figure out what Denise is on about."

Mitch was stunned. "Has this box-shed you talk about got anything to do with the tunnel under that monstrosity of a bed." It hadn't taken him long to catch on.

"I'm pretty sure it does, and there's another thing I didn't tell you. The tunnel wasn't empty. There was a skeleton down there." Matt said this as if it were a common occurrence.

Mitch was again stunned. "Holy crap, not human, I hope."

"It sure was and it frightened the crap out of me when I lay on it. I can still hear it crunching underneath me."

"Who on earth is it? How did it get there?" Mitch was shaking his head in disbelief.

"I've no idea. It could be some poor bugger that either the old man or Jack Smith knocked off, I suppose. Anyway, we better not get off track. We've got to figure out what the detective's trying to tell us."

"What did you mean when you said 'some poor bugger'?"

"That's another story. Maybe I'm wrong. It's not a good thought to think your father is a killer. Maybe it wasn't him, maybe it was Jack Smith. Who knows? You know it was either the old man or Jack Smith who knocked off Mia's mother, don't you? Then there's the bone that Mark, Mal and Danny found up near the Big Rock."

"What bone? What are you talking about?"

"The story is a bit confusing. The three of them were up there planting dope. This was years ago. They found a bone and buried it again. There was some argument about whether it was human or animal. They were all stoned at the time so they couldn't really tell. Anyway, they put a cross on it, but when we found Jane Broadbent's skeleton up in the cave near the Big Rock, the detective threw the cross away. It would be nearly impossible to find it again." Mitch was amazed at what his brother was telling him.

"Denise set it up so that crooked police sergeant would find the skeleton and take the credit for solving the disappearance of both Mandy Lamont and Jane Broadbent in exchange for Mick's freedom. He was after Mick and would have planted evidence about the death of the two women on him. But Denise had plenty on him so they came to an understanding and Mick was let off."

"I never knew any of this. It sounds almost as bad as Afghanistan. Don't tell me there's more?" He was both fascinated and dismayed at what his brother was telling him.

"Well, yeah, there's lots more. The sergeant tried to kill the detective, tried to choke her, but she got away from him and videoed the whole thing. She was always frightened he would get her again. But I've still got the video and the recording. I've kept them hidden all these years."

"It sounds like the detective is quite a woman." Mitch, like his brother, was now thinking of his sister-in-law as the detective and had a new appreciation for all that she was and what she had been through for his family.

He thought of his brother and this woman stuck in their prison cells, their lives turned upside down. His determination to help solve this mystery was strengthened.

"We better get on with it," Mitch said as he followed his youngest brother out the back steps of the house and over towards the boundary of the cleared area around the home. He stopped when Matt stood at the log that had lain there for as long as he could remember. "Where are we going?"

"I haven't been here for years," Matt replied as he went to the knot in the ageing timber of the log. He put his hand around it and grunted as he pulled a large section of the log open.

"What the hell!" Mitch's jaw had literally dropped open.

"Get your torch light on. It's pretty dark down here." Matt brushed a few cobwebs away as he climbed down the steps into the box-shed. It was similar in size to a shipping container and was made of an impervious material.

He had to give it to his father. There was little corrosion or evidence of moisture contamination. Where his father had learned such skills, Matt had no idea. About the only memory he had left of his father was his drinking, abuse and driving trucks. He waited until his brother joined him.

"This is it," Matt explained. "Welcome to Farraday hell hole."

Mitch was gob-smacked at what he was seeing. It was like a museum of all things illegal and dangerous. He gaped as he gazed at the categories of weapons before his eyes.

The metal shelving on all sides of the rectangular room was covered in numerous fire arms, body armour, knifes, cross bows, knuckle dusters, silencers, handcuffs, nunchakus, batons and even a couple of hand grenades. All manner of items that would cause grievous bodily harm or death was on display as though they were collector's items.

The knife collection was impressive. There were knives of all kinds from ballistic, butterfly, flick, sheath, trench knives and even a walking stick that contained a disguised sword.

For a moment, Mitch thought he was back in a war zone. His mind was reeling. All he needed was a rocket launcher and he could start his own private war. He was less interested in the bundles covered with heavy plastic of what he assumed were drugs. It was the array of weaponry that had taken his eye.

Matt was not as interested in the weapons as his brother. His main interest was his father's journals. "Seen enough," Matt asked.

"I could spend a week in here going through this stuff," Mitch replied. "It's amazing. What's it all for? What did he think he was going to do with it, start his own private war?"

"It beats me; looks to me that he just liked collecting weapons. Weapons and women were his thing, besides other things. That's our father, not too many like him, thank goodness."

Matt collected all the books his father had used to keep track of his criminal history. "Let's get out of here and take a look through these. Hopefully, we can work out what the detective was hinting at."

Matt was already climbing back out of the box-shed. "Come on, Mitch. We'd better get cracking. There'll be plenty of time for going through this stuff later."

Mitch dragged himself away and followed his brother. "Who else knows about this place?"

"Besides the detective and Mick, only you and me; there was little point in telling the others. What were they going to do with it? So we just left it all where it was."

They returned to the house. Matt brushed the journals down. They were nothing more than school exercise books. They were the type used by young children.

"Let's see what we can make of these?" Matt began his search.

They halved the books and commenced going through the journals. Good fortune was seldom on their side of late. But fate smiled on them as sheets of paper fell out of one of the journals. Matt picked them up and together they looked them over.

"This must be what the detective figured out," Mitch said. "It looks like she left lists of cities and towns up the coast. Here it is. It's the city of Mackay and she's circled it. Then underneath it, she's written what looks like a place called Sandringham Creek. I wonder where that is?"

"We'll soon find out. You keep looking and I'll do a search," Matt hurried off to get his laptop.

A few minutes later, he said, "Well, would you look at that? It's the name of a truck stop near Mackay. This must mean something. That's what he did for most of his life, drive trucks."

They looked at the map and saw it was south of Mackay.

Their interest was intensified. They looked again at the detective's notes and there in distinct printed letters was the name Geraldine Wright.

"You know who she was, don't you?" Matt asked. His brother's blank expression suggested he had no clue. "She's the third woman who disappeared all those years ago, about the same time as Mandy Lamont and Jane Broadbent."

"You don't think the skeleton in the tunnel belongs to her, do you?" Mitch was horrified.

"I don't think so. Denise is telling us something. She said a strange thing when she spoke to me yesterday. She said that we have relatives up at Mackay. As far as I know we don't have any relatives. What about you, Mitch? You've been around longer than I have."

Mitch shook his head. "I've never heard of any. There's only one thing for it. We'll just have to go up there and find out. From what you said, the detective's hinting there's something up there that we need to know."

Matt agreed with him. "It will have to be you. I can't leave Mia and the children. The way things are, it's too dangerous to leave them alone."

"You and Mia seem to be getting along pretty well," Mitch said. Matt didn't reply. "It's okay, Matt, she's a great girl. You could do a lot worse."

"I know she's different, a bit scatty and vacant at times but I think the world of her." He didn't like to say the word 'love' but the more he got to know her, the more certain what he felt was love. He never stopped thinking about her and couldn't wait to get into bed with her every chance he got.

"What about you, Mitch, how's your love life?"

"I have spasmodic good fortune, but only very spasmodic." His brother replied. "Well, I guess if I'm going to this Sandringham Creek, I'd better make tracks. It's probably better I go anyway as we've been warned not to leave town. It's less likely that I'll be missed than you."

30

Malcolm's thoughts were chaotic. He could not get the image of his deceased wife out of his mind. He kept seeing her body with the gaping hole in her throat slumped over the side of the bed. The blood was imprinted on his mind.

His most hurtful thoughts were those of his daughter. He tried to keep the worst images out of his head as pictures of her being tortured kept coming back to him. He found it hard to eat or sleep.

He had been further questioned by the police and asked a myriad of questions, often the same ones time after time only in a different format. Things like where he was when his wife was being murdered, why was his car at the house, when did he last see his wife and child? The questions were relentless.

He kept repeating that he had been for a drive earlier in the night to get away from the restaurant for a break. He told the police he had gone home about 10pm to check on his wife and daughter who were both asleep.

He was very sure he had locked the house. He had then returned to the restaurant to finish up for the night but as he was tired he slept in his office before returning early the next morning to check on his wife and get his daughter ready for school.

He reiterated that he seldom slept in his office, preferring to go home which he did on most nights but on that particular night he decided not to as he repeated that he was too tired to be driving.

He explained that his Alfa Romeo had run out of fuel which was the reason he took the Yamaha. He told the same story time after time. He had no witnesses to prove he was sleeping in his office. It was estimated his wife had died between 10pm and 4am the following morning.

His office, home, car, computers and phones had been forensically investigated but there was no evidence to prove any involvement in his wife's death or his daughter's disappearance.

There was no murder weapon and no motive for his involvement in these two events. There was extensive medical evidence to prove that his wife had been ill for some years.

The fact that marijuana was found in his wife's remains and in her bedside cupboard was significant but blood tests revealed that Malcolm Farraday did not have any trace of the same drug in his system.

Then the suggestions came that he was tired of having a sick wife and the endless treks to health care providers had worn him down. He denied all of this. He said he was dedicated to his wife and daughter.

But his past sins came back to haunt him. His reputation as a womaniser was well known. His staff tried to deny any knowledge of their employer's love life, but there was too much talk from too many women of the nights he had spent with some of his female staff.

Not that any remained working in his restaurants, but there were other staff who had heard the graphic details of sexual escapades that had occurred in his office.

There was the question of the marijuana. Malcolm did admit to providing this for his wife. He said she needed it to make her feel better. It was about the only thing that sparked her up. Sergeant Andy Brown was very interested in where he obtained his supply.

"I got it from some guy who comes into the restaurant. I don't know his name. I just pay him and get a supply. That's it. It was for Carrie to help her get through the days."

"You wouldn't call it the best environment for raising a small child, would you?" The sergeant had little sympathy for anyone involved in drugs.

"No, it wasn't the best of environments. But Lucia is a well-adjusted little girl. She does well at school, has plenty of friends. Did you know her best friend was Sarina?"

Malcolm could not prevent tears forming in his eyes. He avoided looking at the police officer as visions of Sarina's fate haunted him. Sergeant Andy Brown was a father himself. He had sympathy for Malcolm Farraday—a lot of sympathy. He could not see this man committing any of these vile acts.

He believed he was a womaniser and had provided his wife with illegal drugs but he couldn't see him being the sort of person to cut his wife's throat. It was clearly evident he was totally devoted to his missing daughter.

The sergeant's mind went back to what he knew of the Farraday family history. He remembered that Michael Farraday had been imprisoned for six months for causing grievous bodily harm upon Jack Smith. This had occurred ten years ago.

At that time, Malcolm did have a drug habit. This was well documented, but he was clean now. The Farradays had a murky history which was peppered with bizarre happenings.

The man known as Jack Smith had intended shooting Denise due to his hatred of police, but subsequently had shot Michael instead. Michael had thrown himself in front of Denise to protect her and had taken the bullet instead. Denise had returned fire and had killed Jack Smith.

They were quite a bunch, these Farradays, but they had kept a low profile for a good ten years. The only thing of consequence was that they were now all wealthy. He wondered how that had happened.

Were these past events connected to what was happening now? Because it was certain that someone was after them and intent on making them pay.

Andy Brown could not connect any of the dots but his gut instinct told him that the bad things that were happening could well continue.

Malcolm was aware he was a 'person of interest' in his wife's murder and his daughter's disappearance. His only consoling thought regarding this current nightmare was that there was no evidence implicating the lovely doctor.

Their night of passion was so far undetected. He hoped it would stay that way. Thoughts of her helped keep him sane even though she was gone from his life.

Zaylee could not get their night of passion out of her mind either. But unlike him, thoughts of him were not helping her sanity one little bit. No matter how many walks she took along different beaches, how many motels and towns she visited, his brilliant smile which reached his black eyes was something she would never forget.

Her face was almost healed but she didn't think her heart ever would. She looked almost as good as ever except for the sadness in her spirit.

The doctor knew she would have to return sooner or later. There was little likelihood of ever running into Malcolm again.

If he wanted to see her professionally, she would just refuse. That way she could avoid him for ever.

Besides she still had her search to continue. After all, that was the reason she had come to the area in the first place. Had she known there was such a person called Malcolm Farraday waiting to break her heart, she would have gone in the opposite direction.

But she had vowed as a child to search, and that was what she was going to do. In spite of her efforts in trying to banish him from her thoughts, her treacherous body still lusted after him.

Lucia's world had also turned upside down. All she had in her life now was Mrs Potter. There was no mother or father. Mrs Potter told her that something really terrible had happened.

Lucia was told that her mother was dead. She thought this might be true because her mother had been sick for as long as she could remember. Her mother had been so thin which was why Lucia had seldom been allowed in bed with her because she might hurt her bony arms and legs if she tried to hug her. Lucia was quite prepared to believe her mother was dead.

"If my mother is dead then where is my father?"

Mrs Potter, who had read the newspapers and watched the television news broadcasts, had set herself up as judge, jury and executioner. Malcolm Farraday was guilty of murdering his wife. She didn't need any police investigators to convince her of this.

"Your father had done a dreadful thing, Lucia. He killed your mother." She neglected to tell the child that she was guilty of kidnapping her. As the days went by it became too risky to own up to her misdeeds.

Even though she was very young, Lucia could not believe her father would ever hurt her mother.

"I think you're wrong, Mrs Potter. My daddy would never hurt my mother. My mother might have died because she was sick but my daddy would not have done anything bad to her."

Lucia remembered the night when she had been so frightened; the night when she had phoned Mrs Potter. She remembered the dark figure that came into her room.

She was going to tell Mrs Potter about that frightening figure but the older lady was being so peculiar with her, not letting her watch television, and telling her to stay in her room all the time.

The only time Mrs Potter allowed her out was for meals and at night for a short time. She wasn't even going to school. She had seen none of her cousins for ages.

Lucia heard voices talking to Mrs Potter about her mother and father. When she looked out the bedroom window all she could see was a wooden fence. She wished she could climb out the window but it was kept locked. There were times when she heard sirens. She wondered if it might be something to do with her mummy and daddy.

She felt very lonely in her small room. There was little to do other than read the few books Mrs Potter bought her. She was told to do her 'homework' which consisted of reading various books, different from those used at school.

"Why can't I stay with my Uncle Matt and Mia? Lizzie, Hope and Harry stay with them as well as Rafe and Gabe. Even Arlo stays there, so why can't I?"

"They have too much to do looking after the other children, Lucia. They said you should stay with me."

Lucia was bewildered by this. She was sure she didn't need much looking after. It wasn't as though she was always making a mess like Gabe or Rafe when they ate all those weetbix.

How many times had she heard Mia say that those boys could eat them out of house and home? She wasn't too sure what this meant, but she was always careful to only have one weetbix for breakfast. That way she was sure she would always have a home to live in.

She never got into fights like Gabe and Rafe. They were always in trouble at school. Uncle Matt was often called in to see the principal about them. Lucia had never been in trouble, not once.

Even though she was lonely Lucia did have a secret which she was not going to tell anyone. She knew about Sarina. Sarina had been talking to her since the night she had been picked up by Mrs Potter.

They sometimes had little conversations in their minds. She knew Sarina often had to sleep under a bed and that she had a friend who looked after her. She also knew that Sarina was often very frightened just like she had been on the night Mrs Potter said her mother had died.

The older lady knew she would be in tremendous trouble if it was found that she had taken and kept Lucia. She worried endlessly especially when the police came knocking on her door. It was all she could to stop herself from telling the truth. Tears poured down her face as she talked about Malcolm and Carrie. It was a tale of sickness, illegal drugs, and womanising. But the tears she shed were for her own transgressions and the fear of detection.

There were many times she regretted not telling the truth. As time went by, her continued silence reduced her fear of being caught out with her lies. Mrs Potter had a plan of escape, but could not enact it yet. It involved her brother.

Patience was required. She would wait until the police and media were no longer interested in the Farradays. When it was safe, she would flee with the child. She would live where the name Farraday was unheard of.

With her brother's help, she may have found the means for a more comfortable life.

31

Mitch Farraday was a man with many skills. His departure from the airport and his arrival in Mackay were unremarkable.

No one had cause to remember the inconspicuous man who had taken the particular flight. The only thing that was memorable about him was his size and his walking stick.

The stick contained a concealed single-edged blade taken from the box-shed. Long experience had taught him to be well prepared. Too many bad things were happening. Weapons were his business. There was little point in having these at his disposal if he wasn't going to make use of them.

It took very little time to hire a car and find his way to the Sandringham Creek truck stop. Like his brother and Denise had done years ago, he went to the restaurant and drank coffee while he covertly investigated his surrounds.

It was very busy with numerous trucks, trailers, caravans and other vehicles. People were taking advantage of the restaurant and rest rooms.

When he saw the middle-aged wait person was free, he beckoned her over. The woman had never seen him before. He was not unwilling to make the most of his size and good looks.

He did not have Malcolm's charm, or Matt and Mark's kind nature but he did have an aura of authority. He could command attention when he needed to.

The woman approached and he started a casual conversation with her while he took his time ordering a meal. He said he was passing through and wanted to look up his relatives.

He asked if she knew any people by the name of Farraday. He took a gamble saying this, but if it didn't work he would try the name Wright. He was sure there would be less Farradays than Wrights. Good fortune followed him again.

"Of course I remember them." The woman was warming to her subject and keen to chat to the big, good-looking man. She didn't mind how long it took to order his meal.

"You're joking," he responded in absolute surprise. "I wonder if they are the missing relatives. You wouldn't know where they live by any chance?"

"Would you believe they used to live in that cottage over there." She pointed to a small house not far from the restaurant. "But I haven't seen any of them for ages. I can't remember how long it's been. You know how it is, time gets away."

"I can't believe I could be this lucky," he continued the conversation. "Geraldine wouldn't have been one of them, would she? I haven't seen her since we were kids at school."

"You must be talking about Gerry. She was always coming here for groceries. Then there was a daughter and Maxie. He was a funny one that Maxie. I think the daughter was frightened on him. Poor thing, she was terribly shy, hardly said a word."

The woman was distracted as she reflected on times past. "Well, it's been great chatting with you but I'd better get a move on." The restaurant was filling up. The woman did not have time to mention the other men who sometimes lived there.

Mitch was elated with his discovery. He could not believe his luck. His next step was to break into the house to see what else he could find out, especially about the 'funny one' Maxie.

He was on a roll. He could only imagine how Michael and Denise had felt all those years ago when they had found this place and the people who resided inside the cottage.

Was this the connection he was looking for? He now knew of three people who had resided in the house—Geraldine, the daughter and Maxie. Either one or all of them had used the name Farraday

Who they were was not totally clear. He was now certain that Geraldine Wright was using the surname Farraday. If he knew anything about his father, it wasn't too hard to guess why Geraldine had used his name.

He looked at the house and wondered what secrets and lies this place held. Mitch was a soldier, used to combat, used to weapons, used to death, used to managing men in battle but the thing he was not used to was what was happening to his family.

It was like he was back in a war zone—experiencing terrorist attacks. His family was being decimated one by one. No matter the cause, they were being systematically killed off. Why would anyone resort to such brutal killing?

He became a driven man. Michael, whom he had relied upon for so many years to ensure his daughter was kept safe, was languishing in jail. He was thankful now that he had never met her.

If the people who were attacking his family could take two young children, then there was nothing to stop them from going after his own daughter. Surely if he didn't know who she was, there was no chance anyone else would know.

The only people who knew he had fathered a daughter when he was sixteen were the mother of the child, Michael and himself. No doubt Denise probably knew as well. Her bond with his brother was unbreakable. He was sure they did not keep secrets from each other.

Again he remembered all that Matt had told him about the events of ten years ago. Denise had fought to keep Michael out of jail. Now they were both locked up like criminals. Nothing that was happening was fair or made sense—at least not until today.

It was time to visit the house.

A huge, traveller palm swayed softly as he opened the gate, went up the front steps and from long practice soon had the door open.

The door was in poor condition, badly in need of maintenance. He entered the house not knowing what to expect. At first glance it was very ordinary with well-worn furniture and old kitchen items. He quickly searched each room.

In the main bedroom he found out more about Geraldine Wright. There were feminine touches to the room with frilly curtains and colourful duvets. While searching a chest of drawers, he pulled out some photographs. The first one he looked at was of a baby wrapped in a printed blanket. The photograph was quite old.

There were more photographs as this baby grew older. They showed a dark eyed and dark haired, solemn-looking child. He looked further. He should not have been surprised but was still stunned. There was his father looking as proud as punch holding the child.

He stared at this for some minutes, thinking of his own brothers and his sister. Had he found another sister? He kept looking. There were more photographs of his father and another man.

Then there was a plethora of photographs of Geraldine having sex with both these men in any number of unimaginable positions. His father looked reasonably young and fit in these photographs. He had no idea who the other man was but he assumed it was Jack Smith.

He found further documents in the name of his father and Geraldine Farraday, old telephone accounts, electricity accounts and passports. He shoved a telephone account in his pocket, in case he needed to track some of the numbers.

The photographs on the passports were of Alan Farraday and presumably Jack Smith but not matched by their names. There were none for Geraldine or her daughter but there were further passports of other men. Big strong, dark-haired men who again looked much like Alan Farraday and Jack Smith.

There were various names on these passports, none of them familiar. He committed these names to memory, just in case. There was no Maxie.

The room looked unused as if no one had been in it for some time. It smelt musty much like the rest of the house. He went into the next bedroom which was clearly a girl's room. There were a few dolls scattered on cupboards around the room.

His biggest surprise was the number of religious objects? It reminded him of his mother's prayer room which had always given him the creeps. There was little else of interest.

The third and fourth bedrooms were the most interesting. They had clearly been used by men. How many he wasn't certain. They were big bedrooms and contained two single beds in each. There was nothing neat or tidy about either of the rooms.

There was an abundance of men's clothing—jeans, trousers, shirts and jackets strewn around. Most articles of clothing were in black. Boots of all variety filled the cupboards—all in large sizes. Whoever had used these rooms was by no means small.

There was pornography. Mitch Farraday was no stranger to this type of literature but the images of children disgusted him. Whoever these men were, they were not the type anyone would want near their children. He again thought of his nieces, Sarina and Lucia. His heart bled for them.

Mitch had found out about as much as he wanted to. He went out the back to further check. There was a run-down shed which was so unkempt that no one would bother with it. It was overgrown with vines and tall grasses. It would make a safe home for snakes, spiders and other reptiles.

He recognised what a great hiding place it was. He jimmied the door open. It did not require much digging around to find the stashes of illegal drugs and weapons—similar to what his father had kept hidden in the box-shed at Sunshine.

As he surveyed the cache in front of him, he saw the brown snake lying ready to strike. The concealed blade on the walking stick dispatched it before it could strike. It was about the only time in his life that Mitch was grateful for his father's peculiarities.

The whole set up could have been a replica of Sunshine. There was the house with its mysteries, the woman, the girl and the men who had lived there; there was the shed and weapons.

The small garden contained similar plants, but it had not been tended with the care and attention as that at Sunshine. The area of land was small but it was as if his father was trying to create an imitation Sunshine only on a smaller scale. His father had lived a double-life which mirrored his first.

Mitch wondered if his father had been more proud of these men who had lived in the cottage than his sons. He wondered if they were also his father's sons.

The memory of the passports with photographs of those big, rough-looking men put a shiver up his spine. Surely they couldn't be relatives. His worst thought was that they might be half-brothers.

He had seen enough. He just wanted to get out of there as fast as he could. He locked up and left the place as he had found it. Mitch no longer cared if neighbours were inquisitive about his intrusion into the house.

He breathed a sigh of relief when he returned to his home town. He spent the night considering all that he had found out. He was certain that Denise was spot on with her deductions. All that had befallen his family was almost certain to be connected to the people who had lived in the house at Sandringham Creek.

He informed Matt of what he had found and of his suspicions. They ramped up their security for the children. If these men were targeting them, the most perplexing aspect was why.

If it was the weapons and drugs they were welcome to the lot. All they had to do was ask. Or easier still, take. They had sat undisturbed for years. What good were they to anyone? The firearms were old. The weapons were impressive but these were easily available from various outlets. Illegal drugs of all types were readily available if one knew how to acquire them. It was without question that these men certainly knew how.

Mitch did not know how long the plastic-wrapped packages of what he assumed to be cocaine would last. He did not know if there were 'use by' dates associated with illegal drugs.

32

She was becoming very impatient. Francine had tried many times to see Dr Lang but she was constantly told that she was on leave.

What was she to do? She particularly liked the doctor and felt comfortable with her. She was beginning to panic. She needed confirmation of her pregnancy.

The slow decline of her husband's health continued. It was agony to watch him deteriorate. The only thing she could think of to make his miserable life better was to announce that she was having his child. Surely knowing he was leaving part of himself behind would bolster his spirits.

No one seemed to know how long he would last. No one would give her a time frame. But her own eyes did not deceive her. All the health professionals who helped care for him told her time after time that there was no particular indicator on how long he had left.

While his heart still beat in his frail chest and he kept breathing, he would live. This was what they told her. Her private thoughts were that it could hardly be called living.

She cursed the doctor for the leave that seemed to go on and on. She was totally perplexed. She had done a further home pregnancy test. She could not believe her eyes when it came up negative. What was going on? She had to know for certain.

She was running out of time. It was well over a month since she had contrived to have sex with her husband. There was no doubt this attempt was unsuccessful. But Mr High and Mighty should have been able to fill the gap. He was built like a stallion. Her body could well attest to that.

Then he had a second chance at it but now the tests were telling her that nothing had happened. How could this be? One month she had been pregnant and the next she wasn't.

In the end she asked to speak to another doctor to get the results of the tests. She could not wait any longer for the doctor's return. She was transferred to a Dr Alicia Worthington who was the owner of the practice.

Francine listened to the doctor do a medical interpretation of the results which in her present state of anxiety she failed to understand. In the end she simply asked if she was pregnant and the doctor simply told her 'no' she was not pregnant. Francine managed to stammer out a very quick thank you.

All her worst fears had come true. She had nothing left to give her husband. Her dreams were shattered. Very soon there would not be any husband and there was no baby. What would she have to live for?

All she had were fancy clothes, trinkets of jewellery, a big house and the memories. But memories could never keep her lust satisfied. None of these would ever be enough to fill her lonely heart. She blamed the man for all her troubles. She wanted nothing more than to find him and teach him a lesson.

Francine was fast replacing her anxiety with anger. She made up her mind she would find him. She was unclear what she would if she did find him but she felt like she could strangle him.

He was as big a failure as she was. By the size of him, his sperm should have been strong enough to firmly attach to a dozen eggs, but instead they had failed miserably to do their job.

She made the usual excuses. Only this time she said that something had come up unexpectedly and she was required to go away again. Neither her husband nor Val Richards questioned her. Both could see she was extra quiet and upset.

As she said goodbye to her husband, she cried again and said she would probably be back the next day if things went as smoothly as she hoped. He was much too weak except to smile at her and say goodbye.

She stayed at the same place, even had the same room. This time she didn't care how she was dressed. She wasn't sure that she would be lucky enough even to find him. She returned to the same bar and ordered a beer.

There was no room left in her spirit for any more pretence. She was tired of being sophisticated, pretending she was a connoisseur of fine wine. She didn't even like wine so she drank beer. She didn't like beer either, but her husband had when he had been well and she knew that the man drank beer. The heavy, dark beer that he drank was unpalatable to her taste buds but she persevered. If it gave her sufficient courage to confront him, then she would persevere.

She was on her second when he came in. Their eyes met like magnets. It was like she had extra sensory perception. She knew the moment he came through the door. There he was looking strong and healthy. She couldn't help her treacherous eyes. Yes, he was magnificent.

How unfair was it? Her husband had faded away to not much more than skin and bone while he was tall, strong and with more muscles than a weight lifter.

His black eyes feasted on her. She could feel him caressing her body with his mind. But this time, she would not allow her body to be lured by him. He had a penalty to pay. Somehow she would make him feel as lost and depleted as she was.

He was seated beside her before any words were spoken. Of course his hand was on her thigh, his fingers making small twirling movements that penetrated through the thin fabric of her loose skirt. She pushed his hand away before she lost her courage.

"What's up with you? You don't look too happy," he asked disdainfully.

"You," she replied caustically. "You're what's up with me. And you can keep your hands off me." His big hand was back again rubbing up and down through the stupid skirt she had put on. She should have known better. She should have bought a chastity belt. She pushed his hand away again.

"That's a change. You usually can't get enough of my hands or any other part of me for that matter. Hubby still not well?" He looked at her enquiringly.

She wouldn't have him talking about her husband, not when everything was his fault. "Shut up about him. This is not about him. It's about you, about what a failure of a man you are."

"As usual I don't have a clue what you're on about. Sounds to me like you need a good roll in the sack again. How about you finish your beer before you get too aggressive and we'll head outside." His hand was again on her leg, but this time under the loose fabric of her skirt and no longer just rubbing her thigh.

"I told you not to do that," she repeated breathlessly. It felt good. There was no other word for it. She was reluctant to shift his hand again.

"If you didn't like it you would move, but instead you sit here trying to act all virginal. If you don't want it, why don't you get up and walk out?" He could feel her tremors.

"Don't! Please don't touch me. You know what happens to me. I'm not here for that." She shifted away from him to stop that big hand from torturing her. "You make me so angry."

From the looks she was giving him he was certain that as well as being aroused she was very angry. He could never quite figure her out. One minute she was hot for him and then the next she was pretending she wanted nothing to do with him—like nothing had happened between them.

Sick husband or not, she was good at getting under his skin. "One thing I do know is that you're a crazy bitch. No wonder your poor husband is sick. You probably drove him to it."

These words were her undoing. She lifted her hand and slapped him hard across the face in front of the patrons at the bar. There were few there who had not heard the crack as her hand connected against his face.

"That's enough," he said, taking her hands in his as he pulled her outside.

She was more than getting to him. Now she was making him angry. He dragged her along after him. She stumbled as she realised he was dragging her around to the dark places at the back of the restaurant. There was the fence—dark, hard and menacing.

"Let's get some of this aggression out of your system first and then you might settle down."

"What do you mean? Just let me go," she demanded. Being pushed up against the fence in the dark of night had dampened her bravado.

"You know what I mean. So quit with your nonsense and let's get on with it." He had heard enough of her crazy talk and hysteria.

His mouth came down on hers forcing her lips open. His tongue was inside her mouth as one hand kneaded her breasts while the other returned up her skirt to her thighs.

Her mind was swirling with the sensations he was causing as well as the anger she still harboured towards him.

She didn't know how he did it but the next thing he was inside her, thrusting away, big hard stokes that were turning not only her good intentions but her whole body to jelly.

Eventually she quivered and fell limp in his arms, whimpering and moaning. She felt him shudder inside her as he put her down. She clung to him with tears again starting to course down her face.

"What's making you cry this time?" he asked, with a hint of gentleness.

"Because of what you do to me, because you make me lose any vestige of respect that I have for myself," she answered, still clinging to him as she tried to get her body and mind under control.

"I hate you, you know, I hate everything about you," she told him as she took his hand and pressed it against her breast.

It started again, this time equally as intense and violent. She felt the fence hard against her back. He took her again and she did not object. But it could not last, not in the dark behind a restaurant and against a hard, solid fence.

"Anyone there," the voice came out of the blue.

"Yeah, just taking a leak," was his gruff reply. It brought them both back to reality. He waited until the person had disappeared before he straightened her clothes and tucked in his own shirt and made himself look somewhat respectable.

"Come on, we can't stay here. Are you staying at the same place?" He took her by the hand. She was shaking and unsteady. They were both breathing heavily. She knew she must look a fright. Her hair was mussed up. Her lips were swollen and hot.

She tried to pretend she was an ordinary person walking down the footpath with a man. But nothing about what she was feeling was anywhere near ordinary. Why was she such a fool for this man? All he had to do was touch her and she fell for him every time.

He had taken the key from her and unlocked the door. Again he dragged her inside. He stripped her off making no effort at tenderness. Her clothes were thrown onto the floor. He backed her onto the bed. She landed on her back with a thump. She lay naked in front of him watching as he got rid of his clothes.

She tried to grab at the sheet to cover her nakedness. All he did was laugh and pull the sheet out of her hands. Then he ripped it totally off the bed and threw it on the floor adding to the mess of their tangled clothes.

Then he was on top of her. There was no tenderness. It was as if he had the demons of hell after him. She could not do much more than hang on and feel. When it seemed he had got the worst of it out of his system, he slowed down and began to take his time with her. This was worst torture.

She now had the freedom to have her own back on him. So she took her time, slow and easy. Everything about him drove her crazy. What had he called her—a crazy bitch? That was exactly what she felt she was, crazy because she couldn't get enough of him and a bitch because of what she was doing.

But exhaustion took its toll and they had to stop. "I still hate you, probably more now than before." The vehemence had gone out of her speech.

"Yeah, so you said before. You also told me I was useless." He replied as his hand again started stroking her thighs. "Anything else you want to add?"

She was remembering why she had come to find him again. "You are about the biggest disappointment I've ever had in my life."

"Well, I can't say the same about you," he replied as his hand moved towards her buttocks, squeezing her firm flesh.

This gave her food for thought. "What do you mean? Are you saying that you like having sex with me?"

"What do you think?" he asked as he pulled her back on top of him. He only had to look at her and he was as hard as a rock. She wanted to talk to him more than anything.

"I've only ever done it with two men, just you and my husband. It's different with you. With my husband it was making love, but with you, it's like you're a drug. I can't think straight. I suppose it's what you call lust. What do you think?"

"I think you talk too much. I can't stand a woman who talks too much," he replied, as he flipped her over.

When they had again both settled down, he dragged her back on top of him, holding her close. She felt very safe, safer than she had for ages. His big hands around her back and buttocks were like a great wall keeping out all her troubles.

"What am I going to do when he dies?" she asked. "I'll have no one then. I don't know how I'll be able to bear the loneliness."

She hesitated before asking, "Do you think, maybe, I could see you sometimes, not for a drink or a meal or anything too personal, just for this?" She kissed him again. "I can still come back occasionally when I have business to attend to. They want me to keep up the same schedule, to return every four weeks. Maybe we could meet at the same place."

"You want me for a stud?" he asked, wondering what could be much more personal than what they did together.

"That sounds pretty crude, but I guess that's what I mean." She started nuzzling his chest. "I did something I'm ashamed of—that is besides what I do with you."

"What's this thing that you've done now?" he asked, sounding amused.

"The other day, I tried flirting with some guys that I know, just to see if there was anything there. But I didn't feel a thing, not a thing. There was no tingling, no wanting sex, nothing. Why does it only happen when I'm with you?"

"I thought you said I disappointed you. I've never been told that before but there's always a first time. I'd hate to be the poor bastard who didn't disappoint you. You'd probably kill him from exhaustion." He was further amused to hear her giggle.

She felt as though her world was complete if only for a few hours. She lifted her head and kissed him. It wasn't a kiss of sex, lust or seduction.

It was a kiss that may have had a touch of love in it. He was as surprised as she was as his lips returned the connection. There was a change in both of them. So he just held her close, savouring the feel of her body on top of his.

She couldn't lay still for long. He had his eyes closed when he felt her poke him in the chest with her fingers.

"Open your eyes," she demanded. He did as she asked. It was just as she had thought. His eyes were glistening.

"You know what I think," she continued as he shook his head, slightly ashamed that she had seen his wet eyes. "I think that you even like me just a little. And you know what else I think," again he shook his head, not trusting his voice, "I think that you're very lonely just like me and I don't believe you've got a wife and two kids at home. I think you're as lost as I am. Maybe worse, at least I've still got a husband even if it isn't for long."

He couldn't reply. Everything she had said was true. He did feel lost. He had yet to find his place. She was as near to anything that he felt he could belong to.

"You don't have to say anything," she said as his grip on her grew tighter. "It's enough that we've had these few times together. I guess I've forgiven you. It was just not meant to be."

"I think you're wrong. I've seen some odd things happen in my time. I think you and I were meant to meet, to be here together like this." They were both at ease with each other. He smiled at her as he added, "Even if I am a disappointment to you."

"Oh, stop it. You know I wasn't talking about us, here in bed." She looked him square in the eyes, before she said, "You know how you make me feel. I can't think straight when I'm with you. I was upset about something else, but maybe it's all for the best." She had given up on being angry with him for not making her pregnant.

"I still have no idea what you're on about it. What I do know is that it's damn hard lying here while all you do is talk and wriggle around. Why don't just shut up and be still?"

"Or what, you've had a rest? A big, strong man like you, you can't be that exhausted. If you don't hurry up and do something about it, I might keep right on talking and wriggling. That would drive you crazy."

33

At one time, school days were enjoyable for Gabe and Rafe, but no more. There was nothing enjoyable about being talked about, being the butt of unwelcome jokes, being called the sons of child killers.

They were becoming angry boys, taking offence even when none was intended. They became loners, no longer the bright, talkative and highly achieving twins they had been not so long ago.

Their school grades began to fall. While at school, they kept to each other although while at home with Uncle Matt and Mia and their cousins life was not so bad. They still had some fun and also the freedom to roam the property.

Like their uncles before them, they were able to explore the secrets that Sunshine hid. They had found the cave up near the Big Rock. This was the cave that was reputed to be haunted, the place where a skeleton had been found years ago. There was a time it had been used as a tourist attraction by Danny and Maryanne, but those days were gone. It had all but been forgotten.

It became their secret hide out. It was a long drag walking up the steep hill to get there, but there was little else to do on holidays unless they wanted to play with Hope and Lizzie.

They did more than play pretend in the cave. They decided that as well as having karate lessons, they would also practice other things.

Their sister was gone as well as their cousin, Lucia. Their uncle and two aunties were also dead. The twins had heard enough stories and watched enough television news to know that there was something very bad happening to their family.

Knives began to consume their lives. There were so many knives around the house and in the sheds that no one missed the ones they confiscated. Knives would be another weapon in their defence. They did have rules, but basically only one. When one practiced with a knife, the other brother remained behind the thrower. That way neither could get injured. This became their favourite pastime up near the Big Rock

School was something to be endured. Children had learned to leave them alone as their reputation grew. There were fewer fights. Mitch continued to show them moves to help with protection. They were also learning how to inflict harm.

Not that he advocated harming anyone. All this practice was only for 'just in case'. He didn't add it was just in case someone came for them like they had Sarina and Lucia. They were intuitive enough to understand what he was getting at.

Cricket practice was over. They waited at Sundial Park for Matt. There were swings and play equipment, but they were too old for these.

At that time in the evening, as there were no other people around, they decided to practice their knife throwing. Neither of them noticed the black SUV that had followed them from the cricket field.

Rafe sat on the wooden fence surrounding the park, watching his brother who was further into the trees. The boys had made a pact they would always keep a knife in their bags.

The school had not detected that they had broken the strict school rules. There was no one at cricket practice who cared less what they carried in their backpacks. Gabe practiced while Rafe kept a look out.

The black SUV cruised along slowly, pulling up near Rafe. Gabe remained out of sight in the trees. Rafe watched as two men in black got out of the SUV. They walked casually along the footpath to where he was sitting.

He thought it strange for men to be out walking at this hour. There was no sign of Matt. Rafe was feeling unsettled. He called out to his brother. The men were approaching quickly.

He shifted off the fence. As he did so, one of the men, moving quickly, jumped the fence and made a grab for him. Rafe shouted out knowing this was as good a way as any to fend off an attacker.

Gabe ran out of the trees when he heard his brother shout out. His heart pounded as he saw a big man grab his brother. The other man stood on the other side of the fence near the SUV.

Rafe was being pulled along by the man but still shouting out. The big man used his other hand to place it over Rafe's mouth. Gabe could not believe what was happening. Reaction kicked in. He lifted his arm. He didn't stop to consider his aim or his target. He ran towards the man who held Rafe, and threw.

The big man was an easy target and the knife entered the fleshy part of his buttocks. Rafe was free. He turned quickly, saw what Gabe had done, and then he kicked the man in the knee and then his groin.

The brothers escaped together, running as fast as they could into the thick bush. They were unsure of the thickness of the trees or how far the bush extended. All they knew was to run as far and as fast as they could and to remain within the safety of the trees.

Before they had gone too far, they found themselves on a small, walking bridge. They jumped off it and into the waters of the murky gulley that coursed through the park.

It was preservation that helped them find their way up the small stream until they came to what was the most impenetrable part of the trees. The boys lay flat out on the ground, pulling fallen palm fronds over them. They lay still, not speaking. They listened for any sound that might indicate they were being followed.

There were only the sounds of the bush and the noises coming from the nearby houses where people were either watching television or preparing the evening meal.

"Do you think they're still there?" Rafe asked, hanging onto his brother.

"Maybe, we better stay here a bit longer. You never know what they might do." Gabe was equally frightened by the whole experience.

"Who were they? Where did they come from?" Rafe was beginning to suffer mild shock. His hands were trembling and his speech was coming out in frightened bursts.

"They must be the men who took Sarina and Lucia and caused the rest of what's happened. But boy, it could have been really bad. That man had you and wasn't going to let go. Lucky you called out when you did." Gabe shuddered. "I don't want to think about it."

"Lucky for me you got in that throw or it could all be all over for me. Thanks, Gabe, you probably saved my life or I could have finished up like the rest of them." The two brothers tightened their grip on each other. Their breathing had steadied. Rafe's body tremors were slowing down.

"They scared the living daylights out of me. I hope that arsehole who grabbed you bleeds to death." They lay in silence under the palm fronds. "Did you see that throw? I couldn't believe I hit him. At least he'll have a sore backside for a while. And that kick. You got him good, Rafe, right where Mitch told us to aim."

Rafe suddenly sat upright brushing at his shirt. "Something's biting me, must be ants or worse. Long as it's not a snake. I think we better get out of here. It's getting dark. What do we do now?"

"We better go somewhere where there are plenty of people. How about we get out of these trees and run for our life down to that shopping centre? Maybe we can phone Matt from there. He must be out looking for us by now. He'll be worried."

"Okay, on the count of three, we'll hightail it out of here and run like lightning down to the shops." Rafe counted to three.

They rushed out of the trees, not stopping to consider how they looked. Their white cricket uniforms were covered in mud, leaves and prickles. They took off at speed and ran down the streets towards the shop.

They were still running when they heard another vehicle slow down behind them. "Just keep on running, Rafe, and scream if you have to," Gabe called out, not looking behind.

The boys took off again as fast as they could, but the vehicle was catching up to them. They looked around in alarm as Matt pulled up in front of them.

"What are you two up to now? I've been looking everywhere for you."

The boys scrambled inside and in unison, said. "Just get going, Matt, before they come after us again."

"Before who comes after you; what are you talking about?" Matt had a bad feeling as he noticed the scruffy appearance of his twin nephews. It wasn't just the fact that they were grubby and dirty. It was the expression of sheer fright he could see in their faces.

"There were two, big men dressed in black. One of them grabbed Rafe while we were at the park waiting for you." Gabe told his uncle what had occurred. He was still winded from their frantic run to the shopping centre.

"And that's when Gabe got him. That slowed him down and that's when I kicked him right in the nuts. That had to hurt almost as much as the knife." Rafe grinned at his brother.

"What knife? What are you talking about?" Matt Farraday had fearful images going through his mind. He was certain this was another attempt to abduct a member of his family.

As they drove back to Sunshine, the twins gave a full account of what had happened. Their tale was embellished the next day when Mitch arrived. He tried not to show the pride he felt at what these young boys had done. Secretly, he wished he could have fathered his own sons who were as brave and tenacious as these lads.

Neither uncle was overly concerned about the knives the lads had been carrying. It was clear this is what had saved Rafe, if not Gabe. It took all their powers of persuasion to persuade the boys not to tell Hope or Lizzie. The two girls did not need to know there had been another attempt on their family.

Mitch decided it was time he left his unit in Tewantin and live full time at Sunshine. He was certain that these men were connected to the photographs he had seen at the cottage at Sandringham Creek.

Why the violence perpetrated upon his family kept happening was unclear. There had been no contact from them other than these attacks. If it was weapons or drugs they wanted, he would have expected some approach by now.

Unless it was just the outright desire to destroy all the lives of the Farradays.

34

Their hot anger was palpable. Maria felt it as soon as they walked through the door. The two men were alone. The other monsters had gone off somewhere.

Two angry men were more than enough. There was vile swearing and cursing. Her ears should be used to such words but they still sent a shudder through her. At first she couldn't understand what had stirred them up until she saw the blood on the hands of one of the men. It was at the same time, she noticed he was limping.

She listened more attentively and finally worked out that the man had been stabbed. This pleased her no end. Her only regret was that the injury hadn't been right through his heart.

They looked to her to tend the injury. She regarded them blankly. What did they expect her to do? She was no nurse or doctor. If the injury was that bad then he would have to seek help elsewhere. See a doctor like normal people did, only none of them were normal—certainly not herself.

It became clear this was not an option. More swearing and threats convinced her that she would have to perform some sort of miracle to fix the wound. When she realised the wound was on the buttocks, she found it hard to suppress a smile. She wondered who the courageous person was who had inflicted this punishment.

Had she been brave enough she would have clapped her hands in glee. Instead, she kept her silence and quietly suggested the man have a cold shower.

She went through her meagre supply of wound coverings. She picked out what she thought would suffice. There was little left in the way of supplies, having used all she had on treating Sarina's hand.

Not that she cared. He would just have to make do with what she had. Eventually he came out of the shower. It gave her great pleasure to see him expose his naked and still bleeding buttock. She had more joy when it was apparent he was embarrassed. After all the degradation they put her through, this was a tiny piece of justice.

She shoved a pad of thick cotton gauze over the wound and taped it on, knowing it would fall off as soon as he moved. If it didn't fall off with his movements, she fervently wanted it to stick to his wound so it would hurt like hell when it came off.

Maria hoped with all her heart the injury would become infected. If it didn't, it wouldn't be her fault. There was no hand washing involved as she applied the dirtiest dressing she could find. Finally, it was done.

It was an awkward time as the two men hung around, grumbling and swearing. Maria escaped to her bedroom. There was no point in locking the door. If they wanted her they would just force the door open.

Fortunately, they left her alone, too absorbed in their own plight. Maria was fearful they would remain longer than usual which would prevent her from checking on Sarina.

Solitude was becoming too frequent and painful for both Sarina and Lucia. They did not realise their isolated feelings were those of depression. They were both lonely, missing their families.

Sarina kept practicing her ability of sending messages to Lucia. She was not sure if Lucia received them but she knew that Lucia was being held similarly to herself. She sometimes saw Lucia in a room lying all alone in a bed and crying. She knew there was a woman there as well.

Their sad lives were already changing them. Their hope was dying as well as their spirits.

35

Matt informed Michael and Denise of the attempted attack on their sons. This weighed heavily on both of them. They were in an intolerable situation.

Matt did his best to minimise the event and related what had occurred in as blasé a manner as possible so that if their conversation was being monitored, it would sound like nothing more than a school-boy scuffle. Knives were not mentioned but both parents were canny enough to grasp the full extent of what had occurred.

Michael knew he had to take drastic action. Their committal hearing was drawing close. They both intended pleading not guilty and take their chances with a jury. He could not risk both of them being found guilty. There had to be one parent to protect and nurture their boys.

He made up his mind. He would plead guilty to the charges. He would claim he alone had committed the offences he was charged with.

He could not say the word murder—not to himself, not to anyone. He hoped this would deflect any involvement implicating his wife. It would minimise the results of a court case and would leave his wife free to care for their sons.

When Denise heard of her husband's plans, she screamed out her horror at what he proposed to do. But he explained his reasons, knowing she was far more capable of protecting and nurturing their children than he was.

She experienced unimaginable grief to think that her beloved husband would be incarcerated for years. After more thought, she saw his point of view but still had grave concerns about this strategy.

There were many stages in the process before this could occur. But the first step had been taken. When the media caught whiff of Michael's alleged confession, the story went viral. Here was another revelation in the saga of what was becoming known as the 'Fiasco of the Farradays'.

This brought into fresh focus all the other issues concerning the Farraday tragedies. Where was Lucia Farraday? There were reports of her having been seen in many foreign countries.

There were more fearful reports that she had been taken by paedophiles or had been sold into child slavery. Beautiful, golden-haired girls with perfect skins were a prize. The focus of her disappearance was no longer directed towards Malcolm. But he did not escape speculation of involvement in his wife's murder.

There were those people who believed the two crimes were connected. Their speculation was that Malcolm had murdered his wife and had given his daughter away to the highest bidder. Even to the police investigators, this was far-fetched. But there was no stopping speculation.

As for the deaths of Danny Smythe and Tiffany Farraday, the gossips were certain that it was Maryanne Farraday who had somehow caused their demise. She could hardly be blamed for doing away with her no-good husband who had been playing up with her brother's wife. The decent thing would have been to find someone outside the family.

It was no more than they both deserved even if the punishment was somewhat harsh. This was a definite view of those husbands, wives and partners who had ever been subject to unfaithfulness in their relationships.

But Michael's admission of guilt topped it off. It was the most heinous crime imaginable. What father could murder his beautiful daughter? And not just murder, but mutilate as well. He deserved the death penalty—if there was such a thing. It should be brought back.

It was generally hoped that he would get the book thrown at him. Keep him in jail forever, never to be released. The police were kept busy trying to run down leads, perform endless interviews, collect and analyse evidence. Computers and phone records were constantly checked.

The only thing of significance was the wealth the Farradays had accumulated in a relatively short space of time. Dax Webster was questioned again but maintained Denise had been left monies by her parents and due to good and clever investments, the Farraday's had speculated successfully.

One person who maintained a keen interest in the 'Fiasco of the Farradays' was Superintendent Bill Boyd. Secretly, he was thrilled to see the tragedies that kept occurring. His conscience did prick slightly when he heard that there were children involved. It was one thing to have fun with children but another to do away with them.

It reminded him of his nemesis of ten years ago when the then Detective Denise Davidson had as much as accused him of being a paedophile. Temptations never stopped but he had not fallen again. He was an upright citizen—a highly decorated and respected police officer.

Knowing Michael Farraday was pleading guilty stunned him until he realised that this may be a ploy to allow his wife to go free. Superintendent Bill Boyd was quite certain he did not want this to happen.

He wanted her to remain in jail just like her 'killer' husband. He knew she still had the evidence of the time when he had tried to choke the life out of her. He vowed he would do all he could to make sure she stayed right where she was.

Sergeant Andy Brown was perplexed by the entire Farraday disaster. He kept an open mind in spite of all the media reports and idle speculation. From what he could see, and from what his instincts told him, it was hard to believe that any of the Farraday family was guilty of what was being attributed to them.

They were a close mouthed bunch of people. It was difficult to read them. From what he could tell, they had kept quiet profiles for ten years, going about their business, not bothering anyone.

Then it seemed as though all hell began to break loose around them and they were as perplexed as he was.

He had heard rumours that the children were having a hard time at school which he could well believe. He was particularly concerned about the twin sons of Denise and Michael Farraday. Their loss was enormous but like their uncles and parents, they said little.

He had no doubt they could lie like the best of them if they had to and were already adept at maintaining their silence. He also noticed that the Farraday and Smythe children were always accompanied by one of the Farraday men. The children were never left alone except in the school yard.

Mark and Malcolm, who had both suffered great tragedies, slowly began to pull themselves out of their grief and were seen with the children as often as Matthew and Mitchell.

Sergeant Andy Brown could not blame them for this as two little girls had disappeared. He also wondered if there was more reason for their concern. It was doubtful the police would be informed unless it was something very dire or unavoidable

He made note that the Farraday brothers still had charges pending following the scuffle that had occurred when Michael had been taken into custody. The sergeant was certain that this was the least of their problems. There still remained many questions concerning Maryanne and the deaths of her husband and sister-in-law.

The body of Carrie Farraday had been released by the coroner for burial. There was another funeral to plan. The Farraday brothers were left to decide on these arrangements.

Miriam, their mother, was too distraught to assist with any funeral arrangements. With all that had happened to her family, another tragedy was too much to deal with. She also had her sick daughter to care for.

Maryanne had as yet shown little interest in her three children. She saw them regularly and she talked to them about school and cuddled Harry but she showed no inclination of wanting to be a full time mother.

Maryanne's mental state was tenuous. To the outside world she appeared fine, but for those who knew her, she was anything but fine. She would sit for hours staring out at the world and then would either start cursing her no-good husband or profess her ever dying love for him. Then she would spend the next few hours crying. It was not a healthy environment in which to rear three children.

The chore of planning a funeral weighed heavily upon the brothers. What little they knew of planning a funeral was what they had leaned when Danny and Tiffany were buried. Now there was another funeral. They should be experts but it wasn't any easier. None of them had strong religious beliefs. They had all been to church with their mother, but this was years ago.

They had all married in a church except Mitch and Matt who had yet to take this step. But that was as far as it went. Their spiritual beliefs were well-buried. There were hymns and readings to be discussed.

"The only hymn I know was the one that Ma used to sing out on the creek bank," Mark said. "You know the one about Amazing Grace, the one where it talks about being a wretch. That's exactly how I feel. I think it would take a hell of a lot more than grace to make me feel any better, amazing or not"

He thought of his deceased wife in the front seat of an SUV with his brother-in-law.

"I once was lost but now I'm found, was blind but now I see," Matthew continued the words to the hymn.

"One thing's for sure," Mal agreed, "I'm still lost about all that's happened and I'll never be able to see why all these bad things just keep right on happening. If I live a thousand years, I'll never figure it out."

His mind formed a picture of his dead wife and missing child. He also thought of the lovely Zaylee who he had sent out of his life.

'Well, how about we stick with the hymn and get onto the readings. I've got to tell you, this isn't my cup of tea. It's more like women's work." Mitch was of a similar mind to his brothers.

His thoughts were on Malcolm's deceased wife. It was a miserable business. There was little reason for the celebration of this most recent life that had been lost. Maybe Carrie might get her appetite back and have as much marijuana as she liked once she was in heaven or wherever it was she had finished up. He never gave much thought to the afterlife. He was too busy trying to get through this one.

Mitch studied the numerous readings on the computer screen in front of him. None seemed to reflect their wretched lives, especially Carrie's. He found one from Lamentations and read part of it out to his brothers.

> *'My soul is deprived of peace,*
> *I have forgotten what happiness is;*
> *I tell myself my future is lost,*
> *All that I hoped for from the Lord.'*

"That about says it all. Let's keep it short and sweet. What do you say, Mal? Does that suit you?" Mitch was at a loss to comfort his brother.

It would have been more appropriate to have more uplifting words, but their sombre mood and expectation of more danger negated anything more inspirational.

The brothers were only too happy to hand over the rest of the funeral service to the priest. The funeral was held in a sad atmosphere. Carrie was laid to rest near her sister-in-law, Tiffany.

There was little enthusiasm for a wake as there were still children to be protected. Malcolm's missing daughter was uppermost in their minds.

None of the brothers visited the grave of their father or Jack Smith. There was a strong belief that all the bad that was happening was strongly connected to Alan Farraday's secrets, sex, and lies.

36

Sadness entrapped her. Francine sat beside her husband, watching his struggle to breathe. She would not leave his side. Guilt ate her up. Her faith in herself had shrunk. Her feelings of failure were doubled.

She had failed to provide her husband with the gift of a child and in doing so had compromised all her beliefs. She supposed she could lie to him and tell him that she was pregnant but she was too sick at heart to even do this.

Instead, she told him how much she loved him. She tried to be brave and to keep her frequent bursts of tears at bay. It was as if their roles were reversed. He was the one who was comforting her even though it was hard for him to breathe and to voice his words.

She had numerous support people available to her, but no one that she felt completely at ease with. Her good friend, Mia, visited when she could. Mia said little about her own situation but Francine could tell that her friend was both happy and sad.

Francine was aware that Mia was again mixed up with the Farraday family. Francine had known this family ten years ago when they had all experienced difficult times. It was due to Michael and Denise Farraday that she had got her start in the fashion business.

Had she not been so involved in her own unfortunate situation, she would have paid more attention to the tribulations she knew the Farradays were now experiencing.

Val Richards remained in the house, close at hand and ready to assist as necessary. There were numerous health professionals to give advice and provide kind words.

Val sat with Francine as Brad Hamilton took his last three breaths. They were watching the erratic rise and fall of his chest. There were two quick respirations then a gap where there was no chest movement, then one final deep breath.

They sat watching for the next breath but it did not come. Brad had departed this world.

What to do next? She could not think straight. Her own parents had left the area with her two siblings years ago to live closer to the mining town where her father worked. She seldom saw or heard from her family any more.

It was as if they all wanted to leave her behind, to not have anything to do with her. She had always felt out of place in her family, never had any sense of belonging.

There was Brad's family as well. Not that she had ever had much to do with them either. As far as she knew, there was only his ageing mother who lived in a retirement home down south.

The one positive aspect of her life was that she had the finances to attend the funeral arrangements for her husband as he had requested.

She organised for transport of his body to where he had grown up and where his mother still lived. The ceremony was a lonely affair being attended by a meagre congregation of his mother's friends.

So she said a final good-bye to her husband. She would take his cremated remains back with her to Tewantin.

Her loss was immense. Brad's mother had her friends to comfort her but Francine was alone. She had told Val Richards that she didn't know when she would be back and asked that she lock up the house.

She stayed a couple of days to be with her mother-in-law but realised that she was more of a hindrance than a help to the older lady. Conversations became stilted. Francine decided if she was going to be lonely she might as well be lonely in her own home. She flew back to her home with her husband's ashes cradled in her lap.

She tried to keep herself busy with tidying up her home. It was too soon to get rid of her husband's possessions. She was also faced with the dilemma of what to do with his ashes. She could not bear to part with them, not yet, probably not ever.

In spite of her profound grief and loneliness, the image of the man kept popping into her head.

As far as anybody knew, Francine was still out of town. She had not notified anyone of her return. Memories and desires kept invading her grieving body. She couldn't help the feelings that overwhelmed her. Like the weak-willed woman that she was, she returned to the restaurant and bar where she had previously met him.

She prowled around for several nights but he was not there. She was unsure what she would do if she did locate him, probably fall back into bed with him again. She told herself that more than anything she just wanted to talk with someone so as to relieve the aching loneliness of her heart, even though he had made it clear that he did not like women who talked too much.

She knew she was kidding herself and consoled herself even further that 'grief sex' was supposed to be good for a person. It made the person feel better and more able to cope.

With a despondent heart, she returned to her home late at night. Not so long ago, she had two men in her life; albeit one she saw infrequently who was just a temptation and someone to assuage her lust. Now it seemed she had none. Her mind was on her own sorrow as she let herself into her home.

That was when she was grabbed from behind and thrown onto the floor. As she hit the tiled floor, she would always remember the feeling of knees pressing into the centre of her back and her face being shoved down onto the coldness of the porcelain tiles she had lovingly had the tiler lay.

She was terrified at what was happening to her. She had heard about home invasions and the extraordinary fear that people experienced. Her heart felt as though it would leap out of her chest.

Her entire being was affronted. How could this be happening? Didn't they know she had just lost her husband? She tried to scream but there was a hand clamped around her mouth. So she wriggled and squirmed trying to ward off her attackers.

She knew there were two men. She had heard their voices, deep and gruff, speaking vilely and calling her offensive names. It was as if they knew her.

It was crazy what went through her mind. She lay on the floor with her legs tied together with plastic ties. For once she was grateful that she had worn jeans and not some short, ridiculous skirt when she had been checking out the bars and restaurants looking for the man.

It was just like him not to be around when she needed him. Had she found him, she probably would have been lusting after him, while all the time pretending she didn't want to have him touch her. If he had been in the restaurant, she could have been curled up beside him in the motel room.

Instead she was on her cold, porcelain-tiled floor being assaulted by two evil men.

It all happened at incredible speed. Her hands and feet were tied, a gag placed over her mouth as she was hauled into the back of a large, black vehicle. Her head took the brunt of the landing into the vehicle. The left side of her head hit the floor first. She blacked out.

She awoke some time later, unsure of how long she had been unconscious. Francine knew she should be keeping her wits about her, trying to estimate how far and fast the vehicle was travelling, what sort of noises she could hear along the way, but she could not do any of these things.

Her head ached and her eyes were blurred. Instead she kept her eyes closed shut and screamed in her mind for someone to help her. Terror overcame her.

The vehicle stopped abruptly. Then she was being hauled out and carried over the back of one of the men's shoulders and taken to a small building.

She heard a door rattle as it was opened, then she was taken in a few more paces until she was dumped on a bed. She landed with a thud. Again she felt her head hit up hard against the metal bed-head. Her arms were screwed up behind her. She had no purchase to break her fall. She was winded and terrified. She lost consciousness again.

When she awoke, she heard the man walk back out through the door. She heard it rattle again when he locked it. There was nothing she could do but to remain in her petrified state and cry.

Francine had no idea how long she lay on the bed, was unsure if she had slept or lost consciousness again. Although it hardly mattered to her which. She longed to be out of this nightmare. Her eyes were blurred and her head hurt so much.

She was in a dream-like state when she heard a small voice whispering to her.

"Are you all right?"

She rolled over to face the voice and saw a young child looking at her. Francine momentarily forgot her own desperate plight as she looked at the saddest face she had ever seen.

She was uncertain how to reply. Should she tell this child that she was far from all right when it was so obvious that this young girl was also far from all right? So instead she pointed to the gag across her mouth. The little girl pulled it down.

Francine managed to speak even though her throat was dry. "Hello, my name is Francine. What's your name?"

"Sarina," the little girl replied, looking at the lovely lady who was tied up on her bed.

Francine was stunned as she began to process all that she remembered about the daughter of Michael and Denise Farraday. She was supposed to be dead. Surely there couldn't be two Sarina's who had dark hair and eyes. "Are you Sarina Farraday?"

The little girl nodded. "Do you know where my mummy and daddy are?"

Her voice was so mournful, that Francine again commenced crying. "Your mummy and daddy are both okay. But they can't come to get you, not yet, but maybe soon."

What did one say to a child who had been kidnapped? Did you give her some hope or let her go on living in despair? How did she console her?

"Don't cry," the little girl said. "Maria will look after you when she can. She has to wait for the monsters to disappear before she can visit."

Francine was astounded as it was the small child who was consoling her.

"Who is Maria?" Francine gently asked, trying to sit upright. The little girl tried to help her. It was then that she noticed the child's bandaged hand.

"I think Maria must be a saint. That's what I secretly call her, Saint Maria. She saved me from the monsters when they threw me into the dumpster and left me there. She fixed up my hand when they cut off my finger."

Francine gagged and almost threw up at these words. "They cut off your finger then threw you away?"

What terrible fate awaited her if they could do this to an innocent child?

"That's why you have to be quiet. They don't know I'm here. I hide under the bed when I hear the door rattle. If it's Maria, I get out from under the bed and we talk and she brings me food. You have to be very good because of what they do to Maria. They cut off two of her fingers and they do other terrible things to her all the time."

The little girl looked at the beautiful lady trussed up on the bed, before she added, "You know, what adults do. Maria doesn't like it but she's too frightened. She says they will kill her if she doesn't do what they say and then what would happen to me. No one else knows I'm here."

Hearing these words, Francine's other worst nightmare was more than possible. She commenced crying again. The little girl put her arms around her, held her and gently helped her lie down again on the bed.

"You should try to rest now. I'll pull the gag up over your mouth so if the monsters come, everything will look the same. I'll hop back under the bed." The little girl gave her a gentle kiss on the forehead as she looked into Francine's eyes, sensing her deep despair. Then she scrambled under the bed.

"I'm sad that the monsters took you as well, Francine, but I'm really happy that you're here with me. I feel a lot safer." The little girl was already sucking on her thumb and had her wooden circle pressed into her hand.

Francine Hamilton's heart was breaking all over again. There was little hope in her heart but the fact that this child offered her comfort was overwhelming.

37

Work was so therapeutic. Dr Zaylee Lang was back. Hard at it, working all the hours that would help her forget. Her time for feeling sorry for herself was well and truly over. Whether it was grief or stress or whatever it was, she had put it behind her.

She still felt guilty for the time she had taken off. But that was now in the past. She concentrated on the myriad of patients who came through her door and did her best to assist them overcoming their problems and ailments.

Her face had healed. There was no sign of the black eyes or bruises. Instead she focused on being fit and healthy. She jogged every morning no matter how early her start time at work. She was becoming a fitness junkie. She even thought she might take up some martial arts training. But at the moment she was too busy.

She continued to avoid reading any of the local newspapers or watch any television news programs. She did watch television though. She focused on anything that contained a touch of comedy. Anything that would make her laugh and lift her spirits was her main source of therapy and entertainment. There was no viewing of romance programs with happy endings or action shows with good-looking men. These programs were not for her.

She never stopped to listen to any of her colleagues gossiping about community events. Nor did she spend time chatting with her patients about local happenings. She was totally focused on her work.

At night, she read her old text books from university which quickly put her to sleep. She had no inclination to know anything about her ex-boyfriend Dave or the treacherous Malcolm. Of the two, it was Malcolm who had totally fractured her heart. Dave had almost fractured her eye socket but Malcolm's injury was far worse and more enduring.

She had found another furnished unit to live in. She had her wardrobe of fine clothes. She wore the beautiful suits and dresses that she had purchased from Lady Francesca, even if they were dowdy. She wore them every day so that she could focus on being the consummate doctor, going about her business, caring for the sick, injured and disabled. She was becoming more highly regarded than ever with her endless dedication to her patients.

But how long could she keep living in this sterile state? She was a woman of hormones and desires.

Of course she could not close her mind off completely from thoughts of that flashing smile and dark eyes. She tried to keep her mind completely devoid of thoughts of him. But the nagging need to hear his voice remained. She would never know how it happened. It wasn't planned. It was as though her hand had a mind of its own. Before she knew what she was doing she found herself on her phone waiting for him to answer.

When he answered, all he said was "Hello". There were no endearments. What did she expect? She thought she would cut him off, but then muttered out her own "Hello".

There was a pause before he spoke again. "Oh, it's you Doctor. I'm sorry I missed my appointment. If it's okay, I'll reschedule for late this afternoon."

She was taken aback by this response. "Yes, of course," was all she could think to say. That was the end of the conversation. She was at a loss. What on earth was he up to now? He had no appointment to see her. He had made it perfectly clear he never wanted anything more to do with her.

She told herself she had to be professional, to sit through whatever was wrong with him. How hard could that be? He was just another patient. The day seemed interminable. She watched the clock. The minutes seemed to drag. It was well into the evening, way past her finishing time before he arrived.

There were few people left in the offices when he was finally shown into her consultation room. She took one look at him.

"What on earth has happened to you?" was all she said as she saw how haggard he looked. He had lost weight. He was no longer clean shaven and his clothes were rumpled.

"Hello to you, too," he replied. "What the hell do you think has happened? If you don't know, then you must have been living on another planet." He was looking at her as if she were either dumb or mentally disturbed.

"I've been away. I've been sick," was all she said. His demeanour changed. He immediately looked concerned.

"Are you all right now, Doc? I didn't know you'd been sick. You had a black eye but I thought you'd recover after a few days. I just didn't want you involved in any way. It was all I could think of to get you out of there in a hurry. I'm sorry for being so abrupt and rude."

"Involved in what?" she asked, not sure what he was referring to.

"You mean you really don't know what happened?" It was hardly possible she hadn't heard. "About Carrie and Lucia," he added.

She was beginning to get a bad feeling. Sure she had slept with him, but it was hardly possible anyone else knew about it. "Did your wife find out about us? Has she left you?" She felt guilty and full of remorse.

"You really don't know, do you?" They stared at each other. "Carrie's dead, Doc, and Lucia is gone."

She stumbled then fell into her office chair. This was totally unexpected. "Oh no, I don't believe it. How? When? I don't understand."

Her eyes were wide with concern. She was having difficulty taking in what he had said. Then she remembered that she was supposed to be the doctor, taking care of him. Instead she had fallen into her chair in shock. She quickly tried to pull herself together. She stood up, only meaning to just touch him on the arm, to show him empathy.

This was the wrong move. Her professionalism flew out the window. One touch of her hand on his arm, and their feelings for each other exploded. She was in his arms. He was kissing her. She was kissing him. There was touching and feeling. Then she was crying. Between their hungry kisses, she took a moment to look into his eyes and saw that he was crying too. She pulled back away from him.

"I think you'd better sit over there and I'll sit here," her voice trembled. "I'm supposed to be a doctor. I'm not supposed to be kissing my patients." She smiled at him as she wiped away more tears. "You better tell me what's happened?"

He retold the events that had occurred on the night he had made love to her. She listened in astonishment. It was this retelling that made her realise why he had treated her as he had. It was to protect her and her reputation. She couldn't keep away any longer. She was back in his arms.

"Let's get out of here," she finally said. "I want to be with you."

"That's not a good idea, Doc. Someone's after us and I don't want anything to happen to you as well. I don't know any place that's safe. I think we are all being followed. This was the only way I could think to see you without arousing suspicion. I can't see you any more until all this is over."

His hands were again all over her. She was enjoying every second of it, even though she had a strong sense of his pain and loss.

"I think what might help both of us is some therapy, Mr Farraday."

Dr Zaylee Lang was well known for her workaholic status. She told the last of the staff to leave and that she would lock up. This was no surprise to her colleagues.

"That was quick," he said as she returned. "What sort of therapy did you have in mind, Doc?"

"The best sort." She was already loosening her hair as she approached him.

"If you touch me again, I'll have you down on that carpet before you know it." As he said these words, she was again in his arms, her hands around his back pulling at his shirt.

"That's the whole idea. It will be much better for you than any pill I could prescribe."

"You're the doctor. You know best. What do I have to do?" he asked. For the first time, she saw the smile that she loved so much.

"You don't have to do a thing. I'll take care of you."

It was the longest and sweetest patient visit she had ever conducted. All her ethics and values were forgotten. All she wanted and needed was to be with him. Their love making continued until there was no energy left. They lay spent in each other's arms.

"Thank you, Doc." he eventually said. "That's the best therapy I've ever had. I just wish I could keep having more of the same. But I've got to take care of you. I don't think I could go on if anything happened to you as well."

"I'm sorry I didn't make contact with you sooner. I deliberately didn't want to know anything about you. It hurt too much. So I ran away. When I said I was sick, I was. I was sick inside because I thought you didn't want me." She snuggled into him further. "I think I'm in love with you."

He laughed at her, "Well, I just don't think it, Doc. I know it. I never thought I could ever love anyone as much as I love you. With Carrie, she was there for me when I was young and she helped me. That's why I could never leave her." He paused momentarily as he thought of his daughter.

"With Lucia, I love her more than life. I don't know what's happened to her, if she's dead or alive. It's driving me crazy. I can't sleep, can't eat. When I think about her, I get churned up inside. I miss her so much." He strengthened his grip on her.

"I feel bad that I had so little faith in you. I should have tried to figure out what was going on. I was selfish, only thinking of myself. I didn't want to know anything more about you, so I shut myself off. But your daughter—what's happened to her is unimaginable. But what do you mean when you said you wanted to take care of me? Why would anyone be interested in me?"

"It's a long story, going back years. At least that's what we think."

He told her about their family history. She was familiar with some of it. It was difficult to explain. Their history was so complex. He tried to make her realise the gravity of his fears for her especially when he retold the implications of his brother's recent trip to Sandringham Creek.

"What are you saying? That these men who lived at Sandringham Creek are attacking your family?"

"We don't know for sure, Doc. But there's a connection. I really don't know why they are after us, but it could be because they want something from us." Malcolm Farraday pulled her tighter in his arms, his hands cradling her.

"Want what. Just who are these people?" she asked.

"We're not really sure, but they could be relatives. They may be using the name Farraday."

"I don't understand. Relatives—are they cousins?"

He took his time answering, "Probably more like brothers, or half-brothers."

"What? More brothers, how could there be more brothers?" She was stunned.

"Another long story, but my father could never keep it in his trousers. He had women everywhere and it looks like other children as well."

"Oh! This is unbelievable, more family. But why cause you harm? Surely they would want to get to know you. Isn't that what families are all about?"

There were so few of her family, she would welcome more brothers and sisters.

"It's not that simple. My father had a half-brother who was a nut case, not that my own father was much better. His name was Jack Smith. He was an evil man." He was silent as he remembered his own suffering at the hands of Jack Smith.

"What did he do?" she asked, intrigued by these revelations.

"Well, for a start he raped me when I was much younger." He had finally said the words. These were the words he had dreaded telling anyone, let alone the woman curled up in his arms. He waited for her reaction.

She didn't speak for some time. She always sensed something bad had happened to him, but never this. "I'm so sorry. That must have been dreadful for you. How did you cope? You seem to be pretty much together now."

"It was Carrie who helped me get through it. She was there for me when I needed someone." This was a very private moment between them. "That's why I could never leave her, no matter what my feelings for you were. I hope you can understand how hard it was for me, falling for you and still caring about Carrie. She was sick all the time and then she's murdered and my little girl is gone."

"It's not fair what happened to you, what's still happening. When it is all over, maybe we can be together. All I want is to make life better for you, to love you. Where is this Jack Smith now?"

"He's dead. Do you remember my sister-in-law, Denise?" He waited for her to acknowledge that she remembered Denise. "She shot him straight through the forehead after he had shot Mick. The bullet was meant for the detective, but Mick threw himself in front of her."

The sadness of their present situation hung heavily upon them.

"Did you know that Mick plead guilty to the charges concerning Sarina? He did it so that Denise could be released to take care of the twins. They were attacked as well. That's another reason why I don't want to have any contact with you. The risks are too great."

"I understand your fears and the need for safety. But do you think maybe you could visit me sometimes late at night, here at the practice. You've got more than enough reasons to need a doctor. A weekly visit would not be out of the question. Now that I've found you again, it's not going to be that easy to live without you."

Their need for each other was again ignited. Their future was uncertain but the silence of the night only strengthened the feelings of lust and desire that overcame them.

38

Mitch remembered the dry lands where he had fought. He would never forget the explosive devices that were so well hidden. It was so easy to trip one and then devastation was sure to follow.

He remembered the young men under his control who had lost limbs, been horribly injured and others who had lost their lives.

He compared the two situations. They weren't exactly alike but there were similarities. The people who were after his family also struck without warning. The attacks were full of stealth and just as horrible.

He was also certain that they were his own kin, unknown to any of them, but full of hate and deadly vengeance.

He had planned as best he could to keep his family safe and to stop the rampage. What he wasn't prepared for was the kidnapping and the demand for ransom. The phone in the house rang. He did not recognise the number. He said "Hello".

Always expecting the unexpected, he was ill prepared for the muffled voice that said, "A million dollars and you can have her back. You owe us big time. You'll hear from me again in three days; no police or she's dead."

Then there was nothing more.

He stared at the phone, mulling over what he had heard. It was not hard to understand. The instructions had been very clear. All the same, he was still shocked. He immediately thought of his brother, Malcolm. It was now certain they had taken Lucia.

He had no options but to inform his brothers. It was one thing to protect them, but quite another to come up with one million dollars in three days. He didn't have that sort of money but he assumed his brothers did.

The other three brothers were sitting gloomily in the kitchen at Sunshine trying to decide what to cook the children for dinner. Mia was with Harry at the child care centre which was as safe a place as any.

The expression on Mitch's face was serious enough to stop the attempts at peeling potatoes.

"What's up?" Mark asked.

"Trouble," was all he said. "They want a million dollars in three days or else they will kill her."

Malcolm gasped. "They have Lucia. At least she's still alive." He sat heavily on a kitchen chair, rubbing his hands through his hair in both anguish and controlled excitement. "I can't believe anyone could do this to a little girl."

He thought of Carrie and how she had suffered at the hands of the people who had stolen their daughter. "We'll get the money; that shouldn't be too difficult and then we'll have her back."

"Have we got that sort of money? Can we raise that amount in three days?" Mitch asked.

"The restaurants should be able to raise that much. I'll see Dax and get him started on it." Malcolm had a million thoughts running through his head. Get the cash and then get his daughter back. Could it be that easy?

"What will you tell Dax? He'll want to know what it's for. We can't involve the police or they will kill her. You can bet your bottom dollar that the police are monitoring our finances. There's got to be a better way that won't cause any suspicions." Mitch was trying to think of all the scenarios that could complicate the safe rescue of his niece.

"Between us all, we should be able to come up with the cash. That way, it might not be as noticeable." Matt was doing estimates in his head. "Mia's rolling in it. After all, it was due to Denise and Michael that we all got a start. When this is over, I can sell my house and pay her back. What do you say we get started?"

Each brother devised their own means of coming up with the cash. Three days did not give them much time. Matt had misgivings about asking Mia for money but their bond by now was very strong. Besides it was to save a child. In Mia's mind, nothing could be more important than that.

The cash was collected. If the financial institutions from which they had obtained the cash were suspicious of the large withdrawals, there was no indication of it. Mitch now had to decide how to pack it and how to track it once it was handed over.

The retrieval of the cash was not the point, but the kidnappers who had taken the child would have to pay. It was not revenge. It was a simple matter of justice for a little girl.

The easy part was done. The hard part was the waiting. The third day was interminable. Nerves were beginning to fray so that when the phone rang, even though it had been expected, they all jumped. Mitch answered the call.

"Have you got it?" the muffled voice asked. It sounded like the same indistinct voice that he had previously heard.

"I've got it."

"Good—now for the next step," the voice continued.

"Not so fast," Mitch replied. "First I want some proof of life. You supply that and then we can do the exchange."

No answer came for some moments before the voice again spoke, "Five minutes. You'll have your proof in five. Be ready."

Malcolm was tense with anxiety. Mitch handed the phone to his brother who would be more likely to recognise his daughter's voice. The five minutes were up and still no ring. As happened previously, when it did ring, they all jumped.

Malcolm answered, "Hello."

"Please help me." The voice was female, faint, but clearly adult. It was also fraught with fear.

"That's not her," he shouted out to his brothers as well as into the phone. He was on the verge of losing any semblance of control that he had. Mitch took the phone off him.

"You listen to me. That voice wasn't her. So the deal's off unless you produce her or you give us more proof of life. The game has changed. You know where we live. You be here tomorrow at 10am with her. Then you can have your money."

"The game hasn't changed," the evil, muffled voice said, "All that's changed are the circumstances. You've just screwed her over—your fault. Remember, no police or there will be more deaths."

The brothers looked at each other in shock. They had not expected it to play out this way. Why were these people playing this game with Lucia's life? The money was there, all ready to be picked up. It made no sense to have a woman pretend to be the child. There were only two possible explanations.

One was that Lucia was already dead and they had to have a woman provide a female voice or else the child was badly injured and could not speak.

Both options were equally horrific. "So what's next?" Mark asked. No one spoke for some time as the implications of what had occurred sunk in.

"Offer them more money," Matt finally said. "That's what's important to them."

"Let's wait. Maybe Lucia was too frightened to talk or was crying. They'll phone back. As you say, they want the money." Mitch paused as he considered the changed circumstances of their situation. "The game has changed, but the prize is still the same. If necessary, we'll offer more but we'll wait and see. They've kept her alive this long so it's unlikely they'll do anything to harm her now that they are this close."

More waiting—all the mundane tasks in the world could not relieve the tension. The children were picked up from school. Nothing was said to them about their cousin Lucia. The twins took off by themselves with Billy Bob. They did this most afternoons when there was no cricket practice or other sporting events.

Once school was over for the day, Arlo and Hope became an item. They talked endlessly about school, their teachers and other students. Lizzie had found her place by helping out in the kitchen. She was very young but she had lots to offer in the preparation of meals. Her uncles, particularly Mitch, found her very engaging and doted on her.

Mia arrived home with Harry. Matt was there to welcome her. They no longer tried to keep their relationship a secret. They comforted each other but kept their displays of affection under control in front of the children.

Malcolm was close to falling apart so he phoned to make an appointment with Dr Zaylee Lang. He was given the last appointment for the day. Stress relief was provided but it still did not lift the heaviness in his heart.

Mitch remained on edge. He had moments in his mind of being far removed from his present situation. He had dreams and memories that lightened the burden he was carrying. He wished he had something more physical than memories but it was neither the time nor the place.

Mark was a man of few words. He had his son, his tools and mechanical equipment to keep him occupied. He seldom spoke of his deceased wife but the sadness remained.

39

Sometimes Sarina did not know when she was dreaming or when she was having visions. When she was at home she remembered she used to wake up screaming. This was when she would hop into bed with her mother and father and they would talk to her.

She also remembered that they were very worried about her because she seldom slept through the night without having dreadful images coming into her mind.

There were various doctors and other people who tried to help her stop having such nightmares. Her descriptions of blood, dead people and helpless little children even frightened the people who were trying to help her.

Since she had been taken by the monsters, the dreams or visions had almost disappeared. She had not experienced many horrid images until Francine was put into the room with her. She still sent messages to Lucia. She knew Lucia was very sad much like herself but she was not injured. She had not had her finger cut off.

Francine cried a lot. Sarina did what she could to make her happier. Maria also came as often as she could. She helped Francine to the toilet but never undid the ties that bound her. She said she was too frightened at what would happen if the monsters thought she had untied her. Maria didn't say the words, but Sarina knew she meant that the monsters would kill them both.

Sarina's dreams returned. Terrible images of blood, pain and dead people invaded her sleep. She was afraid of screaming out and alerting the monsters. When she started moaning as the dreams commenced, Francine would call out to her and bang on the wall with her tied feet. This always woke her up.

At times she would be so frightened by the images that she would scramble out from under the bed and hop in beside Francine. Francine could not hug her like her mother used to because of her tied hands, so Sarina would put her arms around Francine and hold her.

Three times she fell asleep holding Francine until Francine woke her up and told her she had better return to her hiding place under the bed in case the monsters returned unexpectedly.

Sarina knew that something very bad was about to happen.

Maria could feel the tension and anger as soon as they returned. She had no idea where they went during the periods when they were away from the house. They drove up silently in their big, black SUV's. They seldom spoke until they were in the house and away from any risk of voices being heard from outside.

She knew the situation was very bad from the first moment. As silently as possible, she retreated to her room waiting until she was summoned. By the feel of the anger, she knew nothing good was going to happen tonight. Her prayer was that she had left Francine as she had been instructed. That she had not made any mistakes.

The men proceeded to the small granny flat. The door rattled and opened more quickly than it ever had before. Sarina barely had time to escape under the bed while Francine lay trussed up on the top.

Maria had been instructed to attend to her toileting needs and to provide nourishment. She had done that but was too afraid to do more. Francine's hands and legs were still held with plastic ties.

They stood large and angry in front of her. Francine quivered with fear. She had no idea why she was being held. Maria could not enlighten her. The young woman had been kind and helpful to her but could shed no light on her kidnapping. Her fear of these men stopped her from any attempt to obtain her release.

There was also the question of Sarina to be considered. It did not escape Francine's notice that Maria appeared to be very pregnant. The three of them could not have been in a worse plight.

"Get her up and untie her hands but keep the gag in. Let's get this over and done with. Tell Maria to get ready; that she'll be needed." The man who was obviously in charge waited while one of the others pulled Francine up into a sitting position. Another of the men shoved the gag further into her mouth. She thought she might suffocate.

Sarina huddled as far back as she could under the bed. She could feel the wall against her back. She shoved her thumb in her mouth and pressed the wooden circle with the picture of the lady on it into the palm of her hand. If she had an extra hand, she vowed she would cover her ears with it. The monsters were back and they were incredibly angry.

"I don't know what the fuck they're trying to pull. They want more proof, well, they'll soon get it." The main monster was furious. Francine was hauled up and her hands held out in front of him. "Which one, little lady, which one don't you want?"

He held both her hands, looking at them, studying them. Francine was petrified. She had no idea why he was so interested in her hands. Then she thought of Maria with her two missing fingers and Sarina with her still bandaged hand. Francine started screaming, making an eerie, muffled, screeching sound that was held in by the gag.

She now realised what was going to happen to her. The main monster looked her straight in the eyes. As she stared back at him, she recognised a resemblance to the man she met in the motel room. Or was she just imagining it. Why could he not be here to save her? Why was she going through this torment?

The monster had his knife in his hand. It was fine-bladed and looked very sharp. He studied the fingers. "This looks about right. We'll take the ring as well."

He picked up her left hand, held it over the rim of the metal bed head, pushed her other four fingers back, pulled out the ring finger and brought his knife down swiftly. The first cut did not go right through, so he cut again, bone crunching under his hands, blood starting to pour out.

"Put this bloody thing in a bag," he said as he handed the finger over to another man. "Push the ring down further so it doesn't fall off. If that's not enough proof, there are plenty more left."

Francine stared incredulously at her bloody hand. She thought she would faint. She wanted to faint. She wanted none of what was happening to be true. The man let go of her hand. The pain was terrible. She could still hear the crunching of bone as he had tried the second time to cut the finger off.

She grabbed her bloody left hand with her right hand and tried to staunch the bleeding. One of the monsters threw her a towel and told her not to make a mess. She pressed the towel tight over her hand. She fell back onto the bed as she held her bleeding and broken hand up in the air. But then her right hand was roughly grabbed again and cuffed to the metal bed head.

Sarina heard everything that had happened to Francine. She wanted to help her but fear kept her hidden. She curled up under the bed. The muffled screaming was more than she could bear so she used both her hands to keep the screaming out of her head.

She dropped her wooden circle. She watched in horror as it rolled out from under the bed and came to rest near the feet of one of the monsters. The pretty swirls of the roses on the carpet in front of her eyes no longer brought her any relief from the horror she knew that had occurred to Francine.

The monsters were ready to leave. One had already left to get Maria. As another turned to leave, he saw the wooden circle near his feet.

"What's this?" Sarina heard him say as he picked it up and put it in his pocket.

She felt bereft as she watched those big, ugly hands pick up her circle. It was as if all her hope had disappeared out the door as the big, black boots walked through it. Francine was still screaming under her gag. Sarina was about to get out from under the bed to help her when Maria rushed into the room.

"Stay there, Sarina, don't get out yet." Maria spoke firmly as she took one look at Francine screaming under her gag.

"I can't take the gag out yet, Francine, but I can help with your hand." Maria gently took Francine's hand in her own and tended to her wound. The pain was excruciating. Maria was quick and efficient as she dressed the hand. Like Sarina, she applied plenty of padding so as to avoid any further trauma. She gave Francine tablets for the pain and propped her hand up on a pillow.

"Your hand needs to be elevated higher, Francine. I'll be back in a minute." Maria left quickly.

Sarina was well aware that there was no rattling of the door. She had become so used to it.

"Francine," she spoke quietly as she slipped out from under the bed and loosened Francine's gag. "She forgot to lock the door. Should we try to escape?"

"I can't, Sarina, I'm tied to the bed." Francine's voice was weak and interspersed with weeping. "But you run, Sarina. Run as hard and as far away as you can. At least one of us will have a chance. Pull the gag back up and run. Go now." There was urgency in her voice.

Sarina kissed Francine gently through her tears, pulled the gag back up and ran to the door. The sun's rays were dimming. The day was almost gone. Darkness was fast approaching.

Sarina had been out of the granny flat only once before when Maria had taken her for a walk. She knew the general direction of the back gate. So she ran towards the back fence. There was the gate. She could hear voices coming from the house. She was so frightened.

She reached up to the latch that held the gate closed but could barely reach it. Unbelievably the gate was not locked. She jumped up and knocked it with the bandage on her sore hand. It lifted up. She pushed on the gate and then she was outside.

Sarina vaguely remembered where Maria had taken her. There had been playground equipment in bright blue and orange. She found a foot path but was too frightened to follow it in case the monsters followed her. Instead she found a track that went into the bushes. She followed it until she could see the playground equipment.

The playground equipment was very welcoming. She could see the swing where Maria had pushed her up and down. But her instincts kicked in. Instead of going towards the swing, she hid under a small walking bridge. The ground was dry. She remembered when she had been there with Maria that there had been water present.

Many people walked their dogs at various times of the day and evening in Sundial Park. It was not a dog park but it was used by all those who lived in the neighbourhood for this purpose.

Usually it was boys on bikes who rode up and down the dirt hills. Or else the boys came on their skate boards and tried to do tricks and jumps. At this time of the evening, there were no boys on bikes but there was one man who liked the quiet and peace of the late evening.

Sergeant Andy Brown had acquired a young Alsatian dog. He liked nothing more than to walk it each evening when he finished work. This time provided him with relief from the stresses and strains of his job.

He was well aware he should not have let the dog off its leash. It was against the law but there was no one else around to notice or complain. What harm could it do? Besides big dogs needed space to run around and Sundial Park was certainly big enough for a dozen dogs.

Sarina remained hidden under the small bridge. The dog sniffed and scampered around the park. Sarina and the dog saw each other at the same time. She was not frightened of it in spite of its size. As she scrambled out from under the bridge, she patted it. Just for a few moments her fear subsided.

Andy Brown whistled his dog. The dog looked up as he approached. Sarina still had her hands on its neck rubbing its soft hair.

"Hello," he said. "Do you like dogs?" He was alarmed to find a young child in the park at such a late hour. He was fearful of frightening her.

The little girl looked at the man. He didn't look like the monsters. He looked more like her daddy and her uncles.

"Yes," she replied, still patting the dog.

"It's getting very late. Do you think you should go home now? Won't your mother be worried about you?" It was then that Andy Brown noticed the bandage on her left hand.

"What's wrong with your hand?" he asked, noticing her lovely, brown eyes and her dark hair.

The little girl looked up at him soulfully. She didn't know what to tell him about her hand. She could hardly tell him that monsters had cut off her finger. Who would believe her?

He had also asked her about her mother. She wanted to tell him that her mother had not come for her. It was then that she heard another voice calling out for her.

"Where are you, darling?" It was Maria. Sarina could see her in the distance. She looked very ruffled and worried. "It's time to come home now."

"There's your mother now," the man said. "You'd better hurry or you might miss out on your dinner. You don't want her to be angry with you. Off you go now." He watched as the little girl ran off towards the woman who had come looking for her.

He stopped and watched the two of them walk quickly back through the bushes. The child had intrigued him. It was not just that she had been very pretty but she had been so sad. The memory of her face remained with him. She reminded him of someone but for the life of him he could not remember who.

There was tension in the air as they waited. They had asked for 'proof of life'. They did not know what to expect or when to expect it. Lucia was alive. But why had they used an adult female voice? It made little sense.

Mitch wanted to change the game. He wanted to be the aggressor instead of being the aggrieved. He set up traps and weapons. 'Sunshine' was no longer a property depicting the happiness that Michael had intended when he had named it for the joy he had found with his wife. 'Sunshine' was now a place of misery and pain.

For the children's sake, they tried to keep things as normal as possible. They packed lunches, got the children ready for school before driving them into Tewantin. There was still shopping to be done, meals to be prepared and household chores to be attended to.

There was also a daily mail delivery service. The letter box at the entrance to 'Sunshine' was in the form of a drum. The mail was usually delivered during the morning. The drum was always kept locked.

Mitch made it his business to pick up the mail daily. He walked the few hundred metres to the property entrance. He had become a suspicious man and was wary of what could be put into the mail box. Their foes were formidable. As he approached the box he noticed ants crawling up the pipe that held the drum in place.

He unlocked the back of the box. He felt inside and pulled out a few letters. There was nothing of interest. He glanced down again to take a further look into the drum, brushing more ants away.

This was when he noticed a small clip-lock bag. He pulled it out and looked at it. The first thing he noticed was a ring. It was gold in colour and gleamed brightly in the sunlight. He held up the bag to examine it further.

He had seen many atrocities in war. What he saw now was enough to cause him to dry retch. He stared at the white, lifeless finger. It was sliding around loosely in the same type of bag that he used daily to pack his nieces and nephews lunches.

He leaned up against one of the big gums that kept the property entrance partially hidden from the outside world while he steadied himself. It was clearly not a child's finger. The ring and the beautifully manicured and lacquered nail were proof of this. Neither could belong to Lucia.

He did not know what to think. If the finger did not belong to Lucia, then who did it belong to? Numerous thoughts passed through his mind. What were these men playing at? He looked at the bag and its contents again as he brushed away more ants. It had belonged to someone. The ring was a puzzle. No doubt it was a wedding ring. He thought of all his family members.

He was certain the finger was female due to the state of the nail. There weren't too many female members of his family left. Maryanne and his mother were safely secured with the old doctor at Miriam's Place. Mia was busy in the house looking after Harry. Besides, she did not wear a wedding ring. She wore plenty of others but no gold wedding band.

He briefly thought of the woman he occasionally saw. Yes, she wore a wedding ring. But she was not from around these parts so it could hardly belong to her. Besides, no one knew about their encounters. It couldn't be her.

There was no one else. He had a daughter whom he had never seen. She no longer lived in the area. Her family had left years ago.

The only other person who had any attachment to his family was the unknown daughter of Geraldine Wright and Alan Farraday. Presuming she was connected to the people who were causing havoc to his family, it was unlikely that it was her finger in the bag.

He returned to the house where he confronted his brothers with the gory sight of the bag containing the finger. Their reaction was the same as his own. It also brought back the dreadful memory of what had happened to Sarina. More discussion took place. None of them could shed any light on the owner of the finger. The only certainty was that it had belonged to someone.

Malcolm excused himself, went outside and immediately phoned to ask if his doctor was available. He was put straight through.

"Are you okay, Doc?" His voice was fraught with tension.

"Of course," she replied, immediately aware of the anxiety in his speech. "What's up?"

"Nothing," he replied as he breathed a sigh of relief. "I just wanted to hear your voice."

"Maybe we could get together," she asked.

"Not yet, Doc, soon; I've got to go." The young doctor remained puzzled as she said goodbye. Malcolm re-joined his brothers.

"We'll just have to wait for the next phone call. I don't know who they've got. But whoever it is, I pity her. She's not going to last long going on the past incidents. If they don't get the cash, they'll kill her for sure. I say we do the exchange as soon as possible. I don't want anyone's death on my conscience. There's been enough death." Mitch had made his decision. His brothers concurred. They all wanted this ordeal to be over with as soon as possible.

They had little to do but wait, but this time the phone call arrived sooner than expected. After the first few rings, Mitch answered.

"Was that enough 'proof of life' for you?" The same muffled voice said.

"Yes," he replied. "You deliver her out here and you can have your money."

"Sorry, the price just went up." This time the voice remained muffled but held a hint of cruel laughter. "We want another million. You leave the first million at the mail box today. Have the second million ready in three days and you can have her."

"We don't have that sort of money," He responded. "A million is all we could raise."

""Don't mess with me. You get it or she's dead. You've got three days. Expect my call. There are still nine fingers left if you need more 'proof of life'." Then the phone went dead.

He relayed what had been said to his brothers. "What do we do now?"

"We'll have to find the money somehow. Someone's life is in the balance so we have no option." Matthew remained pensive. "They can have my house for collateral. There must be more properties we can sell. We'll have to see Dax as soon as possible. If he asks too many questions, then we'll just have to tell him what's going on. For all we know, they might come after his family as well."

The scramble was on to get the next million. They confronted Dax Webster. At first he was reluctant to assist in getting the cash together. Eventually they felt compelled to tell him what was happening, hastening to add that it was not beyond the realms of possibility that his own family could be involved. Dax Webster wasted no further time in argument.

Mark had the skills to set up a video camera near the entrance to Sunshine. Because of the isolation of their property, it would be an easy task to obtain a record of all the vehicles that passed by.

Not that there would be many, as Sunshine was one of the properties nearest to the end of the road. There was the Smythe property, then a few more, until the road petered out. The countryside was too mountainous and rugged for the road to continue.

Mitch left the money in a black backpack which he carefully covered with leaves and branches near the letter box. He took one last look at it. Satisfied that the camera was well concealed, he thought of the woman who had lost a finger. He didn't want another finger to confront him in the letter box. If it cost another million for the safety of this person, then so be it.

The day was overcast and grey. No rain had yet fallen. The brothers kept an eye on the hidden camera taking note of the cars that went past. Most of them were familiar to them. None of them stopped.

They heard from Dax several times as he gave an update on his progress. Several times the brothers had to leave the property to sign documents. The children were picked up after school. It was now impossible to keep the tension at bay.

"What's going on?" Gabe eventually asked after Hope and Lizzie had escaped to the bedroom they shared.

"We think they're coming after us again," Matt replied. He didn't mention the finger in the bag or the demand for money. "We have to be extra careful. You have to stay in the house. No going outside with Billy Bob. I don't want you to alarm the girls. This should soon be over."

Seeing the worried expressions on the faces of their uncles, Gabe, Rafe and Arlo were naturally concerned. They tried to emulate their uncles and keep their panic under control. They went to their room where they kept a cache of knives. Guns were out of the question. They were not allowed, but the knives they had confiscated from their grandmother's sheds, were theirs for their protection.

Arlo had been taken into the twin's confidence. He too was becoming competent with a knife. When they weren't playing around with knives, they were playing solitaire.

The sun was setting. The sky was still grey when Mitch returned to the letter box to check on the backpack. At first, he thought he was mistaken as to where he had hidden it. He was unable to locate it from the place where he was positive he had left it. He rummaged around in the grass and leaves certain that he and his brothers could not have missed the pick-up. The bag was gone. The million dollars had been taken right from under their noses.

They again checked all the vehicles that had travelled the road. There were none that were unfamiliar. Of course someone could have walked to pick it up, but from where? It was quite a hike from any of the neighbouring properties.

The Smythe property was the closest and there was no one there other than the work man who managed the property.

They were familiar with all their neighbours. Granted they did not know them well, but it was hardly likely they would be harbouring anyone like these men who were terrorising their family.

Two days to go. Another million to be found and then the woman would be returned. At the back of Malcolm's mind was the faint hope that it would be his daughter who was being returned; that these men were simply playing an evil game with them

41

Though the days were cloudy and grey with scattered showers which were enough to dampen anyone's spirits, Denise could not help but feel a small twinge of excitement. In two days she would be released. She would be returning to her beloved sons. Her husband and daughter would not be there, but at least she could be a mother.

Michael had given up any chance of freedom when he pleaded guilty to the murder of his daughter. This sacrifice allowed his wife to go free.

He would not reveal where the body was buried. He eventually explained that what had happened was a terrible bout of murderous frenzy brought on by insufficient sleep and alcohol. He had initially cut off his daughter's finger in an attempt to get her to stop screaming, but when this didn't work, he had throttled her.

He had carefully plotted in his mind the story he would tell. He hoped he would be sufficiently convincing.

He told those in charge of his case, that he was the only person who knew where his daughter was buried. When he realised what he had done, he had taken her body and buried it. He kept emphasising that his wife was in no way connected with what he had done.

He also said he had left the knife and pillow slip under the spare tire in his wife's car with the intention of getting rid of both as soon as he could. But events had happened too quickly and he had missed his opportunity to dispose of the incriminating evidence.

He refused to say where the body was buried. All he would say was that it was not on their property, that he had taken her elsewhere. He explained that he didn't want his sons stumbling across the body as they frequently roamed the property. He deeply regretted what he had done.

Denise confided in the only person she felt comfortable with—Abigail Jordan. She explained that she was about to be released.

"I'll miss you, Denise. What are you going to do when you get out?" Abagail was always interested in her friend.

"I'm going to spend time with my sons, get them settled and then I'm going to get my husband out of jail and then find out who was responsible for taking my daughter. That's my plan."

"You sound like you mean business. How are you going to get your husband out? Didn't he plead guilty? He's looking at fifteen years if not more." Abagail was an eager confident and keen to hear her friend's plans.

"There are various ways and means," Denise replied. "He's not going to stay there for something he didn't do. If it takes me forever, I'll get whoever has done this to us. Then Michael and I will be together, just like he promised, till the end of our time together."

Denise lay back down on her bunk and dreamed of the good times in her life, when she had a husband, sons and a daughter. She had hung onto these memories during the time she had been incarcerated.

Sometimes she felt as though her daughter was able to speak to her, that she was telling her things. When these thoughts occurred, Sarina always told her the nice things in her life but lately it seemed the little girl could not keep the alarm out of the connection she had with her mother.

Heaven must be a strange place, Denise thought. She did not know much about the afterlife. It had never been of interest to her. But if there was an afterlife, surely little children should be happy, not plagued with worries and concerns.

Sarina deserved that much, surely. Her life had been taken from her. If there was a just god, then her daughter should be allowed to be happy and at peace for all eternity.

While Denise day-dreamed about her past life, Abagail Jordan was requesting to see the prison warden. As part of her requirements for early release, she had been instructed to report any relevant information concerning Denise Farraday.

It was not always possible to determine what was relevant, as Denise revealed very little about herself or her family. But her determination to get her husband out of jail by various 'ways and means' must count for something. When asked what the various 'ways and means' were, Abagail could give no insight other than that Denise had been adamant that she would obtain her husband's release.

Abagail was returned to her cell. As soon as she departed the warden's office, a phone call was made to pass the information on as instructed.

Sarina kept a lonely vigil watching over Francine. The young woman was badly traumatised. The pain in her hand was tremendous. Francine said that it was becoming unbearable. When she realised that her wedding ring was gone as well as her finger, she was doubly upset.

It was as if there was nothing left in her life. Her husband was gone. The man who could not give her a child had not returned. She had been kidnapped for no apparent reason and her finger brutally cut off. The loss of her wedding ring was more than she could bear.

The child could feel her pain, not just her physical pain but her emotional pain. Words did not help. So when she thought it was safe, Sarina would lie on the bed beside Francine and hold her.

While she held Francine, she wondered why her body was so hot. Sometimes she would massage her right arm that was still cuffed to the bed head. At other times she would rub her feet and ankles, trying to help with her circulation. There were times when they fell asleep together.

The rattling door was like an alarm clock. As soon as the first sound was heard, she would jump off the bed and quickly scramble beneath it. The monsters had not returned to the room since they had cut off Francine's finger. It was only Maria who visited when she could.

Maria had been annoyed when Sarina had escaped, but underneath her annoyance, it was clear that she did not blame the child. Had Sarina escaped and it became known that she was still alive then the monsters would surely kill her without hesitation. For how else could the little girl have survived if it wasn't for Maria's interference?

Maria was without hope. There was no way out for her. She was unsure what the monsters planned to do with Francine. She had listened through her bedroom door and heard large amounts of money being spoken about. She also had the dilemma of a baby growing in her belly. She could feel its movements and kicks. This would be the child of monsters.

She thought back to the first time the main monster had taken her. It was soon after her mother had died. Prior to that it had been her mother who had provided comfort but once she was gone, it became Maria's privilege. She cared little which monster was responsible. One was as bad as the next.

She was ignored by them for most of the time except when they wanted her in bed or to cook and clean. There was no mention made by them regarding the child growing inside her. What further plans they had for her or the child she had no idea.

Maria's thoughts were so tortured that she was not certain when the child was due to be born. All she knew was that the kicks and movements were getting stronger as though the infant inside her was angry and anxious to get out.

More than anything, Maria wanted to run away, to get as far away as she could from all her troubles. But she had responsibilities. She was responsible for Francine as well as Sarina. She could not abandon either of them. It was one thing to dream of a peaceful life where there were no monsters or children and women who had their fingers cut off. Reality was altogether different.

Sarina still tried to talk to her mother and Lucia. She was unclear if her mother could hear her but she was certain Lucia could. They had little conversations with each other. Lucia told her that she had a pack of cards and was trying to teach herself how to play solitaire just like Gabe, Rafe and Arlo used to at Sunshine.

Once Lucia told her that she had called her bears after Gabe and Rafe. This made Sarina laugh out loud trying to imagine her twin brothers being teddy bears. Francine heard her laughing and asked her what was so funny. Sarina told her that she often talked to Lucia in her mind and related what Lucia had told her about her teddy bears.

Francine had stared at Sarina as though she was crazy but she still joined in her laughter and said it was a very good thing to be able to talk to someone. Lucia had also told Sarina that her hair was now the same colour as Sarina's and that she also had a new name.

Both Sarina and Francine were very worried about Maria who was in a constant state of anxiety and fear. Not that the two of them weren't as well. But Maria was their life line. Without her, they were both doomed.

They were locked away and totally dependent on Maria. They watched Maria as every day she became more harried looking and was also red-eyed from bouts of crying. The child she carried in her belly seemed to be growing rapidly.

Lucia was trapped in the small house with Mrs Potter. Mrs Potter cut and dyed her hair so that now she looked as dark haired as her father instead of having the golden curls that her mother and father had both so admired.

Mrs Potter again told Lucia that her mother was dead and her father no longer wanted her. She reiterated that her aunty and uncles were too busy to look after her and that her father was in jail.

The days were very long and boring for Lucia. She was becoming very good at playing solitaire. Mrs Potter had told her that her name was now Lucy Potter; that she was her grandmother and would look after her from now on.

Lucia had cried when she was told that her father did not want her. She could not believe it. How often had her daddy told her that she was the most beautiful and precious girl in the whole world? But he never came for her and he never visited. She was beginning to think that perhaps Mrs Potter was right and he was in jail.

Worst of all was that Mrs Potter said that they would have to leave the house they were living in because they could no longer afford to stay there. Very soon, they would be leaving to live in another town where the people were much nicer and where Lucia could go to school and make new friends. Lucia would also be able to meet her new grandfather.

The monsters returned late one evening full of alcohol and good cheer. In spite of her acute anxiety, Maria was keen to know why they were in such high spirits. The alcohol was not something new. It usually made them surlier but for some reason they were all in better moods. She listened in as covertly as possible.

There was endless talk of millions of dollars. She could hear them in the kitchen, drinking, laughing and when she looked out she could see the kitchen table was littered with bundles of notes. She had no idea where the money had come from. As quietly as possible, she returned again to her room. It was only when she heard them talk about having a piece of the bitch in the shed that she came out again.

Maria considered she was already a ruined person without hope. But maybe, she could protect Francine. For once the gods were on her side. As unobtrusively as possible she told the monsters that there was a severe, thunder storm about to happen.

The thunder began to crackle and lighting lit up the sky. As she returned to her room the first of the monsters followed her in. At least Francine had been spared this.

The little monster that was growing in her belly, squirmed, rolled and kicked as they came to her.

42

The scramble to collect the cash was completed by the third day. Dax warned the brothers that if there were any more substantial requests for cash that it would be impossible to get such large amounts together without questions being raised. He had reached the limit of his ability to assist them.

He also added that the Farraday name was already viewed with suspicion. There had been too many incidents over the years. Both policing authorities and financial institutions were most likely monitoring them.

Day three started out with the usual routine. The children were driven to school. Mia stayed at her day care centre with Harry. Mitch was adamant he did not want the children to return home after school. They were to spend the night with their grandmother. This left the brothers unimpeded to sit and wait for the phone to ring—whatever time that may be.

There were two calls initially but not the one they waited for. When the phone rang the third time, Mitch answered.

The same muffled, hoarse voice spoke, "Have you got it?"

"Yes," he replied.

"Good, let's get this over with. You have the next backpack ready and you can have the package. We'll conclude the transaction at three this afternoon at your place. But with only one of you present."

Mitch agreed. "Three this afternoon it is."

The other brothers had heard the conversation.

"What's he mean by just one of us present? Does he think the rest of us won't be here? How's he going to know who's here?" Malcolm retained a glimmer of hope that it was Lucia who would be returned.

"They mean business. As far as I'm concerned, I'll be the one who stays. So if the rest of you don't want to be involved, that's up to you. But if you do, then we'll work it so that the vehicles are shifted but you stay if you want."

There was unanimous agreement that they would all stay. Quickly they shifted their vehicles to the Smythe property and returned together in Mitch's SUV.

They were ready and waiting. Mitch sat on the front steps of the home while his brothers remained out of sight inside. It was twenty minutes to three when the landline rang again. When he answered it, the same muffled, hoarse voice spoke.

"I said only one of you. There are four of you. So unless you want delivery of a silent package, three of you had better leave now. You've got ten minutes to get out of there."

Mitch breathed heavily "Okay, but the package had better be intact."

There was only a gruff laugh before the call was ended.

He summonsed his brothers and explained what had occurred. "How the hell does he know who's here? They must have a look-out somewhere." Matt looked out into the hills.

"Doesn't matter," Mark interjected. "We've got to get out of here as fast as possible. We'll go to Danny's place and wait there. Give us a ring, Mitch, when it's over."

Mitch watched his brothers leave. It was a lonely feeling. The longest ten minutes of his life. He stayed in the kitchen close to the phone in case they called again.

Denise had been released the same morning. She could not wait to see her sons and the rest of her family. She would surprise them. She had not told any of them of her release.

The thrill of release remained with her. Sarina was gone and Michael remained in jail awaiting sentencing. This saddened her but the sadness was lessened by the thought of seeing her sons. It was almost three o'clock. The school bus would soon return her children.

The taxi dropped her at the front entrance to Sunshine. As she got out of the car, she looked around at the place that had been her home for ten years. She looked at the tall gums. She smelled the clean air, stared out at the hills and mountains she had come to love.

She would savour this moment. She decided to walk the back perimeter to the back steps of the house. This was the last place that there had been any contact with her daughter. It was the place where her amputated finger had been found. She needed this closeness.

As she ambled along, she noticed that the gardens needed attention. There was a vehicle present. She assumed it belonged to one of Michael's brothers.

It was not only Sarina who wondered why there was so much heat coming from Francine's body. Maria had also become aware of this. She knew the finger was infected. The monsters were around more often so she did not have any chance to redress the wound. Now, she had another responsibility. Francine's life may well be in her hands.

The monsters returned in the afternoon. They drove into the yard in their big, black SUV's. There was again tension in the air. They briefly came into the house, made some phone calls and then went to the granny flat.

Sarina heard them approaching before she heard the door rattle. Their steps were loud and forceful. She pulled the gag back up to cover Francine's mouth, gave her a quick kiss before scrambling under the bed.

"It's time, bitch. You're going back to daddy. Put her in the back and hurry up." The main monster was directing the others. There was venom in his speech.

Francine stared out of glassy eyes at the four men who stood before her. She had difficulty following what the man in charge was saying.

Sarina lay in a tight bundle under the bed with her thumb in her mouth. She tried to keep her eyes open so that she could count the number of legs in the room but the scene in front of her eyes was too alarming. So she shut her eyes and prayed that Francine would be safe. Her circle may be gone but she could still visualise the image of the lady.

One of the men lifted Francine up over his shoulder and took her out of the room. Her hand was knocked again as he carried her out. She screamed with acute pain. The man could hear her feeble cries coming through the gag, so he clamped his hand over her mouth.

It took only moments to get to the SUV. The door was already open. Francine was roughly thrown into the back. She landed heavily. She felt her head land with force against the hard floor. After that she had blessed relief. She slipped into a pit of blackness.

As she stood at the kitchen window, Maria watched in horror as she saw Francine thrown into the back of the van. There was no movement from her before the door was slammed shut. Maria was uncertain if she should pray for Francine's life or death. Which option would be worse?

All her fears were coming true in front of her eyes. Maria had to take her chances and leave. She would collect Sarina and disappear. But first, she would search the house. She had seen bundles of cash. If she could find the money and disappear, both of them might have a chance.

Maria moved quickly. She went to the room where the main monster slept. It took her only a few minutes to find a black backpack shoved deep into the bottom of a wardrobe. She pulled it out and quickly opened it. Her heart beat faster as she saw it was filled with bundles of cash. She hoped this would help with her escape and not haunt her forever.

She had little experience of driving. Her mother had given her some lessons before she had died. Maria was petrified at the thought of driving the big vehicle. But life was more precious than her fears and anxieties.

She raced to the granny flat where the door remained open. There was no sign of Sarina. Maria was mortified that the little girl had again run away.

"Sarina," she called out. "Where are you?" Maria frantically looked around the room before reaching the bed and looking under.

Sarina lay there, curled up in a ball with her eyes held shut. "Come on out now, Sarina. The monsters have gone. We have to hurry. We're leaving."

Sarina slowly opened her eyes. Maria was looking at her frantically. Her hand with the missing index finger was beckoning for her to come out from under the bed. Sarina slowly moved from her hiding place. She watched as Maria gathered up her few belongings. She emptied out the old cardboard box.

"Come on, Sarina. This is our chance to escape." Maria took the little girl by the hand and hurried to the SUV. She lifted Sarina into the back seat. The seat belt confused her but finally she had the young girl securely seated. Maria ran back to the house. She grabbed the black backpack and another satchel where she kept the documents that her mother had told her were important.

She had few clothes that fit her. Her belly had grown quickly. The only clothes that fit her were a few dresses that she had bought at the second-hand shop. Clothes were not important. Escape was all that mattered. She had to get onto the road that would take her to Cooroy.

She frequently checked in the rear vision mirror. Sarina was staring out the window. Her eyes were not blinking. Maria thought the girl was probably in shock.

"Are you all right, Rina?" Maria asked.

The little girl came out of her reverie. "What did you call me?" she asked, looking at Maria in puzzlement.

"Rina—you have a new name now. Your name is Rina Wright. You're my little girl now."

Maria felt a mountain of guilt. She knew if the monsters ever found out that she had kept the child alive, as sure as day followed night, they would come after the two of them. She had to cover her tracks.

The missing money would be a catalyst for the black rage that would engulf them when they knew the money was gone. There was no doubt they would be looking for her as soon as they realised what she had done.

Maria reached Cooroy then found her way to the main highway where she turned south. She eventually pulled up at a service station. The day was fast coming to a close. As she sat staring at the petrol pumps, she realised she would have to find some shelter for herself and Rina.

She needed petrol but was not sure how to work the pumps. As she sat looking at other drivers filling up their vehicles, she noticed a bus pull up. The monster in her belly was tiring her out.

She quickly helped Rina out of the SUV, gathered their few belongings before speaking to the bus driver. The driver looked at her sceptically as she asked for two tickets to Brisbane. Maria had not planned for the strong movements of the baby in her belly but her flinching soon convinced the bus driver to let them both on board.

The bus driver was happy to take them to Brisbane. He did not want to be accused of leaving a pregnant woman and a small child behind. Maria glanced back at the black SUV she had left abandoned at the petrol station. She doubted there would be any identification of any type left behind. The monsters were very careful not to leave behind any evidence.

43

Silence surrounded him. Mitch listened for any sound that suggested a vehicle was approaching. The ten minutes had passed. There had been no phone calls. There was only the whisper of a slight breeze as it gently waved the large limbs of the tall gums surrounding the house.

At first there was a faint sound, but as it grew louder he knew that the time had come. He left the kitchen and went out to the front veranda. He stood near the steps. He looked up to see an SUV coming slowly up the driveway.

Whoever the woman was, he hoped she had not suffered too badly. The vehicle pulled up in front of the house. It was parked not far from his own.

He realised he was nervous. His heart was starting to thump in his chest. He knew he should be better than this. After all he was a soldier. He had faced worst enemies. These were just rough men, possibly his half-brothers.

It should have been so different. Had the circumstances of their birth been different, they could have had some semblance of a relationship. But much like himself, they were all most probably the off shoots of Alan Farraday's corrupt seed.

As three men got out of the vehicle they opened the back door of the SUV. As he watched them, he noted the legs tied together at the back of the vehicle. He held the backpack firmly in his left hand.

One of the men stepped forward while the other two stood behind. He was clearly the man in charge.

"Show us the money and then you can have her."

The silence of the surrounding hills was unnerving. There was no mild breeze swaying the leaves of the tall gums. There were four men in confrontation. The body in the back of the SUV had not moved.

"How do I know she's alive?" Mitch asked quietly, his voice breaking the silence.

"Would you like another demonstration? She's still got nine left." His question was answered just as quietly, without drama or affectation.

Mitch opened the backpack. It was identical to the first one that had been left near the letter box. "It's all there."

"Hand it over and she's yours." The man checked the bag.

"You get her out so I can see if she's okay, then it's your," Mitch countered.

The man in charge indicated to the other men who went to the back of the vehicle and roughly pulled her out. Again she landed head first on the ground. Mitch heard the sickening thud.

He stared at the figure on the ground in front of him. It was impossible to tell what she looked like or who she was. She was facing away from him. He saw the bandaged hand. He was about to hand over the backpack when he realised that he could not see any rise or fall of her chest. All he could hear was her head hitting the ground.

He kept the backpack in his left hand as he bent down to check on the woman. He lifted her head and turned her face towards him. He was sick with fear and battling blind rage both at the same time as he recognised her.

"You've killed her," he roared. "You didn't have to harm her. What did she ever do to you? If you wanted a fight, you could have come after me, but not her."

Just as the surrounding hills appeared to move with the swaying of trees as the wind suddenly grew stronger, the three men moved rapidly producing their weapons. Mitch was back on familiar territory. He was confronting his enemy. This was what he was used to. He now also had the added incentive of personal revenge and rage.

His hands were lighting fast. He threw the backpack at the man in charge. This caused the diversion he needed. A knife appeared in his right hand. One of the other two men felt its blade piece his chest. He fell to the ground writhing in pain and disbelief.

Mitch moved with all the speed of his extensive training and within seconds the second man was on the ground. He held him in front of him while a second knife appeared in his hand. He cut from left to right across the man's throat. There was gurgling and gagging as the man struggled to hold the flesh of his neck together. This attempt did nothing to stop the flow of blood. The lawns of Sunshine were awash with blood.

He left the man lying helpless on the ground. Small trickles of blood kept flowing as his body emptied out. The man in charge stared in shock at the carnage in front of him.

The man with the knife still visible in his chest remained standing. He looked down at the knife and then back at the man who had thrown it. He was beginning to lift his hands towards the knife as he was again attacked. The movement had only taken seconds.

The knife was removed from his chest. Gurgling and frothing of the mouth had commenced. Just as he had held the man whose throat he had cut, Mitch took this man's head in his strong hands and twisted it until he heard the crack of death. He then let him slide to the ground. The deaths of these two men had taken no more than a few seconds.

"You didn't have to do that," the main man said as he pointed the gun at Mitch's head. He was still in shock but was rapidly pulling himself together. "We would have taken the money and left. You owed us that much."

They locked eyes. Mitch could have asked a thousand questions. He could have asked if he was Alan Farraday's son. He could have asked if they were half-brother. But he asked none of these things.

The woman was dead so the rest of it didn't matter. He was dead inside. What had the woman once said to him, that she thought he was as lonely as she was?

This had been true for so long. But after he had met her, the loneliness had eased. He realised that he had found something worth living for. He closed his eyes while two dead men lay at his feet. He waited for the bullet.

"That's not going to happen," the voice came as if from nowhere. It was soft but full of determination.

Both men looked towards the voice at the same time. Denise Farraday stood a few meters away with her Glock held firmly in her hand and pointed straight at the man's head. There was no fear in her eyes. They were steady and cold.

"Who are you?" the man asked, trying to subdue his surprise. "You're not supposed to be here. The deal was there was to be only one of you."

"I'm the person who is going to kill you. I'm also the person who lives here," she replied. "You can throw the gun down or keep it, I don't care. You're going to die anyway."

The man's own gun was still pointed at Mitch. "We can work this out. If I throw away the gun, you do the same and then that will be the end of it." His eyes were flicking between Mitch and Denise. He realised the dilemma he was in.

"That's exactly right, Maxie. It is Maxie, isn't it? There will be an end to it but only for you. Tell you what, you can close your eyes and I'll end it for you now or else I might just let Mitch here take to you with his knife. He's pretty handy with it as you might have noticed. Between us, we might just carve you up like you did to my daughter before you die. What do you say, Mitch?"

Denise had a tight smile on her face. She glanced at Mitch who remained in front of the two men he had killed.

Mitch could not speak. He was as awed as the other man as she stood there like an avenging angel.

The other man shifted his stance and rounded to face her. She pulled the trigger without flinching or steadying her breathing. His eyes opened wide as the bullet went through his forehead. He had a final thought that it was said people had a third eye. He didn't think the hole in the centre of his forehead was what they meant as he fell to the ground dead.

"That was for my daughter," she said as she approached the body, still twitching as brain waves ceased to work. She pointed the gun and shot him again through the heart. "That was for my husband." She walked to the front veranda where she lay the Glock down.

Mitch was in shock. Not because of the men he had killed but because of Denise's sudden appearance and her intervention.

He again looked at the men who lay near his feet. There was blood all over his clothes and hands.

Denise hurried over to him. "Are you all right?" she asked simply.

He nodded and muttered, "Thanks."

As he shook the blood off his clothes, he wondered again about the woman Michael had married. Everyone said she was clever but no one had mentioned to him that she could kill in the blink of an eye.

She was already with the woman who lay unmoving on the lawn. "You better get over here quick. She's not dead. She's still breathing but unconscious."

Mitch hurried towards the woman who lay on the ground. He kept looking at her, memories flooding back. He was trying to remember all their fractured conversations. He could not seem to move himself.

Denise slapped him hard across the face and screamed at him. "Get yourself moving. Get some help. Get her to a doctor. Get Matt. Where the hell are your brothers? Get them here straight away."

He felt around in his pocket for his mobile. After what seemed like an eternity he found it. Then he had trouble turning it on. His mind was still mush.

"Give the damn thing to me," she said. She quickly found Matt's number. She didn't wait for any niceties. "Get here straight away, Matt, and bring your brothers with you. It's Francine and she's in a bad way. Get the old doctor here or some other doctor to fix her up. And hurry up or else she won't make it. And don't call an ambulance. There are three dead men here. So no ambulance and no police or else we'll all end up in jail."

Mitch was now holding the woman. He had heard Denise call her Francine. He wondered how it was that she knew her name.

"For pity's sake, are you useless?" she screamed again. "Do you want to lose her? She may be yours but sitting around holding her is not going to keep her alive."

She stared at her brother-in-law as he continued to hold Francine. He stared blankly back at her. It was then that Denise realised that he had been unaware the injured woman was his daughter.

"Okay. You hold her and I'll fix her up as best I can." She looked back up to the entrance of Sunshine. "Where the hell are your brothers? They should be here by now."

She ran into the house and brought out blankets, water and towels. By this time, Francine's skin was beginning to feel very cold. She seemed to be stirring and was beginning to shake.

"Wrap her up in these blankets. Then get that bandage off her hand. Whatever's underneath, it doesn't smell too good." She placed a cold pack on the huge lump on the side of her niece's head. As she gently washed Francine's face, she spoke to Mitch.

"Do you think you could get one of your knives and cut the ties off her legs?"

He looked at her mutely. "Mitch," Denise spoke firmly again. "I know this is a dreadful shock but you have to snap out of it. Go," she commanded. She glanced at the two knives he had used on the dead men. "Don't use one of those. Get a clean one."

Mitch finally recovered from his shock. He let go of the woman and hurried back inside the house. He knew there were knives and scissors in the kitchen drawer. He pulled out a pair of scissors. Then he returned and cut the ties that were holding the legs of the woman. He now knew her name. She was called

Francine. He looked at the bandage. He smelled the odour. Quickly he cut the bandage around her hand.

When the bandage was totally removed, both he and Denise looked at the stump of her ring finger. It was becoming black. The smell was horrific.

"This does not look good. Where the hell is that doctor?" She proceeded to pour warm, soapy water over the black and suppurating area where a finger had once been. Red streaks were travelling up her hand into the lower portion of her arm.

"Keep her warm," she told Mitch. "I'll be back in a minute."

He did more than keep Francine warm. He took her in his arms and cradled her, wrapping the blanket around her shaking body. This was so different from the times when he had held her, when she had cried in his arms, when she had told him how much she had hated him, while at the same time making love to him.

The torture he was going through right now was far worse than anything he had experienced in Afghanistan.

Denise returned. "I don't know if this will do any good; it's all I've got."

She poured Dettol onto the infected hand. Then she smeared Vaseline over gauze and placed it against the wound. She then wrapped the hand again in a large bandage with plenty of padding underneath. By this time, Francine was slightly more alert. She opened her eyes and looked at the man holding her.

It took her a moment to realise it was the man whom she had desperately sought out. She reached up to touch his face, but he took her hand in his and kissed it. She thought she saw tears in his eyes. He smiled at her and then told her that she was safe. Francine closed her eyes again then lay back in his arms.

The man, who lay hidden high up on the hills amongst the tall gums with his strong binoculars, could not believe what he had just witnessed. He slumped to the ground in shock. How had it all gone so wrong?

Zaylee was happily attending to her patients when she received a desperate call from Malcolm. It was a garbled conversation but it involved Francine. It took her a moment to recall who Francine was. He asked her to come quickly to Sunshine as he frantically told her that Francine may be dying.

She told him to call an ambulance, but he replied they couldn't. There was too much at stake. He was frantic and begged her to come right away. The entire conversation annoyed her as she did not understand why, if Francine was so ill, she would not be better off in hospital.

Then she thought of all he had been through with the loss of his wife and child. She was already in too deep with Malcolm Farraday. Their twice weekly sexual encounters on the floor of her consultation room were enough to get her deregistered.

The doctor knew her visit to Sunshine would not be a quick one so she told her colleagues that she was sick and had to go home. Knowing the dramas that she had already faced with this family, she restocked her doctor's bag with every kind of emergency medication she could think of. She then set off.

Minutes later, the three brothers arrived. They stared in astonishment at the bloody scene in front of them. The biggest surprise was their sister-in-law who was busy dumping blankets on the ground beside the bodies of three dead men. She said a quick hello before speaking.

"Is there a doctor coming?" she asked, looking impatiently at them.

"Yes, Denise, Dr Zaylee Lang will be here soon. Do you remember her?" Malcolm replied.

"Yes, I do, she was very good to me but can we trust her to keep her mouth shut?" she asked, pointing to the three bodies. Before Malcolm could answer, she continued. "We'd better shift these bodies. It's too much to expect her to carry a burden like this around. It will be enough if she can take care of Francine."

"What's up with Mitch?" Mark asked as he watched his oldest brother cradling Francine. It looked like he was almost crying.

"What do you think?" Denise replied.

Mark did not know what to think. He could see that Francine looked to be unconscious and very ill. He assumed Mitch's emotional behaviour had something to do with the three bodies that lay in front of them.

"Get a move on," was all she said. "Shift these bodies into the nearest shed. We can work out what to do with them later once Francine has been taken care of." She looked at the spot where the bodies lay. "And get those knives and guns out of sight and hose off that blood."

"Hell, what a blood bath," Matthew followed Denise's lead and started rolling the first body into the blanket. Together, the four of them dragged the bodies into the nearest shed.

Denise was not yet finished with her instructions. "Mark, get rid of this SUV. Put it into one of the other sheds, then cut it down and dispose of it. Do what you have to?"

They carefully lifted Francine onto a blanket and carried her inside the house where they placed her on a bed. Mitch remained with her. Denise again regarded her husband's brother. She disappeared for a few minutes and when she returned, she handed him some clean clothes.

"Change out of those clothes before the doctor gets here and get rid of them. Clean yourself up." Mitch did as she instructed.

Malcolm remained on the veranda waiting for the doctor. She arrived soon after.

"What's happened?" she asked as he greeted her.

"It's Francine. They took her and cut off her finger. It looks like it's gangrenous. Who knows what else they put her through?" He explained as much as he knew about Mia's friend.

When she entered the room, she was appalled at Francine's appearance. She remembered the beautiful woman whom she had first met at Lady Francesca's boutique and then again in her consultation room. This was when Francine had wanted clarification of her pregnancy. A pregnancy made possible by a one-night stand.

She asked Mitch to leave the room while she examined Francine. She remembered him from when she had first been to Sunshine when Sarina disappeared. She was taken aback when he refused. He told the doctor he would not be leaving Francine's side and to get on with it.

Dr Lang was used to giving orders but she was now out of her depth. The big man was not leaving and she did not feel up to arguing with him. She had no idea why he was with Francine but it did cross her mind that he might have been the one-night stand. As far as she knew, there was no family relationship. She would ask Malcolm about it later.

She had become mixed up with a tragic family so it was more than likely that Francine was somehow related.

It did not take long for Zaylee to determine the seriousness of Francine's condition. She was appalled by what she saw. She again repeated that the woman required hospitalisation. Zaylee had only met Denise Farraday under the tragic circumstances of her daughter's death so she was not prepared for the strong, determined woman who said to her, "Fix up Francine and don't be frigging around".

Mitch Farraday again was amazed at the strength of his virtually unknown sister-in-law's absolute determination.

The doctor was in dangerous territory. She always had colleagues to consult about any difficult medical issues. This time she was on her own. She commenced the antibiotic therapy that she hoped would improve the condition of the horrendous wound she had tried to clean.

Francine's head injury showed some signs of improvement. She was remaining conscious for slightly longer periods and could take sips of water. When it was apparent there were definite signs of improvement, Denise decided it was time for Francine to be returned to her own home.

Zaylee was about to object but one look from Denise convinced her to shift Francine to her own home. Mia had returned with Harry. When she saw her friend, she began to fall apart. Again Denise made it quite clear that this was not the time for hysterics and Mia had better pull herself together if she was going to help her friend. Matt agreed he would care for the baby.

While the doctor was taking care of Francine, Denise called the brothers together to determine the best way of getting rid of the bodies. When they asked how the three men had been killed, she told them there would be time for discussion after the bodies were disposed of.

Various suggestions as to how this should be done were made—like weighing them down in the creek, or dragging them up to the cave at Big Rock. Matt could not get his mind off the skeleton that lay in the tunnel under the house.

"How about we leave them in the tunnel?"

"What tunnel?" Denise asked.

They told her about the tunnel they had found when they had tried to shift their parent's iron bed. Matt did not mention the skeleton that was already there. Time was of the essence. It became imperative that Francine, Mia and the doctor leave Sunshine as soon as possible.

Denise told Mitch she needed to see him outside; he was reluctant to leave Francine. She explained in her no-nonsense voice that she had to speak to him urgently. It was the first time he had left Francine's side since he had recognised her.

She told Mitch of their plan, not seeking his approval but to ascertain if the tunnel would be a hidden and secure burial place for the three men. His experience of death was more extensive than hers. She assumed he knew more about the disposal of bodies. He agreed with this decision.

Francine was carefully lifted into the back of Mitch's SUV. Following instruction from Mia, Mitch drove the few kilometres to Francine home. The doctor followed in her own car.

Once they were gone, the rush was on to unscrew the bolts that held the bed secured to the floor. They then lifted the bed up and over the cement cover that kept the tunnel hidden. After this was done, the difficult part of dragging the bodies from the shed, up the stairs, through the house to the main bedroom commenced.

Matt elected to go down into the tunnel and pull the bodies along as far as they would go. There was no clear reason why he did not tell his family that there was another body buried under their home. Maybe it was to keep the ghosts at bay. Since the cover had first been lifted off the tunnel, there had been nothing but mayhem.

The bodies were very heavy. Their clothing was searched for any identification but there was none. There were no mobile phones, driver's licences, nothing to identify these men. The only significance was that they were all big, strong men with black hair, dark eyes and similar features. Their knives and guns were buried with them.

They were all very quiet while they entombed the men. The most difficult part was for Matt as he hauled the bodies along the narrow tunnel until he reached the end. Then he had to squeeze himself over the top of the bodies to return to the entrance so as to pull the next one along. He covered each body with more blankets.

When it was done, he surveyed his handiwork under the glare of his torchlight. At least they were covered up. This made him feel better. If they were his half-brothers, at least they were all together and not out in the open. In spite of everything, he said a silent prayer for them.

They hauled Matt out of the tunnel, lifted the cement cover back on and then dragged the iron bed back into place. Mark found his tools and bolted the bed back onto the floor.

Matt thought of the nights he had spent there with Mia. Such nights were now over for him. He doubted that any of them would think of Sunshine in the same way ever again.

When it was all done, Denise went outside and vomited. She collapsed onto the ground not far from where she had killed both Jack Smith and the man she assumed was Maxie. She began shaking. Then she started screaming uncontrollably. Her nightmares had not disappeared. They had just increased.

The brothers lifted her up and carried her into her bedroom and lay her on the bed that she had once shared with her husband.

They were in a stupor. There had been a terrible deed committed on this day. They had all participated in another terrible deed when they had entombed the three men. What use was conversation when confronted by such horrendous events?

There was no beer or whisky that could make their minds forget. There was not enough water in the world to wash off the stink of death they had been involved with.

They sat in their mother's prayer room and stared out onto the hills, listened to the soft, gentle wash of the creek as they heard Denise's sobs gradually lessen. It was sometime later when they heard a noise in the kitchen. They looked up to see that she had showered and changed and was making tea.

She brought in a tray laden with cups, tea bags and biscuits. They ate and drank slowly until she eventually spoke.

"Before we go any further, you all have to get cleaned up, clean up the house and get rid of anything that may be construed as evidence. If you want another cup of tea, then you better hurry up. Anything you don't want, put it into the garbage and we'll get rid of it."

The brothers had thought their ordeal was finished until she had spoken to them. They roused themselves and did as she directed. There were clothes left in cupboards, so after they had cleaned up the marks of the men they had dragged to and from the shed, across the lawn and into and through the house, they showered and changed.

They put their clothes into a garbage bag which Mark said he would get rid of. She told them to tell Mitch to be mindful of any evidence that might link him to the disappearance of the men.

After it was done, she again made fresh tea sweetened with sugar and produced more biscuits that had gone soft. When they were finished she spoke to them again.

"Mitch killed two of them. He knifed one of them and then cracked his neck. He cut the throat of the second. I shot the third man. It was all over very quickly. It looked like Francine was dead, that's what set Mitch off. The last man was going to kill Mitch, so that's why I had to shoot him. I think he was the one who took Sarina. That's what happened."

They all looked at her in stunned amazement until she spoke again, "I don't think we need to speak of this again. It's probably best we shut this place up as soon as we can. I need to see my sons and then I'm getting Michael out of jail. Will you bring the boys back tomorrow, please, Matt?"

That was it. It was over and done with. The terrorism was finished. The terrorists were dead. Denise left the brothers with their tea and the biscuits that had gone soft. She went back to her bedroom where she lay on her bed.

She tried to connect with her daughter as sometimes she thought she could hear her calling to her, but this time there was nothing there. Her daughter was silent.

45

What do you do after such an event? Mark went to his mother's home and collected Arlo. He said very little as was his way in spite of his son's constant questions. He told Arlo that he could now live back at their home. Nights spent at Sunshine with his cousins were over. He also added that he would be very busy over the next few days.

Matthew stayed with Denise until he was satisfied she was settled. She had told the three brothers to leave, that she was okay, to go and do what they had to do and be with whom they had to be with. Denise looked to be asleep when he left.

He collected Harry and then drove straight to Francine's home. After he settled the baby, he sat with Mia watching Francine battle her infection. Mitch was also there.

Matt did not ask why Mitch was so concerned about Francine. His oldest brother was living in a world of his own. Matt rationalised this was probably the result of having killed two men and seeing Francine lying helpless and sick in front of them.

Malcolm also went to Francine's home. He had never been there before. The house was very impressive, but was of no interest to him. For a few moments he had hoped the person being returned was his daughter; that somehow the men had been playing a cruel game with them all.

But this was not so. He did not try to rationalise why they had taken Francine, Mia's friend. He could only assume it was for that very reason, because she was Mia's friend. He waited for Zaylee to leave Francine's bedside. He looked up as he saw her approach.

"I think she's over the worst. She'll be okay." She sat down beside him. He wanted to hold her but knew that she would have a myriad of questions for him. He was still feeling numb from what he and his brothers had done.

"Are you okay?" she asked, holding his hand.

"Not really; how about you?"

"Not really. I don't understand what's going on. I could get into big trouble for this. She should be in hospital," she replied.

"She probably should," he replied. "It was either you or Sam. He's just too old although his mind is intact."

She considered what he had said. She knew he meant old Dr Sam Calhoun. "I think you'd better tell me what's going on."

He breathed heavily before answering her. "It's another saga in what's been happening. They took Francine and cut her finger off. They demanded a ransom with no police involved. We paid the money and they returned Francine. You know the rest. At first, we thought she was dead. Thanks to you, Doc, she's now going to live."

She tried to absorb what he had told her. "But why Francine, she's no relative of yours, is she?"

"No" he answered, "but she and Mia have always been close, like sisters. Matt and Mia are an item. I guess that's why she was targeted."

"Who are these men?" she questioned.

"We're not really sure. Like I said, they could be our half-brothers. My father had a lot of women and seems like a lot of children."

"So what's happened to them?" she asked, watching the tired expression come over his face.

"They're gone. They went away. It's all over. There won't be any more incidents. We're safe now."

"Why did they come after your family?" her enquiring mind was still full of questions.

"I don't really know. They said we owed them, whatever that means. For all I care they can have Sunshine and everything on it." He looked at her. "We're going to close the place up. Shut it up and leave. It has bad memories and karma. I don't ever want to go back there again."

"Trouble seems to follow you Farradays," she commented, leaning her head on his shoulder.

"Are you sure you want to get mixed up with us," he asked. "If you want out, I will understand."

"Well, I tried that and it didn't work. I guess I'll just have to see it through. At least if what you say is true, we can now use a mattress and not the floor." She kissed him briefly on the cheek. "I have to check on Francine. See if you can find a bed. There seems to be plenty of rooms in this place. I'll join you as soon as I can."

He watched her walk back to check on Francine. Lust for her was the last thing on his mind at the moment. He briefly wondered if it would return but as he watched her bend over to examine Francine, he looked at her legs covered professionally by a smart skirt. It was one problem he would not have to face.

Francine murmured and tossed in her sleep. Night had long since fallen. Her body was now neither burning hot nor freezing cold. Her temperature was returning to normal. Mitch stayed by her side. He had sent Mia to bed. She lay curled up beside Matt in one of the many bedrooms in Francine's house.

He watched her throughout the night, giving her sips of water whenever she woke. She was able to stay awake for longer periods. Each time she woke, she looked at him intensely as he held her hand. He stroked her forehead and wiped away the sweat.

Towards morning, she woke again. Her head was much clearer. She looked over at him and saw that he had nodded off. A warm feeling passed through her. At long last she felt totally safe. He was with her and she knew he would keep her safe always.

He opened his eyes. "Hi," she said. "My name's Francine."

He smiled tenderly at her. "Hi," he replied. "My name's Mitch."

"I think I'm much better," she managed to say. "What happens now?"

"What happens now," he said as he squeezed her hand, "is that I'll never leave you for as long as I live. That is if you'll have me."

"I hoped you'd say that," she replied as she closed her eyes again and drifted back off to sleep.

Denise slept fitfully. She woke with a start many times during the night but as morning approached she finally slept more peacefully. Sleep or lack of it was not her primary focus at the moment. She was anxious to see her sons, her beautiful boys, so much alike and yet so different.

She gave herself the luxury of lying in bed for a few minutes before getting out. She could not wait to look at Sunshine, to see what had happened to the place while she had been away. She would have Michael home with her soon—where ever her home might now be.

She knew how she would get him released. She would give herself a few days to spend with her boys, to get her brain functioning properly again and then she would leave Sunshine. She would then make her move to be reunited with her husband.

She walked around the house, looking at the mess that was in every room. She thought it was the most marvellous sight she had seen. There was the daily carnage of having a house full of children. She briefly wondered if she and Michael might have more children.

When she looked in Sarina's room, her heart was devastated, but then she saw the clothes, shoes and toys that Hope and Lizzie owned and knew she would have to harden her heart for a while longer until Michael returned. Then they could mourn her together.

The prayer room was also on her list of priorities. She stayed there for a few minutes. She stared at the blind statue remembering all the secrets it held. She would have to talk to Michael about what they should do with what remained of its treasure. It had been there too long. They might as well give it away to charity.

Denise also remembered the envelope she had found with the letter 'M' written on the outside. She had given it to Miriam. It could not have been very important as Miriam had chosen not to mention it ever again.

She kept away from the main bedroom that Alan and Miriam had shared for so many years. It was a room of secrets much like the prayer room. *The secrets of the Farradays*, she thought. Was there no end to them?

She walked outside. The dew was still on the grass. It glistened like diamonds. There was no sign of the carnage that had occurred the previous day. She wondered if she would ever be able to forget it. It had taken her a long time not to see Jack Smith's body with a hole through his forehead lying on the front lawn.

Now she would have to deal with the image of another man who had lain in almost the same spot with a hole through his forehead; as well as another with his throat cut. The dreadful, unmistakable sound of a neck being cracked and broken would remain with her forever.

She shrugged her shoulders and knew that what she and Mitch had done was justifiable. They would just have to live with it as best they could. Life was to be lived not to be bogged down with endless troubles.

Her thoughts turned to Mitch. She had only met him a few times over the years she had been married to Michael. She remembered the time when she and Michael had contrived to organise a meeting with his daughter, Francine. But fate had another idea and the meeting had not occurred.

She would never forget his stunned expression when he must have realised that it was his own daughter who was lying seemingly dead in front of him. His shock had to have been far worse than what she had experienced.

She remembered hearing the sound of the vehicle pulling up and the angry male voices which had alerted her to danger. When she saw those men with guns pointed at Mitch, she had no hesitation in shooting the man. She and Mitch had done what had to be done.

She would overcome all this evil. She looked around at the trees, hills and mountains that surrounded her. Sunshine had been good to her, but the time was coming when she would leave. She would give it a few days, and then she would pack up and shift out with her boys.

Sunshine wasn't in the pristine order she and Michael usually kept it. She looked around at the grass that was too long, the shrubs that needed pruning back and the flower gardens that were withered.

She wandered around and noticed that the peace lilies were dead. These were the lilies that had been a monument to Mia's mother whose body had lain for so many years buried under a shed. The shed had slipped into the creek that had raged with anger at that fateful time when so much had happened.

It was the day that Michael had been shot when he had almost given up his life for her. It was the day that she had shot Jack Smith. It was also the day when Alan Farraday had taken his own life when Michael had revealed to him that Mia was the child he had fathered by his own daughter, Mandy Lamont.

She put these memories aside. She noticed the black backpack that Mitch had hurled at the man she assumed was Maxie. She had no real idea of what had brought on the confrontation between the four men. She gathered it had to do with a ransom.

Denise picked up the backpack, glanced inside it and saw bundles of notes. She had no interest in the money. She picked it up and carried it and the Glock into her bedroom. She put them in the bottom of the wardrobe.

She had a bite to eat as she eagerly waited the arrival of her sons. She heard the vehicle before she saw it. Matt drove to the front of the house. Her sons got out. She could see that they had grown and were more handsome than ever. She could see Michael in both of them. She was already crying as she flew down the steps and gathered them into her arms.

They kissed and hugged. She told them how tall they had grown. They were almost as tall as she. They all laughed and cried together. She wished she could hold them forever, but growing boys were not all that keen on being kissed and hugged by their mother.

Once the initial reunion had over, it was clear that they had enough of touching and hugging. What else could she do but to make them tea and give them biscuits? It wasn't on the top list of a young boy's favourite diet but they could hardly disappoint their mother.

So they drank tea and ate biscuits while she encouraged them to tell her all that had happened to them. They were very guarded about what they told her especially when Rafe had almost been snatched by the men. They made no mention of knives. They were learning to protect their mother. She had lived through enough. She didn't need to know every bad detail.

Matt stood to one side while Denise, Gabe and Rafe got to know each other all over again. Matt and Denise always had a strong connection. Eventually the boys scampered to their room. This gave Denise the opportunity to ask if he still had the video and photographs that she had taken so long ago. He told her he did. As they were talking, Mark and Malcolm arrived.

Malcolm told them that Francine was improving and that Mitch remained with her. Mark said he intended taking the black SUV still locked in the shed back to his place where he could dismantle it. This was where he kept all his tools and machinery.

He had also dismantled the video camera that had been set up at the entrance to the property. The three brothers left with the promise that they would return soon. Denise settled down with her twin sons to enjoy her first full day of freedom

46

It was a day full of joy. They ate, drank tea and went for walks around the gardens. Matt had left Billy Bob with them. She told her sons that she had decided to close up Sunshine and live closer to Tewantin. They had mixed feelings about this. They loved Sunshine where they had the freedom to wander around the hills and play in the creek as their uncles had done.

But if they were closer to town they would not have to be reliant on buses or their relatives to pick them up after cricket practice.

When they asked when she intended leaving, she told them very soon. She did not want to risk any penetrating odours emanating in or around the house. Not that she thought this could happen because the cement seal was very firm.

She would leave her house of secrets tomorrow. She would leave behind all the lies, the memories of Alan Farraday's lust and the subsequent horror that had haunted them for so many years.

She would leave Sunshine as a place of silence where more dead now lay buried. Whether they rested in peace, she hoped not. They had taken her daughter. No one could forgive that. She knew she would never be able to bury her daughter, not now.

Matt returned later in the day. Rafe had decided they would have pizza for dinner as a celebration. His mother laughed and said she would enjoy this. Rafe went with Matt to buy pizzas for the evening meal.

First they went to check on Francine. Mia was busy cooking. She said that chicken soup would be ideal for Francine. Matt said he would buy some in Tewantin.

Gabe stayed with his mother. He watched her sitting out on the front veranda gazing out at the hills. Eventually she dozed off. He decided he wanted to be helpful and start packing up.

If there was any way he could ease the pain of what his mother had been through, then he would do it. He thought he would start with his father's clothing. It would be painful for his mother to have to do this. He knew she missed him so much.

Denise woke suddenly as she heard her son standing behind her. It was not like her to doze off. She looked out at the blossoming trees and shrub; there were so many. The grevilleas and bottle brush were superb. The butcher birds and crows were at high pitch. Denise thought she had never seen a more beautiful spectacle. Her heart was saddened knowing this may be her last day at Sunshine.

Gabe told his mother that he was going to take Billy Bob for a walk. She told him to have fun. She returned to her bedroom. She was feeling incredibly tired. When she considered all that had happened since she had arrived a scant twenty-four hours previously, it was no wonder. When she lay on her bed she fell asleep instantly.

She did not hear the man enter her room. Her sleep was so sound. Her first indication of the attack was when strong arms held her down on the bed and her mouth was forced open. The man straddled her, holding her body firmly by his legs so that she could not move.

She tried to scream but he was already pouring the bottle of tablets into her mouth. He clamped her mouth shut with his big hands so that she had no option but to swallow. She fought him, trying to push him off. She tried to splutter, to push the tablets out of her mouth. But he held her mouth firmly shut.

She could taste the bitterness of the tablets. She looked into his eyes while trying to kick upwards with her legs. He just laughed at her feeble attempt to free herself. A million thoughts were passing through her mind. She could feel the effects of the tablets beginning to work. How long would it take? Her limbs were becoming languid, her brain foggy.

She tried to maintain eye contact with the man as she became drowsier. She had a faint hope that maybe if she showed enough hate in her gaze, it might be enough to drive him away. Her thoughts were beginning to slow.

She saw her beloved daughter waving to her, blowing kisses as she went off to school in her uniform. She saw her wonderful sons, so much alike, growing tall and strong and so handsome. Her last thought was of Michael. She saw his face, she kissed him. She lay with him under the stars. She felt his tender love making. She smiled as her heart stopped and her brain went to its final sleep.

Before he left, the man waited for the expected phone call. He left the hand piece dangle down beside the body of Denise.

Matt and Rafe collected pizza and the soup that Mia had requested. They stopped at Francine's home and stayed chatting before heading back to Sunshine. Rafe was anxious to return home to his mother. As they were returning, they saw Gabe and Billy Bob walking back towards the house.

"Pizza smells good," Gabe commented. "I bet mum will enjoy this. It's gotta be better than what she's had recently."

They walked into the house together with Billy Bob trailing behind. As soon as the dog entered the house, it started barking. Matt told him to be quiet. The dog pushed past them and ran down the hallway towards the bedroom. He kept barking.

No one cared any longer if the dog came into the house. They were leaving soon so what harm could it do.

They had bought enough pizza for the entire Farraday family, just in case they all turned up. None of them would go hungry. All they had to do was to use the microwave, and hay presto, hot pizza.

For the twins, this night that they were looking forward to was a bit like saying goodbye to their old life and a step into a new life. They had their mother back and she had told them that soon she would also have their father back with them.

Sarina was gone but the rest of them would have to live on and make the best of what they had. They needed some pretence at normality. Maybe someday it would all be normal again.

"I'll go and get mum," Rafe said. "She must be still asleep." He walked down the hallway. Billy Bob was still growling. "Shut up, Billy Bob. You're nothing but a rowdy nuisance."

Rafe walked into the room. His mother remained asleep. He thought that she must be really exhausted. It was not like her to have two sleeps in one day especially this late.

"Mum, come on, wake up. It's time for pizza." He approached his mother. She lay so still. He stood and watched her for a few moments. He was amazed that she could stay asleep with all the noise that Billy Bob was making. She still did not move, so he touched her on the arm. Again there was no movement. He became frightened. He didn't think it was possible for anyone to sleep so soundly and not move. Something was not right.

He left her and returned to where Matt and Gabe were unloading the pizzas. Matt glanced at him as he entered the kitchen. Rafe was white and trembling.

"What's the matter, Rafe?"

"It's mum. She's not right," he answered.

"I'll go get her," Gabe replied, heading back down the hallway.

"No, you'd better not. I think Matt better go and see her."

Gabe stared at his brother. "What are you talking about?" Rafe shook his head and stared back at his twin.

Matt was already down the hallway and had burst into the bedroom. He took one look at her, touched her and knew immediately she was dead. He collapsed back onto the bedroom chair that stood close to the bed. The boys were already at the door. He looked over at them. He was beyond words. They came into the room together.

"She's dead," he managed to gasp.

They stood and gaped at him.

Gabe started screaming, "No, she can't be dead. She's just asleep. We've got to do CPR. She's had a heart attack. Get her on the floor, quick."

Matt could do nothing more than stare at his nephew as he dragged his mother off the bed and spread her out on the floor. He started pumping her chest.

Gabe tried to remember what he had learned in the first-aid course he had attended. His father had made him learn the basics of CPR when he had taken them surfing.

"Call an ambulance. Call 000," he screamed at Rafe. "Come on, Matt, help me."

Denise lay still and silent while they tried to breathe air into her lungs and pump her chest. They did not stop. Matt knew it was too late. Life had left his sister-in-law. They heard the sirens in the distance. Help was on its way. Gabe and Rafe kept going, trying to bring their mother back to life.

When the paramedics came to the door, the twins still did not stop. The men asked them to leave, but they refused. It wasn't until Matt told them to move away and let the paramedics do their job that the boys reluctantly left her side.

The men were on the floor beside her. They started examining her. They pulled her dress open to place a stethoscope on her chest

"They shouldn't be touching her like that," Gabe shouted. "Do something, Matt?"

Matt spoke evenly. "Come outside. We'll sit on the steps and wait." He took Gabe by the arm and led him outside. Rafe followed. They sat on the front steps. Billy Bob lay curled up beside them.

There were more sirens. The trio watched the police cars pull up in front of them. It was the wipers on the car swinging back and forth that alerted Matt to the rain. He realised that it was raining, not heavily but enough to wet the grass. He wondered why it often rained when bad or sad things happened.

Sergeant Andy Brown and another two police officers approached them. Andy Brown spoke to them but Matt could manage no more than a few words of explanation. The twins stared vacantly at the police officers. Matt had worked with these men not so long ago. He knew all of them. Andy Brown entered the house followed by the two police officers.

Andy was a quiet, observant man. He was pleased to have left the police station where there were a series of high level, important meetings taking place with his senior management.

He preferred doing active policing than being bogged down with endless managerial talk.

The scene that confronted him was sad and very final. The paramedics looked at him and shook their heads. They spoke a few words together. The empty Temazepam bottle was pointed out. There were also traces of white powder on her chin. He noticed the disarray of the room; the bags of clothes stacked in one corner.

The scene had been well and truly contaminated by the family's attempts at resuscitation. He saw the empty tablet bottle and the phone hanging idly beside the bed. He left it where it was for forensic testing. It appeared as though Denise Farraday had taken her own life. But with everything that had happened to this family, he was not taking anything for granted.

He and his officers were further examining the scene, when his own mobile phone rang. He listened disbelieving at the information that was being relayed to him.

He thought back to the person that he was now hearing about. He remembered the man's immeasurable grief. Now there was another death in the Farraday family. How did he tell two young lads that not only was their mother dead but their father as well?

Andy Brown was reasonably young for the substantial rise he had made in his career. He was good at his job and very dedicated. But the mystery of this family was puzzling.

It did not seem possible for one family to undergo so many tragedies. If they had been affiliated with criminal gangs or other organised crime, he could understand the deaths and disappearances. But all investigations proved that they were ordinary folk, going about their business, raising their families. There was no hint of criminality.

He would never believe that either Michael or Denise had anything to do with the disappearance and alleged murder of their daughter.

Now it was up to him to deliver the double whammy. Did he tell Matt that his brother was dead and let him tell the twins or did he do it himself? He knew what he wanted to do. He wanted to pass this task over to Matt; to escape this next horrendous piece of news.

They were still sitting on the front steps with the dog beside them. They weren't speaking, just staring out at the hills. The slight drizzle of rain continued. It was light and in any other place and time would have been refreshing. He walked up behind them, cleared his throat and then spoke.

"Matt, boys, I'm afraid I have more bad news for you."

Matt stood up and looked at the sergeant. The twins did not move. There surely could not be any news that could be worse than what they had witnessed. Matt was perplexed at the expression on the police officer's face.

"What's up?" he asked.

"I'm afraid I have to tell you that your brother Michael is dead. He was killed this afternoon in the yard at the jail." Andy Brown battled to get the words out without tearing up himself.

People reacted differently to both bad and good news. Matthew slumped down again onto the steps, grabbing hold of Billy Bob. He was gasping for breath.

"No," he said. "This cannot be true, not Mick. It can't be Mick. There must be some mistake."

The twins stared at Andy Brown. He was unsure if they had comprehended what he had just told them. Then Raphael blessed himself. He started murmuring words which only he knew. The sergeant assumed he was saying some sort of prayer.

Gabriel's reaction was quick and savage. He stood up, and belted the railing of the steps with both feet. He started swearing, words that surprised even the experienced police officers.

"I'm going to get the fucker who did this to my father if it takes me the rest of my life," the young lad shouted out. By this time, there were more police arriving. They stood in a group as Gabe pulled the flick knife out of his jeans pocket, and screamed at them again. "If I ever find out that any of you lot had anything to do with my father's death, I'll slit your throats while you sleep."

He kept the knife in his hand, as he kicked the railing one more time and then ran off, up through the tall gums, following the creek until he reached the hills and was able to climb to the top of the Big Rock.

He screamed out at the pain that was inside him. He cursed the hills and mountains that had once been his refuge. The rain was still slight but it was scarcely enough to wash the tears from his face as he fell to the ground in torment.

47

Francine improved slowly. She had more moments when she was awake for longer periods. Mitch stayed with her. He gave her water and chicken soup. Mia hovered around but it became apparent that she was more of a hindrance than a help. She waited for Matt to return.

Zaylee felt confident enough to leave Francine in Mitch's capable hands. Matthew had told them that the twins were celebrating their mother's return and that pizza would be on the menu if any of them felt up to it.

He emphasised how different the twins were now that their mother was home. They all said they would join Denise and her sons for pizza. Mia asked if she could go as well. Harry was becoming restless and needed to be taken outside where he could toddle around.

Mitch fed Francine again. She was slowly becoming stronger. He tried not to look at the burns and bruises that were around her ankles. He could not imagine what she had been through. His rage was barely under control as he wondered what else had been done to her.

The lump on the left temple area of her head was still large. The cold packs were slow to reduce the swelling. Francine also had a further lump on the back of her head which meant she was only comfortable with her head on her right side. Her hand was also elevated on several pillows. The pain was gradually subsiding.

"What do you remember about what happened?" He gently asked as she became further alert.

"I remember that I went looking for you after I returned from Brad's funeral. I couldn't find you so I came back here," she said, indicating her own home.

"I wasn't angry with you this time," she smiled at him. "I just wanted to be with you. I was so lonely. I remember driving home, walking through the door then being grabbed from behind. I remember my face being pressed into the cold tiles, then being tied up and being thrown into the back of a vehicle. I think I must have been knocked out for a time. I know in my heart that bad things happened to me after that but I don't remember. Except when I woke and you were here with me."

"You've done well. Don't try to remember any more. Go back to sleep. I'll be here when you wake up again," he said, touching her face.

"Thank you," Francine kept a grip on his hand while she fell back to sleep.

Mitch leaned back in his chair. His biggest regret was that the men had died so quickly. Unlike Francine, they had suffered very little. If there was any justice in this world, he hoped their souls would be trapped forever in the dark, damp tunnel under the iron bed.

Pizza and beer was what they all looked forward to as they drove to Sunshine. There was a sense of great relief. Francine was going to make it. Malcolm contacted Mark and asked if he felt up to returning to Sunshine to have dinner together with Denise and her boys. He replied he and Arlo would be there shortly.

But there was to be no celebration to welcome home their sister-in-law. Instead, the unbelievable scene of ambulance vehicles and police cars was what welcomed them. Matthew told them of the indescribable horror that had occurred.

Matt took Mia in his arms while they held Harry. He heard Mia say for the third time in her life.

"Other than Francine, Michael Farraday was the only person who ever cared about me when I was young."

The young toddler was a life saver for he still cried and squealed when he didn't get what he wanted. He still had to be cared for.

It was total disbelief. Their sister-in-law who had fought for them was lying dead inside the house. Their brother, Michael, who had always cared for them since they were young boys, was lying somewhere dead on a cold slab. He was the father that Alan Farraday could never be. He was the man they looked up to. He had been their role model. He was the best person any of them had ever known.

Grief was deep and cutting. It was mixed with anger, rage and soul ripping hurt. None of them believed that Denise would take her own life as the very important, senior police officer was trying to tell them.

They were told that the most likely scenario was that when Denise was notified that her husband had been killed with a shiv to the kidneys when he was involved in a melee at the jail, it was surmised that this was what pushed her over the edge.

Mitch was notified by Matt about what had happened. When he heard this he had to escape outside. It was one of the few times he left Francine's bedside. He remembered looking at the shiny porcelain tiles which she had described when they had thrown her down.

He shook and trembled at this most recent horror that had been described to him. In the cold, rational and analytical part of his mind, he wondered if there were more than three. If there was a fourth or a fifth person out there who was intent on harming his family.

He also wondered what had happened to the two million dollars—the two bags of one million dollars each.

His other concern was that the name of his daughter had died with Michael and Denise. Now he knew that his hope of finding her was fruitless. He would never find her. The pain in his spirit just got deeper. He stayed outside until the rapid beats of his heart had slowed down. Then he returned to Francine.

"Are you okay?" she asked as she saw the slight tremor of his hands.

"Sure," he replied. "As long as I have you, everything will always be okay."

"You'll always have me," she answered as she closed her eyes again.

Sam was with Miriam when the phone call came to tell them that their son and his wife were both dead. Sam took the call. He stumbled and fell to the floor when he heard this news. Michael, the man who should have been his son, was dead. Miriam rushed to pick him up, but he pushed her away.

"You better sit down, Miriam," he said, panting in pain as he held onto his hip.

"What is it? What's wrong, Sam?" she said as she fussed around him.

'Sit down, Miriam," he spoke more forcefully. He remained on the floor. Miriam grabbed a chair and sat down beside him. She could see he was in pain.

He swallowed and clasped his hands together. "It's Michael and Denise, they're both dead."

Miriam could do nothing more than gasp. Then her eyes rolled back in her head; she started to breathe rapidly before her head lolled over to the side and she slid off the chair onto the floor.

Hope and Lizzie were playing outside. They heard Sam calling out for help. They ran inside to see both their grandparents on the floor. They quickly ran to get their mother. Maryanne was in her bedroom. When she came out, she looked at her mother and Sam on the floor.

"Has something happened?" she asked, looking enquiringly at the two of them. Her mother was gasping for breath. The old doctor was trying to crawl over to Miriam.

"Mum," Hope yelled at her mother. "You have to call an ambulance. Grandma is sick. Look at her."

"She doesn't look well at all," Maryanne responded. "You had better call the ambulance, Hope. I think I'll go and lie down." Hope watched in dismay as her mother walked away. She knew she would remember her mother's action all her life.

Lizzie was crying and trying to put a pillow under her grandmother's head. "Mum, come back here, please help us," the little girl called out, desperately watching as her mother strolled back to her bedroom. She knew her mother was sick, but what sort of sickness could cause her mother to be so unfeeling?

Hope ran to the phone and dialled 000. She stammered out what had happened. She told the operator that her grandparents were both lying on the floor. The operator asked if they were both breathing. She told them her grandfather was but she didn't know about her grandmother. She also said that her grandfather could not get up off the floor. The operator told Hope to keep her grandparents as comfortable as possible and that help would arrive soon.

The two girls stayed with their grandparents. Sam groaned and held his leg. Their grandmother was still breathing, but her eyes were staring straight ahead; she was not blinking. Miriam did not speak. The side of her face drooped down and fluid escaped out the side of her mouth. The girls were terrified.

When the paramedics arrived they found the two girls crying but still doing their best to comfort their grandparents. As the paramedics loaded Sam and Miriam into the ambulances, they asked if they had anyone to care for them. Hope looked embarrassed and told the man that her mother was lying down in her bedroom.

The man went to find Maryanne. Just as her daughter had said, Maryanne was lying on her bed, looking out at the gardens and listening to music. When he asked if she was okay, Maryanne said that of course she was, why wouldn't she be?

The paramedic then phoned the police and explained the situation. The police were aware of the latest in the Farraday family saga of tragedies. They collected the two girls and took them to their family at Sunshine. Maryanne was collected by another ambulance and carted off to the nearest psychiatric unit.

Later that evening, Gabriel returned back to his home. He was wet and dirty and carrying a metal fence post. He did not stop to change. He did not speak to his uncles or the police officers who were still present. Instead he went into the prayer room where his twin brother, Raphael, was sitting. Rafe was alone and seemed to be praying.

Gabe ignored his brother. Instead he lifted the fence post and started smashing the smallest statues and icons that his grandmother had always kept there. The sound of breaking pottery, glass and picture frames smashing onto the floor was heard throughout the house. Gabe had started with the small stuff and was working his way around the room.

"Useless, hopeless, bloody things," he said as he continued his rampage.

Rafe was initially stunned by his brother's outburst. When he saw the carnage, he jumped out of his chair and ran at Gabe, trying to grab the fence post off him.

"Put it down, Gabe. You'll ruin everything."

Gabe threw his brother off. He had reached the blind statue. The one he had always hated.

"You are the ugliest of the lot. You never open your eyes. You've never been able to see what's happening here. You let her die. You let them both die." He lifted the metal fence post into the air high above him and was about to strike when Rafe tacked him to the floor.

The brothers started wrestling, landing punches and kicks. They had never before physically fought between themselves. Sergeant Andy Brown was the first to respond to the melee that was going on around them. He hauled Gabe off Rafe and pulled the iron post away.

"Cut it out," he shouted to them. "Have some respect. Your parents are both dead. Do you think they'd want you fighting like this? Wake up to yourselves."

As Mark and Mal entered the room, the sergeant told them to get the twins out of the house. As the twins were taken out of the room, the blind statue remained upright on the wooden stand. There were no eyes that could hint at the remains of the treasure that lay beneath it. The statue remained as cold and emotionless as it ever had. Mark marched the boys out of the house and along with Arlo, took them back to his home.

In the ensuing days all that could be done for Sam Calhoun was done but he did not survive the fracture to his neck of femur. He was too old and frail. Miriam hung on, drifting in and out of consciousness. She had suffered a massive stroke.

She was paralysed down her left side, her power of speech was gone and parts of her memory were missing. She would never again be able to reveal the secrets and lies that she had held in her heart. Her silence was sealed.

48

It was time for another goodbye. Michael and Denise's bodies had been released for burial. Their time together had not been long enough. They had vowed to remain together till the end of time. Who would know that this time together would be cut so brutally short? All the plans and dreams they had for their future would have to be played out in the afterlife.

Their children's lives were already irrevocably changed. Gabe was filled with rage, anger, and hate. Rafe had turned to spiritual redemption. Their bond remained strong in spite of their brawl. The loss of both their parents had set them both on different paths for the future.

Sarina was gone. She would remain a sad and tragic figure who did not deserve the fate that had been awarded her. Her family would grieve for her forever.

The service for the celebration of their lives was difficult for all concerned. The brothers again had to find some words that would carry them into eternity. In the end they chose a reading from 1 Corinthians 13: 4-7.

It was usually said at weddings, but the brothers thought it most apt for Denise and Michael. It stood for everything they had believed in. It was read by Matthew. He was understandably emotional as he read out the words,

"Love is patient and kind.
Love is not jealous or boastful.
It is not arrogant or rude;
It does not insist on its own way
It is not irritable or resentful.
It does not rejoice at wrong, but
Rejoices in the right.
Love bears all things, believes all things,
Hopes all things, endures all things".

Denise and Michael were interred on a day of wonderful sunshine when the weather was warm and the breezes gently blew through the paper barks beside the Tewantin cemetery.

They were laid to rest side by side as they had lived side by side during the ten years they had spent together during life. They would now be together forever.

People came from the most unusual walks of life. Police colleagues from when Denise had been Detective Denise Davidson attended. There were people from schools, sporting clubs, the building trades, maintenance workers and charity groups.

There were people from various church groups, patrons from hotels, restaurants and clubs. There were men and women whose lives had fallen on the wrong side of the law who had been jailed at the times when Michael and Denise had been incarcerated.

The saddest group of all were the single mothers with small children and the poorer people of society who had been given a chance of a better life by Denise and Michael. They had been given housing, food and work where it was available. These were the people who were the most vulnerable in the affluent society they had lived in.

They were the people that Michael Farraday vowed to help with the proceeds of his father's crimes. These people did not for one moment believe that he was a child killer. It had become common folk law that he had pleaded guilty so that his wife would be released to care for their sons.

There was a strong contingent of police present. Matthew's former colleagues gathered together in support. Sergeant Andy Brown had many questions regarding the deaths of Denise and Michael.

But the coroner had found no suspicious circumstances regarding Denise Farraday's demise. It was deemed that Michael Farraday had been murdered by prison inmates who remained unknown. Nobody liked a child killer particularly when it was the man's daughter.

The gap they left in the family's lives was enormous. It was as if, for a short period, that time stood still for them all. There was little incentive left to get out of bed each morning.

But the demands of everyday life could not be shelved for long. The grief and disbelief remained, but life had to continue. Very slowly, their lives resumed.

Decisions had to be made. Sunshine was closed up. A gardening and maintenance service was contracted to ensure the grounds and buildings were kept tidy and in good repair. The entrance to the property was locked.

No family members wanted to return there to live. They had taken everything they needed. Gabe and Rafe were technically orphans. But the courts deemed that they could remain in the care of their uncle Matthew, as were Hope, Lizzie and Harry Smythe pending the return of their mother when she was well enough to care for them.

Matthew assured the courts that he had ample funds to care for the children properly. He also said that he lived with his girlfriend, Mia Lamont, who was already acting in the role of mother to the children.

He explained that he had purchased another home with sufficient bedrooms to house his new found family. The home was inspected and deemed suitable. It was also close to where his brother Mitchell lived with his fiancée, Francine Hamilton. The authorities were eventually satisfied the arrangements in place were adequate for the proper care of the Farraday twins and the Smythe siblings.

The last will and testament was read. The bulk of the vast estate was left to their three children and Michael's siblings. The body of Sarina Farraday had never been located. It would be years yet before she could be declared deceased.

Michael's brothers had been appointed executors of the will. Dax Webster was also handsomely rewarded for his services. He was left with instructions that he was to continue to give advice with the handling of the estate as he had during the lifetime of Denise and Michael.

There were strict instructions that the legacy the deceased couple had left of providing affordable housing for lower income families was not to be revoked. Dax remained straight faced when this section of the will was read out.

He had always wanted Michael to invest in the luxury market but this was always refused. He had a clear memory of the time when Denise had pulled her then boyfriend off him, when he suggested they get involved with luxury accommodation. Michael had not been the sort of man who would be crossed.

Dax wondered how malleable his brothers would be to suggestion. There were great opportunities and a lot of money to be made. But one look at big Mitchell Farraday with his quiet demeanour and bulging muscles sitting silently as the will was being read was enough to convince him to keep his mouth shut.

There was also the question of what to do with Miriam's Place. They had a small service for Sam Calhoun and cremated his body. His ashes were left to be buried with Miriam when the time came.

Miriam recovered sufficiently to be transferred to the aged care facility at Cooroy. It was the place where she had said she would be happy to end her days. She loved the big trees, the numerous birds and the spectacular gardens that were to be enjoyed. Miriam never spoke another word but she did recognise her children.

She tried to smile and speak when they visited. She took delight in her children and grandchildren. It was only when Matt and Mia visited together that she became disturbed. It was then that she desperately tried to speak. To put voice to her words seemed to mean so much to her. This was a mystery to them both. When they visited separately she showed no such agitation.

The family decided to keep Miriam's Place as it was. It was still the show piece that Sam Calhoun's first wife had decorated. It was filled with priceless and tasteful artwork of all types. There was a first-class security system put into place.

It was Zaylee Lang who was the driving force in keeping the place from being sold. She suggested it be used for local charity groups. Both the gardens and home were spectacular. It would be a great venue for fund raising for various charities.

The same property manager who looked after the Smythe property was appointed to look after Miriam's Place. He was given carte blanche to use what other labour was required.

It was hoped that Maryanne would be home soon to care for her family. It was understood that she would need regular mental health assistance to ensure her stability continued.

Mitch waited anxiously as Francine gradually regained her health but it was her psyche that was most damaged. She could never recall what had happened to her during the time she had been kidnapped.

The missing finger was her greatest torment. She had always been a person who took pride in her appearance. Mitch was never sure what he was supposed to do with the finger and wedding ring that had turned up in the letter box of Sunshine.

He never knew what had happened to Sarina's finger. It would have been something to bury with her parents, some mark of recognition that she had existed; some comfort for her brothers.

He had kept Francine's finger in the freezer at Sunshine. He collected it before the place was closed up. In the end he buried it in the rose garden at the home he shared with Francine. He kept the ring hidden with his few belongings.

His resignation from his position with the military was regrettable but understandable. He had served his country well. His efforts were well recognized. He had a bunch of medals to prove his valour.

He now had two jobs. One was to love Francine and the other was to help his siblings sort out the massive task of following the instructions left by Michael and Denise regarding their estate.

The cottage at Sandringham Creek bothered Mitch. He spoke to Dax and left instructions to find out as much as he could about ownership. He was surprised when the deeds were quickly located.

The property had belonged to Alan Farraday so, in the event of his passing, it had subsequently been left to Miriam. Miriam's power of attorney was now her surviving sons.

He told Francine he needed to go away on business. She was upset at his leaving, but knew eventually he could not remain solely with her forever. She told him she would be fine. She would get Val Richards to stay with her. His trip north this time was more leisurely.

Now that he knew the family owned the cottage, he had no qualms about entering the empty house. The outside was unchanged but as he entered the house, he found it had been stripped bare, nothing remained.

He went out the back to the overgrown shed. He could see that the vines and weeds had been pulled aside. Again he was not surprised to find all the weapons and drugs were gone.

This made his decision easy. It was a home without any personality. It was full of bad karma. When he returned, he asked Dax to get rid of it; to give it away if he had to.

When the brothers met for discussions over the handling of the estate, the question always arose about what had happened to the two million dollars. Before they packed up, they had searched the home at Sunshine carefully for the second million. No one could remember exactly what had happened on that fateful day. Mitch retold how he had thrown the backpack at the man in charge. After that he had no idea what had happened to it.

He assumed Denise had picked it up along with her Glock but neither was ever found. He did not state the obvious to his brothers but he was concerned that there was another person out there who had escaped with the money and the Glock.

The first million had to be somewhere. Someone had it or else it was languishing in banks. They had endless discussions about the disappearance. None of them was hell bent on its recovery. It felt like blood money. What they did want to know was what had happened to it? It couldn't be spent by dead men.

The mystery of the weapons and drugs in the hollow log was kept between Matt and Mitch. Mark and Malcolm had enough to endure with having lost so much. It was one issue that they did not have to concern themselves about.

They decided to leave the contents of the box-shed alone. How the log remained preserved they did now know? Whatever their father had used to keep it intact was a mystery. There was no deterioration. There were no white ants or rot or rust causing destruction.

It was further indication of just how intelligent their father had been. He had been a skilled and clever man. The biggest pity was that he had few saving graces and little love for the children he had fathered by Miriam.

Zaylee Lang was badly affected by the deaths of Michael and Denise. She had scarcely known them but the impact of their deaths was far reaching. She would watch Malcolm sit and stare vacantly out any window he sat beside. She could almost read his mind.

She often saw him with tears in his eyes but he would quickly look away and pretend to focus on whatever was outside the window. He repeated the story of how Michael went to jail for him years ago. The loss of Lucia was stronger than ever. He was often awake at night watching television or just sitting in the lounge. His flashing smile was seldom seen.

The need for family was strong in her. She frequently phoned her own parents and visited when she could. She and Malcolm had not discussed children. It was too soon for him to be thinking about more children. His missing daughter was too fresh in his mind. Besides, she had her career and much more to achieve before she could think of having children. She spent every spare moment of her time on the internet looking up various sites. One day he asked her what she was doing. She replied that she was trying to locate her birth parents.

He looked at her in surprise until she explained that she had been adopted at birth. The only thing she knew was that her parents had lived in the local area and that it was proving almost impossible to gain any further information about her parentage. Malcolm was stunned by this revelation.

The Farradays had issues that were ongoing. There was still the case pending regarding the scuffle they had with the police when Michael had been arrested and jailed.

The brothers could care less about any sentencing that might be handed down. There was nothing that could come near to what they had all already lived through.

It was a long and exhausting bus trip to Sydney. Maria and Rina had a stop-over in Brisbane. Maria asked when the next bus was leaving. The man behind the counter asked in what direction. Maria had answered south. He then told her there was a bus leaving for Sydney in thirty minutes. She bought two tickets.

She hustled Rina along to await the next bus. Maria was feeling very uncomfortable. The baby monster inside her was extremely active.

When the call for departure was announced, Maria handed over a small case, but kept the backpack and her own hand bag with her. Rina was becoming sleepy. A lot had happened this day.

As she lay with her head against the window, Rina wondered what had happened to Francine. She had loved Francine, just like she loved her mother, father, her brothers and Maria. But Maria was now a bundle of nerves. She was also very angry.

Rina knew it had to be the monsters that were worrying her. They had taken Francine. Even though the monster had picked her wooden circle up off the floor, she prayed to it that Francine would be safe.

The bus was soon in darkness. There were few lights to be seen outside. Maria sat nervously beside Rina. The little girl noticed how often Maria clutched her stomach, saw how she could hardly sit straight in her seat, how she could not sleep. Rina also saw Maria's belly move.

They finally arrived. The trip had been exhausting. Maria booked them into a hotel. They both needed proper rest. The little girl followed Maria through the hotel lobby and up the lifts that took them to a room that overlooked the city.

Rina looked out at the city. It was so huge that she could not see the end of it. She had heard of Sydney. Her parents had talked about it. They had even been there. She used to listen to them talk about it and about other great cities they visited.

She wondered again where they were. Why they had never come for her? Maria had told her she didn't know anything about her parents but was sure they loved her. But now she was a different girl and her name was now Rina. Sarina was gone and Rina had taken her place. Maria again told her that she was now her mother.

Rina could not understand how Maria could now be her mother. She didn't know how adult people could change so quickly. She couldn't imagine how you could have one mother and father not long ago and then have another mother so soon afterwards.

The room they stayed in was very nice, much nicer than the room where she had spent such a long time under the bed. Her hand also felt better. Maria told her they would leave the bandage on until they could find a better place to live.

The young girl enjoyed a wonderful sleep. She thought the bed was the most beautiful bed she had ever seen. She asked

Maria if there were only beds like it in Sydney or did other places have such lovely beds as well.

Maria reminded her again that she now had to call her mother but then added that there were lots of lovely beds in the world and when they found a nice place to stay she would buy her one. Rina told her mother that if she did buy her a bed to make sure there was enough room underneath it in case she had to hide again from the monsters.

The following day Maria left Rina in the room by herself and said not to let anyone in. Her new mother told her that they had to find another place to live. Mother did not mention the bulge in her belly but Rina knew she was very worried that the baby monster would soon be coming out.

Her new mother came home later that day and said she had found somewhere safe for them to live. Rina could not wait to see it. The next morning they left in a taxi to travel to their new home.

It was a long trip. She saw many amazing buildings that reached up to the sky. She was alarmed when they suddenly went under the ground. The taxi driver exclaimed that they were in a tunnel. Her mother seemed equally as awed as Rina.

They finally arrived in a quiet street where Rina could hear children playing. She looked over and saw a school. Then the taxi pulled up in front of a single-story, brick house. It looked very nice with tidy gardens. The driver helped Maria out as she was very awkward with the big bulge in her belly. He then carried their few belongings to the front door.

After being in the granny flat for so long, Rina thought it was a wonderful house with lovely furniture in all the rooms. She quickly ran from room to room. Which one would be her room? She looked at all the beds.

There was one bed that stood high off the floor. She asked her mother if this could be her room. Mother didn't seem very interested so Rina put her few belongings in the room. This would be her bed. There was plenty of room underneath.

Mother seemed very uneasy. She kept clutching her stomach. She told Rina there was a shop at the corner where they could purchase everything they would need. Together they walked the short distance to the shop where mother bought food and milk. Mother told the shopkeeper they lived close by.

Mother then said they had to hurry home. She told Rina that she had to learn to be an invisible person and never talk to people if she could help it. Rina was more confused than ever. Not only did she have a new name and a new mother as well as being a different girl from Sarina. Now she had to be an invisible person.

While mother put their groceries away, Rina went to her room and thought about all that she was now supposed to be. Mother said the monsters were probably angrier than ever. They had to take every precaution that they were never found.

Mother spent the afternoon lying on her bed. Every now and then she would cry out. Rina went to her several times and asked what was wrong. Mother told her to go away.

The night came and Rina could still hear mother groaning and crying out. The groaning got louder. Rina could not sleep. Not even when she lay on her new bed could she sleep because of the noise coming from mother's room.

Rina went back to see her mother. Mother was lying on top of the bed, moaning and crying. She also had her legs wide open which was a shocking site for Rina. Mother was breathing short, sharp breaths and sweat was pouring off her head.

Rina could not take her eyes off what was happening between mother's legs. She now understood that the baby monster was coming out. She timidly came into the room. Mother did not seem to mind any more. She wasn't angry and didn't tell her to go back to her bed.

It was very frightening. Mother groaned and screamed again and Rina saw the head of a baby come out of mother's body. She was waiting to see what a monster baby looked like. Mother pushed and screamed again and the baby slipped out. Rina was again amazed. It was just a little thing much the same size as Harry had been when he was born.

Mother lay back on her pillows. She looked exhausted and started shaking. Rina kept looking at the baby. It was covered in what looked like slime and blood. She didn't know what to do. It looked so naked. Rina looked around and saw a towel lying on the bed beside mother. She placed it over the baby.

Mother started to moan and groan again as more bloody stuff came out of her. Rina thought it was another baby but it looked different. It too was very bloody and slimy.

"What's happening, Mother?" Rina asked, her voice high pitched in alarm. She was very frightened. There was so much blood. The baby that had come out of mother was starting to make little crying noises.

"Get a knife, Rina. Run to the kitchen and get a knife." Mother was again sounding frantic.

Rina did as she was asked. But she was alarmed all the same. She could not imagine what mother wanted a knife for. She thought of her finger that had been cut off by a knife and had a dreadful feeling that mother might have something similar planned for the little monster.

She returned with a serrated-edged knife in her hands. "What do you want the knife for, Mother? What are you going to do with it?"

"For heaven's sake, cut it off, Rina and hurry up." Mother was still shaking.

"Cut what off?" the little girl asked, thinking she wanted her to cut the baby up.

"The monster, that's what. Cut the cord that's holding it together." Mother pointed to a bloody thick rope that was attached to both the baby and the other bloody thing that had come out of her.

Rina didn't think she could do this. She started shaking her head in horror.

"You had your bloody finger cut off. You know what that's like so just cut it," Mother was angry, shouting at her.

So Rina got the knife and sawed away at the bloody cord. It wasn't easy because it was so slippery. Finally, the knife slipped through. There was more blood. Rina again did not know what to do.

There was blood now coming from the baby. She had to stop it. She pulled the rubber band that held her long hair in a ponytail and then twisted it around the part of the cord that was attached to the baby.

The blood stopped oozing out. There was blood all over her shaking hands. The little girl again did not know what to do. Mother was just lying there staring up at the ceiling. Her shaking was not as severe. Finally, Rina rolled the baby onto the towel and wrapped it up just like she had when she had been given a baby doll for Christmas.

Rina was beginning to think more clearly now. She remembered about baby Harry and she also remembered playing with her baby doll. What she had to do now was to keep the baby wrapped up and put it in a cot the same as baby Harry. She looked around mother's room but there was no cot.

She carefully put the baby on the floor. Then she ran back into the kitchen and found the rubbish bin. It was square in shape and quite deep. She emptied out the plastic bags and paper towels that mother had put there when they had come home from shopping.

She returned to mother's room with the bin. The baby lay very quiet. Rina knew what it was like to sleep on hard floors. It had been all right for her but she was not a baby. The baby would need something more to protect it.

She ran back into her room and got more towels from the bathroom. She folded them up, then placed the rubbish bin on its side, pushed the towels as flat as she could into the bin and then gently laid the baby inside it.

She put another towel over the baby to keep it warm. This house in Sydney was much colder than the room she had been in when she had to lie under the bed. The baby was very quiet and seemed to be sleeping.

She returned to mother who was now moving around in the bed. "Get the plastic bags from our shopping trip, Rina, and put this bloody mess into them. Then wrap the plastic bags in newspaper and throw the lot in the bin outside. Can you do that for me?"

Rina did as mother asked. When she had it all wrapped up she went to go out to the rubbish bin outside, but the door was locked. She hurried back to mother who was now out of bed. Mother had walked over to the baby sleeping in the bin on the floor.

Mother had her hand over the baby's mouth.

"What are you doing, Mother?" the little girl asked. It didn't seem right that mother should have covered the baby's mouth.

Mother quickly pulled her hand back and sat back heavily on the floor. The baby moved but did not cry out.

"You take it into your room, Rina. I don't want it here with me." Mother pushed herself away from the baby in the bin.

"But it's your baby, Mother. You should look after it."

"No, Rina. It's not. It can be your baby if you want it. Do you want it? Otherwise it will have to go out." Mother was very serious.

Rina was not sure what mother meant by saying the baby would have to go out. She surely didn't mean out in the bin. No, Rina didn't think this was possible. Mother had told her that she had pulled her out of a big metal bin when she had been called Sarina.

She looked at mother again and saw that she was crying. Mother must be very tired and sick.

"I'll take the baby, Mother. It can live with me in my room." Rina carefully picked the bin up, kept it on its side and dragged the baby into her room. She placed it beside the bed. The baby stayed asleep. She returned to mother.

"I'll clean up your bed first and then you should have a good rest, Mother. But first I'll make you some tea." Rina knew how to boil a kettle and make tea. Her other mother, her real mother had taught her how to do this. She bought the hot tea with milk and sugar back to mother.

Then the little girl pulled the bloody sheets off the bed and rolled them up before putting them in the laundry. The blood had gone through onto the mattress. Rina couldn't do anything about this so she put extra towels that she found in the laundry cupboard on the bed and dragged a clean sheet over them.

Mother was covered in blood as well. Thankfully, she seemed to have more strength since she had drunk the tea. She stood up unsteadily and managed to walk to the shower. Rina heard the water running. She looked in at mother several times. She was just standing there staring at the wall in front of her while the water poured over her.

Rina found some clean clothes for mother and helped her put them on. Then mother hopped back in the bed and lay there quietly. Rina stayed with her until she thought she had gone to sleep. Then she returned to her own room and looked again at the baby. It was still sleeping.

50

It didn't seem fair that the baby that mother had called a monster should sleep in a bin on the floor while she slept in a beautiful bed. So Rina dragged the duvet off the bed and lay down to sleep beside the baby. She felt very tired.

She was woken by a strange noise she thought was a cat. It took her a few moments to realise it was the baby. It wasn't a cry, more like mewing. Rina saw it was morning. She got up and pulled the baby out of the bin. It looked very dirty with dry blood and slime all over it.

She knew she should wash it just as she'd seen Harry being washed when he was an infant. But she was too small to wash it in the bath or the sink so she got some warm water which she poured into a saucepan.

She carefully wiped the baby with some paper towels that mother had bought at the shop. The baby again mewed. This was alarming. It wasn't so bad when it had cried properly before mother had put her hand over its mouth. She got half the blood off it before the mewing commenced again.

Rina desperately wanted the mewing to stop in case mother became angry again. She wrapped it up again in another towel. She rocked it back and forth as she sat back on the duvet. It eventually stopped its strange noise and went back to sleep.

The baby would have to be fed. She did not know how to do this. It was only mothers who could feed babies. They held them again their chest and the babies drank. She knew that much. Timidly she went into mother's room. Rina saw that mother was now awake.

"How are you, Mother?" she asked, wary of what mother would say when she had to tell her that the baby was hungry.

"I'm much better now that I've got rid of that little monster."

Rina was afraid of what mother's answer would be. "The baby is hungry, Mother. It needs feeding."

"You're its mother now, Rina. That's your job." Mother said as she very slowly got out of bed. She avoided looking at the little girl.

"How do I do that?" the child asked.

"If you're going to keep it, then you better go to the shop and get a baby bottle and some milk. I'll give you some money. The rest is up to you, Rina. You know I don't want to have anything to do with it. I don't even want to see it."

"Why don't you want to see it?" The little girl asked quietly knowing that mother might get angry again.

"Because it's a monster. It's just like the monsters that cut off your finger and threw you away, Rina. You still remember what happened when you were a different person, don't you?" Just as she thought, mother was becoming angry.

She wanted to say that it wasn't a monster, that it was just a little baby but thought better of it. Then mother started speaking again.

"You remember what it was like when the monster was born. You remember the pain, the blood, the mess. That was you, Rina. That was your baby being born. Make sure you don't forget it."

Rina was confused again. Mother was speaking as if she, Rina, was the person who had pushed the baby out from between her own legs. Mother was changing. She wasn't kind and nice like Maria had been. She seemed to be angry all the time.

Rina went to the shop and asked the man for a baby bottle and some milk. The man laughed and said, "Congratulations, I knew it wouldn't be long. Your mum was the size of a house."

He took her around the shelves as he picked out a baby bottle and some formula. He also said that you couldn't have enough nappies with a baby in the house. He loaded all these items into a bag. He asked how mum was doing. For a minute Rina was again confused thinking he was talking about her but then she realised that he meant mother.

""Not so good," the little girl replied.

"Did she have a hard time of it," the man asked.

"Yes, yes she did," she replied. The picture of the baby being born was fresh in her mind. It all looked very hard.

"It's not that easy having a baby," the man continued. "I've got three of my own. It can be a good time or a desperate time, depending how things go."

Rina thought of mother saying the baby was a monster. "It was a desperate time," she told him.

"Then you'll have to put Jude in the name somewhere, after Saint Jude. He's the patron saint of desperate cases. Doesn't matter if the baby's a boy or a girl? Jude won't see you wrong. I had to put Jude into one of mine. It helped things along. By the way, is it a boy or a girl?"

Rina hadn't thought about this. She tried to remember. Then she said quietly, "A boy."

"Well if you need anything more for that baby, little girl, you come straight back here and we'll fix you up. If I'm not here then the wife will be."

Rina trudged home with her parcels. They were quite heavy and bulky. She was weary by the time she returned. She was pleased to see mother had showered again and changed her clothes. Between them they had very few clothes. Mother was back lying on her bed.

She went immediately to check on the baby. He remained lying contentedly in the bin. His eyes were open and he was looking around. Rina waved to him and told him that she was going to give him his breakfast. She returned to the kitchen where she washed out the bottle. Her real mother had told her that you should always wash everything when you first bought it.

She tried to read how to mix up the formula. She could read some words but not the big ones. In the end she looked at the scoop in the tin. It had spoons on either end. She rationalised that a very little bottle would only need a little scoop, so she mixed it up with water and poured it into the bottle. She used warm water as she could always remember that her aunt Maryanne used to shake the milk over her arm to see if it was too hot or too cold.

The baby had its eyes open. She laid it on the duvet that she had slept on. She removed the towel that she had wrapped him it. She was dismayed to see that there were marks on the towel like the baby had opened its bowels.

She cleaned him up with another paper towel then tried to put the disposable nappy on him. It was a long time before she got it to stay on. Every time she thought she had the nappy on properly, it would fall off. She was becoming desperate until finally the nappy stayed on. The baby was so small the nappy came right up under its arms.

The baby began to murmur. She thought he was probably cold, so she quickly wrapped him in another towel. The towel supply was getting low.

As she held the baby in her arms with the bottle poised to put into his mouth, she spoke to it for the first time, "Hello, Jude. My name is Rina and I am your mother."

She put the teat into the baby's mouth. She thought babies were supposed to suck but Jude only lay there with his eyes open. He looked to be staring at her.

"You better hurry up," she said. "The milk will get cold."

Still the baby did not suck. Rina did not know what to do. She wanted to go to mother and ask her for advice. But she knew she could not do this. Mother would just get angry with her. Rina tried again to get Jude to suck but he couldn't.

Eventually, she got a spoon from the kitchen and spooned the milk into his mouth. She didn't know how much he swallowed but she kept trying until some of it was gone. The baby fell asleep.

She kept feeding Jude whenever he woke. He had stopped his mewing sounds and generally when he woke he just looked around. Rina thought it was funny that he never cried but she was pleased as well because she was sure the crying would just make mother angry.

The days went by and they settled into a routine. Rina stayed mostly in her bedroom with Jude. He still did not suck so she fed him off a spoon. She often went to the shop.

That was one thing that mother was good about. She did not mind giving Rina money as long as she kept Jude quiet and out of the way. The shopkeeper and his wife always helped the little girl out.

Rina asked about clothes for the baby. The woman showed her the baby section in the shop and helped her choose little clothes for the baby. When the shopkeepers asked about mother, Rina said that mother was still very tired and not well. The shopkeepers wondered why mother visited the shop to buy groceries but never anything for the baby.

One day mother came to her and told her that she had booked Rina into the school across the road. Rina was terrified. How would she be able to care for Jude if she was at school? Who would feed him? Mother said that he would just have to survive as best he could.

So Rina went to school. It was a much bigger school than the one she had gone to with her cousins. There were hundreds and hundreds of students. At first she was terribly lonely but then she remembered mother's words saying she had to be invisible, that she was now a different person. Rina thought of herself as being two people. The one she was before the monsters took her and the person she was now.

Her baby stayed in the bedroom while Rina went to school. She had a plan for Jude. She would get up very early before the sun rose, before she heard the pigeons and doves cooing outside and she would start to feed Jude.

He still only took his milk off a spoon, but now she was crushing up plain biscuits and mixing it with his formula. He seemed to like this and began to eat more. He still did not cry.

While she was at school, Rina worried about Jude. He had nothing to do but lay in the big box that she used for a cot. He had grown too big for the bin. In spite of the little toys she bought for him, he showed no interest except in staring out around the room. She had asked the man at the corner shop for one of his boxes. She told him she wanted it for her toys. He always asked how the little boy was coming on.

When school finished, Rina would run home and immediately start feeding the baby; she would feed him until she fell asleep at night. She still slept on the floor beside the box. Slowly he was beginning to grow and put on weight but he never cried or smiled.

Mother never asked about Jude. As far as she was concerned he was not there; he did not exist. Mother cooked a meal every night for herself and Rina. She would ask Rina about her day at school.

Rina went to great lengths to tell her all she had learned. She told mother that there were so many children there from so many different countries that she was already invisible. No one took the least notice of her.

Mother always emphasized that Rina had to be invisible, that she was a different person now, a mother. Rina started thinking that she must really be two people, the one she was now and the one she used to be. There were so many confused memories in her head.

51

Mrs Potter watched the television news late at night when Lucy was asleep. The older lady was fascinated by what had happened to the Farraday family. She saw grainy shots of Malcolm when he attended the funerals of Denise and Michael.

The funeral made the local news services. She was pleased to see Malcolm looked strained and gaunt. *What was it about these Farradays that was deserving of making news headlines? Serves him right, he should learn to take better care of his family.*

The time came to leave. Mrs Potter planned carefully. She was living in a rental house. She told neighbours and the real estate agent that her brother was extremely ill and she would be leaving the area to look after him.

She paid all her accounts. She left no forwarding address. She sold the car she had used to get to the Farraday home when she worked there. She only used disposable mobile phones. She closed her bank accounts. She covered her tracks.

Her brother told her he had a plan that would keep them comfortable for ever. He couldn't wait for her to arrive with Lucy.

Mrs Potter purchased two bus tickets to Sydney in the name of Mrs Potulski and her granddaughter Luce Potulski. They carried little baggage. Most of her personal belongings were disposed of. She had long ago destroyed the phone she had given to Lucia.

The girl cried quietly as she clutched onto her black teddy bear as she waited for the bus. Her dark hair hung down around her shoulders partially covering her face. She was crying because Mrs Potter had told her she could only take one of her teddy bears with her.

Lucy was devastated that she had to leave one behind. It was like dividing her heart into two pieces. In the end she chose the bear she had called Gabe. She left Rafe behind. She always wondered what Mrs Potter did with Rafe.

Lucy continued to ask Mrs Potter where her mother and father were. Previously, the older woman had dismissed her constant questions. It was as if the child's mind could not comprehend that her mother was dead. Mrs Potter said she had a big secret to tell her. She would tell Lucy the secret once more and then they would never again speak of it.

She again said that her father was a very bad man and had killed her mother. If he knew where Lucy was then he would probably hurt her as well.

Lucy did not want to believe this, no matter how often Mrs Potter told her. But then she again remembered the dark figure that had come into her room that night. She never thought it was her father. Now she couldn't be sure. She was very confused. She started crying.

""Don't cry, Lucy. You're safe with me. Haven't I taken care of you? I won't allow anyone to ever hurt you again." Mrs Potter wiped the girl's eyes and pulled her hair further around her face.

"I have another secret, Lucy. You're going to have another name. Your name is now Luce Potulski. You're no longer

Lucia or Lucy. Your first name is Luce." Mrs Potter watched the puzzlement on the child's face. "Say your name, say Luce Potulski."

The child's face trembled as she said, "Luce Potulski." The last name was hard to say, so Mrs Potter told her to say it often, to keep practicing.

Lucy said the name time after time while they waited for the bus.

"That's good, Luce. I have a new name too. My name is now Mrs Potulski and I'm now your grandmother. We're going to live in a big city with my brother, Mr Potulski, and he is going to be your grandfather. He's always said he would like a little girl of his own."

Lucia Farraday tried to work out all these changes in her young mind as she sat beside Mrs Potulski on the long bus trip to Sydney. Her head started to hurt as she tried to get all the names right. She had been Lucia Farraday for such a long time, then she was Lucy Potter and now she was Luce Potulski.

She hugged the teddy bear close to her and wiped her tears on its face. But there were times when she felt she would like to rip its head off. She often stuck her fingers into its soft fur when she thought of the father who never came for her.

Not even Gabe or Rafe had come looking for her. Of all of her cousins, she thought at least Gabe would have come busting through Mrs Potulski's door to take her home. He had often teased her, had called her Goldie locks and pulled her pig tails. But underneath it all, she knew that he really liked her.

Her tears started again when she tried to listen in to Sarina. But Sarina no longer spoke to her. She had not heard from her for ages. Everyone who she had loved had deserted her. She pressed her fingers harshly into her bear.

Whenever she made the mistake of calling her new grandmother Mrs Potter instead of grandmother she felt the older lady's fingers pinch into her upper arms. Sometimes she even had the skin on her arms bruised. The child soon realised that Luce Potulski had to learn very quickly about another way of life if she was going to avoid being pinched and bruised.

Luce remained very quiet beside her new grandmother on the long journey to a place called Sydney. She stared in awe at the endless number of buildings that she could see out the window of the bus. There were so many cars and people. Eventually the bus stopped. She stumbled down the steps of the bus behind her new grandmother.

There was a man who looked scruffy and old waiting for her. He was much, much older than her father had been. He was not nearly as handsome either. He had long, grey hair and a big stomach. He hugged Mrs Potulski and then got down on his knees to look at Luce.

Luce stared at him. The first thing she noticed were his dirty teeth. He also had a strange voice. It was high pitched. She thought he sounded like a woman. He laughed and smiled at her but she could not bring herself to smile back at him. He reminded her of one the cane toads that came out in the late afternoons where she used to live. She thought he looked bloated up and ugly.

He went to give her a hug but she stepped back from him. He again pulled her to him and put his arms around her. She wrinkled her nose up as she smelled him. The smell was repellent.

"What a beautiful girl you are, Luce. I'm glad that I'm now your grandfather. We're going to have lots of fun together."

The man who was now her grandfather gave her double hugs. Grandmother watched in delight.

Her new grandmother and grandfather chatted together as they drove along many streets. Luce did not like the place where they eventually pulled up. It looked like an old house made of brick with a red-tiled roof. It was double storied. There were tall trees out the front which stretched gloomily upwards so that the front of the house was difficult to see.

She was taken inside and shown to a room which her grandparents told her was to be her very own bedroom. Grandfather told her that if she was a good girl she would be able to have two bedrooms.

"Are you going to be a good girl, Luce?" he asked her. She just nodded her head. Her real father, the one that her new grandmother had told her was a very bad man, had always told her that she was the best girl in the whole world. It was the only concept that she knew. She was a good girl. She had always been good. She did not know how not to be good.

Luce spent much of the next few weeks in her room. Her grandparents only saw her at meal time. She was used to being by herself when she had been with Mrs Potter. She played with her teddy bear. She also played solitaire with the pack of cards that she had brought with her the night that grandmother had picked her up from the big house she had lived in.

One day her grandmother came to her while she was in her room and told her that she would be going to school in a few days. Luce was both frightened and excited. She was told that it was not the same school as the one she was used to. Luce hoped that her cousins would also be there. She had a new name but she was sure they would still know who she was.

Before she went to school, her grandparents called her into a downstairs room. It had nice furniture with soft, thick carpets. Luce thought it was a lovely room. She could not understand why her grandparents kept her upstairs in her own dull room.

They told her that she was to have two types of education; the one that she learned at school and another type of education that they would teach her. She had never heard of such a thing.

Before she was taken to her new school, grandfather said he was starting her other education. He asked her what her name was. She replied Luce Potulski. He seemed pleased with her answer. Then he told her that when she went to her big school or anywhere else she was to remember five things. Luce was quite sure she could do that.

"What five things?" she asked timidly as she stood before him.

"You have to remember this, that when you live with us, that there are rules. If you break the rules, Luce, then there are consequences."

He watched the expressions sweep across her face trying to fathom what he meant.

"These are the rules, Luce. One, you don't talk to anyone; two, you don't laugh; three, you don't touch; four, you don't eat; five, you must be perfect. You are not allowed to do any of these things without your grandparent's permission. Now repeat them after me."

Grandfather looked at her menacingly as she repeated the five rules after him.

"Now you say them by yourself, Luce," he demanded in his strange voice.

Luce tried to repeat the rules. She got mixed up. All she could remember for sure was that she must not do certain things unless she had permission. He made her repeat them time and time again until at long last she got them correct.

Luce was in turmoil. How could she go to school if she didn't talk or eat? She didn't care if she never laughed or touched anyone ever again. She didn't even care if she didn't eat. She did not know what perfect was. But she knew at school that she had to talk. The teachers always asked her questions.

Grandfather asked her if there was anything she wanted to know about going to school. She burst into tears and told him that she didn't know how she was not supposed to talk. Grandfather told her not to worry, that she was going to a school where many of the children did not talk because they were disabled. All she had to do was to pretend that she could not hear or speak.

She was again puzzled. "But I can hear and I can speak."

"We know you can, Luce. But if you pretend then you won't have to speak. When you come home from school, your grandparents will talk to you and I'll tell you when you can speak."

"No, that's not right. School isn't like that. You're supposed to talk. The teachers always ask what we did in the holidays and on weekends. You have to answer questions, read books out loud and even sing." Luce could not understand why grandfather was being so stupid.

"What did I just tell you, Luce? You have already broken the rules. Grandfather is already upset with you. Remember what I told you. If you break the rules there are consequences."

"What are consequences?" she asked in a weak, troubled voice.

"I'm going to teach you what consequences are," grandfather replied.

He then asked grandmother to take her upstairs to the happy bedroom and get the box.

Grandmother took her up the stairs to another room. There were no lights in the room as they entered. Grandmother turned on the bright lights. It was a strange room with a huge bed in the centre. Grandmother told her to get up on the bed. There were many pieces of strange equipment also in the room.

Grandmother put the box on a small table near the entrance of the room. Luce watched as grandfather opened up the box and pulled out a needle. Then he went and played with one of the strange pieces of equipment that was at the end of the bed.

"Sit down on the bed and take your shoes off." Luce was again terrified. She hurried to remove her shoes and socks. Grandfather started talking, not to grandmother who stood in the background. It seemed like he was talking to himself.

She sat on the bed with her feet out in front of her. Grandfather came over to her and took her left foot in his hand. She remembered looking at his dirty nails, when suddenly he picked her foot up and kissed it. This horrified her. He then rubbed her foot against him. She shuddered and tried to scramble backwards on the bed but he held her foot firmly in his hand.

Then he quickly got the needle and shoved it firmly up under her great toe nail. He pushed it right in and then held it there. The little girl was in shock.

"Now do you realise what consequences are, Luce. You must never break the rules," he repeated.

Luce screamed and screamed until finally he pulled the needle out. There was blood already trickling out from the front of her toe. Grandmother just stood and watched. Then grandfather put her great toe in his mouth and sucked and sucked on the blood that was pouring out of her foot. He kept talking to himself until her screaming stopped. Then he went back to the strange piece of equipment.

Finally, he spoke to grandmother, "We've made a good start. Take her back to her room."

Luce lay on her bed, crying and holding onto her toe, trying to stop the pain. She could not believe what had happened. It must have been someone else whose toe had been stabbed with the needle. It could not have been Lucia Farraday. Then she remembered that she was no longer Lucia Farraday. Since she had been Lucia, she had been another person called Lucy Potter and now she was Luce Potulski.

She grabbed her teddy bear and hugged it to her. She held it to her toe so that the pain would stop. But the pain did not stop. She threw the bear at the wall and screamed at it.

"I'm not calling you Gabe anymore. You don't care about me. From now on I'm calling you devil. You're now black devil. I hate you. You don't help me. You're just like my real father. You don't care about me. You never came to save me."

Luce got off her bed and kicked the bear again and threw it again at the opposite wall. She could not stop crying because the pain in her toe would not stop.

Finally, she lay on her bed and stared at black devil, lying on his side against the wall. Eventually when the pain was less, she limped out of her bed and picked up black devil. She went back to her bed and curled him into her arms and cried until she fell asleep.

So began Luce's double education plan.

During the day she went to a school for disabled children. It was very strange. A few days before she attended school, her grandparents placed a little object into her left ear. They explained that it was a device to help her hear. She dare not say again that she could hear everything.

Her grandparents told her she had to keep it in her ear, to practice keeping it there. It didn't hurt but it was a nuisance as sometimes it fell out. When this happened she put it straight back in again. It didn't stop her hearing and it did not help her hearing. Her grandparents told her it was there so that everyone would think she really was deaf.

So it stayed in her ear while she was at school. As soon as she was home she took it out. Luce didn't mind going to school. It was in some ways like her other school. There were mostly older children there. Some children could not walk; others could barely talk, while others had any number of difficulties.

Some of them spoke but it was often difficult to understand what they were saying. She listened to everything that was said by her teachers and by those students who spoke differently.

After a time she realised that some students just watched other people's lips when they were trying to understand what was being said. Luce thought this was very clever and decided she would learn how to do this.

Every time she wanted to say something she thought of what grandfather had done to her, so she did not speak. She heard everything that everyone said. She even began to understand the strange hand movements that some of the students made when they communicated to other students.

It was easy not to laugh. There was nothing much to laugh about in her life, although as she came to know the other students she realised that those who could not hear, had a laughter of their own. They often told jokes and even tried to make her laugh. But she knew better than to speak or laugh.

Grandfather's third rule was that she must not touch. This was a very easy rule to follow except when one day another little girl held hands with her as they waited to be picked up after school. The little girl reminded her of the friend she had known a long time ago, a girl called Sarina.

Grandfather was so angry when he saw the two girls holding hands. He took her straight to the happy bedroom. Grandmother went to get the box out again. The ritual was the same. Luce had to endure the unbearable piercing pain of another needle being shoved under her great toe nail, then watch as grandfather sucked on her toe and rubbed her foot up against him.

She screamed and screamed. Grandfather again played with the equipment in the room. Luce was still screaming when grandfather spoke to grandmother.

"That was better than last time. It's time we asked Uncle Lucas to visit."

The young child was traumatised. She hobbled off to school, never speaking, never laughing, never touching and only ate what grandmother packed for her. Her teachers asked grandmother what was wrong with Luce.

Grandmother spoke to the teachers each morning, while she held Luce tightly against her. Luce heard the teachers often talk about grandmother, saying what a wonderful lady she was and how sad it was that she had a disabled granddaughter.

When the teachers asked what was wrong with Luce's foot, Luce heard her grandmother say that she had an ingrown toe nail. Grandmother explained that as Luce was growing so quickly, her shoes became too tight which made her feet sore.

Luce was crying and screaming in her head that everything grandmother was saying was a lie. She wanted to shout out the truth but the memory of grandfather and his vicious needles prevented her.

She found salvation in the computers that were provided to all schools. Luce was an intelligent child although she did her best to pretend otherwise. She spent as much time as she could learning about computers. Luce had found an outlet for her miserable life.

One day grandfather told her that uncle Lucas would be visiting. He also spoke threateningly to her; he said she had to do whatever uncle asked. Luce just nodded her head. She could not remember any of her uncles being called Lucas when she had been Lucia Farraday. She was glad she had another uncle. She hoped that he might take her back to where she had lived before.

Uncle Lucas arrived. He took little notice of Luce until her grandparents took her to the happy bedroom. Then he became friendly, smiling and touching her. Luce did not feel safe with him in spite of his friendliness.

Uncle Lucas asked grandmother to help Luce into her new dress. It was a red dress which Luce thought was very pretty. It was made of red lace. Grandmother helped her get dressed. The dress was very tight on her. Then grandmother placed a red band on her head which had two little horns attached to it.

Uncle Lucas told her to stand up on the bed. The dress was long, hanging down to her feet. He stood near the equipment at the end of the bed. Luce now knew that this was some kind of camera. Then Uncle Lucas told her to repeat after him.

"My name is Lucifer. I am red Lucifer. I am the guardian of your dreams." As she said this, she was to lift up the end of her dress to above her knees. She was not to laugh or smile.

Luce was so nervous that it took her several practices until she got it correct. Grandmother stood at the back with the box in her hands while grandfather held the needle in his hands. Her lips trembled as she spoke the words that she did not understand.

When they were satisfied, grandmother took her back to her room where she was told she could have a treat. Grandmother told her she must never eat too much or she might get fat. Nobody wanted a fat Lucifer. Very soon she would also be black Lucifer. Grandmother gave her four chocolate lollies as she told Luce that she was becoming a perfect little girl.

52

The school bus was hot and the trip home seemed to take forever. Lizzie Smythe was pleased she was back at her real home with her mother. It had been such a long time since she had lived there. She had been to many homes with different uncles and cousins. But now that her mother was home, she could play with her dolls and toys in her very own room.

She also played solitaire, the card game she had learned when she had been with her cousins at Sunshine. She was very happy that at long last she had her own room and did not have to share with anyone else.

Lizzie missed Hope and Harry. When she asked why Hope and Harry did not return to their real home, her mother told her that she didn't think she could look after three children all at once as she was not well enough.

Hope was delighted that she did not have to live with her mother, although she was wise enough to pretend otherwise. She desperately wanted to stay with Matt and Mia. She never told anyone, not even Arlo, that she was secretly frightened of her mother. She had terrible memories of her mother when her grandparents were taken to hospital.

Maryanne said she did not mind in the least if her eldest daughter lived elsewhere. She seldom showed any interest in

Harry. She never asked about him, picked him up or nursed him. He was her forgotten child.

Maryanne had been allowed home under strict supervision. Initially, care support workers came daily to check on her progress. She had numerous mental health checks. She had medications to take several times daily. So far, she was coping well. Her thought processes were clear. Except for only wanting her middle child, she appeared quite normal.

Lizzie missed her father. She often looked at the wedding photo of her parents. Her mother was happy and smiling. Her father had his arm around her mother and was looking down at her with love.

Even though she was very young, Lizzie had heard the rumours about her father and Arlo's mother. She didn't know exactly what it meant, but knew it was an adult thing.

She sometimes saw the man who looked after the property. He lived in the granny flat where her grandfather used to live when he was alive. When Lizzie first came back to live with her mother, she seldom saw him but then he was always visiting her mother in the house.

She kept out of his way. He was a big man with black hair and dark eyes. He frightened her, but her mother seemed to like him. Lizzie stayed in her room when she heard them talking together in the kitchen.

Lizzie came home from school one afternoon and found the man drinking coffee with her mother. This annoyed her as she knew the man had his own kitchen in the granny flat. She was also annoyed at her mother because she didn't want Hope and Harry at home but she was quite happy to have this man in their house.

He seemed to keep busy on the property. He also went to her other grandparent's property, Miriam's Place, to work there as well. If Lizzie saw him coming, she would go in the opposite direction. But the day came when she came face to face with him.

"Hello," he said. "You must be Lizzie. It's nice to meet you at last. Your mother talks about you all the time."

Lizzie wondered who else he thought she could be. There was no one else around. She was also sure her mother never talked about her. Her mother never showed any interest in her. She never asked about her day at school or how her sister or cousins were.

"Yes, my name is Lizzie. What's your name?" she asked.

"Leon," he replied.

"Leon who?" she asked.

"Leon Jones," he answered her. He was looking at her with keen interest as if expecting her to talk to him, but Lizzie didn't want to talk any more so she ran away.

She missed her brother and sister especially on weekends. After school was finished during the week, she would watch television before having dinner. At times she would play solitaire before going to bed. The king of spades was her favourite card. It reminded her of Rafe who she always thought was very wise, as he used to talk to her about many things.

But on weekends, the time dragged. Uncle Matt usually picked her up to take her to karate or dance lessons. But if he did not come, she just stayed home. Her mother did not care what she did.

When Maryanne first came home from hospital, her cousins and uncles often visited but as time went by they visited less and less. She saw her sister and cousins at school, but they were older than she was and had their own friends. Not even Rafe talked to her any longer. She hardly ever saw Harry.

Rafe was a big disappointment to her, as was Hope. Rafe spent most of his time trying to keep Gabe out of trouble. Gabe was always in fights and arguments with other boys. Lizzie often saw Uncle Matt at the school talking to the teachers. At one time she heard that Gabe had been suspended. She wasn't sure what that meant but knew it was bad.

It was as if Hope had forgotten all about her. Just because she was now one of the big girls in school, it didn't mean she should ignore her. Lizzie knew Hope hung around with Arlo whenever she could. They always went to each other's houses especially on weekends.

Her biggest worry was the man called Leon. He was often in their house even when her mother was outside. She found him one day looking through the drawers in her mother's room. He didn't know she had seen him so she quietly went outside to avoid him.

Leon did not work on weekends. This was his time off. He drove away on Friday afternoon and returned on Monday morning. Lizzie decided that if he could look through their house then she could look through his.

Her mother often slept through the afternoon. She told Lizzie it was because of all the tablets she had to take. Lizzie noticed that her mother was getting bigger. Not exactly fat, but she was much bigger than before she got sick.

The young girl knew her mother would not surface for ages. She went to where Leon lived. The door was locked but she knew of a way to get inside.

When her grandfather had been alive, he had shown her where there was a loose plank amongst the floorboards. If you lifted it up, you could push yourself up from underneath the granny flat and crawl inside. That is, if you were small enough.

Lizzie had never been brave enough to crawl under the granny flat, but she was determined she would bolster her courage and crawl underneath. It would be tit for tat—if he could spy on them, she would spy on him.

The dirt under the granny flat was loose and soft. Lizzie knew her jeans would be dirty, not that her mother ever noticed such things. She crawled under the floor boards until she came to the loose plank. It was about one metre long.

When grandfather had lived there, he kept a rug over the top of it. The granny flat had all polished floors with rugs everywhere.

Lizzie lay on her back as she pushed the plank up with her foot. At first it would not budge. She was very disappointed. She tried again with both her feet kicking upwards with all her might. The plank moved. She kept pushing until finally it shifted.

Just as she thought, when she looked up she could see the floor rug. She pushed with all her might until the rug shifted. Lizzie was jubilant. She turned sideways and then pulled herself up through the hole. She was inside.

She looked around but was disappointed that everything looked the same as when her grandfather had lived there. Lizzie explored further. She had expected to find something that would prove to her mother that Leon Jones was not a nice man.

Lizzie went into the main bedroom. As she looked outside the window, she saw her mother walking around. She would have to get back out through the floor in case her mother started looking for her.

When she got through the hole she was faced with another dilemma. How was she going to get the rug back in place and at the same time put the plank back? If she didn't smooth out the floor rug, then Leon Jones would know someone had been in his flat.

She knew she couldn't do both. So she crawled back inside, put the plank back, straightened the floor rug and then went into the main bedroom. She would have to crawl through the window and jump down.

As she sat on the window sill, she overbalanced and fell. Lizzie lay on the ground stunned. Her ankle and arm hurt. She wondered if she had broken any bones. Slowly she got to her feet. Her arm was scratched but her ankle was the worst. It was beginning to swell and pain. She brushed herself off and limped back to the main house. Her mother was in the kitchen drinking tea.

"What happened to you?" she asked, looking at her bedraggled daughter.

"I fell out of a tree," Lizzie answered.

"You'd better clean yourself up then," Maryanne told her. She did not attempt to help her daughter as the young girl struggled to her room.

Lizzie spent a long time under the shower. Her ankle was still swelling and thumping with pain. She knew enough to put a packet of frozen peas on her ankle to stop it swelling further. Lizzie hopped onto her bed and held the frozen peas against her throbbing ankle. Her mother did not go near her.

It was several weeks before Lizzie could walk again without limping. When she was at home, she kept to herself which wasn't hard as her mother seldom came near her. But the day came again when she could not avoid Leon.

"How is your ankle?" he asked.

"Almost better," she replied.

"Then you had better be more careful when you climb trees or anything else," he replied. "Otherwise worse things might happen to you."

He walked away from her. Lizzie started at him, not sure what he meant but thinking it was the window she had left open. She vowed to herself that she would search his flat again when her ankle was fully recovered. The way he looked at her made her very uneasy. She was very concerned that her mother was so fond of him.

Public holidays were good fun because there was no school. Children got to play on their skate boards or scooters, go to the movies or the beach. All Lizzie got to do was spend time alone with her mother who probably didn't even know it was a holiday. Lizzie got up early, ate breakfast, cleaned up her dishes and went back to her room.

It wasn't long before she heard her mother laughing with Leon Jones. The laughing and giggling went on and on. Lizzie became so angry with her mother's giggling that she went to find her. She wanted to tell her not to be so stupid; that she sounded as silly as Harry.

At first she could not work out where her mother's voice was coming from. She was usually in the kitchen drinking tea with Leon Jones. Lizzie could hear her mother making strange noises. She realised the noise was coming from her mother's bedroom. Lizzie went to her mother's room but stopped at the door which was wide open. It was then that she saw Leon Jones on top of her mother. They were both upside down on the bed.

Lizzie gaped in shock. She could do nothing but stare. She knew she should not be looking. It was the thing that adult people did. She was about to run away, when Leon Jones looked up and saw her. He didn't stop what he was doing. He locked his eyes on Lizzie then smiled and licked his lips.

Lizzie was terrified. She couldn't go to her room, so she turned and ran as fast as she could. She ran into the bushes and headed up the track towards the high hills and the Big Rock. Tears poured down her face as she could not get the image of Leon Jones out of her head. She kept seeing his evil smile and the way he had licked his lips.

Lizzie had never been up to the Big Rock by herself. But she had walked up there with her cousins when she had lived at Sunshine. Even though she was on the other side of the Big Rock, she was certain she could find it by herself. She ran and ran. But it was too far and too high. She stopped and sat down. She could not go home, not yet. She could not face her mother and Leon.

When she had calmed down, she remembered it was Friday and that he would be leaving that afternoon. If she could wait longer, he would be gone and she could avoid him. As the sun went down, she returned home.

His vehicle was gone so she went into the house. Her mother was drinking tea. Maryanne told Lizzie to get her own dinner as she was too tired. She showed no interest in her middle daughter.

Lizzie could not believe that her mother could be so cold and uncaring towards her, especially when she could lie upside down on her bed with her fat legs wrapped around Leon Jones.

The time had come to again spy on him. Her ankle was better. This time she was better prepared. She waited until her mother was asleep before placing a ladder outside the window of the main bedroom of the granny flat.

As she crouched down to crawl under the floor, she heard a scrambling noise. This alarmed her. She lifted her head quickly to see a frill lizard escaping through the soft dirt. Lizards did not frighten her, not like snakes.

As she watched the lizard, she noticed a black bag lying on a stump under the granny flat. She pulled it down then opened it. It contained photographs, an old mobile phone and other items. Lizzie did not want to look at any photographs. Seeing her mother with Leon was enough to last forever.

She shoved the black bag back where she had found it. She though it an odd hiding place and wondered who could have put it there. It held little interest for her. It was Leon's secrets she wanted to find out about. She doubted it belonged to him as he was too big to fit under the granny flat.

This time she was quicker. There was little to find that looked important. As she looked through a drawer in the main bedroom, she found a box which held letters and documents as well as some smaller notebooks. Lizzie had seen these little notebooks before. Rafe had told her that if she ever had to go overseas she had to have a passport.

Lizzie looked at the passports. There were so many of them with photographs of men who looked very similar. Lizzie did not want to be too obvious, so she just took one passport. That was her plan. Whenever Leon Jones did something bad to her then she would do something bad to him. She would steal whatever she thought looked important.

Her escape was much easier. She climbed out the window, put the ladder back and then hid the passport under the beams with the black bag.

Lizzie was so pleased with herself that when she encountered him on the Monday morning before school, she just ignored him when he spoke to her. She could not believe how stupid her mother was as she heard the start of more giggling.

At school she was dying to tell someone about what she had discovered in the granny flat but her sister and cousins were too busy to talk to her.

Her afternoon routine was unchanged. Her mother no longer cooked an evening meal, so Lizzie helped herself to what she found in the refrigerator.

Before she went to sleep, she always played solitaire. What woke her was the movement of the mattress. She felt a weight on top of her. Lizzie opened her eyes. Even though it was dark she knew straight away that it was Leon. She knew he didn't like her but in her young mind she had no idea what he was doing on top of her in bed.

There was a hand clamped across her mouth so she couldn't call out to her mother. Not that her mother would probably hear her after she took all her pills and tablets. He held her down on the bed.

She tried to remember some of the karate moves she had learned. She tried to hit him in the face with her hand and then her elbow. But he just gathered both her hands together and held them up above her head. Her meagre strength was no match against his.

"Are you going to be quiet, Lizzie?" he asked as he removed his other hand from across her mouth.

As soon as he shifted his hand, she tried to scream but he used the palm of his hand to slap her hard across the side of her face. Her head snapped over to the side.

"Are you going to be quiet, Lizzie?" he asked again.

Her face was burning with pain but she still managed to glare up at him. Even in the dark of night, she could see the evil in him. She was about to scream again, when he pulled out the knife he had placed under her pillow. He let go of her left hand, dragged her right hand down and knelt on it.

"You are going to be quiet now, Lizzie," he said as he slowly dug the knife into the outside tip of her left little finger then dragged the blade along the length of her hand as far as her wrist.

Lizzie was screaming in her head. The pain was intense even though she knew the cut was not that deep. He then grabbed a pillow and wrapped it around her bleeding hand. She lay gasping for breath, holding the pillow around her left hand.

"My bad, beautiful Lizzie," he whispered into her ear. "You've been very bad Lizzie, very bad, everyone has to pay eventually."

The mattress again began to move. Lizzie was in shock. She did not know what was happening to her. She didn't know what he was doing. Did he think she was her mother? But she was not a mother, she was not grown up. She was only a little girl.

Lizzie then went into the glorious world of blackness. She did not know when he left or what else he did to her. She gradually came out of her blackness. Everything hurt. Her hand pained. Her whole body hurt not just her arms and legs but her whole being.

She tried to return to the blackness but it had disappeared. She then decided if she couldn't go back to her black world then she would live in a grey world. She let her mind float off in grey. She lay for hours on her bed seeing the world in charcoal colours. The sky was grey, the grass was grey.

Lizzie kept her world grey as she slowly got out of bed. She looked at her bloodied left hand. The bleeding had stopped but when she looked at her bed she saw more blood. She wondered where it had all come from.

Even the blood was grey. Lizzie liked grey blood better than red blood. So she painfully got out of her bed and showered. Her hand started bleeding again when the hot water hit it. She didn't care any more about the blood. If it wasn't red, then it didn't really matter. When she felt clean she got out of the shower and wrapped a towel around her hand to stop it bleeding.

She managed to get dressed. Lizzie remained in her room for a long time before going out to the kitchen to where her mother was drinking tea again with Leon. She had hoped he would be gone, working as he was supposed to. She nearly vomited when she saw him and tried to run back to her room. But he was very quick. He caught her and held her.

"What have you done to your hand, Lizzie? Did you fall and scape it on the side of your bed?" His words were directed at both mother and daughter.

Lizzie could not reply. Then her mother informed Lizzie that if she had made a mess in her bedroom, she should clean it up.

Leon then spoke to Maryanne. "I'll help Lizzie clean up her room. You go and get your rest." He ushered Maryanne away as he said, "Come on Lizzie, I'll help you get your bedroom straightened up."

Lizzie followed him into her bedroom. There was her bed, covered in blood. It was the bed she had so wanted to sleep in, the room that she could not wait to return to.

She watched as he stripped the bed, washed off the mattress and floor. Then he put a bandage around her wounded hand. She tried to pull away from him, but he just held her hand tighter so that more blood oozed out.

"There Lizzie, that should do it," he spoke cheerily. Then he held her face in his hand as he said, "Your family owes me a lot, my bad, beautiful Lizzie. Not even a million fucks will make up for what your family has done to me."

He carried the soiled linen out of the room. Lizzie stared at his back as he walked away from her. For a short time she had allowed the coloured world back in, but as she watched him, she decided she would return to her grey world. She looked at the bed now made up with fresh linens. She knew she would never sleep on the bed again.

Lizzie Smythe lay down on the floor and stared up at the ceiling.

53

Time passed on for the Farradays and Smythes. Memories began to fade. The past haunts of their lives were behind them. The secrets, sex and lies that Alan Farraday had indulged in all those years ago with ongoing horrifying results were a thing of the past.

The family had been left with a legacy of lies, lust and silence. All the lies that had been told over the years were put to rest. The carnal and material lust had slowly faded. The silence of peace settled upon them.

Desires were mostly satisfied. The cousins still played their games of solitaire when the moments of bad memory came back to haunt them. There was still sin around them. In spite of this, most of the family continued with their lives without any damning effect, except for three little girls.

Their torment did not diminish. The sins perpetrated upon them continued. They were damaged children. There was little peace for them.

Solitaire helped the mind but it did not erase the hurt.

Sin remained. It always would, no matter how they tried to avoid it.

Desire in all its strange and limitless ways was never satisfied. But a small glimmer of desire for a better life remained in three little girls.